KARMA
of the
SUN

BRANDON YING KIT BOEY

KARMA of the SUN

CamCat Books

CamCat Publishing, LLC
Brentwood, Tennessee 37027
camcatpublishing.com

© 2023 by Brandon Ying Kit Boey

Hardcover ISBN 9780744307603
Paperback ISBN 9780744307610
Large-Print Paperback ISBN 9780744307627
eBook ISBN 9780744307634
Audiobook ISBN 9780744307641

Library of Congress Control Number: 2022941018

Book and cover design by Maryann Appel

5   3   1   2   4

 FOR CRISTINA

After a last great interval, a seventh sun will appear
and the Earth will blaze with fire until it
becomes one mass of flame.

The mountains will be consumed, a spark will be carried
on the wind and go as far as the worlds of God.

Therefore, monks, even the monarch of mountains
will be burnt and perish and exist no more—excepting
those who have seen the path.

—*Pāli Canon (29 BCE)*

PART I

There were also monks
residing in the midst of forests,
exerting themselves and keeping the pure precepts
as though they were guarding a bright jewel.

The Lotus Sutra (1st cen. CE)

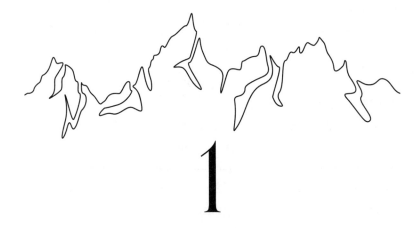

1

THE YAK

*K*arma knows it is a bad omen.

He feels it in his body. A sudden chill in the summer air. A passing shadow in the white Tibetan sky. A hush in the rustle of the yellow grasses.

One moment, the yak calf was with the herd. Now it is gone—the gift for the shaman on his visit. The benefaction. Their offering. Missing.

Karma hastens frantically up the rise, climbing hill and dune as he searches, the little boy beside him scampering to keep up, three little steps for every one of his.

Bad omen. Bad luck.

This day, of all days.

The shaman is to arrive at the village tonight. Soon, the fathers of the valley will bring their sons, and the mothers their daughters, to have their fortunes told, the spirits consulted.

It is Karma's turn to graze the herd. His lot. His fate.

His fault.

Karma's heart pounds as he scales the last hill. The tattered prayer flags of the village outskirts come into view, trembling slightly in the uneven wind. They have been placed here purposely, auspiciously, adorning the rusted ruins of the iron wreckage said to have once been able to fly, a stupa to a miracle of the time before the destruction known only by the name of the Six Suns—six fires said to have consumed all the earth, leaving only the barrens of this remote hinterland. Now the cloth images of the Four Dignities float like ghosts against the sinking of the western sun: the snow lion, the tiger, the phoenix, and the dragon—chained to the east, south, west, and north.

An incongruous form catches the corner of Karma's eye, only paces away from the wreckage like some offering delivered before the stupa: white fur. No movement, except for the fluttering of a few woolen strands. His heart plummets. Before he can even fully comprehend what he is seeing, he already knows it is something terrible.

The calfling.

It lies on its side. Coming down the dune, Karma flinches at the sight of the animal's belly. A large hole gapes from sternum to flank. A jumble of intestines bulges out like a heap of spilled rope from a sack. The ground is a patch of blood so dark it looks black.

Karma is paralyzed at the sight, as if it were his own lifeblood drained to the earth.

No . . . it can't be. Not the shaman's offering . . .

Only hours ago, it was alive and with the herd. Now it is a bloody carcass, viscera baking in the sun.

"What happened?" a boy's voice gasps behind him.

Karma startles. It is his little cousin Lobsang. Karma moves to shield the boy from the sight, but the child is too far out of reach, or perhaps it is only that Karma's legs are too numb.

"It . . . it was probably wolves," Karma mumbles. "Maybe a pack of them, or something . . ."

His voice trails. True, there have been more sightings of wild animals, but his instinct tells him this is something else. None of the meat has been touched. The yak is a calf but by no means small. Looking at the sheer size of the wound, nothing on four legs could do damage that looks like this.

A swarm of horseflies buzzes fiercely, as if to defend their quarry. A feeling comes over him, even more fearful than before. He has been afraid for the yak. But now that he's found it, he is afraid for the village.

If not animals . . . then bandits?

Karma's gaze flickers to the distance, to the flat horizon, the mountains long gone, where the border bandits are known to dwell. Lobsang mirrors his gaze. The vista is empty, but he knows the bandits prefer the night anyway, the better to avoid being shot by the villagers' matchlock rifles. Still, if it was them, wouldn't they steal the calf, not waste it? As depraved as they are, they are more deprived of food, no different from the rest of the Four Rivers and Six Ranges.

But if neither animals nor bandits . . .

Little Lobsang seems to read his thoughts. "Could it be a *migoi*?" he asks in a hushed voice, invoking the name for the supernatural creature that, thus far, to Karma was nothing but a child's figment. "My father says that in the end, the cursed become even more savage because they know that their doom is near. It's like the ghosts who mourn at night because they will never be reborn—"

"That's quite enough, Lobsang. We shouldn't speak of such things."

Karma cannot help a shudder. First the missing yak, then the mutilation. Now talk of migoi, ghosts, and the coming of the Seventh Sun. The day is going from inauspicious to downright ominous.

The wind stirs, and the stink of slowly fouling meat hits them. Karma's little cousin buries his nose in his sleeve, tangling his arm in the necklace of amber and coral that the boy's father gave him that day.

"We should ask my father what to do," Lobsang says, his voice muffled by his sleeve.

It is a perfectly reasonable course of action. Karma has the same urge, to leave this scene and go back to the village. But he feels as if he cannot. He is seventeen, not a child. This has happened on his watch. He cannot go back empty-handed. The bones and the hide. The hooves, the fat, and the tendons. He cannot lose the rest to wild animals overnight. As the son of the scoundrel—it would be unforgivable.

Karma makes up his mind. "There isn't enough time. The shaman's ceremony will be starting soon. We'll have to drag it back with us. Salvage what we can there." He could ask his mother to help him. He meets his cousin's skeptical gaze. "The meat's already turned," he explains. "If I lose the offal . . ."

Your father will lash me for sure, is what he wants to say, but doesn't need to.

Lobsang seems to understand the logic. A look of sympathy crosses the boy's face, and Karma wonders if his cousin, young as he is, actually understands a lot more. If so, he has never shown it. To Lobsang, Karma is not the cursed Sherpa's boy, not the son of the scoundrel. He is just Karma—and for that, Karma has always loved him.

As they begin dragging the carcass away, Karma glances back over his shoulder. The sun is already beginning its descent behind the dusty horizon. Something about the light, the angle of his gaze . . . a memory floods him, searing in its suddenness: an image of his father in this exact place, ten years ago. The entire village is there too. His mother; his aunt; his uncle, the headman.

And a caravan, waiting. But not Karma.

He was only seven years old then, but the memory is clear. He turns his face away.

Father's farewell.

"Are you all right, Karma?"

Karma blinks and the memory vanishes, leaving in its place the empty western landscape, the fluttering prayer flags the only things stirring. A strand of the pennants has come untethered and is snaking now in the air like a loose kite string, whistling as it whips back and forth, back and forth.

His little cousin's head is cocked, watching him. "What is it?"

"It's . . . nothing," Karma says. "Nothing at all."

He nods to resume their movement. But though they continue on to the village, something lingers in the air, sticks to them like the scent of the fouling meat they carry, certain only to ripen even more. A feeling of some ill-fated consequence of the past now finding its way back home.

2

THE GATHERING

If the death of the yak signals bad luck, bringing home its carcass augurs an even worse fate. In hindsight, Karma should have expected the reaction. Fear, anger, blame. He only wanted to do right by the village, thinking of their practical needs. He wanted not to let the people down. Not to anger them or remind them of . . .

Of father.

Wasn't that the truth?

That is why he brought the calfling back, after all. When he should have known better. When he should have seen it for what it was. A sign of the end. A reminder of the Seventh Sun, of the curse that hangs over them, and of the powerlessness of herd or village to afford any refuge. But like a fool, he brought it back. And along with it . . . the ill fate it portends. Now his face stings with shame as he tends the fire in the lodge room alone, stoking the coals, waiting for the villagers to gather.

The door opens, bringing in a draft of cold night air accompanied by the low and wind-like moan. Of course, it is not the wind but the ghosts, who only come in the night, and tonight they are especially restless.

The elders enter first. In the shadows, in the flickering firelight, the sunken stares of their eyes are severe. At the front is Urgyen—Karma's uncle and Lobsang's father, who as the village headman is the one to escort the shaman into the room. The shaman is a grisly sight in his ceremonial garb—a crow's-nest weave of finger bones and mirror fragments, a rosary necklace of skull beads, and a belt holding a flute fashioned out of what looks like a femur. Rattling and tinkling, the reflection of the shaman's mirrors cast slivers of light. He is a burning skeleton on the move.

Next come the visitors from around the valley of Kham. Young men traveling with their fathers to hear the shaman's divinations. Young women pushed forward by their mothers hoping for blessings for their future, and in them, answers about the fate of the world at large.

Last come the rest of the villagers, shuffling in order, his mother at the very end of the line. Their eyes are on him. All look except his mother, who seems to linger, as if holding open the door to an escape into the ghostly land and fractured stars beyond. But then the door is drawn shut and the crowd closes in—only enough room to stand.

One of the fathers speaks. "Is it wise to continue with the ceremonies tonight, Urgyen? With the yak offering the Sherpa boy lost, would it not be more auspicious to wait for another date?"

The Sherpa boy. The scoundrel's son.

Me.

The shaman is the one to reply, with a snort. "Six Suns, six blasts in the sky," he recites. "A seventh one, and the earth will die. Can there *ever* be an auspicious date?" The mirrored crown shimmers as he jerks his chin to the assemblage. "The infant doesn't choose the day he is born, nor the old man the day he departs. What makes you think you can choose when your boys shall become men, or your young girls women?" The shaman casts a jaundiced look at the father who has spoken. "When our days are numbered, how much time do you think your children have?"

The man shrinks back to the crowd. Uncle Urgyen regards the room impassively. They all know the prophecy. They have heard the recounting of the story that had been told to their grandfathers about the six distant blasts that were so bright they appeared like suns in the sky, and about what they did to the rest of the world. An earth if not scorched, then frozen. Dried lakes and drowned deserts. Mountains sunken, valleys leveled. Cities transformed overnight, once-towering structures expended like incense to ash by morning. The destructive force of the blasts would have reached Tibet, would have burned them all, were it not for the tall range of the Himalayas, which have been their only bulwark, their rock and their defense from the winds and the poisons.

But they also know about the telling of one seventh, final Sun—a last and complete destruction. And there is nothing they can do to stop it. The end, they know, will arrive for them too.

Urgyen gives the nod. "The fire," he commands.

Karma immediately pokes the coals, knowing his uncle is talking to him. It is a cold summer night, and the flames have gone down. Karma places more dung chips, then a few precious sticks of juniper brush. The belly of the room fills with smoke, the fire begrudgingly offering more of its heat.

"Move the kettle, or you'll spill the *chhaang*," chides one of the men.

Karma obliges, without emoting so much as a sigh of complaint. The brass kettle burns even through the potholder. He pours the steaming liquid into two bowls and carries them to his uncle. Urgyen takes one to the altar to make a set of seven bowls filled with water, grain, butter, and now—fermented barley.

He hands the other to the shaman.

Despite the steaming heat, the old man tilts the cup to his mouth, slurping the hot brew down his throat.

Uncle Urgyen waves to Karma for more. "Pour it all. Tonight when the spirits speak, they speak for us all."

3

THE FORTUNE

The drums crack and the bells ring, the brass trumpets pulse, and the men sway. The shaman hops and dances to the wailing dirge, the mirrored hat and tinseled robes throwing reflections like shattered stars into the crowded room. The old man shows no signs of wearing out for how long he has been dancing, how much he has been drinking. Somewhere between the music and the chanting he stops to take more swigs of barley brew before resuming his trance.

The first boy they take is Lobsang. Urgyen brings him forward—father and son going to the altar. Uncle Urgyen and Auntie Pema have dressed Karma's cousin in a clean coat tonight, his new amber-and-coral necklace hanging below the paunch of his robe. Karma watches as the shaman shakes and shudders, spitting a mist of alcohol into the fire. The flames hiss as if responding, smoke rising like a spirit winking coal-red eyes.

The diviner comes with barley on his lips, trembling hands outstretched to press the head of the wide-eyed boy. Then with a shout that smarts their ears and a strike of Lobsang's crown, the shaman cries through the vortex of horns and cymbals to summon the spirits. Thus possessed, the shaman's tongue loosens. Now comes the strain of pronouncements about a future of crops and money, herds and horses, and a hopeful reincarnation to another world when this one is gone, before he sends the boy into the world with the protection of dead lamas and enslaved but benevolent spirits.

Next is a girl. The shaman does the same, twisting and gyrating so that the ribbons on his cloak lift like prayer flags on a cairn and he seems almost to float off the ground, sending a churn of incantations along with the smoke from the den to the blistered stars beyond the windows. He swoons when he stops, straining like a nomad's tent in the wind. He strikes her head so hard the girl's eyes water. Her mother, holding her, begins to cry also, jerking to the rhythm of the skeleton drums. And then the utterances pour, fortunes of a fruitful womb and progeny one day like wild foals roaming valleys and hills, while the girl's mother sobs with gratitude—or more likely the grief for what she knows will never be in this life.

Last of all is Karma, who comes alone, without a father to bear him forward. He glances across the room to look for his mother in the shadows but is met only with the glare of the crowd.

"The *Sherpa's* son," the shaman says.

Karma's face flushes with shame, though the appellation is merely a fact. He *is* the son of an outsider, the man from away who came to them with promises of deliverance and sanctuary, only to desert them to their doom.

Together now, the shaman and Karma begin to spin. Around they go, faster and faster. The room is a blur—whistling of flute and jangling of bells, stench of butter lamp oil and yak-dung smoke, brew on the shaman's breath, and wail of ghosts outside. Karma grows dizzy, his feet stumbling.

Just as he thinks he can take no more, the shaman stops.

They swoon, the room still whirling. The shaman opens his mouth to speak, the pink of his gums showing. But then a sudden change comes over his expression. His face sags, his eyes roll. The mirrored crown atop his head begins to tip.

The shaman collapses, sprawling on the floor in a burst of convulsions.

Shouts of alarm. Flurrying of panic. The elders rush forward.

Karma stumbles aside, flustered, head still spinning, heart beating where the drums have stopped.

Bad omen. Bad luck . . .

This day, of all days . . .

Eventually, the shaman's seizures cease. But his eyes remain closed. The men jostle around him, Uncle Urgyen barking orders. A space clears as someone brings more chhaang and food from the offering table, tipping the cup, chewing the meat, and pushing the food into the shaman's mouth like they are feeding a baby. A trickle of pale beer spills down his beard like milk drool.

Slowly, the old man's eyelids crack open. Two inscrutable pupils glint in the firelight, flickering over the circle of faces. Seeking but not finding, his gaze roves beyond the huddle.

A voice with a strange intonation emanates from the shaman's mouth. Within the walls of the lodge room, it sounds strangely to Karma like the ghost-winds outside. He's not the only one to think so, as the elders begin to draw back cautiously.

"The ghosts are suffering," the elders whisper to one another. "It is because they are trapped, no way to be reborn when the earth is destroyed by the Seventh Sun . . ."

"*The son . . . of the Sherpa . . .*"

The elders startle.

The words are coming from the shaman, but they are not his. Not a single voice, but multiple voices at once. Karma's skin prickles as the shaman's gaze falls upon him.

"They know the boy," the elders hiss. "Because of the father. Bad luck."

The familiar guilt floods Karma.

The shaman continues to speak, his mouth as detached from the words themselves as a trumpet from the breath that blows it, incriminating. "*He will follow his father . . . He will go to him . . .*"

A shocked murmur sweeps the room.

Did he say, my father?

No one has dared speak of Patrul Sherpa, not for ten years. Not with anything but a curse. His name has been all but blotted out in the village.

Go to my father?

No one moves or speaks.

Karma's uncle pushes forward through the crowd. "Demons," Urgyen curses. "Deceitful ghosts!" He snatches the bowl of chhaang and makes a motion as if to toss the contents into the fire.

"Wait!" Karma reaches to stay Urgyen's hand, shocked by his own temerity but unable to help himself. It has been years since anyone has openly spoken about his father. He wants to know more.

Urgyen returns a withering look, and Karma's hand falls away.

With a jerk of his arm, Urgyen tosses the drink. The fire hisses and crackles over the spilled chhaang, ejecting a puff of smoke. The ghost-winds shriek outside, trilling in a crescendo. The shaman's eyelids droop. He twitches before going limp on the ground.

Still, Karma leans forward, straining for more, for any other revelation about his father. About himself. Anything.

Please. If only I could just speak to him.

But it is all over. The voices are gone.

The shaman's body is inanimate. There is only an old man in a stupor, dribble seeping from his mouth. In the silence of the room, the mysterious pronouncements merely linger in the air like the vapors of a doused fire, nothing more.

Urgyen now turns to Karma, his eyes still hard. "You should know better."

Karma flinches at the words. But of course, his uncle is right. After all, his father is a fraud, a thief. The curse of Kham. A scoundrel.

"Your father cursed this people once before with his lies," Urgyen says. "Any fortune about him is no fortune at all."

Someone is weeping. It takes a moment for Karma to realize that it is his mother.

"I—I know," Karma stammers, at a loss for what else to say. "I'm sorry."

But surrounded by the elders of the valley, before the unconscious figure of the shaman on the floor, the words of the ghostly prediction hang in the air.

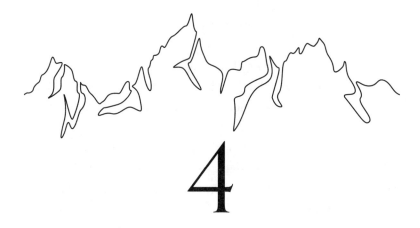

4

THE DARK

The harshness of the cold is a welcome relief to the reeking warmth as Karma bursts out of the lodge into the night. His breath streams in clouded puffs. He has the urge to run, to get as far away from the lodge as possible, from the village, from the whole valley, even.

He will follow his father, the spirits said. *He will go to him.*

The villagers' voices spill outdoors. A drunken song warbles through the air, along with the sound of low, mingling conversation. But Karma does not tarry. He does not join in any of the exchange. He quickens his pace, almost reckless in the dark, anxious to avoid another person. Clouds have moved in, lumbering cold and still, hiding stars behind their cumulus rises. Below, the earth is a different story. The land at night always sways in slow tremors like the motion of a giant sieve, growing then fading, growing then fading. Shifting. Sorting. Unstable.

The residual warmth dissipates, and Karma begins to feel the cold. He slips the dangling half of his robe over himself—the yak-hair wool too warm for the stuffiness of the lodge—pushing his arms through the baggy sleeves and tightening the jute sash. The voices behind him drop away and finally he is alone with the wailing of the ghosts in the blackness of night.

Gravel crunches. Something stirs in the dark behind him.

Karma spins to face the sound, his mind conjuring up the lurking of ghosts . . . or is it a migoi, after all? He was foolish to go off alone. Too hasty in his desire to get away.

But when a shape emerges from the shadows, it is only his uncle. He slowly stalks toward Karma, drinking bowl in his hand, stopping to take a swig when he sees him.

"Risky, to be wandering off by yourself after dark," Uncle Urgyen chides, "especially with how you found the calfling today, wouldn't you say?"

Karma says nothing in reply, taking the remark as the rebuke that it is meant to be. Even in the dark, he can feel his uncle's gaze—probing, judging.

"What you think you heard tonight . . ." his uncle continues. "The problem is that you can't really tell how much it is the spirits talking, or if it's just . . . the *spirits.*" Urgyen downs the rest of the drink, shaking out the emptied bowl with an air of irony.

Is this his uncle's version of conciliation? Karma knows what he heard. The words spoken by the shaman were as clear as they were unexpected.

Urgyen goes on. "The truth is, the future holds the same fate for all of us. The Seventh Sun is coming. No fortune-telling can change that."

Karma remains quiet, hesitant to say what he is thinking. The first six of the "Seven Suns" have destroyed the earth, so that all that remains is the Land of the Four Rivers and Six Ranges—shielded at first by the protective wall of the Himalayas from the blasts. Until now. Earthquakes have come and toppled those mountains, leaving the land just as vulnerable. *All except for one mountain,* his father said. It was this proclamation of his father's that began it all, gave the people hope until he left with supplies and people and money—never to be seen again. But now Karma is beginning to wonder, what if his father was right after all?

In the cover of night, under strange stars so cold and dispassionate, the utterance from the shaman runs through his mind again.

He will follow his father . . . He will go to him . . .

Karma will take the leap. "The shaman spoke of . . . looking for my father."

Despite the darkness, the stiffening of his uncle's posture is perceptible. Karma is on dangerous ground, bringing up his father again. He knows this but has also sensed an opening. Perhaps it is some guilt on his uncle's part, however small, for cutting him off over the shaman's message earlier.

But it is enough.

"Uncle," Karma plows ahead. "What if . . . I tried to find him now?"

The outline of his uncle's shoulders rises. "What if you tried to find him now," Urgyen repeats Karma's words like someone rolling a bitter taste around in his mouth.

Karma tries to explain. "We say that everything has changed because of the quakes. The land. Even the stars are out of place. It's become impossible to orient ourselves with accuracy anymore. What if the reason he never returned is not that he abandoned us . . . but just that he's lost?"

"*Lost?*" Urgyen exhales, the air through his teeth making a cutting sound. "Let me remind you, in case for some reason you have forgotten. Your father was a liar and a thief. A Sherpa trader who came to our village, seducing the people with stories of a sanctuary in the mountains. He asked for men and provisions for an expedition, for horses and yaks. He duped my own brother Tenzing into going with him, leaving the village. And for what? If your father is speaking to ghosts, then maybe he is dead. Good riddance. But my brother was innocent."

The words singe Karma and remind him why he never speaks about his father. So much blame, so much disappointment. But also this conclusion: Even if his father was a charlatan, by now no one knows what has become of him anyway.

"How he could have been so stupid as to believe it, I will never know," Urgyen continues. "And how could your mother fall for such a scheme—and for such a man, looking to some stranger with a faraway promise instead of seeing what was right in front of her?"

His uncle spits in the dark, eyes boring hard and black into Karma. "But the bird always shows its feathers. Not content with what he had *already* taken, he had to steal from us too. It wasn't until he was gone and it was too late to stop him, but we discovered it in the end. *I* discovered it. The money gone, just as he was gone." Urgyen shakes his head. "Lost?" he repeats with a spiteful snort. "No, the reason he never came back is because he never *meant* to come back. Not for us, not for your mother. And not for you. He betrayed us all."

Karma flinches. If his uncle's words in the lodge room had been a slap in the face, these were a kick to his gut.

"Your mother has kept a lot of the truth from you," Urgyen goes on. "Not that she made it any easier on either of you. I would have taken you both in. I would have cared for her as if she was my own wife. But her mind was already clouded by your father's lies. Even now, ten years after the scoundrel abandoned her, she will not accept the fact that she will never see him again. What she even saw in him in the first place, I will never fathom. A Sherpa without a mountain, as useless as a shepherd without a flock." He pauses. "Or a boy without a future."

Karma feels his face warming. An impotent, meaningless reaction, not even bold enough to be visible in the shroud of night. These are all things Karma has heard before, things he knows people say. He has become used to it, but tonight he feels them like a fresh wound.

"I did you a favor back there, nephew," Urgyen says. "Anything to do with your father is karma you don't want."

The ghostly keening in the night rises in pitch, discordant and bone-chilling, whistling through crevices of stone and earth. Overhead, the clouds have drifted from one end of the sky to another, revealing unrecognizable stars. The heaven's skies turn sullen, the night's subtlety gone.

"Could you really do it, anyway?" Uncle Urgyen asks. "And I am not just talking about the improbability of surviving the Borderlands alone. Or what the Minister's patrollers would do to you—not to mention the entire village—in retribution if they catch you leaving the Territories. But could you leave your mother? Could you leave Lobsang, who looks to you like an older brother? Would you abandon them when you know your father abandoned you?"

The silence between Karma and his uncle is heavy, the answer palpable.

"I didn't think so," Urgyen says. "Because deep down you know. You will never see him again. Not in this life. And if you're lucky, not in the life to come. There is no time for looking back. Nor any reason to look ahead. You are needed right here, right now. To prepare for the end. It is coming. Even the ghosts know it. That's why they mourn."

He stops talking then, distracted suddenly by a sound over the wind, barely noticeable, yet conspicuous in its contrast from the keening of the night.

But it is not the ghost-winds this time.

"Listen," Urgyen hisses, "Do you hear that?"

A galloping noise. Coming from downwind, fleeting and hard to make out.

"What is that?"

Growing louder, and then unmistakable: the muffled hoofbeats of horses approaching.

Their understanding is immediate, their conclusion simultaneous.
Bandits.

Curses bound from Urgyen's mouth. "Of all the damned things—" He whirls back toward the lodge. "Riders!" he shouts, raising the alarm. "Bandits in the night! Get the rifles, defend the village!"

The sense of foreboding returns to Karma.

Bad omen . . . Bad luck . . .

Karma tries to follow his uncle, but in the chaos of the night, he becomes disoriented, for a moment unable to tell which direction he is heading. The crack of a rifle's retort, followed by the bass of its echo from the direction of the lodge, pulls him back in.

The sounds of whooping and jeering pierce the night. Hooves clatter around the village. Karma wheels about in rising panic.

Mother! Lobsang! More shots, fire stabbing in the dark. The villagers are firing haphazardly, but at least they are shooting. The char of gun smoke drifts through the air.

But then, as suddenly as they began, the sounds recede, the hoofbeats fade, drifting farther, the whoops of the bandits dimming. Were they abandoning the raid already? Could the rifles, as old and inaccurate as they are, have repelled them so easily?

"Karma!"

Thankfully, he sees his mother stumbling toward him, his aunt in tow behind her.

Relief floods him. "Mother! Auntie Pema! Over here!"

But . . . something is wrong. It is his aunt. She is sobbing, staggering, barely able to stand.

Uncle Urgyen appears, an armed group of the village men with him, rifles and torches in hand. He sees his wife too.

"What is it?" Urgyen barks. "Are you hurt? Where is Lobsang?" He clutches his rifle at the ready, a long, wooden matchlock mounted by a pair of antelope horns like the prongs of a pitchfork.

The groan that comes from Auntie Pema turns Karma cold. For once, the moaning of the ghost-winds does not sound so loud or so terrible, compared to the wail of Auntie Pema's voice.

She crumples like an ash heap. Beside her, Karma's mother sinks to the ground as well, clutching her sister as if afraid she will disintegrate completely. The men's faces are stunned in the firelight. Auntie Pema's next words confirm what they somehow already know.

"The bandits," Pema cries. "They took him. They took our son."

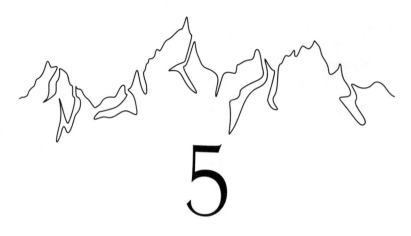

5

THE MINISTER

Daylight brings no trace of Lobsang.

Search parties separate through the valley—to the wreckage of iron and prayer flags to the west, the plains in the north, the stone tower to the south. They bring their matchlock rifles, though what they will do if they encounter the bandits, Karma does not know. They do not venture too far, do not dare to plan a search past the valley. The Minister, or his patrollers, have forbidden it. As the day wanes, they prepare to check the eastern dunes. Uncle Urgyen whips his horse onward. The men follow, but their grim faces speak what they are afraid to say—that Lobsang is long gone.

Riding toward a rising dune, the sound of hoofbeats echoes ahead. At first Karma thinks it's their own noise, but then a flurry of movement and a tide of bright crimson rises suddenly over the crest . . .

Banners. Streaming down the slopes. In an instant, the hills are awash in red—the color, Karma thinks, of the Minister's army.

The men startle. "It's a patrol, Urgyen! They'll see our weapons."

But it is too late to hide them. Too late to stop. They have already been seen. To try to run would be futile.

To resist would be suicide.

Ranks of cavalry stream down, coming now directly toward them. And following the cavalry is a formation of foot soldiers. On their shoulders rides the boxy carriage of a wooden palanquin—carved and gold accented, caparisoned in crimson silk.

This is no patrol.

The faces of the men quail at the realization.

This is a whole troop of the Eastern Army.

Their voices become panicked. "Urgyen, the carriage . . . it's the Lord Minister!"

Karma feels a shudder of dread. Why are they here? It is not the time for collecting the tributes, the four times yearly when the patrollers would come to take their due—yak, wool, ore, and conscripts for the army. Nor would the Minister come himself for that reason. Karma has never seen him before, of course.

But he knows the descriptions of the Lord of the Four Rivers and Six Ranges, who rides on a chariot carried not by horses but on the backs of men.

Like a pincer, the cavalry separates, flanking them on both sides to surround the band of villagers. Urgyen's horse rears. The other villagers wrangle at the reins of their jittery horses. From the head of the formation of soldiers, a single rider canters to the fore, his chain-mail tunic making chinking sounds with each step, like the counting of coins. The voice that hails them through a red, turbaned face scarf is loud and authoritative, the voice of a patroller captain.

"Relinquish your weapons!"

Urgyen drops his rifle to the ground. It tumbles, hitting the dirt with a clunk of surrender. The others follow, throwing their motley arsenal without challenge.

"On your knees!" the captain orders.

The village men cast themselves from their horses. Karma likewise dismounts, prostrating himself on the hot, dry grass. Foot soldiers stomp forward, snatching away their rifles. Then all seems to go still.

From the ground, Karma's uncle stammers, "We—we beg your pardon, sir. We did not know the Lord Minister was here—"

"Who are you to question the Lord Minister's business, bandit?"

"Sir . . . we are no bandits—"

"Rebels, then! You have been caught with arms."

Urgyen flusters. "Please, sir . . . our village was attacked by bandits. They took my son. These weapons are for our protection."

"The Lord Minister is your protector."

"*Captain* . . ." Another voice, much different—softer—speaks.

The captain bows, ceasing his questioning instantly. "My Lord."

Karma risks a furtive glance toward the sound of the other voice. Past the patrollers, past the retinue of banners and spears, a hand parts the curtains of the palanquin window, its arm wreathed in red brocade and golden bangles.

From the lofty perch, a round face emerges, moonlike in its paleness as if untouched by the wind or sun, an arrangement of peacock feathers adorning its crown like the unblinking eyes of some all-seeing deity, and Karma knows for certain now:

It *is* Hanumanda, Lord of the Eastern Army, Minister of the Four Rivers and Six Ranges. His eyes survey the group of villagers before him, crossing Karma's gaze.

Karma lowers his head quickly, fearing reprisal for his impertinence. To his amazement, the voice that comes is quiet, almost kind.

"These men are not the enemy."

"Yes, my Lord," the captain demurs.

The door of the palanquin creaks open, and now the Lord Minister is stepping out. He approaches the men, the sound of his retinue rustling to follow him. He directs his voice to Urgyen. "You say that your son was taken?"

"My Lord, y–yes," Urgyen stammers in reply. "They came into our village and took him . . ."

"Bring the litter," the Lord Minister orders.

Karma risks another glance from the ground.

The retinue parts as two men trot forward carrying a gurney between them.

Karma immediately recognizes the small figure.

His uncle is already on his feet. "Lobsang! My son!"

Karma's heart leaps. But just as quickly, it plummets. His cousin is not moving.

The boy's eyes are closed, his face still and passive.

Oh no . . . oh, Lobsang . . .

The Minister waves the guards aside as Urgyen dashes to him, dropping to his knees beside the boy.

"How did . . . this happen?"

"Your gang of bandits had the misfortune of crossing paths with the Eastern Army last night," Hanumanda says. "In their attempt to evade our troops, there was an accident. But I would not fret. According to my physician, he will wake eventually. I assure you . . . the bandits were far less fortunate."

Urgyen clutches Lobsang to his body, and Karma can see the color draining from his uncle's face. "Thank you." His uncle swallows. "How fortuitous . . . that your Lordship was there."

"Yes," the Minister replies. "Though not strictly serendipitous."

His gaze suddenly flicks back to Karma, catching him by surprise, this time fixing him with his eyes.

"You see," the Minister continues, "we have come searching for someone too."

Karma's uncle blinks. Glancing down at Lobsang's unconscious face, he collects himself, wiping at the corners of his eyes. "Someone, my Lord? In these parts of the valley? If there is any assistance we can impart . . ."

The Lord Minister Hanumanda smiles in return, and for some reason the expression fills Karma with a sense of dread even deeper than before.

"There was a man," the Minister says, "who came from the mountains. A Sherpa."

Dread now turns to shock. The ill-fated feeling of yesterday's discovery rushes back to Karma. And then the feeling of guilt, of destiny coming home to roost, of a curse inescapable—as the Minister says his next words.

"I am looking for his son."

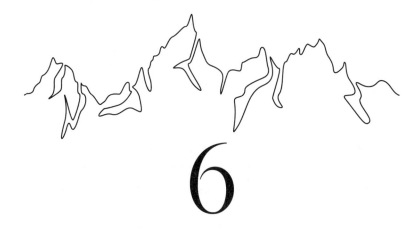

6

THE TABERNACLE

The tent of the great tabernacle of Lord Minister Hanumanda shudders from the winds. Karma and his mother sit within the cocoon of crimson cloth, alone, save for the shadows of servants blinking in and out from behind the curtains.

Karma wondered at first if the structure would hold against the valley's punishing winds. The homes in the valley are built squat and heavy, stacks of rock bracing against the worst of the southwest gales. In contrast, this tent is tall, a miracle of engineering that the villagers gawked at as the soldiers erected it to its full height. Even with the hurling of the winds broadside, the massive spectacle stands.

Now the curtains shuffle. The great drapes part. From the bowels of the tabernacle, Lord Minister Hanumanda strides into the sanctum and ascends a raised dais. Through the dim lamplight and the smoke of the incense censers swinging from the rafters, he studies them.

After a long moment, he speaks, his first words directed at Karma.

"I see Sherpa Patrul's resemblance in you."

Karma blinks. *Did the Minister just say that he knows my father?* He glances at his mother.

"My Lord . . ." she says, her expression equal parts bewildered and afraid, "you . . . have seen my husband?"

"My patrollers arrested him and his companions many years ago," Hanumanda answers, "trying to cross into the Borderlands."

His mother's face pales even more. "M–my Lord . . . I did not know . . ."

The Minister holds up a hand. His clothing tinkles with the movement of embroidered stones. "Rest assured, I did not come to condemn. But on the contrary, to pay honor and respect."

Honor . . . respect . . .

These are not words ever associated with his father. Is this some test? Some form of interrogation? The Minister said they had arrested him. Leaving the Territories was forbidden. Those who did so were assumed to be deserters, rebels, or generally traitorous to the Lord Minister.

Have the patrollers now come because they suspect Patrul's own family of being the same?

"The quakes destroyed what was left of the Himalayan range," the Lord Minister goes on. "Yet your husband embarked on a search for a refuge in the mountains anyway."

Now the worry deepens. Karma remembers what his uncle said to him. The wrongdoing of one could bring punishment on the entire village.

Like a curse.

"My Lord," Karma's mother says shakily, "my husband was a dreamer. He heard sounds. Sherpa horns blowing from afar. He thought it was his people calling to him from the dead for help."

"Your headman seems to believe it was a ruse to steal from the village, no different than the deceptions of so many charlatans and false sorcerers who prey on the ignorant these days."

"Have mercy, my lord," she pleads. "He grieved for his people. He was not in his right mind. I thought it was a gift. I could not stop him."

"Nor should you have," Hanumanda says, surprising them with his answer. "It's why we sent him on his way, with some of our own men to help with his expedition."

Karma's mother looks confused. "My lord . . . you helped him?"

"'Six Suns, six blasts in the sky. A seventh one, and the earth will die,' goes the prophecy," he recites. "There were many fantastical things made by the people from the time before. Things we can barely even imagine. The wreckage of that great iron bird outside your village, amazing to think that it could once fly, carrying people through the skies. But the most unfathomable creations were their weapons, which unleashed destruction on such a massive scale that they rivaled the sun in fieriness, that on command could annihilate a whole civilization in the blink of an eye, even the whole earth. Indeed, that is what has been left of the world now, because of six of those Suns. Waiting, until the seventh and final one finishes off the land of the Four Rivers and Six Ranges."

He pauses, as if to let the words sink in. "Yet, despite this doom, we have also been left with one glimmer of hope. Consider the second verse: 'But gather to the Mount and the Seeing Stone, that the Lama may reveal yet a future unknown.'"

Karma suppresses a recoil. He can feel his mother doing the same. That verse. Those words. It is not that the words themselves, abstruse auguries he will never understand, hold any meaning for him. But according to his mother, they are the very words his father quoted when he came to the village. Karma knows enough about the myth of the Seeing Stone to know that it convinced the villagers.

Or deceived them.

A glimmer of hope? More like a shameful shadow.

The Lord Minister leans forward. "The monks have records going back to the last Lama, to the time before the Suns. They say that the Seeing Stone is the key, that anyone who can look into it can see what has happened in the past, but only a Lama can also see how to change the future. Including how to stop the Seventh Sun. I believe that this Stone was the answer Patrul was searching for—and found."

A lull in the wind turns the tabernacle silent. Karma and his mother stare, stunned.

Karma's mind does not understand. The words make no sense. For so long, his father has been the scoundrel, the liar, the thief. Now the Lord Minister is telling them . . . that his father was right?

The answer Patrul was searching for—and found.

Suddenly the walls of the tent feel untethered, the shaking of the canvas as if the wind at any moment would tear it away to reveal an unsheltered sky.

"My father was right after all?" Karma blurts out. The outburst is impudent, he knows it immediately. For someone of his standing to direct a question at the Minister, without the proper form of address, no less. But the words and thoughts spill out faster than he can contain them. "He was telling the truth about the Mountain?"

But instead of censuring him, the Lord Minister replies gently. "Your mother said it herself: He could hear the suffering of his people who died in the quakes. In the moans of the ghost-winds, the dead were calling to him."

Karma's heart rises in elation. He knew it. Always, deep down, he has believed that his father was faithful. "Where is it, then?" Karma says. "Where is my father now?"

Now Hanumanda pauses, his face becoming somber. "I'm afraid this is the difficult part. Along the way, your father and his Khampa travel companion went missing from the expedition. My men searched for days, high and low, but never did see them again. They were gone. Maybe fallen into the earth. Maybe bandits. Maybe wolves or beasts . . . or worse."

Just as quickly as his hopes rose, Karma feels a crushing weight come cascading back onto him.

"Unless . . ." Hanumanda continues.

Karma looks up at the Lord Minister. *Unless?*

He is afraid of the words that will follow. To the village, under Uncle Urgyen, it has always been as if his father never existed. But somehow that is not as bad as thinking that his father is dead. To Karma it has always meant that perhaps someday, somehow, his father would return.

He has always harbored this hope in secret. Not even to his mother has he dared to bring it up, lest it give her any hope she could not stand to have.

"Maybe he is someplace where he cannot reach us," the Lord Minister says, as if he were speaking of another village in the valley. "Maybe he has found the spirits, but he just cannot find his way back. Not without some help." He fixes his gaze back on Karma, as if waiting for him to say something in return. It is what Karma said to his uncle just the night before, only to be reproved. But now Karma is too confused to speak.

"Why?" his mother says instead. "Why are you telling us this now? What can we do, powerless as we are?" It is not so much a voice of protest or even disbelief but rather heartbreak and helplessness.

The Lord Minister replies with the measured cadences of someone counting out taels of silver. "Because the end is upon us," he says. "And there is no hope of escaping it. 'Six Suns, six blasts in the sky. A seventh one, and the earth will die.' The first six Suns have already destroyed the world outside the Four Rivers and Six Ranges. The Seventh Sun will come soon. Our shamans have seen the signs. Earthquakes and storms unceasing. More blood than water flowing. Beasts become the hunters and man the prey. Stars losing their places and stranding the traveler. This is why the mourning of the ghosts grows louder every night. Because they too know that time is running out."

He holds up two slender fingers, repeating the second verse like a mantra: "'But gather to the Mount and the Seeing Stone, that the Lama may reveal yet a future unknown.' We must find the Mountain and the Lama. We must change the future."

Now it all makes sense. The reason for Karma's unease, for the sense of foreboding. He has felt it since seeing the red over the dunes. Even the day before, at the sight of the blood-soaked yak by the prayer flags. He has felt it all these years, growing, accumulating, as constant as the mourning of the ghost-winds at night. And now he begins to see that it is fate. Uncle Urgyen cannot deny him now.

"The monks say the Lama is a reincarnation from the time before the Suns," Hanumanda says. "Tomorrow, I will leave to join my troops gathered at the Borderlands to search for this Child. What I need now is help finding the Mountain where the Seeing Stone resides. What I need is for you to find your father."

Again, Karma is stunned. Again, it is his mother who responds.

"But my son was born right here in the valley, my lord," she protests. "He knows nothing about the mountains."

"Your husband was led by a gift."

"My husband had dreams. He heard the sound of a Sherpa's horn when no one else did. Karma has never experienced the same thing—"

Haven't I . . . ?

A dream. A shimmer of a glimpse here, an echo of a sound there. He can remember, as a child, being with his father and watching the herd, and hearing a sound—a distant burring.

"What if I have?" Karma says, before he can catch himself, before he's even sure if he's right.

Despair crushes his mother's face, any semblance of hope seeming to drain from her body. Why did he say it? Perhaps he should have kept his silence.

But it is too late now.

"Be glad, mother," Hanumanda says. "Your family is the only hope we have of escaping the Seventh Sun. To save your village and all of the Four Rivers and Six Ranges. The same village that cursed your husband's name when he didn't return. But now they will come to know the truth."

At those words, a lump forms in Karma's throat. Is it possible, is there a chance that he will no longer be the scoundrel's son?

With a mere flick of his hand the Lord Minister summons a servant who immediately appears carrying a pillow with an object wrapped in red silk on it. Hanumanda unbundles it, revealing a knife, one unlike any Karma has seen. The scabbard gleams silver, filigreed and inlaid with gemstones. Its handle looks like ice, crystal clear and colorless, some kind of quartz. When he draws the blade, the metal is black in color and mottled in texture. Instead of the typical, flat shape, it is a three-sided spike.

He comes down from the dais, approaching Karma and his mother with the object displayed in both hands. "This was found by my men. It is a ritual knife, from a time when there were still Lamas. The blade is made of the ore of a meteorite, representing the power of heaven on earth. The handle is crystal, its translucence symbolizing a clear grip on truth. In all the Four Rivers and Six Ranges, I have come across nothing like it." He turns to Karma's mother. "And it was your husband's."

"But I have never seen it before," Karma's mother says.

"No," Hanumanda affirms. "And that is the proof—that he *found* something on that journey."

Hanumanda returns the blade to its silver sheath, startling Karma when he then holds the knife out to him. "It's yours now. A gift, from father to son, just like the other gifts of his that you already possess."

Karma stares at the object. The Lord Minister takes Karma's hand and puts it into his palm. The crystal and silver are cool to the touch. Within the facets of the glass, the light of the incense burners bends and multiplies.

"The monks say that the Mountain is a sacred place. A meeting ground between our world and the otherworld. Find the Stone, and not only will you redeem your father's name, but perhaps you shall also see him again."

Karma swallows, the lump burning within him now as if it has become a coal.

Find the Mountain . . . Find the Seeing Stone. . .

This was his father's task. The duty they said he left unfulfilled.

But Karma has always known better. And now, there is proof. He holds it in his hands. For the first time, there is a hope he'd never had. A mountain sanctuary in which his father has found a stone that could change the future—perhaps even stop the Seventh Sun and save the Four Rivers and Six Ranges.

But most of all, a stone that would let him see his father again.

The keening of the wind outside seems to grow into a faraway cry. The Lord Minister is right. By no mistake of the imagination, tonight they sound even more tortured than usual. More desperate. The pelting of sand and lashing of wind is like the scratching of nails and gnashing of teeth, raging against time and its incessant advance. But is his father's voice among them, among the spirits of the departed, waiting to be freed? Calling to his son?

Find the Stone, and not only will you redeem your father's name, but perhaps you shall also see him again.

Karma's fingers tighten around the knife, gripping the handle as if to grasp the opportunity. It's all he's ever wanted, the one thing he has yearned to do.

He looks at his mother a final time. This time he tries to convey resolve, to reassure her that all will be well, all will be right.

But in her eyes, he sees only fear.

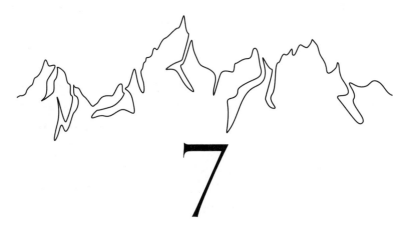

7

THE DAWN

Karma knows he is dreaming.

First, there is the terrain. Not the dry valley grassland, but green and forested earth. Not expansive and flat, but high and mountainous. Then there are the mists. As thick as clouds, rolling downrange, shedding light summer snow.

This is not the valley of Kham.

Around him, people are everywhere. Walking, wandering. Filling the mountain slopes. Karma is walking too, though where he is going, he does not yet know. He has the sense of an endlessness of horizon. Of time, too. Of waiting.

He looks at the people as they walk. Strange faces. Races he has never before seen, with colored eyes and strange clothing. But there is something else—something different about this sea of people that he cannot quite determine. A transparency in their presence, in their movements. A sense of walking in place, without progress, without change, no matter how long they move. As if trapped.

Karma looks around, suddenly nervous. He tries to speak to the people, to get their attention, ask them what is wrong. But they do not acknowledge him. He cannot talk to them. They do not even seem to see him. Despite being immersed in the stream of people, he is separate from their world.

Because this is the otherworld, and they are the dead.

It dawns on him suddenly. These are the wandering deceased. The specters of the ghost-winds. Then this must be the world between death and rebirth. And now his panic grows. Why is he here? Why can he see them?

Up ahead, a white shape darts out from behind a boulder, crouching. An animal. Muscled and snowy-haired. Feline. Watching him, waiting for him.

A snow lion.

Karma knows the mythical animal instinctively even though he has never seen it before, even though he knows it is not real. The first of the Four Dignities from the prayer flags.

This is just a dream . . .

When the animal growls, the low, throaty sound rumbles through the range.

Follow me, its eyes seem to say. *This way.* It lets out a roar. This time the resounding echo of its voice reminds Karma of the blare of a horn. It whirrs through the mists, echoing off the rock. A deep sound. A swallowing sound.

Ommmmm . . .

Follow it.

The snow lion bounds up the slope, away from the multitude of spirits. Karma hesitates, glancing at the stream of spirits. But they do not seem to see the lion or hear it.

Except for one lone person.

Karma sees a man split off from the masses, turning to follow the snow lion up the steepening terrain. Specks of white begin to drift from the sky, snowflakes that never touch the ground. His back is to him, but Karma knows who it is.

Father.

The mountain mist moves in, masking Karma's view, the man vanishing into the perimeter of cloud.

Father . . . wait!

Karma scampers up the slope, chasing after him. Loose scree crumbles, cascading as his footsteps displace broken rock. Rounding a boulder, he sees his father again, even higher. The snow lion by now is nowhere in sight; only the echo of its roar still beckons to them. More clouds drift in. He must keep up or he will lose him.

Ommmmm . . .

The fog thins, as if he is breaking through the ceiling of the cloud barrier. He sees his father perched on a rock, hands cupped to his ears. Listening.

The clouds peel back, rolling away to reveal a triangle of white, looming bright and clear in the dim, gray sky. Massive in size, dazzling in beauty.

Karma stares in awe.

The Mountain! It is real!

He shouts again to his father, joy now suffusing through him.

His father hears the shout, begins to turn around—

A boom shudders the air, wrenching his father's head back toward the sky before Karma can glimpse his face. The earth trembles. Suddenly it heaves. For a moment, all is suspended in midair. A flash of light streaks over the peak, so bright it could be the sun, eclipsing his father's silhouette and filling the sky with a blinding whiteness. Karma cries out, shielding his eyes. But his voice is swallowed up. A wind surges, blasting down the mountain. He is thrown back, flattened to the ground.

Over the horizon, an inferno mushrooms—a raging tower of flame swelling in force, expanding toward him.

Shrieks fill the air. Shrieks, Karma realizes, of the dead. The fire thunders down the mountain. It sweeps across the range. In an instant, it engulfs the heavens, the earth, and everything in between.

Until all that is left is his own voice.

Screaming.

———

Karma jolts awake in his bed, shaking, chest heaving. His vision is blurred. His face streaming with tears.

A dream. Just a dream.

Gasping, he lies there for a moment, his mind still reeling, the dreamworld still leaning on his consciousness like the lingering of a presence once someone is gone. The image of his father permeates his mind, of him turning to look at Karma. But at that moment, the flash had burst over his father's shoulder and the flare had swallowed him up in its light.

I could not see his face. He was there. But I could not see it.

He squeezes his eyes shut, trying to will into existence any other recollection of his father. There is a memory somewhere. He feels it, lingering just beneath the surface. He tries to think back to the things he can remember. Grazing the yak herd together in the haze of a dry windstorm. The two of them watching the sunset as the valley turns to pink from gold, silhouettes in the dark when it was over. And of course, the last memory he has of him. The view as he peered out from the iron wreckage—of his father's back as he called and called to Karma before finally giving up, departing to the west, never to be seen again.

Never to return.

And never a clear picture. The face of his father eludes him still.

All the memories, all incomplete. The memories of a child. And the understanding of a child too. How much did he truly know about his father? Could they really share the same gift?

Would his father even recognize him?

How can I expect to follow in his footsteps?

He hears a quiet sound of sniffling coming from the other side of the woolen partition. He wipes his eyes, sitting up. From his mattress, he glances across the darkened room. Night clings to the corners, though dawn begins to punch through the dusk.

Karma gathers his robes out of the bedding and slips into them, tightening the sash, turning his blanket back into clothing as he slides his feet into the shoes on the dirt floor. Venturing out from the curtain, he finds his mother still in bed, her back toward him, face to the door.

"Mother," Karma says.

Her voice is tearful. "I've said goodbye to a husband before. Must I do the same to a son?"

Uncle Urgyen's question tugs now at Karma's chest. Can he do it? Can he leave her? Or Lobsang, still unconscious?

Karma goes to the edge of her bed, stooping to sit on the mattress corner. Outside, the stars are blinking out. With the onset of dawn, the ghosts are retiring, and the darkness is still.

"The first time it happened," his mother says, "your father woke one morning saying he could hear an echo in the sky. The sounding of the Sherpa horns, he said, calling to one another in the mountains. I thought he was bewitched. 'You are talking about horns that are gone, sounding from people who are dead, in mountains that have collapsed,' I told him."

She pauses. "But the truth is, there are times . . . I think I can hear things, too. I imagined I could hear *him*. Among the ghosts." She curls herself into her pillow as if muffling a moan of pain. "Like he is watching us. But we can't talk to him. We can't see him."

"I dream of him," Karma confesses. "But I can't see him either. Not face-to-face."

"I didn't want to admit it." Karma's mother shakes her head. "But I've always known. And now I know for sure. He is dead. He is gone.

My Patrul is never coming home. And soon my son will leave too. The Seventh Sun has not even come, but already I will have lost everything."

When the village discovered the missing money, Uncle Urgyen and the people declared him a charlatan and a thief. But deep down, Karma knew his mother never blamed him. Despite the trials that followed, she never regretted her marriage, regardless of what her sister or Uncle Urgyen said. She has her son. And to her, that is a blessing far greater than any curse. If Karma is to leave her too, she will have nothing left.

I can't do it, he realizes. *Not this way.*

"I don't have to go," Karma declares. "I won't. Maybe if I just stay, he'll come home one day. Or maybe he won't, like the Minister said, and we should just accept it. Maybe it's like people say, that it was because he cheated death in the mountains that fate caught up to him."

His mother turns sharply to face him, her expression suddenly severe. "No," her voice rises in vigor. "Never say that. You heard the Minister; he did nothing wrong. He was your father—still is—not some condemned migoi they make him out to be. He was not cursed, at least no more than the rest of them. Do they think their fate is any different? Never believe that. Not about him. Not about yourself. They blame him because he gave them hope and now they have no one else to believe in. But it was the world's karma that got us here. Not his."

The anger leaves her face. "It was hope. *That* was why he left, Karma. Not to run away. Not because he believed he carried a curse. But because he could still feel them. He could see his people in his dreams. They should have been dead, beyond all reach, but he could still hear them sounding their horns, just as if they were alive. It was a sign to him that there is something more, something beyond the end. That's why he left us—to find it, so that even if the world ends in the Seventh Sun, there can still be hope."

Karma looks down.

Dreams.

He has those too. Dreams like the one he just had. Dreams that tell him things. But always terrible dreams—because death is always a part of them.

"Your father used to say, a Sherpa's destination becomes his destiny. Though he cannot always see the end. He leads so others can follow." Her voice grows soft. "And that is why . . . I know you must go."

"Mother—"

"You must finish what he started, Karma—as much as it breaks my heart." Her voice quivers. "Or else the curse *will* be our fate, and the condemnation ours."

The low moaning of the ghost-winds crescendos suddenly outside, the spirit voices usually gone this close to dawn. His mother hears it too. "The ghosts of the dead are just as trapped as we are," she says. "When the world is gone, there will be nowhere for them to be reborn. Your father felt that he had to help them. To try to free both the living and the dead from our fate under the Seventh Sun. And that is why you must go, too. Because if . . . if he *is* dead," his mother's voice trembles, "then he is with them now. And he needs you more than ever. We all need you."

Karma swallows, finding the knot that has been in his throat now in his stomach. "What if I end up wandering lost in the mountains?" Karma says. "I heard the horns once, but it's been so long."

She straightens her back, nodding like she has never been more certain. "Better off wandering lost in the mountains than languishing to die in the valley. If there is a future, it's not here."

Karma presses his lips together. He says nothing, knowing the choice is clear.

He clears his throat. "The Minister's guard will keep watch over all of you," he says at last, fighting hard not to let his voice waver. "I will see to it."

To protect the village. To be sure that what happened to Lobsang will never happen to you or anyone else. That alone is worth the sacrifice.

"It is you they must watch over," his mother replies. "Life in the Territories may be harsh under the Minister's law. But the lawlessness of the Borderlands is worse."

"I will be all right," Karma says. "Nothing is safer than traveling with the patroller escort."

"Out there, it's the warlords, not the Lord Hanumanda, who rule," his mother warns. "And if you do go beyond the Borderlands, to the wasteland, you will have yourselves to contend against, because there is only barrenness beyond devastation."

"I will return, Mother."

Karma's mother gazes at him, trying to put on a strong smile. "Yes," she says finally, voice thickening with what must be the courage she is mustering to say the words. "You will. With your head held high."

In the dark of their home, in the chill air, Karma makes an oath before the rising sun.

I promise.

A warbler buzzes outside. They hear the yap of the terriers. On the eastern horizon, the first ray of sunlight shoots out through the valley, reaching the threshold's open door.

8

THE BASIN

L ater that day, the village marches Karma out in a procession to the prayer flags. His uncle leads the people as if he were a captain of one of the Lord Minister's troops himself, but once they see the expedition's soldiers at the flagstaff of the iron wreckage, they halt in a quiet cluster.

His mother's tears. The clapping of the prayer flags with the animals of the Four Dignities surrounding a faded but flaming jewel. The white *khata* scarf his mother puts around his neck, pressing her forehead against his, whispering blessings and good luck. It all seems like a memory of his father's departure in the very same place, so that he almost finds himself looking for his younger self in the spot where he had hidden ten years ago. When the stupa sinks into the distance along with his mother's figure and outstretched hand, he imagines his father looking back at the same scene of unfettered hills and far-reaching sky—a trail of horses carrying the army's expedition due west.

Now the terrain begins to rise, the yellow grasslands breaking into small, rocky outcroppings. The gradual lift would seem to mirror

Karma's rising hopes, were it not tempered by the rifts in the ground from earthquake damage, a sobering reminder of the dangers that may lie ahead. Their plan is to re-create his father's journey, to head west, and then wherever Karma will take them, guided by the horns that his father spoke about—but the sounds of which Karma has not heard in years.

Perhaps soon.

Perhaps when I am at the Borderlands.

For now, he can only wait and hope. The men of the expedition, around two dozen of them on horseback, regard him without words. They are disguised as ordinary nomads so as not to draw attention should they encounter anyone, but all are inconspicuously armed. They bring with them many packhorses carrying supplies. This will be a journey of weeks, if not months.

After many hours, their route takes them toward what looks like a shimmering lake in the distance, but the captain assures them that it is just an illusion. The body of water is dry, he says, having long since been drained by the quakes, leaving this afterimage like some ghost of what was once there. The expedition's captain calls it the Skeleton's Head because the shape is that of a skull.

By evening, they reach the outermost boundary of the valley. The Skeleton Head is inverted from their eastern approach. On the horizon waits a low wall of cliffs separating the Territories under the Minister's control from the Borderlands beyond. The red glow of the setting sun peeks here and there from clouds that have amassed. It bleeds through the hint of gorges and gullies, but otherwise the rock face is dark, vacant. The seeping colors make the basin look like it is stained with blood.

The soldiers immediately bustle about—pitching tents, watering and grazing the horses, preparing the evening victuals. They move without instruction or orders, with the practiced rote and speed of men accustomed to repetition of these tasks. As they mill about, Karma feels out of place, conspicuously idle, sheepish too, at the thought that he is somehow supposed to be their guide to the Mountain. Until he can hear the horn, he will feel useless.

Two of the patroller soldiers huddle over the implements of a fire, bickering quietly. They are brothers, from what Karma has been able to glean, and only a few years older than he is.

He is within earshot of the brothers when they notice him watching them, and their bantering stops. The older one, Osel, gives him the once-over, a hint of suspicion in his eyes.

"Something you need, comrade?" he says, using the formal though less deferential form of address.

Karma offers what he hopes is an affable smile. He doesn't want to appear to be eavesdropping. These men are going to be his travel companions, his escorts. They will be journeying together for what might be a long time, to find this Mountain.

He knows he is an outsider still, but he will be one of them, a group he has long feared because of their mercilessness in enforcing the Minister's law. How strange, but perhaps he has misjudged them—the Minister's patrollers.

Perhaps soon they will be his friends.

"Not at all," Karma replies, "I just wanted to offer my help."

At his reply, the elder gives a snort of derision at his younger brother. "Hear that, Jonang? Even the Sherpa boy is getting tired of watching you bumbling around with that tinder."

The younger brother shoots both Osel and Karma a look of challenge, eyes flicking back and forth between them as if trying to figure out who has insulted him the most.

Osel jerks his head toward a gray gathering of clouds beyond the distant elevations. Storm clouds seep down, smoky and opaque. The winds are blowing hard now, in long, cold gusts. "If you don't get that fire going before the storm, it'll be you explaining to the captain why we're having dried *tsampa* for dinner, not me."

Jonang's face twists into a deeper scowl. For a moment, the two brothers seem to have forgotten Karma. Trying to diffuse the tension, Karma makes a show of shifting his attention toward the cliffs.

"Do you know much about the Borderlands?" Karma asks.

Their attention returns to him. Karma senses their distrust. Probably understandable, being on constant guard for spies. Either that, or they take his question as a kind of provocation.

"I just mean . . . I've never been this far from home myself," Karma adds quickly, the mention of home suddenly bringing an involuntary pang of homesickness.

Osel's eyebrows rise in curiosity. "Yet, here you are."

Karma realizes that his declaration could be interpreted as boastfulness, like he was somehow special. He has to be careful to remember that there could be envy or resentment by the others at the attention the Minister bestowed on him and his family. Gifts. A new horse. Food for his village. Guards to protect the villagers. These soldiers undoubtedly received no such exchange when they joined the Eastern Army. They have come from other villages elsewhere in the Four Rivers and Six Ranges, drafted into the patroller ranks. What makes him so special?

Before Karma can say anything else, Osel imparts another reply. "Let me give you a piece of advice, Sherpa. Forget about home. You won't be seeing it for a very long time, if ever again. But don't worry. The Minister's guards promise that they will keep a close eye on the village, night and day. There won't be a single soul that will come—or go—without their knowing." At these words, the brothers exchange a strange, knowing look, and for some reason Karma feels uneasy.

A sudden gust of wind rushes through, strewing about the embers of the tinder fire that Jonang has been toiling over. The younger brother lets loose a chain of curses. "The damned wind in this damned valley!"

Osel slaps the back of Jonang's head. "It's not the wind, you ignoramus. It's your useless fire. If you had gone and gotten the bags to build a barrier like I told you, you wouldn't have wasted all this time."

For a moment, Karma has the impression that the wind is alive, as if it was not just the current that carried the ghostly voices but the ghosts themselves that blew through the fire. He sees Jonang swivel to face his brother, ready for a fight.

"I'll get them," Karma rushes to volunteer, in part trying to quell the conflict, in part feeling like he's had enough of the brothers' company. "It's no concern, really." He gives what he hopes is a nonchalant shrug and turns to go, Jonang's glower and Osel's searching stare at his back.

Their retorts fade in the growing wind. It is getting dark, and it will not be long before the refrain of ghost-winds rises in full measure. Karma pulls his mother's scarf higher around his neck, shielding his face from the dust.

Reaching the packhorses, he picks two bags. One clinks with the weight of the soldiers' armor, hidden within bundles inside. The other feels like furs for bedding. He totters with them back to the fire.

Only Jonang is there, having regathered the kindling. "Just leave them," he grunts, without bothering to look up.

The sun is almost completely obscured behind the walls of the distant cliffs as Karma goes back to the packhorses for more bags. Meanwhile, storm clouds have gathered in the east.

The sudden rages of weather have worsened in the past year. During spring, the winds blew the village's calabash seeds right out of the soil and they had to gather them back up for replanting. And then, when the long melons finally began to grow, another windstorm tore the young gourds off their vines. The rest were killed in the frost that followed. The Minister was right. The weather was raging. Another sign of the Seventh Sun's approach, so they said.

The silhouettes of the tents make Karma think of evening in the village. He imagines his mother alone in the gloaming of the darkened house, the sound of the ghosts already filling the room. A hollow feeling comes over him, and once again he feels the stab of homesickness.

He's not sure if it's the dust or the image, but in spite of himself, his eyes begin to well.

The wind whips at his face as if to slap him out of it. Karma blinks behind the strands of his hair, feeling embarrassed. Surely his father was not so easily distracted. He takes a breath of resolve, wiping his eyes as he bends to lift more bags. Back and forth, he fetches the saddlebags. As the wind barrier rises, so do the flames. Soon a fire, white and spindly, licks into the blustery night.

But the weather is also worsening quickly, the air getting colder. As Karma returns with another bag over his shoulder, a particularly strong gust unbalances him and he drops the sack, spilling its contents. Clothing strews about—a tunic, a shirt, a pair of trousers, a necklace on a string. Fearing the wind will scatter them, Karma rushes to retrieve the items, scooping them back into the bag.

Amber beads, orange coral. The sight of the object in his hand jars him. Familiar yet somehow incongruous in its appearance in the patrollers' bags.

I know this necklace.

And then the moment of recognition.

This is Lobsang's. The one Uncle Urgyen gave him on the day of the fortune.

His mind goes back to the moment he and his little cousin found the dead calf. He remembers the necklace around Lobsang's neck, so long that it dangled below the boy's belt, tangling in his arm as he shielded his mouth and nose from the foul odor of the dead calf.

Karma's eyes drop to the bag.

It is as if a cold wind has breezed over his body, standing his hairs on end, at what else he now sees.

Masks.

Leather visors. The kind worn by riders to protect their faces against sun and wind and sand. The kind worn by—

Bandits.

Karma's mind comes to a halt under the onslaught of revelations, to the cumulative realization that something is not right.

A whiff of cooking meat floats on the wind—dinner—and he feels suddenly sickened. He tries to tell himself that there must be a good reason . . . that the soldiers merely found these things. But the nausea that follows tells him instinctively otherwise.

Fragments of the soldiers' voices echo over the wind, making him jump. He shifts his eyes from the belongings to the direction of the campfire. In the haze of the wind, in the smoke and dusk, the soldiers look as if they could be anybody. Nomads . . . monks . . . traders . . .

Bandits.

Everything inside him goes cold, though it has nothing to do with the growing chill of the night, but from knowing that he has been deceived. The soldiers are not the saviors they purported to be. The story of their rescue of Lobsang, not true. And if they were capable of lying, of staging a raid . . . if they could commit such a cruelty as to injure a child as a ploy to convince the village, what other atrocity might they subject them to?

Karma backs away from the sack. He wants to run, to go back to warn the villagers.

But how? What is his plan? He glances toward the shadows created by the fire. He'd never reach his horse, not while the soldiers are around. The packhorses, then. Unattended, left for last. Not as ideal as the black Amdowan stallion gifted from Hanumanda, but his only option to flee.

Karma starts for the animals, reaching the one he just unloaded. There is no saddle, only a halter and a lead. But there is no time to choose. He trembles in the chill of the ghost-winds. Doubt fights against action. His absence will quickly be discovered. But he has to try. He has to warn them. Especially since the village is being guarded by soldiers oblivious to the deception—

Because of me.

Because of the deal he made—his service in exchange for the protection of the village.

He reaches for the horse's lead.

"Don't."

The patroller captain steps forward, and Karma's heart stops. The captain studies him. Slowly, he holds out his hand for the rope. Trembling, Karma gives it to him.

"Don't trouble yourself," the captain says. "The men will take care of it."

Immediately, several of the patrollers converge on the packhorses, starting to unload the rest of the bags, leading the horses away. Karma blinks. They are just here for the bags. Coming to tend to the pack-horses. He breathes out, a shaky, quivering sigh of relief.

But then he sees one of the patrollers moving toward a sack on the ground—the one he dropped—within steps of coming upon it. Relief turns back to panic. In his haste to escape, he left the bag out in the open.

Thinking quickly, Karma starts toward the fallen pack. "I don't mind at all," he says over his shoulder, as if in reply to the captain. "We were just using the bags to build a barrier against the wind. I'll just run this last one back—"

He rushes past the patroller just in time to snatch up the spilled contents. The stones in Lobsang's necklace feel like polished teeth, and Karma crams the necklace into the sack, cinching the bag shut before the patroller can see what fell out.

"Sherpa!" the captain calls.

Karma hesitates. His heart is pounding in his chest. The footfalls of the captain's steps follow. Slowly, Karma turns.

Even in the dark, the captain's presence is dominating, his eyes watchful. "A caution," the captain says. "The Borderlands are a dangerous place. Bandits, outlaws, rebel warlords. Restless ghosts and the vengeful damned." He lowers his voice. "You'd do well not to go wandering off. Remember that out here, anything can happen. Your only promise of protection—is us."

Lightning shimmers over the horizon. The distant sky emits a low rumble.

Fragments of ice begin to rain down, tiny crystals pecking Karma's face. The air has the hardness of stone and bitterness of iron.

"A storm's coming," the captain remarks ominously as he heads back toward the tents. "You men, tie up the horses," he orders. "Some spook more easily than others."

Once again, Karma is left on his own. But this time there is no thought of escape. There is no chance of it. Not with the approaching storm and the blindness of night. And not under the watchful eye of the patrollers. Karma is powerless to do anything about it now. His insides grow sick at the realization.

The ghost-winds lash again, and in the howl, the billows whip and the scarf Karma's mother has given him suddenly rips away from his neck. He tries to grasp it, to claw it back from the night. But in an instant, it is gone, leaving his skin naked—

His throat bare against the cold and darkened world.

9

THE BANDITS

Daybreak—and Karma moves like the walking dead, riding on his horse.

He has not slept. How could he, knowing the truth about the guards watching his village? Throughout the night, he longed to sneak away. He imagined stealing a horse and riding to the valley to warn them. But now he begins to worry that even if he could make it home, it would accomplish nothing if he returned without the Seeing Stone. They would only force him to go back, this time under compulsion, erasing any pretense that the villagers were anything but hostages.

And what about his father? The Minister lied. He used stratagem to trick Karma into fearing that there would be no other choice. What else then might he have lied about? Could he even trust what Hanumanda said about his father?

I believe that this Stone was the answer that Patrul was searching for—and found.

Karma wants to believe this. But can he now?

Find the Stone, and not only will you redeem your father's name, but perhaps you shall also see him again.

Why would the Minister send Karma on this search if it was untrue? The dilemma looms before Karma now. In his heart, he does not want to give up the search for his father. More than anything else, he longs to see him again, even if it is for one last time. But he can't just abandon his mother, his cousin, his aunt, and his uncle—*his whole village*—either, knowing the truth of the Minister's subterfuge. Especially knowing that his own father has been accused of leaving them just the same, ten years ago. What would happen if Lobsang awoke with a memory and told the village? The patrollers are known to be ruthless if they as much as suspect insurrection.

Karma makes a decision then. He will go back to the valley first. He will warn the village, come whatever blame his Uncle Urgyen is sure to lay on him. But then he will come up with a plan. He will sneak away and resume his search for the Stone and his father.

The horse snorts, flaring its nostrils in irritation, as if sensing the competing fears in Karma's mind. Already the air is stifling. The winds are gone, replaced by the heat that hangs over them. Today the horse that the Minister called the black moon of Amdo when he gave it to Karma is more like a black cloud, its courtly bearing the day before replaced by a stormy tenseness. It hesitates at Karma's halfhearted signals, eyes darting to the others, tail swishing with suspicious flicks. This is a horse used to a leader's direction, unaccustomed to following from behind.

In the afternoon, they reach the bottom of the Skeleton Head's basin, a narrow gullet entering through the cliffs. Inside the gorge, the passage of rock is striated, alternating between shimmering colors and pockmarked shadows, hinting at a deeper maze of hollows.

The captain never takes his attention away from the canyon walls, with its holes looking like large eyes, watching them back. By evening's onset, they have climbed out of the gully into elevated land, and the horses seem more relaxed, less jumpy. Birds the color of brass swirl through the sky, disappearing into the western sun like sparks from a fire under daylight.

"You don't see a sight like this every day," comes the captain's voice to Karma.

Karma must appear to be homesick from how quiet he has been, avoiding all conversation, speaking only when spoken to and merely in single words. The truth is that he is afraid that he will be unable to hide his knowledge of the truth—as well as his contempt for those who deceived him.

"Where the valley ends, the Borderlands begin, bandit country from here on out, as far as the wastelands," the captain continues. He is refer-ring to the border bandits—scourge of the Four Rivers and Six Rang-es—tribesmen and nomads turned raiders for survival, deserters and herders forced off their settlements in the Territories for failure to pay tribute, now banded together to live by robbing travelers and refugees. "We had an understanding. Each of us was to stay on our own side of the cliffs. The Eastern Army to the Territories, the border bandits to the Borderlands. But all that is going to change soon. The Lord Minister is gathering his army, like the prophecy says. Once he finds the Lama Child and you find the Seeing Stone, we will go west to the Mountain."

The expedition suddenly slows, the soldier in the lead pointing to something on the ground. The captain eases his horse forward to take a look. When Karma's horse joins from the rear, he sees a column of tracks parallel to their course—a sign of recent travel through the area.

"Are they border bandits, sir?" the patroller brother Osel asks.

They scan the rise ahead to the crest of a tall ridge. A small mound has been erected, silhouetted against the white sky. It is a cairn, a me-morial of stones, shaped into a pyramid. From the top, a streamer flutters, almost invisible. They nose their horses up the ridge to inves-tigate further. Around the edifice, they find fresh signs of circumam-bulation around the edifice. The tracks suggest it was a sizable group.

"Not bandits," the captain concludes as he scrutinizes the trail. "More likely outlaw refugees of some sort, trying to go west. A caravan of around fifty people, from the looks of it. Most on foot, some with carts and animals too."

Jonang retrieves one of the stones from the cairn, a flat, gray disc with an inscription on the surface, and gives it to the captain. "'Om mani padme hum,'" the captain reads. "'Behold, the jewel in the lotus.'" From the ridgetop, he surveys the land. The soldiers follow the captain's gaze.

In the distance, at the base of a wooded spur running down from a hill below a bluff, they spot them.

"They're monks." Osel and Jonang recognize the group at the same time.

Even at this distance, their maroon-colored robes are distinct to Karma, who recognizes the clothing as those worn by travelers who pass through his own village from time to time, collecting alms. But those other holy men are sanctioned by the Minister, often traveling with patroller soldiers.

"Shall we detain them for questioning, sir?" Jonang inquires of the captain. "If they're monks, they may know something about the whereabouts of the Lama Child."

The captain tosses the rock to the ground. "True. But these are pilgrims, not outlaws. Detaining them would do no good. We'll talk to them disguised as fellow travelers, instead."

He jerks his chin to the group toward an area below the ridge. "Leave your weapons with the packhorses." But then he points to Osel and Jonang. "You two stay behind with the supplies."

The brothers look as if they are about to protest but think better of it.

The captain nods at Karma. "You'll be coming with us, Sherpa. But remember what I said. Stay close. Should any of them try to speak to you, tell them nothing. Trust no one."

The soldiers mobilize. From the rear of the group, Karma's warhorse strains on its bit as if sensing imminent action. They move out, their hoofbeats rattling off the landforms as they stream down the slope. The tops of the trees are lit with the late sun, its rays scattered over the ridge ahead.

The monks' caravan appears suddenly. The feeling of foreboding, of impending disaster, that has become all too familiar of late comes over Karma. He sees the monks' heads turning, faces animated, maroon cloaks frozen like a group of startled sheep. And then, just like sheep . . . they scatter—dispersing in every direction, some fleeing from where they stand, some running to their handcarts.

The captain swerves his horse, apparently scuttling his original plan of approach. "Fan out!" he shouts to the patrollers, swearing. "Cut them off before we lose them!"

The formation of soldiers instantaneously spreads out. The patrollers veer on the trail of fleeing monks, preparing to head them off. But there is something about the way the monks are fleeing, something that Karma only now notices.

To the left, to the right . . .

Toward us.

As if they are not fleeing the soldiers . . .

But something else.

A rider beside Karma swerves dangerously close, threatening to collide into him. Instinctively, Karma jerks his reins away. But he is going too fast, much faster than he has ever gone. Still unaccustomed to the horse, to its quickness and its power, he feels himself suddenly slipping—sliding from the saddle, the momentum of his body going in one direction, the horse in another. He tries to lean into the turn, to hold on . . .

But he falls and finds himself on the ground beneath bulging musculature and circling hooves. Motion seems suspended. His sight dims. He can see the horse's veins throbbing, the flying of earth. Though he has fallen, somehow he is still moving, still speeding along. It is his foot, he realizes—caught in the stirrup, which is lodged around his ankle. Karma kicks. Miraculously, his foot comes free. He tumbles, rolling to a stop.

For a moment he is immobile, all control of his extremities lost, the only feeling a lingering sense of moving, of earth gliding beneath his body. No pain, but no other sensation either.

He blinks. Once. Twice.

Nothing.

I can't feel anything.

Panic floods him.

He strains to lift his head.

A tingle of feedback twitches in his neck. Slowly . . . thankfully . . . he rises from the ground.

I can move.

He looks ahead in a daze. His horse is nowhere in sight. The other patrollers have continued as well, spread out, oblivious to his fall, chasing after the scattering monks. A pilgrim nun with gray hair lags behind, clutching something as she flees into the woods.

A shrill whoop rings through the air, immediately answered by hoots from the surrounding forests. Karma turns cold at the sound—it is one his people have come to fear. And then he understands the reason for the seemingly illogical direction of the monks' flight. They are not running from the patrollers in their nomad disguises.

They are running from the border bandits.

The surrounding forests stir with the twang of bows and flitter of arrows. The fleeing monks cry out.

Bodies tumble, handcarts turn over.

All at once, there is mayhem. A swarm of bandits suddenly streams from the woods.

The patroller captain is shouting, his voice sharp. He swivels back and forth on his horse.

"Fall back!" the captain screams, his arm waving empty-handed as Karma remembers that the patrollers are unarmed. "Retreat to the ridge!"

An arrow streaks through the air. One moment, the captain's mouth is moving. The next, it stops—skewered open with an arrow. His face goes still, eyes wide and searching. Then another arrow lands, thumping into his chest. The horse sidesteps, an effort to keep him astride, but finally the captain falls.

Karma stares.

At the sight of their captain, the other patrollers panic, circling, turning their horses to retreat. More arrows zip across the clearing. One by one, the soldiers drop from their horses.

A massacre . . .

Snapping out of it, Karma runs.

Toward the woods. Trampling into the foliage. Hemlock bristles. Heads of cassia swoop. Karma ducks, hurling himself blindly, deeper into the tangle. The shadows of fleeing monks flit, helter-skelter.

The patrollers . . . Dead.

We rode into an ambush.

A blur of a figure in maroon clothing and gray hair darts out from behind a pine. Karma swerves, but he is running too fast and the ground is too uneven. They collide, careening down a bank of the forest floor.

He comes face-to-face with the same gray-haired nun he observed a moment ago, a bundled object still in her arms, cradled against her body. For a moment, neither move, staring at each other. But then the forest fills with the shouts of men, footsteps pounding, voices shouting.

The nun scrambles to her feet. She whirls around just in time to face a masked bandit who jumps out, blocking her path. Shrinking back, she swivels in the opposite direction. But that way is barred by another. Still a third bandit bounds out from the periphery. A fourth comes into view, now completely cutting off her escape. She is surrounded.

And Karma with her.

The fourth bandit's face, the only one not wearing a mask, is covered with red grease. He tilts his head toward the object in her arms. "What is that you have there, old woman?"

The nun hugs the bundle close. "We're pilgrims. We have no possessions of value."

"Oh?" the red-faced bandit replies. "Then you won't mind if he takes a look." One of the other bandits strides forward to grab hold of the object in her arms.

The nun pulls away. The bundle's covering unravels. There is the sound of something tearing. A book tumbles to the ground, pages scattering.

The bandit backhands her across the face, and the nun gives out a stunned cry as she falls to the ground. He retrieves the book, handing it over to the red-faced bandit, who is apparently the chief among them.

He studies the pages. "These are maps," he says. "Where do they lead?"

The nun's lip is bleeding. She is shaking. When she doesn't answer, the bandit chieftain starts toward her. Frantically, she begins to slide away, until she is behind Karma.

The bandit chieftain turns his attention to Karma, his brutal face managing an expression of curiosity at this person who is clearly not one of the pilgrims. "And who are you?"

Karma does not reply because he is too afraid. He does not move, because there is nowhere to go. Nowhere to run. As the bandit chieftain takes another step forward, Karma thinks suddenly of the knife the Minister gave him. Karma has never wielded a weapon before, never held an object to fight or to maim another person. But there is no choice. He thrusts his hand into his robe, grasping the handle. He draws it out, tugging on the silver sheath.

Stuck. The blade, lodged inside the sheath, does not come out.

Karma glances down. The scabbard has been damaged, dented somehow at the throat—probably when he fell from the horse. He tries once more, tugging on the handle as hard as he can.

Still no use.

The bandits begin to snicker. A slow, vicious smile grows on the chieftain's face. A stone axe slips into his hand by his leg. Karma feels his insides grow weak, bracing himself, still clutching the undrawn knife like a child wielding a stick. The chieftain raises the weapon.

A sudden crackle of rifle fire pulls their attention away.

The chieftain's smile vanishes. The bandits exchange glances with one another.

"Gangdruk outlaws, Drakpa?" asks one of them.

More rifle shots carry through the forest, followed by shouting.

The chieftain's mouth contorts into a scowl. "Take the book," he barks. Glancing to Karma and the nun, he adds, "Bring them with us."

The bandits start forward.

No . . .

Karma acts, making a grab for the chieftain's axe. He has the upper hand at first, but in the next moment, his palm is empty, the bandit chieftain wrestling it out of Karma's grip.

What comes next takes only an instant, but Karma can see it happening, sees the stone ax-head arcing toward him before he can fully duck or raise his hands to protect himself—

His vision flashes, a rupture of light and pain to his head. He stumbles back.

Earth tilts. Forest dims. Somewhere very far away, the nun is shrieking. The world begins to turn. Like a stone, Karma drops, with the sensation of plummeting into a hole. He feels the darkness closing in, feels the velocity of his body's fall.

A world of blackness unfolds.

10

THE NUN

K arma stands on a broad thoroughfare.

The ground under his feet is hard as stone, but it is neither rock nor mortar. It is completely uniform—a single, endless stretch without breaks or variation or any seams—going as far as the eye can see. Something large hurtles by, startling him, soundless as a breeze but extraordinarily fast, gleaming. Another passes him, going in the other direction. More follow, whizzing by on wheels, without noise, without effort, as if whisked on the very wind itself. He begins to realize that these are vehicles, like wagons, with people inside them. Pale, unseeing faces. They do not look at him; it is as if he is invisible.

He darts to the edge of the thoroughfare and looks off to the side. A bank of towers looms before him. They rise, seemingly endless in height, gleaming pillars in the sun like crystal stupas piercing the very heavens.

Karma looks up in awe. These translucent structures are not made of the stone of the earth, but of iron. Also glass. He can make out figures inside. More white faces. The people are dressed in strange clothing as formfitting as a second skin. Behind the windowed walls they look like bodies trapped under the ice of a frozen lake.

As he stands amid the scene, he begins to hear a distant noise—a growl. He turns in its direction. Somehow, his eyes zoom closer.

He sees a large tiger, striped and yellow, which he recognizes as the second of the Four Dignities. It crouches in the middle of the road. A whirling vehicle courses into its path, sounding a warning blare.

The tiger roars in return. It snatches the vehicle in its jaws, crushing its iron shell. Then it slams the wreckage to the ground, flinging its occupants into the swerving onslaught of other wagons.

This must be a dream.

I am only dreaming.

The tiger turns its head toward Karma, as if hearing his thoughts. Its mouth opens, baring fangs, and Karma feels his certainty fleeing. The throaty rumble of its growl thunders forth. It is a violent sound, rupturing the smooth thoroughfare in a shattering of cracks up to the buildings, splintering windows, splitting metal. Wagons careen to avoid the shower of glass, crashing into one another.

The tiger roars a second time, and this time the sound peals through the air with the crack of lightning, bolts sizzling across the skies and setting the lofty rooftops on fire. A third roar, and the ground ruptures, springs of floodwater course through the thoroughfare, washing away the people as they run from their vehicles. A fourth roar brings thunder and a deluge of rain. A fifth roar comes like the blast of a furnace, a wave of heat evaporating the water into burning steam that melts the skin of every person, sapping even the color of the land to bone-white dust.

It roars a sixth time, and this final burst is like the gust of a violent wind, stripping away the buildings like leaves from a stalk. Then the buildings disintegrate, tumbling, darkening the sky, shadowing the earth, filling the air with a flock of falling bodies.

Karma lurches awake at the bump of a wheel, the rattle of a cart. Darkness surrounds him, the dusty blackness of the night sky, and the half-wheel of the waxing moon hangs low.

Dull throbbing. Movement sends a swirl of pain and faintness through his head. He can sense that he is moving. But where is he? Where is he going?

A shadow appears by his side. Karma sees a gleam of silver hair, hears the swoosh of monks' robes. Flashes from his memory emerge.

Horses, arrows, bloodshed . . .

A stone axe raised to strike . . .

He jolts upright in a panic. A hand reaches for him. The shadow's silhouette leans forward, whispers into his ear.

"You're safe."

A woman's voice.

"Be still."

Karma blinks up at the shadow. Her figure moves beside the cart, leaning into it to help him. White hair gleams in the moonlight. It is the nun from the forest.

"Don't be afraid," she whispers, easing him back down. His head feels inordinately heavy. Like an unwieldy stone. It throbs as it touches back onto the hard floor of the wagon.

She walks alongside, keeping pace. "The Chushi Gangdruk found us. You've heard of the outlaws who help refugees cross the Borderlands?"

He has. They are a legend in the valley. To some they are saviors, fighters that help the helpless. To the Eastern Army, they are like any other outlaw gang—worthy of death for insurrection and breaking the peace.

"They're our escorts through the Borderlands," the nun says. "We were waiting for them when the border bandits attacked."

The cart jounces again, and the bump sends pain rippling through Karma's skull. He winces, a hand to his forehead.

The nun's voice is empathetic. "You took a hard blow."

Karma remembers: a red face. A bandit chieftain named Drakpa. Karma tried to snatch his weapon. A blinding blow followed. Luckily not an axe of iron, and only a glancing blow as they struggled, but enough to knock him out. That was the last thing he remembered.

But isn't there something else? Fire. Roads breaking. Buildings burning. People falling from the skies.

"Six blasts," Karma mumbles to himself, in and out of consciousness. The images slip. The memory is just a dream.

"You were dreaming of the Suns, weren't you?" asks the nun.

Around them is the quiet jangling of stirrups, the steady march of footfalls.

"You were talking in your sleep," she says.

Karma moves his head to shake off the grogginess. He feels naked, vulnerable, and self-conscious. Unsteadily, yet deliberately, he reaches a hand for the edge of the cart. Once more, she gently stops him.

"Where am I?" he says.

"You're traveling west with the monks of the Oracle."

Karma processes the words.

West. Farther from the valley. The wrong direction.

"No," Karma replies. "I—I have to go back."

Once more he tries to sit up. Once again, the nun reaches out to steady him, but this time she doesn't try to hold him back. She doesn't need to. Karma sags against the cart under the weight of his own body.

"You're injured," the nun says. "What you need is to rest."

"I've got to warn them," Karma mumbles.

"I'm . . . sorry to tell you," she says, "but your comrades did not survive."

"What?" Karma says.

"The others you were with. The patrollers."

Slowly, Karma understands. Despite the disguises, she guessed who the patrollers were. And now she must assume that Karma is one of them. He tries to read her face, but her features are indiscernible in the dark.

"The bandits killed your fellow soldiers," she says, "just like they killed many of my own people." Her voice quivers. "Just as they killed our Oracle." She composes herself, steadying her voice. "But you needn't worry. We've said nothing to the Gangdruk. We've clothed you in monk's robes, and they will not suspect a thing."

Karma touches the clothing, his fingers confirming that the loomed wool of his coat has indeed been replaced with a rougher, unfamiliar fabric.

His gaze returns to her. "Why are you helping me?" he asks.

"A kindness for a kindness," the nun replies. "What the bandits took was something very valuable. But had you not intervened, they might have taken my life too. I couldn't in good conscience leave you behind."

Karma recalls the knife. He moves his hand to his inside pocket where it should be, but of course it is not there. He dropped it in the fight, the useless weapon now left behind.

"My name is Reverend Mother Dorje. I keep the history of the monks of the Oracle—what's left of it that we know, at least. The book they took was written by the Oracle's own hand, containing every revelation he had come to discover about the location of the Lama Child."

The Lama.

So the patrollers' instinct to question the monks was not misplaced. Have their paths fortuitously crossed to join on the same journey? *No*, he decides. He is looking for the Seeing Stone. The rest of the prophecy is something he does not even understand. In any case, he already decided that he must go back to the village first. At present, however, he has little choice. His head is beginning to spin again, a sign that his strength is waning.

"Thank you . . . Reverend Mother," he manages to say, addressing her as best he knows.

"But rest now, patroller," the nun says. "We'll speak more later."

"Karma," he replies. "My name."

The Reverend Mother's voice lifts with a sad smile. "And so it should be," she says. "As it is karma, after all, that we should meet."

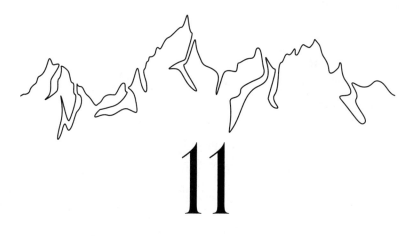

11

THE BURIAL

In the morning, the Gangdruk escorts stop at a field of wild buck-wheat. Filaments from the forest's cotton trees float in the sun.

The outlaw at the head of the caravan is a man named Surkhang. Like the other Chushi Gangdruk, instead of yak wool, he is dressed in skins, the fur side turned in the way of the nomads. His cap is the no-mads' style too. But Surkhang also wears an ensemble of mismatched adornments: bone beads poorly painted to look like expensive shells and glass, a bright feather missing its top, an array of brass buckles polished but fastened without any discernible function. Over the shirt is the trophy—a chain-mail hauberk, ill-fitting and with missing links, undoubtedly taken from some captured soldier, girdled in place by a fraying strip of tiger skin that looks at once too tight and too short.

Karma feels a sense of unease when Dorje and several other monks make their way toward the outlaw. As they speak to Surkhang, two carts trundle up to the clearing from the rear. They hold the bodies of the dead. Some agreement is reached. At an open patch of rock, the pilgrims assemble a cauldron and array of tools. Picking through the implements—hatchets and hammers, cleavers and knives—they begin chanting a prayer mantra.

As Karma wonders what is happening, the Reverend Mother Dorje shuffles toward him. Her eyes are red.

"The Oracle was a good man," Dorje says. "In life, everything he did, he did for others. And so will it be in death." She pauses a moment, lowering her voice so that only he can hear it. "It may be uncomfortable for you to watch this, Karma."

Karma gives her a questioning look, unclear of what she means.

"This will be a sky burial," Dorje explains, "to accrue to our dead even greater karma. As a final act of compassion for the living, they will be rendered into carrion—for the birds and the beasts."

Karma blinks. His eyes flicker back to the monks who have begun to unload the bodies from the cart, chanting as they work. Off to the side, the Gangdruk outlaws are watching, squatting and eating figs in the forest shade. Suddenly, he understands what is about to happen. In his village, they burn the deceased, the ground too rocky to bury the dead deep enough to protect against excavation by animals.

Out here, the monks have another solution. They let the animals feed from them. The Reverend Mother was saying that by acts of selflessness through one's life, the giving of one's own flesh in the end, a person can earn a higher rebirth—a belief in reincarnation. But Karma cannot help but wonder what good that will do when facing the end of the world.

Without the earth, no one will be reborn.

"It doesn't all have to end," the Reverend Mother says, as if anticipating the question. "The Six Suns were not real suns, after all. Only weapons. Powerful weapons, to be sure, but weapons all the same. Men wield weapons, which means men can lay them down. The prophecy may predict the end of the world from the Seventh Sun, but even it provides a way to change the future if we can find the Lama."

The pilgrims now approach the bodies with the tools of excarnation.

Karma stifles a shudder. "I'll be all right," he says. If the Gangdruk are to believe that he is one of the monks, he will stay.

"Very well." Dorje nods.

She covers her head with a fold of her robe and then leaves him to go to the charnel site. The monks begin a prayer, ringing a bell as they speak words that Karma understands to be instructions for the deceaseds' travel to a place in the otherworld. When they undress the bodies, Karma averts his eyes. But he cannot avoid the sounds—the clink of the butcher knife on rock, the sawing of tendons and pounding of bones, the weeping of the pilgrim monks.

Like dogs summoned by the sound of the pan, the winged visages of the Himalayan raptors soon materialize, their shadows circling on the ground. When the monks begin to cast the first bits of flesh, they descend. Hopping and pecking, the beaks of the great vultures strike the blood-soaked rock, joining the tapping and scraping. In the growing humidity, the air soon fills with the odor of meat and butchery.

It is not until the feeding turns into a swarm that the monks take their leave. In a daze, Karma retreats to the forest, going until he can no longer hear the squawking of their gullets and tapping of their beaks.

Karma stops at a downed tree, seating himself on its fallen trunk, head in his hands as if trying to squeeze the images and sounds from his mind.

A few moments later, the Reverend Mother Dorje comes through the trees. She sees him and gestures to the spot beside him. "May I?"

Karma rises to offer the seat. There is plenty of room for them both, so he sits again, with her.

"All is impermanent, nothing lasts," Dorje says after a moment. "I know this. Believing there would be a reincarnation to look forward to, that we might one day reach the final enlightenment together—that was enough. But now all is like a dry well, the world a barren womb."

Her eyes are wet as she stares into the woods. "For years, I walked by the Oracle's side. Following him in search of the Lama Child, who would one day come to save our dead, and rejoin our worlds again before the coming of the Seventh Sun. Now he is gone, and I am to take his place. But he was the one with the vision. I was just the annalist, content to record the journey and study the past. But all the books are gone. The past before the time of the Suns is an almost hundred-year-old mystery, while the future is an even murkier miasma. We are in a limbo of ignorance, and I fear that I will not have the gift of his sight. The monks will look to me . . . but I see nothing."

While I hear nothing, Karma thinks, and he finds that he can sympathize with her. Two people expected to lead; neither knows the way.

The two of them sit in silence.

Dorje wipes back the white hair from her brow and tears from her eyes at the same time. "Listen to me, a rambling old woman. You spill your deepest secrets to a stranger, but never confide in the ones who are the closest . . . until it is too late."

"I thought it could help my village," Karma says suddenly. "If I joined the patrollers. It's the only reason I did. But it's only made things worse. Now I have to go back because I made a promise, even though I still haven't accomplished what I set out to do."

Dorje nods. "Don't worry, I intend to keep my promise too, when I said I would repay a kindness for a kindness. We'll see to it that you have the means to get to where you need to go. But say nothing to the Chushi Gangdruk. They can be suspicious."

Footsteps approach from the forest, and a flustered monk comes through the trees, panting as he addresses the Reverend Mother. He looks panicked. "Something's happened, Reverend Mother. The Gangdruk are changing course. They're ordering us to go to their *dzong* instead."

Dorje frowns, rising. "Their dzong? But they agreed to help us search the Borderlands. This is where the Oracle said we would find the Lama Child. It's what we paid them for. We said nothing about going to their fortress."

The monk nods. "I told them. But the outlaw Surkhang says the circumstances have changed. With the border bandits and the Minister's army both about, he said he's not risking his neck for nothing."

Dorje shakes her head with incredulity. "What is it that he wants? We were just robbed! There's no more money! They agreed to help us with our pilgrimage."

The monk looks as helpless as he sounds. "Not anymore. He says the agreement was with the Oracle. Now that the Oracle is dead, the pilgrimage is over."

The sun has disappeared behind the trees and the clouds. A gray wind has moved in, its swells shaking the boughs of the cotton trees. Downy flecks float down to the charnel ground, which is wet with gristle and blood.

"Surkhang," Dorje calls out as she crosses into the opening. "We'd better discuss the plan of our course now. In the Oracle's last vision, he saw the Child traveling westward through the Borderlands. We know where we must look next."

"Really?" Surkhang shoots back. "Is that the same vision in which he failed to see the slaughter of his own people by border brigands?"

Dorje looks stung.

"Take my word for it," Surkhang goes on, "when I tell you that you're lucky to be alive. You belong behind the safety of our fortress walls with the other refugees, not wandering through bandit country."

"We are *not* refugees," Dorje says. "We are monks of the Oracle. Our pilgrimage is to find the Lama Child, not shelter. But if it's bandits you fear, then by all means—go. We will manage on our own, if we must."

The change in Surkhang is immediate.

"If you mean to imply cowardice," Surkhang answers darkly, "I assure you, Reverend Mother, that you will not find another in the Four Rivers and Six Ranges who has shed more bandit blood than I. It may be my brother who is the leader of the Gangdruk outlaws, but it's the name of Surkhang they know and fear."

There is something dangerous in his voice, something that makes everyone go still.

"Furthermore," Surkhang adds. "It's not just the border bandits you may encounter out here. The warlord Altan Khan has been calling together the clans to join his rebel force, and they're itching for a fight. And perhaps most troubling of all, the Eastern Army has been spotted gathering to the Borderlands. Hundreds, if not thousands, of them. Rumor has it that the Minister himself is leading them. You saw the scouts. They're coming."

Karma stiffens, suddenly feeling conspicuous as he realizes that Surkhang is referring to his patroller escort. But Dorje does not give him away. Instead, she keeps her eyes fixed ahead, before apparently relenting. "It is not my intention to put anyone in danger unnecessarily." She sighs, lowering her head in a short nod. "We will do as you say, for now. When things clear, we'll resume the search for the Lama."

"Good," Surkhang snaps, "because you don't have much of a choice anyway. Now get your people ready." He turns without another word, striding off.

Alone, the monks speak among themselves in hushed tones. They glance at Karma. Dorje whispers a few words, then makes a discreet motion of her hand.

"Come quickly now," she says to him.

Karma does as he is told, following her back into the forest, through the cotton trees into the thick of the evergreens, out of sight of the rest of the caravan.

She stops to scan the woods.

Karma sees what she is looking for—a mule, tied to a low bough of a tree. Someone has hidden it here.

"This was the Oracle's," Dorje says. "I had them separate it from the others when the outlaws were not looking."

She slips off the tie and holds it out to Karma. "I trust it should get you wherever it is you must go."

"Reverend Mother," Karma says, astonished. "How can I take this?"

"Where the Oracle is, he has no need for it any longer," Dorje says. "I assure you, it's quite all right." She puts the reins in his hand. "Take it and go, before they find us."

Bowing, Karma accepts the reins.

He climbs the stirrup. The Minister's horse was taller, more valuable, its saddle of finer craftsmanship, but it is on this animal that he feels more grateful.

"Good luck, patroller."

Karma lingers a moment. "What the outlaw Surkhang said—about the Minister's army," he pauses. "He's right. Hanumanda is planning something. The soldiers are coming. You should take your people as far away as you can."

Dorje studies him, her eyes intent under the gray wisps of hair. "Where we're going, no army will be able to reach us. But first we find the Child. And then indeed we shall leave, far away from here." She is silent for a moment, as if considering this. "Until then, perhaps fate will see our paths cross again."

There is something about the way she says this, and the words, that fills Karma with a sudden sense of having been in this moment before, like he felt when the Minister came to him. A feeling of . . . inevitability.

"You two," someone's voice calls from behind them. "What are you doing?"

A young Gangdruk outlaw, ponytailed and no older than Karma himself, comes out from the trees. "Reverend Mother," he bows when he realizes it is the nun. "Can I . . . help you with something?"

Seeing him, Dorje turns back to the mule, making a feint of rifling through the saddlebags. "We were looking for some thousand-leaf to make a poultice for the wounded," she says, bluffing. "Karma thinks he saw some growing at the edge of the forest."

For a moment, it seems that the young outlaw will question them further, but then he replies, "White blossoms?"

"You know plants?" Dorje says, making an expression of surprise. "I could use your help, if so."

"Some." The young outlaw looks proud.

Dorje and Karma exchange a discreet glance. "Well, in that case," she starts back toward the clearing, "where did you see the herb?" She pivots, indicating for the Gangdruk to follow. She feigns calling over her shoulder, "Don't be too long, Karma," before turning her attention back to the young Gangdruk. "Now, since you're so observant, did you happen to also notice any creeping rootstalk . . ."

Karma watches them, listens to their voices fading in the woods. As soon as they are out of sight, he nudges the mule away, not too fast in case his movements are being observed by anyone else.

A few yards away, he throws another look over his shoulder. No one is following. No one standing in his way.

Karma turns face-forward, preparing to spur the mule ahead until nagging words fill his mind, the prophecy of the Seventh Sun, creeping and unbidden:

But gather to the Mount and the Seeing Stone, that the Lama may reveal yet a future unknown.

The Reverend Mother said that they were on a pilgrimage to find the Lama Child. And then after that, to the Mountain, if they could find it. The Mountain, the Lama. It could have been fate.

A lone finch lands suddenly on the path before him, pecking on the ground. Karma stares at the bird. No, the end of the world is their fate, impossible to change, except by some miracle. Perhaps the monks will find the Lama and stop the Seventh Sun.

But his mother and the village are in danger from Hanumanda's men at this very moment.

He kicks his feet. The finch startles off into flight. That's it, then. Home. Mother. Lobsang. The village.

Then Father.

But as he rides east toward the valley, a creeping feeling remains. A feeling not so much of uncertainty in his direction but doubt suddenly about what lies ahead. A question of what he can even do to change his village's fate, if anything at all.

12

THE REBELS

Karma's way meanders, the tracks from the previous night all but indiscernible on the granite ledge. Forest, ledge, forest, more ledge. The Gangdruk outlaws took this path intentionally, their footprints harder to follow for anyone who might be tracking them. But now, as Karma tries to recreate their route, the trail becomes unclear. He was unconscious for only a few hours in the cart, but nothing about his surroundings is familiar from last night.

In the tedium of searching the terrain, he plays out in his mind the plan for his return to the village. To enter undetected will be one thing. He is fairly certain he can slip in if it is dark. He knows the village well enough. He will go to his mother to relay all he has discovered about Lobsang's abduction, then to his uncle's house to tell them too.

But then what?

How would they warn the entire village? And once they did, what would they do? Fight the patroller guards? Or would they try to escape undetected? Even if they all got away, where would they go?

There was nowhere to hide in the valley. They would be found.

The elders will know.

All I need is to get home. Uncle Urgyen, the shaman, the other clan heads—they will decide what to do.

But then he has another thought.

What if by returning he is putting his people in greater danger? Right now, their captors are maintaining the charade of being the village's caretakers—helping them, protecting them from bandits. Eventually, when the captain's party fails to show up to meet the rest of the army, they will surmise what happened, that there was an attack. And for all they know, Karma was killed with the others.

Perhaps that is best. Perhaps then the patrollers will leave the village. If I simply disappear, there no longer will be a need to hold the villagers as hostages.

The mule's gait slows as if worn out by being strained in two directions. The clouds having cleared, the sun now beats down, a harsh glare on the granite. The heat is rising, heightening the sense in Karma that, indeed, he is lost. He needs to stop somewhere. To let the mule rest. To give himself the chance to gather his thoughts.

At the next grove, he dismounts. Dragonflies dart along barberry shrubs, sunlight glaring on their wings. The mule noses Karma, its dark, clouded eyes gazing into his own. It is no colt, but still strong, still alert. How many miles it must have seen in its years, a life of wandering with the monks of the Oracle.

Karma takes the mule by the lead, entering the shaded wood. There is visible evidence of the quakes here. At one edge of the trees is a break in the earth, revealing a shattered rock ledge below, as if a giant hammer had broken off a chunk of the land, exposing its rocky insides. The result is a steep drop, though not enough to kill someone in a fall.

Karma takes his rest beneath a tall cedar's shade. The trees around pulse with the drone of cicadas. Strange to hear them this early, harbinger of frost so soon. Then again, nothing is usual in the earth anymore.

Between the growing quakes and violent storms, the strange skies and ghost-winds at night, nothing is as it once was.

Fishing through the saddlebags, he finds some millet, but what he craves is water. He takes the food and rests against the trunk of the tree. Overhead, high boughs lean close together, a gap in the canopy exposing a window of white clouds. The sight of this jogs Karma's memory of seeing a narrow strip of sky from last night. Perhaps this is where they passed. But when he looks at the ground, he sees only some fox and marten droppings, none of the signs of foot traffic he would expect had they come this way.

Lost already.

Karma peels off the upper garment of his robe from his sleeves down to his waist, letting the monk's cloak hang over his belt. He has been anxious to make his way back to the village. Now, he is not even sure where he is going. The mule nibbles at the grass, teeth clacking as it chews. Its dark eyes continue gazing at him, as if waiting to know what they are to do next.

"Your guess is as good as mine," Karma mumbles.

He shuts his eyes to think, allowing the shade to cool his brow, trying to picture the trail from the night before. But all that comes to him are images of the sky burial. The monks spared no part of the bodies. To turn the unclean into the meritorious, they even smashed the bones—rolling up the broken fragments with bits of meat for the vultures to feed on.

There was to be nothing left behind but the blood that soaked the earth.

A shaking of leaves rustles from his periphery. A twig snaps.

Karma's eyes jerk open. The hairs on his neck prickle.

Two faces peek out from behind a bush. It takes only a moment for Karma to recognize them: Osel and Jonang, the two patroller brothers who were left behind to guard the packhorses.

"Mother's corpse!" Jonang swears, rising from a crouch. "It *is* him!"

Before Karma can react, the brothers spring from the undergrowth. They reach him before he can get up, pinning him to the ground with the weight of their patroller armor, pieces of leaves and forest debris stuck to the chain mail. Karma gasps, both stunned by the blow and upset that he forgot about the brothers. Made to stay back, the pair didn't join the raid and survived the ambush. The brothers stare at him with similar disbelief, their ruddy faces dirty and sweat streaked. Their eyes go from the mule to Karma's monk clothing.

"Why are you dressed that way?" Jonang demands. "Where have you *been*?"

A bitter taste of bile rises in Karma's throat—an anger returning once more at the patrollers for what they did to Lobsang, and again at himself for being so careless. "Let . . . me . . . up," he grits through his teeth.

Osel gives his brother a nudge and Jonang relents—only a little—allowing him to breathe. "All right, Sherpa. Start talking."

As Karma catches his breath, he tries to collect himself. *Stay calm,* he tells himself. If he is to stand any chance of getting out of this, he will have to keep his wits. "There was an ambush."

"Yes, we know," Osel harries him. "But who was it? And where did they take you?"

"They were border bandits," Karma answers. Instinct tells him not to mention the Gangdruk outlaws.

The younger brother lets out a hiss of air. "I knew it," Jonang says. "It was an idiotic thing, the captain riding out like that with no weapons or armor."

Osel's eyes narrow on Karma. "Yes. But that doesn't explain what happened to you, Sherpa. How did you get away? And why are you dressed like one of the monks?"

"I was injured," Karma replies. He points to the area on his head where he was struck by the bandit chieftain Drakpa. "The pilgrim monks helped me. But then we went our separate ways."

The brothers eye the physical evidence of the bruise. Apparently satisfied, Osel gestures to Jonang. "Let him up."

They step back, giving him space to get to his feet. Osel dusts the front of Karma's robe where his knee was embedded in his chest. He glances around the forest. "Sorry about that, comrade. Can't be too careful, you know? The Borderlands teeming with spies and rebel fighters as they are. No hard feelings, right?"

He retrieves something from his belt. Karma recognizes the silver scabbard of the knife that allegedly came from his father.

"See?" Osel says. "We found this, along with the captain and the others, but not you. That's how we realized you were probably still alive." He pauses a moment before handing it to him. "The scabbard was bent. Took a few hits with a rock."

They eye him as if watching to see what he will do. Slowly Karma takes the knife. The thought crosses his mind to turn it against the brothers. But he knows that he's no match for them.

Osel nods. "You must be hungry and thirsty. We still have the packhorses, at least. How about something to eat?" He takes his brother aside. The two of them confer quietly, Jonang's eyes flicking to Karma as they talk. Without a further word, Jonang disappears into the woods, presumably to fetch the horses.

Osel comes back to Karma, moving in slow, casual strides. "My brother is right—for once," he says with an exaggerated chuckle. "It was a mistake, the captain sending the men out without weapons like that." He lets a moment pass between them in silence. "But it was an order, and as far as things go in the Eastern Army—you do not disobey orders." He stops abruptly. "Just like what they asked us to do at your village."

Karma blinks.

"You know what I'm talking about," Osel says. "The raid. Kidnapping the boy. Your cousin. You saw the necklace, didn't you? Again, my idiot brother's fault, his idea to keep the plunder." The words come matter-of-factly, divulging what Karma indeed discovered already but is now afraid to hear him say, wondering what it means that they have dispensed with the facade. "You see, it was the Lord Minister Hanumanda's plan to scare your village, to motivate you to help him find the Stone."

Karma's insides twist, the same feeling of nausea coming back to him as the night he discovered Lobsang's belongings in the packs.

Osel raises his hands in a sign of blamelessness. "I understand how you feel. Jonang and I—we were only following orders. But I swear to you, we didn't want to hurt the boy. Just like we don't want to hurt you now, either."

The sickening feeling grows, but so does the anger. First his cousin, now they are threatening him.

"What is it that you want?" Karma manages in reply.

Osel glances at Karma's mule, and then out across the forest. "I think that maybe you're thinking, I need to warn them, I need to go home. But do you remember what I told you? You need to forget about home. Forget about them. Because now that you know what the Minister is capable of . . . you can never go back. Not ever. For their good as much as yours."

Karma stares at him, anger replaced by a sinking sense of helplessness.

"Right now, they will assume that we're all dead," Osel continues to explain. "And that's a good thing for you and your village. Do you see what I'm trying to tell you? We're free now. You too. We can choose where we go. We could stay in the Borderlands, if we wanted to. Or, if, say, we choose to go to the Mountain, we can do it." He pauses now. "If we want to get the Stone for ourselves, as powerful as they say it is, there's *nothing* to stop us."

Now Karma understands. It is the Seeing Stone the brothers want. Whatever they think it can do for them, they want to use him to obtain it.

Osel becomes more animated. "We could use it." He pounds a fist into his hand. "My brother and I—we can help you."

Karma remains silent. He agreed to the expedition because he believed that he could save his village, and that he might somehow see his father again. But all at once now, he sees how naïve he was. How little he knew before embarking on this, about the Mountain, about how his father and his travel companion had found it by following the sound of phantom Sherpa horns. How little he knows now still. Except for one thing—he knows he will never again trust the patrollers.

Osel's conspiratorial demeanor is suddenly interrupted by a thrashing of footsteps, Jonang bounding through the trees. He has neither the packhorses nor the supplies with him.

"Armed riders!" Jonang sputters. "Approaching!"

Osel's face sharpens. "Border bandits? One of ours?"

Jonang's eyes are wide. He shakes his head. "It's a caravan. Rebel fighters, maybe? It looks like they have *prisoners* with them."

Osel tilts his ear toward the sound of their approach. He frowns. "Come on," he says, reaching for Karma's arm. "We have to get out of sight."

Together, they bustle through the trees, heading toward the break in the earth and the rock ledge Karma found earlier. They find cover behind a toppled tree, its roots half buried, half exposed to the sky.

"They're over there," Jonang whispers, pointing.

Peering down the winding approach, they see a column of horsemen advancing, ascending the rise, trailed by a train of tethered bodies.

"Must be one of the Khan's prisoner caravans," Osel says grimly.

"Mother's corpse," Jonang curses.

"Keep quiet," Osel hisses. "Stay down. They'll pass us by soon. No need to panic."

Silently, they watch the approaching party. Karma is rigid, not with fear, but with anticipation at the opportunity that is upon him, that he knows he can now take.

The brothers are preoccupied, Osel's back to him, Jonang's as well. The fall from the ledge is not lethal, only a drop down a wooded slope—but perhaps just enough to let him get away.

Time to act. Another moment and it may be too late.

Suddenly, Osel glances back at him, as if catching wind of his thoughts. His eyes flash.

Now!

Karma shoves the brothers as hard as he can. Osel lets out a grunt. At first it seems as if the shove has no effect other than to stun him. But then his arms wheel, his body leans. Jonang, too, teeters.

Karma doesn't wait to see what happens. He needs only to get away. He turns now, bursting into a sprint. He hears shouting but does not linger.

"You!" the younger brother's voice rings out. "Come back!"

Karma does not stop; instead, lengthening his stride, he vaults over rock and root. The mule sees him and sallies forward, trotting by his side. The edge of the forest beckons, but he can hear the thrash of footfalls nearing in pursuit. He darts in and out between trees, ducking their limbs.

A clearing appears, a drop down a hill.

He feels a hand clapping onto his back, so fast, and spares a moment of surprise at how quickly they have caught up to him. A sharp push. His body totters, his balance tips.

He goes into a dive. Down the slope. Down the hill.

He tumbles to the bottom, rolling to a stop.

The mule is no longer beside him, open sky now in place of the forest canopy. Footsteps pound, then he sees the reddened face of Jonang. The brother grasps him, clenching him by the collar.

"You . . . little . . ."

He drives a punch into Karma's gut. Karma doubles over but stays on his feet and sees Jonang raising his fist again.

"Trying to pull one over on us?"

Another blow rams into him, this time into his side. Again, Karma groans, dropping to the ground. He tries to stumble away, but he can hear Jonang following.

"Osel!!" Jonang calls out. "I got him! I got the little Sherpa bastard. Now you're going to pay."

Jonang's voice tapers off suddenly. His steps freeze.

From the corner of his eye, Karma sees a train of riders filter into view. Hooves clomp, chains clink. The caravan they observed from above now comes to a stop, arrayed before them.

Jonang, clad in his patroller's armor for all to see, begins to make a startled retreat until finally stopping, realizing he has nowhere to go. His hand hovers by his sword, but then seems to falter. He raises both arms in surrender instead.

Karma feels a wave of relief. But as he glances back to the caravan of horsemen, the feeling quickly fades. Behind the column of riders, he glimpses the trail of fettered figures, shuffling along a cable of chains and ropes.

Prisoners.

And just like that, Karma knows he is never going home again.

PART II

He made do with what little he could get
and never hoped for anything finer,
unaware that in the lining of his robe
he had a priceless jewel.

The Lotus Sutra (1st cen. CE)

13

THE GROTTO

The cry of cicadas is like the sound of metal across a whetstone.

Shriek . . . shriek . . . shriek . . .

It repeats, piercing Karma's ears, drowning everything out.

Blindfolded, hands bound, he sits on the ground, waiting. He can tell it is nighttime. He can feel it in the blindness, in the sweat-dampened chill of his body. His feet are blistered from the march, the feeling a dull pain now that they have stopped moving.

Voices approach, men speaking in unfamiliar languages.

Hands take hold and yank him to his feet. A sharp tug and the blindfold tears away to a dusky blur. Shapes and silhouettes. The hint of a fire-lit village. Blinking, Karma's eyes come into focus. A shove from behind propels him forward.

"Move," a voice barks at him.

Karma glimpses other captives—similarly bound, shuffling together like a stock of wrangled animals. There is no sign of either brother that he can immediately see, the line moving quickly.

The trees are black against the darkened sky, the surroundings a mass of shadows. Men stride about, dressed in tunics of the type that he has seen on traders. But these men are armed, and they shout and strike the prisoners, herding them toward the flickering lights.

Out of the forests, smoky torches reveal the outline of ramshackle dwellings and rambling shanties. Dogs with sunken rib cages roam about. Through lightless doorways, mud-faced figures peer, eyes like vacant sockets. Beside one of the hovels, a goitered old man moves his bowels in a tumble of weeds, only to scamper away when he sees the train of prisoners coming, as the dogs rush in to consume the excrement. The air stews with the filth.

But the train of prisoners carries on, passing the dwellings and heading toward a massive hill. Its hump breaches the sky like an eclipsed moon, crowned by a halo of broken stars. Torches light a path around the landmark, oily fissures spewing smoke from their flames into the night.

As they approach, Karma hears a chorus of tapping, the clink of metal on stone. The noise grows louder as they round the bend, coming to a gaping pit in the side of the hill. In the reddish firelight, he sees an army of bodies moving. Clinking and scraping, clanging and hammering.

A string of figures makes a human chain: Men shoulder baskets of rock up an open-cut mine. At the top, hunchbacked women rinse the broken ore in wooden troughs. The runoff of sediment washes back down to the writhing laborers in a river of sludge, while guards keep watch.

Karma tenses as they near the entrance to the mine, thinking that they are to join them. But they continue on to the great hill, to an opening in the rocky side. It is a cave, Karma realizes. He has seen crevices in the rocks of the valley Kham before, but nothing of this size, and he surmises that they must be far west now, where the terrain is higher and rockier, the remnants of the broken range.

Several guards stand watch at the mouth. An orange glow spills from the gaping cavern like a great tongue lapping at their approach. Voices reverberate within, distorted.

Their captors usher them inside. The air is immediately dense. The voices become louder, the passage descending quickly into a cavernous arena.

A crowd swarms a stone pit, reminding Karma of an underground nest of termites. In the light of smoky torches, he can make out different faces—Mongols and Pamiris, Mustangs and Magars, Paharis and Hans—and tribes he cannot recognize. They fill the stone arena, their shouts thundering off the walls. They jeer and spit as the guards jostle the prisoners down stairs that are sticky with sputum.

Karma chokes on the air, as humid as an outhouse and reeking of sweat. Rancid butter offerings cake over rocks of graven deities. To Karma's horror, at the bottom of the arena, a trio of dogs—woolly mastiffs of massive size—strains against chains, barking and snarling, lunging at the center of a pit where two men stand trembling, bloodied, and naked.

This is a ring, Karma realizes. A fighting pit.

He freezes then, suddenly recognizing the pair.

Osel and Jonang.

"Keep moving," a guard growls in his ear.

Karma swivels to see a face tattooed with deer antlers, horns branching out over each cheek. The guard swings the butt-end of his spear at Karma's leg. "I said, move!"

Karma staggers into the prisoner in front of him, the two of them tumbling into the crowd. The other prisoner wrenches away, flashing Karma a warning glare. To Karma's surprise, he sees that it is a girl— likely no more than a couple of years older than he is. People laugh, pawing at them. The guard shoves Karma and the girl back in line.

Karma staggers on, a feeling of terror growing. The line of prisoners reaches the bottom of the stairs. They are herded into a holding pen of bamboo poles. The gate claps shut, Karma the last in, the door pressing him into a crowd of bodies.

They push and scuffle, panicking. From behind the bars, Karma peers out at the two brothers. Osel and Jonang stand facing the crowd, like prisoners facing an executioner—naked, their patroller armor arrayed on the ground in display. The crowd crows. Though their shouts are a mix of languages and dialects, Karma understands—they are shouting for blood.

At the front of the spectators, from a seat of prominence weathered out of the stone steps, a man rises. Like the guards, he is dressed in a long, fur-trimmed tunic and peaked hat. His face, too, is covered with the same antler tattoos, but his are even more elaborate, multiple branches forking out like the points of a large buck. Around his neck is a necklace of bone fragments. It reminds Karma of the one the village shaman would wear. Like a man of medicine or magic. The man holds up his hand. The shouting subsides.

"These patrollers," the man proclaims, pointing to the brothers, "were found not in the Territories, but here—in the Borderlands. Scouts, undoubtedly. For those who say the Eastern Army isn't coming, remember that every stick comes from a tree. Here is your proof!"

The shouting of the crowd turns into a roar of booing. The brothers stare haggardly back in silence, as if beaten and cowed beyond speech.

The man turns back to the crowd. "It is time, comrades, to put aside each and every petty difference, in the face of a common peril. A much more dangerous evil." He begins to pace as he continues to address the people. "When the Six Suns destroyed their country, the predecessors of the Eastern Army fled here to the safety of the Tibetan highlands. Your great-grandparents accepted them; they had no choice. That was three generations ago. Now, the mountains of the Himalayas have crumbled away, and the danger is no longer from outside, but within. The Eastern Army is still here, grown in power, seizing more and more of the Four Rivers and Six Ranges, taking more control. Today, they

KARMA OF THE SUN

have been sighted in the Borderlands. Not just these scouts, but vast gatherings of troops—right at our doorstep."

More hisses rise from the crowd at the mention of the Minister's army.

The man nods. "Some may say, perhaps we should join them. They say, we should do like the border bandits, those thugs, and become Hanumanda's ally." He stops his pacing. "Let me disabuse you of that folly, should you think that it will save your skin. Hanumanda's loyalists are dispensable, like arrows in a quiver. The Minister is all too happy to use the border bandits to scare away the refugees who try to leave his territories, or to harass his enemies. But what do you think he will do to them once he gets what he wants? He will obliterate them! Just like he will obliterate anyone else who can threaten his power. For let there be no mistake about it, what he wants is *absolute* power."

The booing swells. The man's eyes glint as he pauses, on the brink of some even more damnatory reveal.

"And this is the reason, I have heard, that he is in the Borderlands. It is because he believes that the Child Lama is here. And I believe . . . he is right."

Murmurs of curiosity ripple through the crowd.

"It is a fool who laughs at prophecy. The monks were right about the Six Suns. They will be right about the Lama too. This Child will control the future. And that is why we must work together. Only together will we be able to search the land. Only together will we be able to find the Child—before the Minister can."

Slowly, heads nod, agreement growing, spreading throughout the audience.

"Hanumanda knows that if you are divided—warlord against warlord, tribe against tribe, band against band—you will be easy to overcome, as we were in my own land. We stood no chance. The only way to win is to win together. And that is why I propose . . . an alliance, of every clan, every tribe, every gang, every outlaw band. A united rebel army!"

The cave booms with cheers. They echo through the chamber, multiplying on the force of their own reverberations.

The man raises his hand, more to declare now that he has their agreement. "The first order of business: eradicating all traitors and spies from our midst. They're either with us—or they're against us."

He turns toward the pair of brothers. "Instead of resisting the Minister, you joined his army," he says. "Instead of joining the rebel movement, you became patrollers. You are traitors to your own people. And now . . . you deserve a traitor's death." He gives a flick of his hand.

The three hulking mastiffs are released. The dogs charge, lunging at their victims.

Osel and Jonang try to shield themselves, to cover their naked genitals, to turn their bodies away. But it is in vain. The ground is soon slick with their blood, and they lose their balance. The teeth of the mastiffs latch on. The brothers go down, a pile of snapping jaws and clawing paws over flailing limbs.

Karma turns his eyes away. But he cannot shut out the sounds, the hungry snarls, the mauling paws, and the screams, until mercifully, they are drowned out by the lusty roar of the crowd in the grotto.

A chant begins, repeating what appears to be the man's name over and over. "Altan . . . Altan . . . Altan!" And then, "Khan! Khan! Khan!"

The dogs are subdued, the carcasses dragged away before their hunger can be satiated.

The Khan swivels now toward the bamboo cage, gesturing to the prisoners inside. "Even many of the so-called refugees are the Minister's spies in disguise. Bring out the next two for interrogation."

The crowd bursts into wild cheers once more. The guards stride toward the pen and fling open the door. Karma tries to back away, but being the last one into the cage, he is the closest, and they seize him.

He stumbles, tripping as they drag him toward the pit. Although they have strewn chalk to soak up the blood, his feet still slide on the rock.

When the crowd sees him, they begin to laugh, pointing and taunting. It is his clothing, Karma realizes—the maroon robe. They think he is a monk. The guards drag out a second prisoner. Now the crowd is leering, heckling. With a glance, Karma sees that it is the girl with whom he collided on the stairs.

She struggles, raging and kicking. Unlike Karma, it takes several guards to restrain her, one man for each of her limbs. They pick her up, the braid of her long hair dragging on the chalk as they carry her to the pit. She is strong, and their movements are strained. The girl's eyes meet Karma's. While he is panicked and fearful, her gaze is dark, more angry than afraid. Dirt and grime do little to cover the expression of contempt on her face.

The same guard that struck Karma with the spear now whispers into Altan Khan's ear.

"Fight! Make them fight!" the crowd chants.

The Khan holds up a hand as he takes a moment to study Karma.

"You, monk—you were seen running from the pair of patrollers," he says. "Why?"

Karma's heart is pounding. He can hardly breathe under the smokiness of the torches, the fresh smell of blood, the thronging of the crowd.

"They . . . ambushed me," Karma stammers, the reply true enough that he does not have to think.

"A monk traveling alone in the Borderlands," Altan counters. "A risky proposition."

Karma is too close to death. He must keep talking. They are of the belief that he is a monk and this belief could be his best chance of survival. "My companions were killed by bandits while we were . . . looking for the Lama Child," he says, forming his reply more quickly this time, having just heard the Khan's words.

The remark elicits haws of laughter from the crowd, but Altan jerks his hand up in a command of silence.

"So you're telling me that you're a monk of the Oracle?" Altan's voice registers mocking skepticism, but his eyes peak with interest.

Karma pauses, suddenly unsure of himself. But he has no choice. He must continue the pretense. "Yes," he swallows. "They—they killed the Oracle, and then they took our texts. There was a map."

Altan's face changes, suddenly dead serious as he leans forward.

"A map, you say?" Altan says.

"Yes."

The guard with the spear jabs Karma in the ribs. "Yes, *Khan*," he barks.

"Come now, Bataar," the Khan reproves the guard. "That's no way to treat a monk. Didn't you hear him? He's on the pilgrimage, just the same as us." He looks back to Karma appraisingly. "But the Borderlands are vast and dangerous. How did you all ever hope to find the Child without any help?"

Karma winces from the pain to his ribs. He knows he has to be careful, that he is being tested, but he is overwhelmed. "The Chushi Gangdruk outlaws," he mumbles, before he can think it through. "They were going to be our escorts."

Now it is the Khan's turn to pause. "Indeed," he says.

This is not going well, Karma thinks. *Do they know I am lying?* From the look on the Khan's face, he cannot tell. Thinking to bolster the authenticity of his claim, Karma quickly adds, "One of them is called Surkhang, but it is his brother who is the leader. We were traveling to their fortress—somewhere on the river."

As soon as he says it, he knows he has made a misstep, though how or why, he does not exactly know. Inexplicably, he feels the gaze of the prisoner girl burn into him like a pair of hot pincers. More murmurs ripple through the crowd.

The brow of Altan Khan crooks up in a curious expression. Karma sees that he has convinced him. But at what cost? It feels like a trap has been sprung.

Too late now.

"The Chushi Gangdruk outlaws," the Khan repeats. "How fortuitous, as we seek them as well—to join our confederacy. They would be a tremendous help to us, in our fight against the Eastern Army. As would you, monk, in our search for the Lama."

That is it. The gambit has paid off. Altan nods at the crowd, then the guard. "You see? Fortune is on our side. Take this one to the cells, Bataar. It would seem that fate has other plans than the mines for the young monk."

The crowd cheers as the guard with the spear signals to two other guards, who take Karma by the arms and march him to the stairs. As Karma passes the girl, again his eyes meet hers. Again, a look of anger. But there is something else this time—a feeling of loss and longing, of something in common. Perhaps it is just pity, he thinks. Or in his case, maybe it is guilt, knowing that he is being spared while worse awaits her. The sensation washes over him with such force that he cannot ignore it, and his eyes search hers, hoping for some clue.

But the look she returns is only one of fury and disgust—as if to say, as he is led up the stairs and away from the burning torches and rank air of the grotto, that he has made a terrible mistake.

14

THE PRISONER

The prisoner cells are in a cave a short distance from the grotto. From inside, Karma can still hear the crowd. The hiss and sigh of their cheers. The piercing of the prisoners' screams. The barks of the guards' voices.

I can't be here. I shouldn't be here.

In the light of a single waning torch on the wall, he tries to examine the bamboo posts of his cell. They are thick, lashed together with fibers, reinforced with hardened tar. If he had his knife, perhaps he could cut his way through, but someone has taken it from him. At the door, an iron padlock secures a chain fastened around the bars. As much as he tries to pry it loose, it does not budge. His shadows flicker in the adjoining pen, like another prisoner stalking his movements.

My uncle warned me. Why did I think I would succeed—me, the boy with no future?

The light from the torch begins to sputter. It snuffs out, dousing the room in blackness. In the dark, the nearby shrieks of the prisoners seem louder, the cries of the rebel council lustier and more terrible. Karma cringes at each crescendo, his mind replaying the attack of the dogs as they mauled the brothers. His thoughts go to the prisoner girl, at the rage in her eyes as she watched him go. He begins to feel sick.

Yellow light flickers at the cave's entrance.

Voices approach. It is the same guards. Karma backs away from his cell door. Torchlight fills the room.

The guard Bataar enters wielding his spear and a torch, his two companions following. Behind them, a prisoner is led by rope.

Her mouth is bloodied, some of it smeared on her cheek. But as she stumbles toward the adjoining the cell, Karma recognizes her—the girl. Bataar removes a key from around his neck, unlocking the door to the neighboring cell.

"Tie her down in here," he orders. "Make sure it's tight. After all, she's quite the fighter, isn't she?" His expression is leering.

As one of the guards fight to hold her in place, the other leashes the rope from her wrists to a bamboo post on the far side of her cell. The second guard does not look like the others. He is darker-complexioned and thinner, with no tattoos on his face.

"Come on, come on. Hurry," Bataar barks.

As the rope is knotted, Bataar hands one of them the torch while he stands over the girl, a lecherous grin growing on his face. He begins to loosen his belt.

The girl's foot thrashes out suddenly, heel to the groin.

Bataar jounces backward, knocking out the torch in the other guard's hand. The light tumbles, the cave plunges momentarily into darkness. When it flutters back, they see Bataar wrapped between the girl's legs, his face purpling, his arms flailing. His two companions rush to his aid, trying to pry him loose from her chokehold. A kick sends them reeling into each other and crashing into the bars. The darker-skinned guard cups his nose. The other doubles over, grunting with pain.

Bataar scrambles away, streams of unintelligible profanity raging from his mouth. "You . . . rotten, little wretch . . ." he heaves.

The darker-skinned guard spits out a chunk of red mucus onto the floor. "My nose," he wails. "I think she broke my nose."

The girl starts forward on her feet but jerks back under the leash. The two guards quickly stumble out of the cell, leaving Bataar alone within, still cursing.

"You think you're tough, don't you?" Bataar growls. "A refugee, are you? I don't think so. Fighting like that."

"Let it go, Bataar," the other guard moans. "Let's just leave her be."

"Like hell," Bataar curses. Still, he hobbles from the cell, slamming the bars shut. "This is not the end of it." He slaps the lock shut. "Mark my words, we'll see just how tough you are."

The three guards slink away, glaring at Karma as they pass, swearing all the things they will do to make her pay. Then once more the cave plunges into darkness, the harsh voices of the guards fading away.

For a moment, all is still, silent.

In the dark, Karma can make out little more than a shadowy bulk in the corner of the next cell. But as his eyes slowly adjust, he detects movement.

"Are you all right?" he whispers.

"Am I *all right*," the girl spits back through the dark, "asks the coward and the traitor?"

Karma blinks, stung by the venom in her reply.

He can hear her moving now, grunting and straining against the bamboo bars. "I guess you think you're safe, don't you," she says, "helping the Khan? Taking them to the Chushi Gangdruk's hideout?"

"I never—"

"I heard you! The dzong on the river. Giving up their names!"

Perhaps she was right. But he hadn't really told him anything, had he? He was only posturing, trying to buy time. Yet from her reaction, it is as if she has been personally wronged. "I—I don't actually know anything—"

"That much is clear," she cuts him off. "You *don't* know anything. Not the consequences of what you told them, not what they're going to do—"

Karma is at a loss. "I was just trying to avoid the dogs."

"And in that you've succeeded—*for now*," the girl says scornfully. "What do you think, that they'll just let you go on with your pilgrimage when all is said and done? Do you have any idea who you're dealing with? That's the warlord Altan Khan. That's the rebel council!"

Karma swallows. She is right. Even more so when they discover that he can't tell them anything else they might want to know. "You're right," he replies at last. "I don't know what I'm doing. I have no idea."

The girl says nothing else. Karma can hear her still moving about, her breaths heavy.

"What are you doing?" Karma says.

The girl stops moving. "Listen," her voice comes back at him. "They're going to torture us for information, and when they have what they want, they're going to feed us to their mastiffs, just like those patrollers. Do you understand? You may think you have a different fate coming, but I assure you that is not the case. We have got to get out of here."

If she is trying to scare him, it is working.

"How?" he says.

"I have the key."

At first Karma doesn't know what she means. But then he remembers the key around Bataar's neck. She must have taken it in their tussle when the cave went dark. With their bodies hurting and their egos hurting worse, they hadn't noticed.

"The problem is that I can't reach the door," she says. "They've tied my hands." He hears her jerking on the rope, the bars creaking. "So, I'm going to have to throw the key to you. You will unlock your door, then you'll come unlock mine and untie me."

Karma's mind races. His heartbeat doubles like a drum in his chest. If they were discovered . . .

"Are you hearing me, monk?"

He snaps out of it. "Yes," he says. "All right."

"Stand away from the bars," she says. "Listen for where the key lands."

Karma does as he is told. He holds his breath and shuts his eyes to focus on the sound, even though in the dark he is already practically blind.

"Ready," he whispers.

There is a moment of cringing as he imagines the key sailing through the air. What if it strikes one of the bars and they lose it? What if he can't hear it?

The soft clink of something landing near him signals that the key has made it through.

He lets out a sigh of relief.

"Do you have it?" the girl hisses.

Karma gropes the ground. He feels something, but it is just a pebble. *Where is it, where is it . . .?*

"Tell me," the girl insists.

"Not yet," Karma says. "It's somewhere, I heard it."

"Hurry," she urges. "They're going to come back."

Where did it go? The cell feels suddenly huge. Crawling on all fours, he sweeps his hands across the floor. He wonders if the key bounced back into her own cell after all.

"I can't seem to—"

His hand brushes over something. His fingers close around it, scooping it up. A small object. Thin. Metallic.

"Found it!" he says. "I've got it!"

The girl's relief is audible. "Now the door," she directs.

Karma rushes to the door of his cell, feeling for the padlock. The key goes in.

Yes.

He tries to turn it, just as he saw the guards doing. It does not budge. At first, he panics, then thinks to reverse direction. This time the key swivels. He begins turning it. Faster, round and round, unscrewing the lock.

The shackle slips, the chain slides. It clatters with its weight. Open, swings the door.

Karma stumbles out.

"Quick," the girl calls.

Karma steps through the dark, feeling his way to her cell now. He fiddles at the lock. In a moment, he has her door open too.

"Over here!"

He follows her voice, finding her hands. Her body is trembling, soaked from sweat.

"Untie my hands."

The knot of rope might as well be a knot of wood. Karma presses, pushing and prying, but it does not move. Outside the cave, the swell of the crowd's cheering climaxes, startling them both. Another prisoner meeting their demise.

"Come on!" the girl says. "We're running out of time."

Karma tries again, wincing as it pulls away on his fingernails. It is of no use. He has untied hitches his entire life as a herder—but in the dark, this one is impossible.

"What?" the girl demands. "Why are you stopping?"

"I can't do it," Karma says. "I can't see it and it's too tight. We'll need to cut it."

She goes quiet. Karma swivels his head about as if to look around him, though he can see nothing. How long would it take to search the cave for a rock that was sharp enough?

The girl pauses. "The mine."

"What?"

"There are *tools* in the mine," she says.

Karma stares through the dark. The mine. That was the last place he wanted to go near. Those guards. Those prisoners in chains. He would be seen and he would be caught. It would be mad to try.

"You have to," she says. "We have a deal."

Karma hesitates.

"All right," he replies finally. He can't stay here, anyway. He turns to go.

"Wait, monk . . ."

Karma pauses, hopeful she has thought of some other solution.

But there is only a nervous warning. "Keep off the trails. Stay in the shadows."

Karma swallows.

"And one more thing," she adds. "Don't you even think of leaving me. Do you hear me? Or I'll . . . I'll scream so loud it'll raise an alarm."

Karma nods as he heads for the door.

"Monk?" she repeats. "Do you hear me?"

"Yes," he finally replies, remembering that she can't see him in the dark.

With breath held, he plunges now into the night, into the crisp, chill air. Past the shadow of the entrance, stars prick the sky. The hillside is dark, save the slant of torches over the landform. The noise of the crowd sharpens, and he crouches down behind an outcropping of rocks to study the clearing.

No guards in sight. Across the way, he thinks he can make out the path toward the mines. He imagines he can hear the clinking of irons, the bark of commands.

Keep off the trails. Stay in the shadows.

For a moment, he considers going back to the cave to try the knot again, but he knows it will be useless. The solution is out there.

Unless . . . I just leave.

The thought breezes through his mind, shocking in its seductiveness. By now the clouds have drifted, the gibbous moon casting a faint glow over a slow rise of hills in the distance. Every moment he is out here is a moment closer to getting caught.

Karma turns his gaze from the horizon back toward the woods of the open-cut mine, with its hunchbacked figures and black and silhouetted forms.

He lingers.

Another gush of the crowd issues forth from the grotto.

He takes one last look at the hills, toward freedom.

Then silently, decisively, he turns the other way. Like an arrow from its bow, he shoots forward in the night. Streaking toward the woods, toward the mine, the girl in the cave waiting behind.

15

THE KNIFE

Dark branches claw at him, pine needles scratch. Karma plows through the forest, following the girl's admonition to stay in the shadows. But as the wood deepens and the trail does not reemerge, he begins to worry that he has wandered too far. He slows, then stops, arrested by the increasing fear that he has gotten lost.

Between branches, a faint flickering of light catches his eye, the telltale glow of a fire.

Karma ducks down, flattening himself in the brush. Holding his breath, he watches, wondering if it is a torch, somebody approaching. He waits. The light keeps still, for a long moment neither coming nor going. Eventually, Karma raises his head, squinting through the trees.

Not the flicker of a torch, he realizes, but a stove fire, burning under the bulbous shape of a black cauldron. He begins to make out the silhouette of a table, several benches.

It's an outdoor scullery.

He exhales with relief. A scullery means utensils.

Knives.

There are no signs of anybody there. Still, he makes himself pause, scanning the scene to be certain. Slowly, he creeps forward. He is only a few paces from the scullery when voices sound.

Karma immediately drops back down into the brush, onto his belly. Only paces away, three men emerge, so close their shadows nearly touch him. His heart plummets, chest gripping in panic when he recognizes the guard Bataar and his two companions.

Chairs slide. Cups slam. A bottle and basket of something bangs on the table as they gather around.

The thin, brown-skinned guard with the broken nose plops down on the bench morosely, hands cradling his face.

"Look at him, Chuluun." Bataar gestures with his chin. "Look at what that tramp did to the Mustang's face. She broke your nose, boy. Are you going to let her get away with that?"

The guard grunts through his bloodied nose. "She'll pay."

"The Khan said not to harm her, Bataar," the one called Chuluun warns. "He suspects there is more to her than meets the eye. That's why he had us lock her in the cells."

Bataar slams a fist on the table. "He only spared her because he suspects that she's one of the Minister's spies! Well, we'll get her to talk! By the time I'm done with her, she'll tell us anything we want!"

From their slurred speech, Karma can tell that they have been drinking. Still lying prone, he lowers his head. What to do now? He is trapped, sure to be detected if he makes any attempt to move.

Bataar reaches for the basket on the table, a rattan case with a lid tied on top. He flips it open, standing over the receptacle. To Karma's surprise, the basket twitches; something moves inside. Bataar thrusts his hand into the box.

Out comes a flicking, black shape. A snake. Jaw stretched, fangs bared, tongue scenting the air, it twists agitatedly around trying to strike at Bataar, who holds it by its neck. Karma watches in alarm as

Bataar reaches for something under his belt. The object gleams in the stove fire.

Karma's eyes fix on the glimmer.

A crystal hilt . . . a silver sheath . . .

My knife!

Bataar draws the blade. Turning the snake over, he presses the tip to its smooth underside. The snake kinks into a tortured twist. But Bataar only grasps it tighter, cutting further. Setting the knife down, he proceeds to reach his fingers into the incision. As Karma watches in revulsion, Bataar plucks out a dark sac, tugging sharply to tear it free.

A piece of viscera dribbles blood onto the table. The snake's tail slashes wildly. Bataar flings the carcass into the stove, retaining the organ. The snake lands on the coals, immediately writhing in the fire, coiling and uncoiling uncontrollably before crispening into flames.

The wine flows. Bataar punctures the organ and the men slide their cups to collect a dark ooze. Snake bile wine. Karma has heard of this before. With a throaty curse, they lift their cups to their mouths. The drink goes down. They slam their empty tumblers on the table.

Bataar pushes the snake basket to the guard with the broken nose. "Your turn, Mustang. Go."

The guard pauses, eyes wide and incredulous.

"Man or mouse, Mustang?" Bataar harries. "It'll stop the bleeding, turn you hard as rock. Show that wretch what she gets."

Still the man hesitates.

"Be a man!" Bataar shoves the basket closer just as the guard pushes away, their movements colliding. The basket tips. It topples onto the Mustang guard's lap.

A black tangle tumbles out. The Mustang leaps to his feet with a cry, stumbling over the bench.

A single snake dangles from the Mustang's arm. It hangs there, fangs sunken into his wrist, twisting like a ribbon in the wind. Then it drops to the ground, slithering away with the others into the shadows.

Bataar and Chuluun jump back from the table. "Clumsy idiot!"

Karma goes rigid, imagining the slithering forms zigzagging toward him. He fights every instinct to get up and run.

"I'm bitten! Bitten!" the Mustang shrieks, clutching his arm. His nose has begun to bleed again.

Chuluun swears. "Mother corpse . . ."

The Mustang guard is wailing now, doubled over, the sound nasal through his broken nose.

"That's enough," Bataar snaps. "Stop your groaning. You're not dead *yet*." He jerks his head to Chuluun. "Go on, get him up. We'll take him to the grotto."

"What about the snakes?" Chuluun says.

"Leave them." Bataar grabs the bottle. "Here," he says, tipping the spout into the Mustang's mouth. The guard coughs, choking it down. "Now you won't feel a thing."

They pull the whimpering Mustang to his feet, dragging him back in the direction of the grotto.

The knife.

Karma realizes suddenly that in the confusion, they left it—his knife. He can see it. On the ground, behind toppled cups, the hilt of quartz winking in the light of the stove fire like sparks from a flint.

Karma cannot believe his good fortune. Still, he makes himself wait, counting to twenty until their voices vanish. When he is sure they are gone, he leaps to his feet and scampers to the scullery. He ducks under the table quickly, grabbing for the knife.

A winding shape zigzags out. He startles, pulling his hand away just as it slithers by. With a shudder, he picks up the knife and starts to back into the forest, but not before grabbing a waterskin. Through the trees, toward the cave he sprints, until the forest clears. He overshoots the hill at one point and has to double back, hugging the edge of the woods to track his position. Voices materialize, a glow of torches, the smell of stables emerges.

He sees a group of guards, talking loudly, laughing, surrounding what looks and sounds like a wrestling match. The sounds turn out not to be the grunts of fighting, but the groans of someone sick. Peering through the foliage, he realizes they are surrounding the Mustang guard who was bitten by the snake, holding him down as they try to tie a tourniquet around his arm.

Karma hurries on. Just down from the stables, a single animal is hitched to a tree. Its head perks up as it hears Karma's approach. To Karma's surprise he sees that it is the mule—the one Dorje gave him. Apparently, the rebels found it. It appears to recognize him too, clacking its mouth as Karma runs by. Karma makes a mental note of the location and keeps moving.

Over the clearing, to the rocks. Clouds have moved in, adding additional cover to the darkness. Still, he can make out the entrance to the prisoners' cave. For a moment, he has the panicked fear that he will find the guards have already beaten him there and are waiting for him, but then he remembers that they are with the Mustang.

He barges in, panting, chest thumping. He hears the girl's startled movement from her cell.

"I've got the knife!" he rasps.

Her relief is audible. "Wh–what took you so long?" she says, her voice breaking from tension. "Just cut me free!"

Karma bends to her hands and slices the knot apart. The bindings fall to the ground.

"We need to find horses," she says immediately.

"How about a mule?" Karma replies.

She tilts her head, as if reappraising her initial judgment about him. "Fine. Lead the way."

At the door of the cave, Karma pauses, looking out once more to the recognizable, blinking stars to the east, then back to the unknown hills to the west—wondering again where he is to go from here.

"Well?" the girl says.

Another moment of hesitation, another decision. They are both escaping. But where to?

The girl turns him to face her. "You said your people were looking for the Chushi Gangdruk to help you find your way through the Borderlands, were you not? Well, *I'm* one of them."

She's . . . a Gangdruk outlaw?

It all made sense now. Before he can say anything in response, she has dashed out the door. In another moment, her figure will melt completely into the night. Can she help him? There is no more time for thinking ahead. Right now, he needs to get out of the grotto.

Taking a deep breath, he checks the periphery. Then he plunges after her. Once more into the void.

Once more into the unknown.

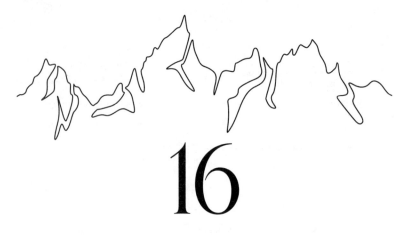

16

THE FOOTHILLS

The sun is only one of many.

He sees it now for what it is: the egg of a phoenix. Onto the horizon it rolls, over darkened hills that resemble coals. Mists from heavens spew, dawn from earth erupts. The darkness cracks, morning spills light.

A wing stretches.

From the egg, its feathers are flames, its plumage the inferno. A halo crowns its head as a cloud. She has the face of a woman, with hair of golden light, coiling like offerings in a fire. She rises, beautiful, spreading her wings, expanding her body. Ash floats quiet as snow.

When she stands in her glory, the light of a thousand scars pricks through her body, signs of a thousand deaths defeated. He sees her—the third of the four Tibetan Dignities. She waits for him.

By now, Karma is afraid of what will happen next. The same that has happened to the others he has seen—the snow lion and the tiger. One in one corner of the world, and the other in another. Both destroyed, both decimated by the Suns. And now here is the third Dignity.

Run, he wants to tell her.

Run now.

The Sun is only one of many, and the seventh is coming!

It is coming.

The greatest . . . and most terrible of them all.

It is too late though. Just as she begins to take flight, it comes—out of the hills. Nonexistent one moment, a large orb of white light the next. It fills the sky in a flash, a sphere that reaches the heavens.

The phoenix climbs, but the flames climb higher. Wings, feather, hair. She is swallowed by fire. Fire begets fire, and now, too, fire destroys fire.

He sees it now for what it is.

The Sun is one of many.

And after the many Suns, no one and nothing will be left.

Karma awakes in the saddle to a growing glare, burnished light flooding through his eyes. His vision blurs, then refocuses. The horizon is the horizon, and the sun is the sun. The ground pans beneath him with the lolling hitch of the mule. In front of him is the girl, morning glare on her hair. She turns her head.

"Alive back there, monk?"

Karma straightens up under a spasm of protest from his neck. He realizes he has fallen asleep. She has been carrying his weight. He wipes a hand across his mouth, embarrassed.

They rode like madmen, in silence, fearing pursuit in the night. With the breaking of dawn and the feeling of danger abated, he must have succumbed to exhaustion.

"I'm sorry," Karma replies. "I didn't mean to sleep."

"Rest if you like," she replies. "We're out of the Khan's territory now."

Karma glances at their surroundings. Tall hills border them—not quite mountains, but more elevated than any terrain he is accustomed to. A different world from the dusty valley of Kham.

His heart sinks. How will he find his way back now?

But then, he remembers. A possible solution in this girl.

He is desperate. He can see now that he cannot do this on his own. He needs help for his village. But will she help him?

At some point in the night, they told each other their names. Hers is Nima. She was captured by the Khan's rebel fighters while she was out spying on the Eastern Army's movements. Will she help someone from a village under guard of the Eastern Army's patrollers? In her mind now, he is a harmless monk on a pilgrimage to find a long-lost Lama. If he tells her the truth—that he has been sent by the Lord Minister Hanumanda himself—what will she do? Leave him stranded? Take him prisoner?

Worse?

Yet . . . he knows of the Gangdruk's reputation as fighters who help the oppressed. They allow refugees leaving the Territories to gain safe passage through the Borderlands. They rescue the monks. If he explains what happened, how his people are held captive by the Minister's patrollers, perhaps they can aid his village too.

Carefully, he clears his throat. "The Gangdruk dzong," he says. "Is it far from here?"

"Another two days' ride," Nima replies. "But at this speed, and with the Khan's rebels looking for us, we'll be better off taking the river."

So that is it, then. She will be taking him there. Only after they arrive, will he tell them the truth and plead for their help. But for now, he will have to maintain his false identity as a monk.

As they continue to ride, his gaze turns back toward the brightening east. The burning sun suddenly brings to mind the image from his dream. An image of destruction, of a mushroom cloud and pillar of fire reaching the heavens.

The Seventh Sun will come soon.

Time is running out. He feels like he has no choice. He has been lied to as well, by the Minister. The present is the result of a chain of circumstances—and decisions—of the past, something he cannot change. He cannot worry about the effect his actions will have on Nima, someone he has only just met, in the future. This is a time of action. He will suffer the consequences later, just as his father suffered the consequences when he took it upon himself to go searching for the Mountain, and as he himself has suffered the karma of the son.

At midafternoon, they reach a row of shaded foothills. Storm clouds infringe the horizon and shadows deepen. The sky is all gray and brown, a growing mass of haziness accumulating in size in a slow but unavoidable approach.

Karma's stomach growls. When has he last eaten? Scenes of home gnaw at his resolve: the shuffle of his mother's shoes on the dirt floor, the crackle of barley kernels roasting over hot sand, the scrape of the corns sifting through the sieve, the smell of butter tea trickling into steaming dough.

Instead, they drink rain. A curtain of moisture billows down, half frozen, sweeping into their faces. Nima opens her mouth to the sky. Karma does likewise, tilting his head back to the cold, hard taste down his throat, and catches a smattering of ice in his mouth.

Eventually, Nima stops the mule, nodding for Karma to dismount. "We go on foot from here."

Karma looks around. "Where are we?"

"Not far from the river. I have a canoe stashed in the trees. But it'll be dark soon. We'll have to spend the night."

She begins untacking the mule. "Out here, there is a saying," she says, as she slips off the bridle, stooping to remove the breast collar. "The earthquakes grow worse every mile you go, and the weather every minute."

Tiny ice crystals collect on her hair like white blossoms as she works, here one moment, melting away the next. She finishes with the saddle, removing it from the mule and setting it on the ground.

"That knife of yours . . ." she says.

Karma has forgotten about it. His hand searches for it in the pouch of his robe. He feels the hardness of the crystal hilt, the softness of the silver scabbard. Gone now is the pride he felt when first hearing the Minister's story about how it belonged to his father. He doesn't know if it is true or merely a fabrication to get him to undertake the journey—a lie, just like the bandit raid on his village. And what about the discovery of the mutilated yak?

His people feared a migoi was stalking the flock—a man damned by some act of such evil that not even death would grant him mercy, a man doomed to wander the earth until its end. But now he wonders if that, too, was part of another ploy to scare the village and add more cause for him to embark on the Minister's quest, knowing people were superstitious.

Handing the knife to Nima, he feels a sense of relief to be rid of it, like a thorn in his shoe that he can finally remove.

Nima studies the implement. The genuine awe on her face is an unguarded glimpse of a side of her he has yet to see until now. "Remarkable," she says of the obscure features, the black blade, the ice-like handle. With a look of regret over the mundane task for which she is putting the knife to use, she begins slicing the saddle string.

"You might as well just hold on to it," Karma says when she finishes cutting.

She gives him a curious look but doesn't say anything. He is just a monk after all, in her mind. He said that border bandits had killed his fellow travelers. She is probably not surprised that he never wants to see another blade again.

She picks up the saddle. "Time to go."

Karma regards the mule, its wearied, dark eyes, its matted coat. He strokes its neck a final time before striking it with a hand across its hindquarters, and the animal that had once been the Oracle's trudges forward, head bobbing as if nodding at a command.

Go on, Karma thinks to it. *Go free. Until you reach your home, wherever you wish it to be. Or until the Seventh Sun.*

Nima is already making her way uphill, stopping for a moment to forage at a hedge. Karma follows her. She has found a yellow gooseberry bush. Together they pick the fruit, Karma cramming the morsels directly into his mouth. His hunger revives with the sting of their tartness. But Nima eats little herself, collecting the fruit in her pockets instead. "We need to catch some real food," she says.

They leave the bush to climb the hill. The slope is spotted red with barberry and ilex, white with daisies and everlasting, petals drooping in the gray rain everywhere. At the top, Nima discards the saddle over the edge. It tumbles down into the foliage, disappearing from the view of anyone who might be tracking them.

Following an escarpment of wet sandstone, they reach a grove of mossy oaks. Here the ground is covered in sphagnum moss, thick bunches of bracken sprinkled with the occasional bloom of pale aster. Under the ledge, plants form a drip-line leading to a small stream. This is where they are to make their bed for the night, Nina informs him, under the shelter of rock. Tomorrow they will follow the stream the rest of the way to the main artery of the river.

Next is a search for viable firewood, not an easy task in the rain. They stack the pieces under the shelter of the ledge. Certain sticks are set aside for building a trap. Nima uses the knife to whittle these into double-ended stakes, instructing Karma to dig a small pit in the ground using a rock for a spade. She stabs the stakes into the soil in this hole, creating a pitfall of spikes concealed under a layer of brush. From the salvaged saddle string she fashions a lasso, tethering the strips together to form a long length of cordage with a small loop tied on each end, running one through the other.

Karma watches as she works, the concentration on her face even as the wind and rain mats her hair, the water rolling down from her jaw to the nape of her neck. He is amazed as she bends, pressing down on a sapling to test its spryness, fastening the cordage and hitching it to a stake in the ground before laying the loop gently over the trap. As a last step, she takes the berries from her pocket, scattering them over the brush. Bait for the prey.

She glances up. "What?" she says, catching Karma staring at her.

He averts his eyes, blushing. "Nothing," he mumbles. "It's just . . . how did you learn to do all of this?"

He senses that his own father was like that. He grew up in the mountains just before the last of the ranges crumbled in the quakes. His mother told Karma stories recounted from his father about tracking, guiding, trapping, hunting. Nima seems to have the same skills, with the addition of one other ability he saw—she can fight.

Nima gives a shrug. "I was not that much different from you. We all were, when we joined the Gangdruk. Settlers, nomads, deserters. We've all lost something—people, homes, families." She gives a wistful shake of her head. "Everything. But the Gangdruk gave us something back. They gave us something to live for—and then they taught us how to get it."

"What?"

Nima slaps the knife shut, the trap completed. "Revenge," she replies.

Back under the outcropping of rock, they scour their collection of firewood with the knife for dry or rotting pieces. For kindling, Nima shows Karma how to scrape bark from a tree, explaining how the layers saturated with oils do not absorb moisture. They assemble the pieces into a small heap under the outcropping, out of the rain. Nima goes to the stream, searching along the banks. She brings back a flat stone, rough and bluish in color. Aiming the rock at the pile of kindling, she strikes it against the dagger's iron. With a few tries, it begins to spark.

A wisp of smoke curls up, followed by the whiff of ash. Slowly, she bends over, cupping the tinder into the shape of a bird's nest in her hands, blowing into it. A tiny glow emerges. Coaxing the wadding into the pyramid of firewood, she continues to breathe into the smoldering pile. Within moments, the kindling crackles. Flames catch and lick out. The wood spits. A wave of warmth emanates.

A thrashing rustles from the direction of the trap. They leave the fire to retrieve a small gray rabbit hanging by its throat, its neck broken. The contraption has worked.

Nima takes the rabbit from its noose, bringing it to the fire, but not before resetting the trap. As Karma prepares a makeshift spit, Nima skins the rabbit with the knife. Hunting around the cracks of the rocks, she finds wild fennel and sage, and rubs the coarse herbs into the meat. Soon a tiny carcass is turning over the fire. They sit waiting, watching the meat darken.

"I was a child," Nima begins suddenly. "My family had just arrived at the settlement. There was so much work. Fields to plow, rocks to clear, stones to carry. One day, when it was time for the labors, I'd had enough—I didn't want to do it anymore. So I hid. My parents came out, searching the fields, calling my name, looking for me. I could hear them. But I was stubborn, I would not come out. Next thing I knew . . . I heard screaming. From everywhere. The border bandits. I kept hiding, but now because I was afraid." She stares intently into the fire. "So I stayed there, in the grass, hiding, until the screaming stopped. I didn't call to them. I didn't run to them. I didn't even . . . see them die. All I did was listen—to the sound of them, screaming my name."

Karma feels a knot in his stomach growing. The story is awful. For all that he may have suffered in his own life, he realizes that the hardships of growing up in the valley pale in comparison to the brutality of the Borderlands. He feels sheepish suddenly at the singlemindedness of his own concerns—his pining for his lost father, his fears of the villagers' judgment of him, his worries about his mother and cousin.

Her eyes blink, seeing his reaction. "Like you, I was one of the lucky ones."

She turns back to the fire, lifting the blackened carcass of the rabbit from the spit. Drippings steam as she uses a stick to scrape at the burnt skin. "And then one day I hear that, with the Eastern Army assembling, preparing an incursion into the Borderlands, the clans were joining the Khan's rebel alliance. That even the border bandits may reconsider their allegiance."

Now Karma understands—the reason she has gone on this mission, the reason she allowed herself to be captured. She had hoped that the chief of the border bandits would be at Altan's rebel council.

Revenge.

She stops the scraping, letting the spit rest on her knees, steam curling up from the charred meat. "For too long, the border bandits have enjoyed the Eastern Army turning a blind eye as they act as a deterrent to the refugees fleeing the Minister. Thousands have been killed and pillaged at their hands, just like your monks, just like my parents. But with the Eastern Army's gathering at the Borderlands, the chief of the border bandits is not going to have many options. Either he joins the Khan, or he joins the Eastern Army. I thought he would not be so foolish as to trust Hanumanda. I thought he would be at the meeting of the rebel council. But I was wrong." She stares into the fire. "This time."

Silence falls upon them. She makes no move to speak. Neither does Karma. After a moment, Nima looks at him as if suddenly remembering that he is still there.

"I know what it's like to have your loved ones taken, monk," she says. "Some people say the Chushi Gangdruk are the protectors of the

Four Rivers and Six Ranges. We're nothing that noble. Fighting to find peace is not the same as fighting for peace. But it's all we have."

She digs her stick into the rabbit's flesh, breaking off a bit of meat and offering it to Karma. The inside is stringy and pink. Steam rises into the rain, while evening falls somber as the mists.

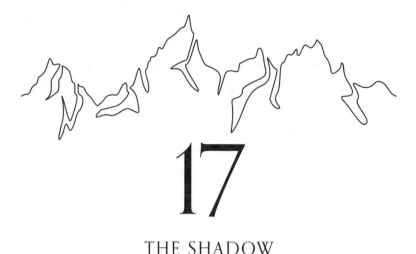

17

THE SHADOW

Sleep does not come easily. Thoughts of his mother and cousin flood Karma's mind. His village. A vague memory of his father telling stories of the mountains.

A Sherpa's destination becomes his destiny. Though he cannot always see the end.

The deathwatch knocking of the insects, the rustle of the wind. Karma's eyes open suddenly, just when he has finally begun to drift. He squints now—at what, he's not sure—in a trance of exhaustion. A fog trundles through the trees, over the banks, dampening light and sound. Like a spell shrouding the land, as if in a dream.

But he is not dreaming.

Something has woken him. Was it the cold? The thoughts running through his mind? Another dream?

A chill suddenly shivers down his shoulders with the sense that someone—or something—is watching.

He props his body up.

In the darkness, his eyes see nothing. Yet somehow, he can sense a change in his surroundings. It is the quiet . . . an unnatural absence of sound. No hoot of the wood owl, no sibilation of mists in the trees, no burble of the stream . . .

No ghost-winds.

That's it.

His mind quickens upon this realization, becoming fully alert now. The dead are silent. A stark contrast from the growing lamentations of each night, mourning the approaching end of the world. Lying there, in the sudden consciousness of this void of sound, a drift of insight comes to Karma. His father believed that the Stone gave the living the same freedom as the dead—to see unbounded through space and into the past—as well as the ability to talk to them. Ghosts are disembodied. No longer part of the physical world, their perception is no longer constrained by temporal barriers. Past, present, and future make no difference to them. But, estranged from the living, they cannot communicate what they see. The growing voices, then, are not just mourning the coming destruction of the earth and the fear of their never-ending limbo, no world into which to return. The ghost-winds are something more. They are pleas to the living for help.

To do something about it. *Before it is too late.*

Now the silence is not a void but a held breath, the darkness a legion of eyes watching him, waiting to see what he will do. And he wonders, afraid of the thought, What if his father is among them? Restless, unable to be at peace? Trying to speak, but unable to be heard?

Karma feels his skin prickle. There has never been a night he could not hear the haunting of the ghosts before dawn. But although the only perceptible noise is the deep whisper of Nima's breathing, he knows—they are not alone.

He glances toward her. They had retired in their separate corners beneath the rock outcropping, backs turned to each other. He hesitates, then whispers her name.

"Nima—"

She startles awake immediately. In the void of silence, she goes still.

"There's something," Karma whispers. "Or someone, I think, out there—"

Nima cuts him off with a shush, rising with deliberate quickness. She can sense it too. Something is moving in the deep blackness. Some animal in the woods? He can hear the whisper of Nima drawing the knife. His knife, now hers. They stare, waiting, watching. A long moment passes, so long Karma begins to wonder if they only imagined it, the thing that seemed to be watching them.

And then he sees it.

Two dark pinpricks like a pair of eyes, looking out at them, unblinking.

The same involuntary chill runs down his neck.

But there is something else. Another darkness appearing to grow. Advancing swiftly from the background. An emerging shape, taking on the figure of an upright form. The suddenness turns Karma immobile, simultaneously filling him with the instinct to flee. In the corner of his eye, he sees Nima likewise frozen.

Until—a thrashing sound. The two pinpricks jerk away. The sharp whiplash of a branch, sticks snapping. And a scream of agony so shrill it makes Karma's ears go numb with ringing, as if bitten by the wind.

The trap!

Karma shrinks back, bumping against the wall of rock behind him. An image inexplicably flashes in his mind. The silhouette of his father and Uncle Urgyen's brother. The village in the half-light of morning. And then the farewell of horses and men.

A broken stare.

Weeping. They blur in rapid sequence. He can barely feel Nima as she pushes him behind her, stepping out with the knife raised to face whatever might come their way.

The forest exhales. The blackness recedes. The foreground retreats into the back.

Trees quiver, water burbles, the hint of shadows overlap innocuously. The chattering of insects whirs. A sliver of the moon reappears, tipping its light onto the ground.

All is normal. The night resumed.

"What . . . was that?" Karma whispers.

In front of him, Nima is still watching, still waiting, still wielding the knife. After a long moment, she lowers the weapon, though she does not put it away yet.

"I don't know," she replies.

Together, they continue to stare out into the darkness.

But the darkness has no answers.

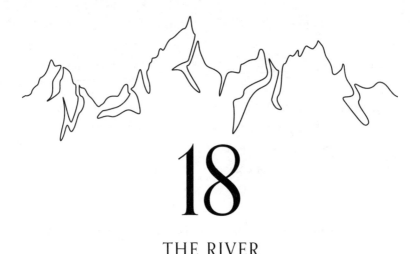

18

THE RIVER

This day is clearer and brighter, though the ground and bushes are still wet from yesterday's rain. They find the trap sprung, the hole caved in, spears smashed with blood on the spikes. The signs suggest some large creature—wolf, bear, jackal, leopard—but Karma finds himself thinking back to the fateful day when he and Lobsang found the yak with the hole ripped in its belly, and his cousin's frightened question: *Could it be a migoi?*

The migoi are a myth. A tale told by shamans and parents as a fable about wrongdoing. A migoi, it is said, is a person who committed an act so vile that no form of reincarnation can ever account for the karma of their life. For such, their punishment is to be deprived of even the mercy of death, condemned instead to walk the earth in the eternal torment of their sin, knowing no relief until the end of the world—or the absolution of a Lama. Karma always wondered if some evils accrue too much wrong to be borne by the collective karma of the world, whether those responsible for the Seven Suns deserve the fate of bearing the weight as migoi. Unless . . . such blame falls on a whole generation and, now, their descendants.

They make their way toward the river. Stray strands of moss capture sunlight through ragged treetops above. A pair of birds lands on a high limb. They fan their wings, once, twice, mirroring each other, then one of them flits away as quickly as it appeared, leaving the other to haw at its absence in the boughs, a haunting cry that follows them as they pass.

Karma's ankle itches. He bends to scratch it and his fingers come into contact with a wet lump. A black slug, thin and stippled with gold stripes, is clamped to his leg. He kicks, repulsed, trying to shake it off, only to be startled to see another on his wrist, latched onto a sleeve and crawling. Suddenly they are everywhere, a speckled hive of bloodsuckers scenting them, cockling up on the leaves and branches.

"Leeches," Nima exclaims. "Get away from the bushes!"

Karma follows as she runs. The leeches rain down, dropping from the trees, landing in their hair. Karma bats at his head, feeling one on the lobe of his ear. The trees open to the blue sky by the river's edge, and they suddenly hear the chatter of water.

They begin to tear off their shirts. There is disgust but no shame, as Karma glimpses the mottled skin of his own belly and the same on Nima's back. He can feel the leeches suckling on his neck, in his armpits. He tears off the rest of his clothing and his boots too. They are even in between his toes. He claws at them, pinching and flinging the slowly engorging bodies off his skin. Blood trickles from the lesions.

"Careful!" Nima calls out to him. "If they regurgitate the blood, it'll infect the wound!"

She runs down the shore, splashing into the water, scrubbing at the bite marks. Tearing off the last of the leeches, Karma follows her. The water is freezing, much colder than he expected. It surges around his ankles, rising to his knees. He pauses at the edge. He has never been to a river before. He does not even know how to swim.

Nima has no such hesitation. She dives beneath the surface, coming back out in the sunlight, black hair gathering over her back.

Karma lowers his eyes to the water, embarrassed now that the initial panic is over. He turns, busying himself with washing. Sunlight dances over submerged rocks visible in the shallows. A cloud of red emanates from the bites. Silt swirls. Naked, he ventures farther into deeper water.

After a while, he grows accustomed to the water. It is refreshing, and in a moment of courage, he bends his knees, dipping himself neck deep. The cold is brutal, and he lets out an exhale of shock. He tries it again, this time bracing himself with a deep breath. His head goes under, all the way.

He can feel the cold in the roots of his hair, in the pores of his skin, every part of him tingling with the shock of it.

When he finally returns to the shore, his clothes are laid out, Nima nowhere in sight. The sun is high and strong, baking the stones on the banks. Karma collects the monk's robes, checking them carefully as he puts them on. Under the intense sunlight, the leeches are gone, having retreated into the shade or under rock.

After a few minutes, Nima appears from the trees fully dressed, pulling a canoe behind her, the one she said she had hidden away.

"Parasite spawn," she curses. "It's like the earth's gone mad. Of all the creatures to thrive, why those wretched life forms?"

They clear the boat of the debris and branches used to hide it, a small yak-skin coracle stretched over a frame of sticks. Inside are two oars, more poles than paddles. They carry the canoe to the water's edge. Karma tiptoes hesitantly.

"Stay to the right of the river and you'll be fine," Nima says, pointing to the center of the waterway. "Away from the churning."

Karma follows her finger. Halfway across the wide ripple of swiftly running currents, a trail of eddies swirls just beneath the surface.

"What is that?" Karma asks.

"Rocks," Nima says. "Sharp as blades. This looks like one river, but it's actually two separate channels pushed together. One flows in one direction, the other the opposite. Sometimes they merge, sometimes they change direction. This side takes us downriver, where we want to go. Cross over to the left, you'll go upstream instead. Get stuck in the middle . . . well, half of you is liable to go one way—the other half, the other way."

Karma stares.

"Just stick to the right and you'll be fine," Nima says. "Get on."

After a moment of hesitation, Karma wades out toward the front of the boat as she holds it steady. With a ginger step, he climbs in. Nima immediately follows, shoving off with a thrust. In an instant, the river catches their craft, bearing them downstream. For a moment, the nose begins to meander, but then Nima dips her oar into the water and their course straightens out.

River willows bend along the eastern bank like old women washing in the water. Crows take flight along the channel. Karma cannot help but smile. The sensation of being borne up, of riding upon water, is no less miraculous to him than if he were floating on air. He turns to watch the motion of Nima's paddle, then mimics her movement. Dipping and digging. Dribbling as he does it again. As he paddles, he peers overboard. Sunlight gleams serpentine upon its surface, but the bottom lurks unseen.

"Don't suppose you know how to swim, do you?" Nima calls out from behind him. Karma shakes his head. "Then do yourself a favor, keep your body in the boat. These aren't built for stability."

Karma can see now what Nima was talking about. While the current moves downstream swiftly on their side—on the other, dead logs drift aimlessly in the opposite direction. There are two separate rivers indeed. Across the water, the shoreline is a stretch of toppled trees. They form a half-sunken forest, an embankment of eroded earth and mangled trunks.

Nothing stirs. Even the light over the stretch of land seems muted.

Karma cranes his neck toward the scene. "What is on the other side?" Karma asks.

"Nothing good," Nima replies. "About ten years ago, when the earthquakes started getting really bad, the mountains started to fall. The range had been the only thing stopping the winds, so when it finally fell, the poisons came. Gendun says they were from the Six Suns, from the burning. Anyway, the dying started from the west, and every year it has gotten closer. Soon it'll be all wasteland, west of the river."

Perhaps it is just Karma's imagination, but the denuded trees appear to bow across the river, as if shaking at the mention of the great quakes. The slow crumbling of the mountains—this was why his father left his own people to come to the valley and why, when the mountains finally fell, he worried about them, wondering about the dead, hearing their voices in the ghost-winds.

But Hanumanda seemed to believe that his father has found his way to one last mountain—the home of the Stone. Karma turns back to Nima. "Did *any* of the mountains survive?"

She shakes her head. "If you think that's where you're going to find your Lama Child, you're wrong. There's nothing in the wasteland. No one goes there. Not even outlaws."

Karma slowly turns back to the front. *Nothing. No one.* His father, vanished.

The river pulls them on, growing in speed and depth, as Karma sinks into the repetition of the paddling and the mire of his thoughts, until Nima's voice suddenly breaks through.

"The bandits who ambushed your caravan," she says, abrupt. "What can you tell me about them?"

The question catches him by surprise.

"Did they wear masks?" she prods, when he doesn't respond right away. Was she examining his story? Suspecting that he had not been telling the truth?

Yet as Karma thinks back to the ambush, he can picture them. *Masks? They did.*

"Yes," he says.

"What kind?"

Karma's apprehension grows. An interrogation. It is a convenient time to test him. His back is to her. He cannot swim. If unconvinced he is telling the truth, one swing of her paddle and he will be drowning in the water.

"They wore leather visors," he answers. "With holes cut out for eyes. And markings drawn on them."

"Border bandits." Nima swallows. The answer seems to be what she is looking for. "Did you happen to see their leader?"

Now Karma understands why she is asking. Not because she is suspicious. She wants to talk about the brigands. He can sense it now, the fixed focus she has on this one thing, her drive for revenge.

"Their chieftain," she presses. "Any chance you saw *him*?"

Karma remembers. The one who questioned Dorje, who took the nun's book and maps.

Nima pushes further. "Someone by the name of Drakpa?"

Drakpa.

The red-faced bandit, the only one not masked, who struck Karma unconscious with a stone axe.

Karma twists around with the recognition. "That was what they called him."

Nima stops. "They called him Drakpa?" she echoes.

Karma nods, turning and pointing to the welt on his head. "He was the one who did this."

Nima's mouth tightens. "Where did the ambush happen?"

"In the Borderlands."

"*Where* in the Borderlands?"

Karma searches for a way to describe the location. For someone who until recently knew nothing of what was outside the valley, the geography still resembles a mystery. His village is in the valley, at the western edge of the Minister's Territories. The attack was past the cliffs, where the Borderlands begin. "It was by the cliffs in the eastern end of the Borderlands," he says finally. "Not far from a dry lake they call the Skeleton's Head."

He is glad he can provide this detail, but the answer does not seem to be something that Nima recognizes.

"This place, would you be able to find it again?"

Karma fumbles with his paddle, the wooden implement feeling as unnatural and cumbersome as the charade he is maintaining. More and more, the pretense of being a monk weighs like the lie it is.

"Look," Nima continues. "That brigand Drakpa *robbed* us of our loved ones. He killed your Oracle. He killed my parents. I know you monks believe in karma, not bloodshed. But part of karma is retribution, isn't it? This is where they pay for what they've done. This is where you either act or are acted upon. Where you make your own fate. So *if* you know how to find him—"

This must have been her hope all along. In hearing that his caravan of pilgrims was waylaid by the border brigands, she opened up to him, hoping for more information about how to find Drakpa. She trusted him.

"Nima . . ." Karma says. He has to tell her. They are not yet at the dzong, but close enough. This is his opportunity to admit the truth. To explain what he has been trying to do.

He opens his mouth to say more.

A sudden fountain of water shoots up, splashing down around them in a shower of droplets, followed by a gush of bubbles in the river.

Karma startles. He looks back at Nima, hoping to see from her expression that this is normal. But her face reads alarm and fear. Before either can speak, another splash erupts, this one from the other side of the boat.

Then, all across the river, the water begins to roil.

A disturbance rising, growing rapidly, bleeding to the gray surface in a reddish foam, like water to blood.

Karma grips the edges of the canoe. "What's happening?"

Her reply is the one everyone dreads. "Earthquake." She grips her paddle, thrusting the scull into the water. "Paddle," she shouts. "Paddle to shore now!"

But a sudden lurch pitches them forward. They feel themselves rising from water to air, for a moment weightless as if suspended in time, cresting waves frozen around them. Then all at once, the prow drops, the bottom slamming down so hard it rattles Karma's teeth. Water sprays in the sunlight. The weight of the hull jerks Karma's paddle forward, trapping it, raking his knuckles over the edge. He cries out, but in a blink, the shaft tears from his grip, the paddle disappearing beneath the swell.

The boat is spinning now. Nima digs deep with the remaining paddle, but the river is too wild, sunlight and water too blinding. Ahead—a trough of rocks flashes in their path. Karma understands now what she was saying about the danger. Their jagged shapes are as pointed as knives. And their canoe is speeding right for them.

"Hold on!" Nima shouts. "We're going to hit!"

The boat still spiraling, Karma braces himself, losing his direction. There is no impact where he expects it. In the dizzying whirl, he hopes they have somehow avoided the hazard—

The crunch of the bow tells him otherwise.

Karma flies forward. He slams against something hard, grunting as his chin meets solid rock. In the next moment, he is submerged. The shock of cold. A slit of pain. A cloud of red balloons before his eyes. He wonders ludicrously to himself if it is blood or silt, or both mixed together.

I can't swim!

He tumbles, topples. Underwater—corners scrape and edges scratch. Something snags at his robe, lashing him around the rocks, pinning him beneath the force of the prevailing current. The river's current is a thunderous roar in his ears. His eyes, mouth, and throat fill with its rush.

He swallows water.

Can't breathe . . .

The end is here. He is sure of it.

I'm going to drown . . .

His chest tightens. The waters darken.

An image flashes before him. A vision of his village. As clear as if he is seeing it with his eyes. A memory of himself as a child with his father riding the herd together. They are watching the sunset, looking toward the west, toward where the mountains had been, now gone. Look to the Mountain, he remembers his father saying. *Look to the Stone. Listen for the dharma horn, to take us home.*

The sky is darkening, just as the waters are closing above, caving in. And now something else calls from memory. Just beyond the edge of perception. Barely detectable.

A sound.

In the tumult of waters and tumbling of stones, he hears it. A tingle of an echo, but whether it's happening in his memory or in his ears, he cannot tell. Yet he knows . . .

I'm hearing this now.

It fills his ears, muted by the waters, distinct in its resonance. A low, long hum, whirring through the darkness, echoing in the depths of the river, in the rocks and in the earth, in the bones of his body. A deep sound. A swallowing sound. The sound . . . of a horn.

Ommmmm . . .

Karma's flesh convulses with its reverberation.

I remember.

He feels himself come untangled from the rock. His feet find resistance at the bottom.

The sound of the Sherpa's horn.

He points his body, angles his legs. He gives a hard thrust. Head rising, water clearing, his body hurtles upward, breaking through the surface. Sunlight, burst of foam. But then he sinks back down again. His hearing muffles. The river rushes. He kicks again.

Once more his head breaks through the surface. Something is reaching for him—Nima's hand—grabbing his collar.

"I've got you!" she shouts, pulling him onto the rolled craft, hugging one arm under his armpits, the other hanging on to the boat. "Now climb!"

The boat leans as they pull themselves up, tipping, righting itself back to its normal pitch. They scramble aboard, tumbling into its hold. The coracle is misshapen, water ballooning in different areas. But it still floats.

Karma retches, both stomach and lungs heaving at the same time. He spews water, as his ears throb with the lingering echo of rushing waters.

But all he can hear, all he can think of, is the sound.

The horn.

Calling to me.

The Sherpa's horn.

I have heard it!

He strains to listen again now that he is out of the water, expecting its resonance to be even clearer. The river's motions subside, the gushing having petered out to a hiss. But gone too, is the sound.

I didn't imagine it. I know I didn't.

Nima crouches before him, studying his face. Like him, she is soaking wet, breathing hard. Like his, her paddle is nowhere to be seen.

"Are you all right?"

I heard it.

Karma blinks at her. Registering the question, he gives a haggard nod.

Whatever it is, it's real.

Nima leans back, exhaling heavily. "We were fortunate. These quakes—the last time was so severe, the river actually reversed course. Sent everything back upstream. I honestly thought we were done for."

Karma's eyes widen. "You didn't mention that."

"You said you didn't know how to swim," Nima replies. "There was no point in scaring you." To Karma's surprise, she laughs suddenly. "Like I said. Fortunate."

Slowly, Karma smiles in return. Then he begins to laugh too.

I heard the horn. Fortunate, indeed.

Nima looks out to the river, studying the surface as if watching for aftershocks. "It's only a matter of time, though," she says. "The earthquakes. The storms. The winds from the Six Suns. The changed stars. It's the motions of an earth reeling. Like the convulsions of an animal on its last breath. They say it's a sign the end is near. The Seventh Sun is coming." She turns to glance at him. "You monks really think the Lama can stop the end of the world?"

The question catches Karma by surprise, and for a moment he forgets that he is not a monk. He has always accepted the prophecy of the Seventh Sun. Even after Hanumanda's visit, he only thought of the journey as an opportunity to find his father—to see him one last time *before* the end. But now, in the robes of a monk, having heard the horn, the two things suddenly seem within reach.

But gather to the Mount and the Seeing Stone, that the Lama may reveal yet a future unknown.

"I hope so," Karma replies, speaking the truth of what he suddenly understands his mission to be: To find the Stone so that a Lama can see the future and stop it from happening. But also, to see his father again—whether in the flesh, or as a ghost through the Stone.

"I hid too," Karma says, unexpectedly. "On the day my father left. I thought I could stop him. I thought if he couldn't say goodbye, he wouldn't go. That if he loved me, he would stay. I could hear him, calling my name, over and over. My mother too. But I just sat there, hiding in the wreckage. Like a coward, or a fool. And even after he was gone, when he didn't come back, when they called him a scoundrel, still I said nothing. As if I didn't know that he wasn't a fraud, the whole journey not a lie. Even though I knew all along . . . it was true."

For some reason Karma's hands are shaking. Perhaps it is just the cold, the wet clothing. "I never got to say goodbye," he says. "But the worst of it is, I never let him say goodbye either."

The boat becomes very quiet now. For a moment, neither of them speaks.

"That's why you're out here," Nima says. "Trying to take the same pilgrimage."

He sees something soften in her gaze. Slowly, she gestures toward him. "You're bleeding," she says. "Your chin."

Karma feels a warm liquid dripping down his neck. It must be from when he hit the rock.

She leans across, gently pressing the wound between her fingers.

"There," she says after a while. "Keep holding on, just like that."

Karma's fingers rest where hers were only moments before. "Thank you," he mumbles.

The river is rounding a bend now. Here the eastern banks are thick with giant bamboo, broken up by fingers that jut into the land. The boat turns the corner to a waterlogged shore, a cluttered marsh of bamboo and grass. Past the bamboo thicket peek crowns of birch and pine. The sun's glare over the water is so strong it hurts his eyes.

"We're here," Nima says. "And none too soon. This thing is going to sink."

The announcement surprises Karma. Nima begins to paddle with her bare hands. Karma joins her, the two of them stopping now and then to bail water from the ballooning yak skin. The abrasions on his back chafe against his clothing. With the effects of the excitement of the earthquake wearing off, he begins to feel a dull ache in his side, becoming more pronounced.

As they near a willow, Nima grabs hold of the wiry branches, pulling the crumbling boat into the thicket. She begins to climb out.

"Nima, wait!" Karma winces at his side as he climbs out after her.

This is it. My last chance to tell her.

"Not much farther," Nima waves ahead, forging on through the overgrowth.

Karma clasps a hand to his rib cage, now throbbing with pain. Insects whir, mosquitoes swarm in the humid air. The bank rises to solid land. Pillars of green bamboo tower, bristling with bladed grass. He tramps through the shaded grove after her, sunlight filtering down in streaks and shafts.

Then he sees it—hidden by the clutter of bamboo until now.

Walls.

The fortress.

The Gangdruk dzong.

The structure is mud brick reinforced with cane and timbers and spiked with battlements. Nima shouts up to a tower. A head appears through a slit momentarily, then disappears. They round the corner to a pair of doors facing an open field that looks like it was recently cleared.

"For planting," Nima explains. "To feed the refugees." She is visibly glad to be home.

"Nima," Karma tries to get her attention again, wincing between breaths. The pain in his side is reaching a peak. "I need to tell you something."

She looks at him, noticing now the pained expression. "Easy, monk. We'll soon have someone look at your wounds and get you into some dry clothing."

He shakes it off. "I'm not who you think—"

The gate creaks on its hinges and swings open.

Out rushes a column of Gangdruk outlaws, weapons brandished, surrounding them.

Nima waves for them to stand down. "It's all right," she says. "He's with me."

But rather than putting their weapons away, they seize Karma instead, throwing him to the ground. He grunts from the pain, but knows he has no right to resist.

Nima wheels on her fellow Gangdruk outlaws, shoving them back. "Didn't you hear me? He's just a pilgrim!"

"We know who he is," a man's voice comes out at her.

Karma glances up from the ground. A figure strides through the midst of the outlaws. Karma sees boots; he recognizes the familiar tiger-skin girdle.

Surkhang.

The Gangdruk looms over him, his gaze shooting from the soggy figure of Karma to Nima. "But he's no pilgrim."

19

THE FORTRESS

Alone, nursing the dull ache in his side, Karma sits on the floor in the room where they are holding him and studies the space. The straw scattered about. The late afternoon sunbeams igniting flecks of dust. The rough-hewn timbers of the ceiling. The unadorned but neat mud-brick walls. The square windows, through which he can see other buildings and hear the braying of animals.

His interrogators listened to Karma's story and pleas. He left nothing out, not about his father the Sherpa, or the Minister and the Mountain. When he was finished, they gave him dry clothes and then left, presumably to deliberate over his fate, leaving only one guard to watch the door. The dzong is a fortress, after all. Where can he run? And the Gangdruk are still his only hope of freeing his village from the patrollers.

But what will happen if they don't believe me?

And then another thought.

What will happen to Nima?

That look on her face when she realized Surkhang was speaking the truth—a look of betrayal at the realization that she had been misled, that in her zeal for her own revenge, she made a careless judgment—cut deep under his skin.

Suddenly the woolen cover over the doorway parts and a dusty wedge of light sweeps into the room. Karma straightens up from the floor. When he sees Norbu, his face immediately reddens at the memory of the ruse that he and the nun used to distract him.

There is something in Norbu's hand. Karma wonders if it is a weapon. Has he come to get even?

It is Karma's nose that identifies it first. Not a weapon, but sustenance.

Norbu crosses the room and squats before Karma, balancing a dish in front of him. A halved egg, some meat, pickled cabbage, and a lump of something that looks like raw sugar. Karma's stomach stirs loudly. It has been almost a full day since the rabbit.

Norbu gives a lopsided smile. "Thought you might be hungry." The young outlaw extends the dish. "Go ahead. Just because they're deciding your fate doesn't mean you have to starve in the meantime."

The thought occurs to Karma that perhaps the food is poisoned, but his hands are already shoveling one mouthful after another, cradling the plate in his arms as he crams the food past his teeth. The meat is warm, wonderful. He is ravenous, the ache of hunger seemingly only growing the more he eats. Both halves of the egg follow in one bite. The pain in his rib cage returns as he chews, but he ignores it.

"You caused quite a fuss when you left," Norbu says. "I've never seen Surkhang angrier. With me, as well." But then he lets out an airy laugh, showing that he begrudged Karma no ill will. "Looks like you didn't make it very far anyway."

The drapes over the doorway stir, another pair of feet appear outside.

"Somebody else wants to see you." Norbu nods.

Nima?

Karma swallows. He has a hope it might be her—mixed with equal part apprehension. Though if Norbu is in trouble for letting him slip away, Nima must be in even worse straits for bringing him to the fortress. He was desperate for the Gangdruk's help, but at her expense. He regrets it now, not just because they may not agree to help him. But because he has been selfish about it, when she trusted him.

But instead of Nima, it is the nun Dorje who opens the curtain.

"Reverend Mother," Karma says, rising. The movement hurts his rib cage and makes him wince at the pain.

"Sit, sit," Dorje says. "You're injured."

Together, Dorje and Norbu help him lie down. She presses her hands on his side, palpating the area over his rib cage. Though she applies little pressure, the pain is acute.

"You have a dislocated rib, Karma," Dorje concludes. "Lie on your side."

Gingerly, he does as he is told.

"Our paths have crossed again, after all," she says as she feels his ribs, digging with her fingers to isolate the ligaments in between. "How miraculous, the workings of karma." She finds what she is looking for, a feeling of something protruding out of place in his lower rib cage.

"Take a deep breath," she instructs, positioning her hands over his side as his torso rises with the expansion of air. "Now, exhale." Gently, but firmly, she presses down.

He feels a sharp crack of something being pushed back into place. The pain takes his breath away, but a moment later, the earlier debilitating ache in his side is gone.

"Better?" Dorje says.

Voices approaching from outside cut off Karma's reply. The curtain parts again. The Gangdruk leaders have returned. This time, Nima is with them, though she avoids his eyes. Their sober faces remind him of the village elders.

Norbu takes Karma's plate discreetly, withdrawing to a corner of the room.

"What's the nun doing here?" Surkhang snaps. "We didn't say anything about visitors."

Dorje steps between Karma and the Gangdruk, the shadow of her small figure stretched long in the light of the window.

"The boy is not the enemy," the Reverend Mother says.

"And you know this, how?" Surkhang mocks. "Another vision?"

"It's no accident that our paths have crossed," Dorje replies. "He is looking for the Mountain. We are looking for the Lama Child. We need each other. He's here because of fate."

Surkhang snorts. "He's here because some of us are more easily duped than others."

Karma sees Nima give a visible flinch.

"It's not her fault," he says, before he can stop himself.

The room turns to him. He cannot help it. Even though he needs the Gangdruk's help, he cannot sit by and watch them blame Nima alone.

"I came here . . ." Karma stammers, "to ask for your help. You, the Protectors of the Four Rivers and Six Ranges, who help the people who cannot help themselves. The thing the Minister wants—the Stone—I do not know where to find it, nor would I give it to him even if I did. But my village is being held prisoner until I do. *That* is why I have come to you. Because I do not know who else to turn to, or where else to go."

Surkhang dismissively scoffs. "You came because the Minister Hanumanda sent you. You came because you are a *spy*."

"That's enough, Surkhang," Gendun, the leader of the Gangdruk, cuts him off.

The outlaw captain looks and acts nothing like his younger brother. The whisper of gray on his head and chin hints at his seniority in age. Turning to Karma, he speaks deliberately but firmly. "You wish that we liberate your people from the Minister's patrollers. But we're outlaws, not a rebel force. We cannot take Hanumanda's army head on in his own territory, outnumbered as we are. And therein is the predicament. Because you have seen our hideout, your knowledge is a liability to everyone here."

Karma's heart sinks. The light in the room dims as the sky clouds over outside.

"You won't help him, but you won't let him go either." The Reverend Mother shakes her head. "What shall we do, then? Throw him in the river?"

"Trust me when I say we've done far worse for far less," Surkhang replies sharply.

"He's been a help to both of us—to me and one of your own who was a captive of the rebels!" the nun protests.

Gendun makes a gesture of silencing his brother again. "I agree with you, Reverend Mother. That's why . . . we will give him the choice of joining us."

Surkhang's eyes widen. "What?"

"If what the Reverend Mother has said is true," the Gangdruk captain says. "If the signs show that the Child Lama is waiting to be found, then there is no greater cause—for any of us. Bandit chiefs, warlords, patrollers . . . kill one, another takes their place. Nothing changes. Meanwhile, our karma accrues."

Surkhang shakes his head. "What are you *talking* about, Gendun?"

"I'm talking about the killing," Gendun says. "The bloodshed. What good has it done? How has it profited us?"

Surkhang's expression of incredulity grows. "Our profit is our wages for the safe passage we provide at the risk of our own necks. The good is the world being rid of one less lowlife. We're outlaws, Gendun. This is what we do!"

"I *know* what we are," Gendun replies. "I know what we've done. I only mean that perhaps . . . fate will now have us profit in another way." He turns back to the Reverend Mother. "If the Lama's time truly has come, you'll need help—finding the Child, keeping him safe, and taking him on his pilgrimage to the Mountain."

Dorje looks grateful beyond speech. "We . . . cannot pay you."

"Perhaps the clearing of our karma will be our payment, to redeem us from our past, if we should be so fortunate," Gendun replies.

Surkhang blinks as if he cannot believe what he is hearing. "You can't be serious, Gendun. Karma? Fate? Reincarnated Lamas and Seeing Stones? And from monks who have wandered in the wilderness their whole lives with nothing to show for it? Their Oracle is dead! He failed to predict his own death! What does that tell you?"

"*I* had a vision last night," the Reverend Mother Dorje declares. "In my dreams. I saw a child approaching in a lake of blood. It is the Lama, I know it."

"A lake of blood," Surkhang repeats. "Now it is utter nonsense. Why do you persist in continuing to entertain this drivel, Gendun?"

But Karma perks up at her last words.

A lake of blood.

He knows such a place by appearance. He recalls the scene in his mind. Wind sweeping across the basin. The pair of patroller brothers bickering at the fire. The patroller tents. Karma's fateful discovery of Lobsang's things in their bags.

The skull-shaped lake, red in the sun.

Skeleton's Head.

"I know that place," Karma says.

Slowly, all heads turn.

Gendun frowns. "You have seen a lake of blood?"

"It's an empty lake now," Karma replies, "in the shape of a skeleton's head. But in the setting sun, it resembles a pool of blood."

Silence follows. Dorje bows her head. "Truly, this is fate."

Surkhang juts a finger at Karma like someone catching a thief in the act. "This is another ploy. He's trying to lure us to his village!"

From the back of the room, Nima blurts out. "For heaven's sake! This is ludicrous. He's not lying about the lake."

Surkhang's face purples. He wheels about. "What is ludicrous—is to think your opinion is of any consequence after the lack of judgment you displayed."

"He mentioned the same place to me, when—"

"When you spent the night with him?" Surkhang's eyes pierce Nima's. She stares back at him, a look full of the hate Karma saw in her eyes at the grotto, multiplied.

"That's enough, Surkhang," Gendun snaps. The room falls silent.

He looks at Karma. "If we take you to the valley, will you be able to lead us there?"

"I . . . can try," Karma replies.

Gendun pauses. "If you do, and we succeed in finding the Child, then we will see what we can do about your village."

Surkhang's indignation burns in his eyes, but Karma's heart leaps with joy.

"Yes, sir," Karma breathes. "Thank you."

"I make no promises," Gendun warns. "Acting as an escort is one thing. Facing the Minister's army in the Territories is something else entirely." The Gangdruk leader turns to the rest of the room. "We will escort the Reverend Mother. Whether this vision is true or not, the outcome will speak for itself."

"And what if the outcome is failure?" Surkhang derides. "If all this talk of a Lama is nothing but a fantasy, and instead we meet with the Eastern Army?"

Gendun returns a sober look to his brother. "Then heaven help us, for then there is truly no hope before the end—or after it."

20

THE MISSION

Beyond the fortress walls, the sun is setting, shadows gathering. Karma follows along behind Norbu across a hay-filled yard. Though the space is smaller than Karma's village itself, there are many more people. He can feel their eyes on him.

The guards on the walls. A pair of girls fletching arrows of bamboo. An ironsmith suspending his hammer as they pass the bellows. Men laden with baskets on their shoulders carrying loads to a storehouse. Refugees from the Territories and Gangdruk outlaws.

People who have reason to hate the Minister . . . and those who serve him.

Norbu glances back at Karma, seeming to read his thoughts. "They're just scared. All this talk about the Minister planning an incursion into the Borderlands. Now your story about the Seeing Stone. It just confirms what we know. It's why we built the dzong. The Eastern Army is coming." Norbu slows, lowering his voice, his jaunty expression growing serious. "I understand why you did what you did," he says. "I would have done the same if I thought I could save my family. It was brave of you."

Karma looks at him, surprised by the sentiment. But of course what Nima said to him is true. They all lost people. Karma has been without a father since he was seven, but there are so many like him. They are all mourning something.

"Thanks," Karma says.

"Don't worry, Gendun is a good man. If he says he will help you, he'll do it." He clears his throat and gestures ahead. "The armory's just up this way."

Beyond the yard is a planting field. Though the sun is already well below the fortress wall, there are still people at work, turning the soil, digging irrigation ditches. Karma can see a patch of what might be young barley. Off to the side, baskets of potatoes and squash are being stacked, carried into a nearby storehouse, doors open to silhouettes of dried peppers and calabashes hanging from rafters.

The fortress is a nest of interwoven sections, rising the farther they go, past animal pens of bleating goats and clucking chickens, all the way to an elevated keep where stupas festooned with prayer flags face the eastern gates of the dzong. It is in this bailey below, lit presently by evening torches, that the Gangdruk fighters are mustering, assembling with their horses at the gates.

Karma and Norbu enter an enclosure by a corner palisade. It is the armory—well stocked, still filled with weapons despite having already been picked through. A stand on one wall holds riding lances and bamboo shields. On the opposite side, a rack holds a collection of long bows next to a half-dozen odd matchlock rifles. Norbu slings one of the bows over his shoulder, filling his quiver from a basket of arrows before moving on to the spears, selecting one for himself. He turns to look at Karma.

"Ever ridden with a lance before?" Norbu asks.

Karma gives him a blank look.

Norbu smiles. "Every horseman needs a spear. If you're coming with us, you'll need to be armed." He goes down the row, selecting the shortest pike. "Here. Try this."

Karma takes the spear in his hand—a wooden shaft reinforced by a metal band with the polish of the hands of those who have wielded it before. The tip is iron, like a needle's point. It is heavier than it looks.

"And . . . here," Norbu adds a sword to the arsenal. "A saber to go with it." As a finishing touch, he slaps a helmet onto Karma's head. "Now you look like a proper Gangdruk outlaw."

Karma stares at the weapons in his hands. His mind goes back to the raid by the border brigands, the sight of the bodies of the sky burial. He might look like an outlaw, but he doesn't feel like one. If anything, he felt more certain of himself in the monk's robes.

The doorway darkens as someone enters the armory. This time it is Nima. A quiver hangs on one hip, a sword and bow on the other. With a leather tunic and breastplate, she looks ready to go to war.

Her gaze roves from Norbu to Karma. "What do you think you're doing?"

"Gendun said to get him fitted out so . . ."

She marches up to them and snatches away the spear and sword from Karma. "As a *guide*," she says.

Karma removes the helmet from his head. They stand in uncomfortable silence.

"Leave us," she says to Norbu. He obliges, throwing a sympathetic glance at Karma on his way out.

When he is gone, Karma starts to speak. "Thank you for what you said to Surkhang—"

With a swift move of Nima's hand, a knife flashes out. Karma startles, bumping into the rack behind him just as she brings the blade up to his throat, too fast for him to do anything but stare wide-eyed at the black blade and crystal hilt—his knife.

"Let me be perfectly clear," she punctuates her words with a jerk of her arm. "I wasn't defending you then, and I'm not trusting you now, either. You tell a good story, *Sherpa*. You've got them convinced, all this talk about your father and the end of the world, just like how you had me convinced. But know this—I'll be watching you. And if I so much as get a whiff of something foul . . ."

She drives the knife into the tabletop, the gesture saying all that is needed to be said. "You'll wish I left you in the grotto."

She tosses the sheath to the table. "Consider us even," she adds, as it clatters beside the knife. "Get to the gate. We leave for the valley now."

PART III

<hr>

Strike the great Dharma drum,
blow the great Dharma conch,
rain down the great Dharma rain all around.

The Lotus Sutra (1st cen. CE)

21

THE SCROLL

I n the beginning was the void—so it was said.

Void was the world, and of the void came the world, at the sound of the heavens.

Ommmmm . . .

Rumbling forth from the darkness. Traveling, rippling, like the echo of a thunderclap in the distance, filling an expanse.

From its sound, a division of light from dark. It is a wall of fire. Churning, roiling. Winds like the blast of a furnace. Vapors rising into clouds.

Ommmmm . . .

Next were the roaring waters. The deluge of rains. Rushing, crashing. Waves overflowing. And on these waters also, the sound moved.

Molten floes from the deep, their heat mixing with the seas, form rock. Diverging, transforming, converging . . . into the first, primordial mound. Dry land. Colliding, cresting, pressing toward sky. The *Himalayas*—the Land of the Snows—rise.

The Four Rivers and Six Ranges, whose valleys hold the cradle of life. Trees, plants, flower. Herb, root, and seed. Fish swim, fowl flock, foal roam the land. And other beasts.

Pa Trelgen, the ape man, who walked upright and climbed the Mountain. Who here communed with the traveler from the stars, and in their union, formed man and his race. Thus began the six tribes. And these are their ages: the first, the second, the third, and the fourth.

Truth.

Loss.

Discontentment.

Vice.

From whence we came, to thence will we return. As the sun rises in the east, so it shall set in the west. So, too, must our bodies return to the earth. For as dust we are, and to dust we will go.

Yet, if all things need be as they first were, then to the final place will we also return. To our place among the stars. *Look to the Mountain,* Father said. *Look to the Stone. Listen for the sound of the dharma horn to take us home. Look before it crumbles, returning to the sea. The sea of fire, the sea of glass. The sea that sees all, and what will come to pass.*

I go to find it, Father said. *I go to call the others. The sleeping, to wake. The wandering, to gather. From the high country to the low. Along the lengths of the Four Rivers, up the heights of the Six Ranges. The herders, the sowers, the tent-dwellers, the settlers. The mountain people and the sky people. I go to save them all.*

You will know when I am there. The whole land will know.

You will know by my sounding the dharma horn, calling you to the Stone.

⊹————•⊷——⊷

Birds fill the sky. Not the hill pigeons of the valley dunes, or the forest finches who flit in the sun, or redstarts and larks with their birdsong.

These ravens and crows, these griffon vultures, these birds of the borderland—are heralds of the otherworld, carriers of the dead.

Only days since the fateful day when the patroller captain had ordered the soldiers to approach the pilgrim monks, Karma has returned to the same spot. At the edge of the forest, at the site of the ambush, a few bodies are still strewn over the ground—corpses of border bandits left behind by their gang in retreat, slain horses and animals, and the patrol escort.

The Gangdruk outlaws rove the site, scouring the area for anything that might be of value. A weasel retreats to the woods. A brood of crows scatters, flapping sulkily away.

The Reverend Mother Dorje lowers herself from her horse, head heavy as she regards the scene. The ground is littered with debris from the pilgrims' stolen sutras. She begins picking up some of the pieces. Torn pages of parchment, scraps of palm leaf, a shattered tablet. Fragments of scrawled text now loose and scattered.

Karma and some of the others begin to help, gathering whatever shreds of the dispersed sutras they can, for whatever use they will be. As they work, Karma finds himself glancing around, watching for Nima. She has said nothing to him since their encounter in the armory. He wonders if she will ever trust him again, even if he can lead them to the Skeleton Head.

I had a vision last night, the Reverend Mother Dorje said.

In my dreams. I saw a child, approaching in a lake of blood.

But what does the Reverend Mother expect she will find once they are there? Karma has seen the place, a desolate basin at the edge of the valley, a no-man's-land between the wilds of the Borderlands and the Minister's Territories. There were no people there. No villages or settlements. Certainly no children. Very few have been born of late—another sign of the world coming to an end.

Karma tells himself that he can't worry about it. He will soon be home. In two days' time, he will meet the ruins of the iron bird and the mast of the prayer flags. He will see the brown hills and the squat homes of his village just as their roofs will be turning red under the setting sun. Gendun said he would try to help the village. What Karma needs now is to focus on a plan to extricate his people.

I'll sneak in. Wait till nightfall, go to Mother first.

He pictures himself hiding behind the rocks, waiting for dark. He sees himself creeping into his village like a thief in the night, past the Minister's guards to his own home. His mother will be startled to see him, perhaps even think it is his ghost, that something bad has happened to him. Will she cry out in alarm? He will have to tell her everything quickly. From there, they will go swiftly to his uncle's home. Again, he will relay all that he has learned—that it was the Minister who orchestrated the attack on the village, who kidnapped Lobsang. Then they will find a way to escape in the night, perhaps while the Chushi Gangdruk create a diversion posing as bandits themselves. Together they will journey on to the Mountain. After all, Karma has heard the sound of the horn. He is sure he hasn't imagined it, to the point that he can almost feel its lingering resonation in his body even now. If he can hear it, he can follow it. And if he can't, well then at least the Gangdruk can take them to the safety of the dzong.

But then he has a thought.

What if the villagers don't want to leave? What if, even after learning the truth, they choose the bondage of the Minister's security over the dangers of the unknown? Their current safety is only an illusion, but he will be asking them to leave their homes, everything they know—to openly defy the Minister. Once they go down this path, there will be no turning back.

He continues searching for the scattered papers, following the trail into the woods. A sheet of parchment crackles under his step. He glances down, expecting another torn page of script, but it is a picture that catches his eye. Faded colors—a landscape scene, on curled paper. He stoops down to pick it up.

It is a piece of *thangka* scroll. A ring of mountains circles a lesser ring, their peaks all white-capped, depicting snow. In the center of the page is a large, white, perfect pyramid like a gleaming jewel, with bands of color streaking down the page like rays from the sun. It reminds Karma of the gems drawn on the backs of the wind-horse prayer flags.

There are other images too. Between the rings are rocky valleys, dark forests, icy glaciers, flat lakes, wild animals. On the bottom of the page gapes a cavernous pit from which ghoulish faces look up in expressions of rage, while overhead, atop curlicued clouds, serene-faced deities gaze benevolently down.

"It's Kailash."

Karma turns to see the Reverend Mother Dorje. He suddenly realizes that they are where their paths first collided, two strangers facing the same fate at the hands of the border bandits. Immediately he feels ashamed of himself, of his selfish single-mindedness for his own family's welfare. Here is a person who has lost everything, every possession of value, who has seen the slaughter of her own people, including their beloved leader. How difficult this must be, the trauma of returning to the very place it happened, even for the most ardent believer in the otherworld.

But there is no condemnation, no censure in the old nun's eyes, only a heaviness in her spirit, in the bend of her head as she takes the folded paper to study it.

"The name for the Mountain comes from a Sanskrit word that means crystal," Dorje says. "It was said to be so perfectly pyramidal in shape and perpetually white with snow that it resembled a gleaming crystal seen for thousands of miles, a mountain so pure that climbing it was forbidden. But circling it once would erase a lifetime of sin. In the years before the Suns, pilgrims would come from all corners of the Four Rivers and Six Ranges, and even beyond. Traveling a step, then bowing a step, prostrating face-down in prayer. Step, bow, pray, crawl. Rocks, sand, snow, gravel. Every inch. A journey of tears and penitence. Those who completed the pilgrimage would wear their clothing to tatters, their skin to leather by the end, but their karma . . . would be as clean as the driven snow—and they would be transformed. The Mountain was sacred then. A pillar of another world."

Karma blinks as he hears this. A pillar of another world—the otherworld? Could this be the same mountain?

"The Oracle had a dream," Dorje continues, "of a sanctuary of learning inside this Mountain. Where we would one day be taught by the Lama from a great library of lost books. Books that would tell us everything we have been blind to: where we came from, why we are here, how the Suns came to be, and where we are going." She picks up the shreds of paper from the ground. "Years of carting these sutras around in hopes of one day joining them to its archive. Now look at them. Tatters, scattered by the wind." She lowers her voice as one speaking of the dead. "Just like his own body, taken by fowl over the four winds."

She turns to face Karma. "I was all but ready to give up after we lost the Oracle. But then *you* came along, a miracle of fate. I know you made a promise to your family to return to the valley. I made a vow too. For forty years, I walked by his side. For that many years I followed him. Like you, I miss someone. Like you, I would want nothing more than to be reunited—with him. But that reunification can never last in the Seventh Sun."

Karma lingers on these words. Something is stirring in him, something that was awakened on the day he found the yak, that has grown since he learned about his father.

"What can we do?" he asks finally.

Dorje fixes him with her gaze. "You really want to help your people, Karma? Then help us. The answer is not in the valley. The Stone is not in your village. It is out there." She points westward.

"Six Suns, six blasts in the sky. A seventh one, and the earth will die. But . . . gather to the Mount and the Seeing Stone, that the Lama may reveal *yet a future unknown*," she recites. "When we find the Child and Mount Kailash, we will find our answers."

A silence settles around them, and suddenly too peaceful a feeling, despite past bloodshed. The horses are being mustered. The Gangdruk are calling, readying the company to move out. As Karma ponders her words, he begins to wonder—whether or not the Reverend Mother is right.

22

THE SKULL

It is sunset when they arrive at the cliffs overlooking Skeleton's Head, the shadows of the wall slowly stretching across the empty lakebed.

The outlaws set up camp quietly, careful not to disturb Dorje, who assembles her tent apart from the others, the flap open to a view of the basin below, even though it will soon be too dark to see. As they work, Karma looks out through the dusky afterglow. Even in the onset of twilight, the shape is unmistakable. On the far side, at what would be the crown of the Skeleton's Head, the land is wreathed in an orange halo. Two sunken impressions give the appearance of hollow eye sockets, and immediately below them, crumbled sections of the cliff resemble a missing mandible. As the gloom deepens and the light of the moon appears, the skull fills with a silvery shimmer that could be mistaken for water, an apparition in the night.

Someone is watching him. A figure stands off to the side. The light is just enough for him to recognize Nima. His heartbeat quickens. He understands why she is angry with him. His lie has cost her, has harmed her standing with her people. The worst of it was that his betrayal hurt her. But now, he hopes, she can see that he is not untrustworthy. He promised to bring them to the Skeleton Head lakebed, and now here they are. Perhaps now she can see that he never meant any wrong.

Karma faces her, feeling hopeful, when he startles at someone else's approach from the opposite direction. He turns, finding Surkhang.

Karma's pulse again quickens, but for another reason entirely. A feeling that he is suddenly close—*too close*—to the edge of the cliff. He glances quickly back at Nima, but by now she is gone.

"She's only watching you because she doesn't trust you," comes Surkhang's voice. "You can imagine why. You and the nun may have convinced my brother. A Child Lama come to free the people from the karma of the world's misdeeds? Wipe away the blood on our hands? How convenient. No wonder Gendun wants to believe. He has as much blood on his hands as mine, if not more." His eyes bore into Karma in the dark. "Lucky for me, I'm not troubled by blood. Because all this is a delusion. You know that, don't you? There's no Child. No savior coming to rescue us from our fate. The only help you can rely on is that of your own sword. No Seeing Stones required."

He circles Karma, venturing to the edge of the cliff and the black sky. "Coming here was a fool's errand. The old believers had their chance, prophesying about the Seven Suns. But all the prayer wheels and chants in the world couldn't stop the first six. No reason to think the seventh will turn out any different. My brother will come to realize this, sooner or later. And then there will be no excuse for you, for there are many here who harbor a hatred for the Minister deeper than you know—*and* for those who support him. Soon comes the moment of truth. How do you think it will bode for you, boy, when tomorrow comes and no Child appears?"

Karma feels himself go cold. The outcome will speak for itself, Gendun had said. If the trip proves unfruitful, what will the Gangdruk do—to him, to the plans to help his village?

"You've been warned," Surkhang says, withdrawing from the edge. "If I were you . . . I'd get as far away from here as you can—and from Nima."

⸻

Karma sleeps restlessly, dreaming of weapons like the ones the Minister described. Objects shooting up in clouds of smoke, crisscrossing the skies, spewing streams of fire and destruction. He counts them as they thunder through the air, watching them from the distance in vision after vision.

One . . . two . . . three . . .

He sees them, flying in the face of one another but never touching, never stopping, intent on only one thing.

Four . . . five . . . six . . .

Fire, cloud, smoke.

Seven . . .

It waits, somewhere in the dark.

Karma wakes with tears in his eyes. A few persistent stars peek down through the open night air, unfiltered, twinkling. A bright moon, slung low, casts an aura over the land. The camp is an unmoving collection of shapes and silhouettes.

The ghost-winds abrade the tents. They seem to echo Surkhang's words.

Soon.

The moment of truth.

With each hour, it creeps closer. What if Surkhang is right? Karma has gotten this far. Perhaps he should do as Surkhang told him and leave before sunrise. He could take a horse and be back in his village by day's end. But stealing a horse is an unforgivable offense. A part of him wonders if this is what Surkhang intended.

Is it worth the risk?

His mind is running, he realizes. He sits up in his bedroll, shivering. They are sleeping in the open, all except the Reverend Mother. The cold air chills his skin. He stands up, somewhat unsteady in the dark, pulling the layers of his robe tighter around him. He thinks he hears something moving about, but when he strains his ear, the only movement he detects is the whisper of the wind over the rocks and the ground.

Slowly, he wanders toward the edge of the cliff. Once more, he feels as if someone is watching him. Yet when he scans his surroundings, there is only the slumbering camp. He turns toward the east, out to the basin. There at the edge of the precipice, under the glow of the moon, the basin is a silvery well, like moonlight on water.

He stays there, for how long, he doesn't know, contemplating his options. By now the sky is changing, softly tinted gray, seeping through the horizon.

He sees something—moving below. On the surface, a single figure.

It moves slowly, so slow it could be mistaken for a shadow. But it is a shadow set apart from the others, a single mote from where he stands, venturing silently onto the plain. Karma squints. He tiptoes to the edge, navigating the rocks.

"Where are you going?"

Karma wheels around.

Nima faces him, one hand on the handle of her sword. She has been there, watching him.

"There's . . . someone down there," Karma tells her, lest she thinks that he has been trying to sneak away.

Nima steps forward, her hand still on her sword. She peers down. He sees her head straighten immediately.

"Stay right there," she barks. He sees her stride back to the camp. Noises and commotion. Someone goes to Dorje's tent, calling out. In a few moments, voices rise.

"She's not here! The Reverend Mother's not in her tent!"

The outlaws flock to the precipice, crowding the edge.

"Is that the nun out there?"

"Move! Make way." Gendun strides through, his brother Surkhang at his side. They stare down at the emptied lakebed.

The Reverend Mother is walking alone, toward the slowly rising sun.

Surkhang scoffs. "What does she think she's doing?"

As they watch her, the first colors of the morning begin to creep over the horizon, darkness shifting to sepia and golds, the rocks appearing molten at the touch of the sun's fragile first rays. A sense of inevitability grows in Karma. His moment to escape has passed. They have found nothing. He wonders what will happen to him now.

Norbu's finger stabs at the air suddenly, pointing toward the horizon. "Look!"

All turn their heads in the direction of his gesticulating. Across the basin to the east, at the area of the crown of the skull, now lit by the sun's ascension, a smattering of tiny figures appears.

Unmistakable. No illusion. Moving out toward them.

A caravan.

They stare, stunned.

Surkhang frowns, cocking a hand to his brow as if to blame the sunrise for this inexplicable vision. "What is this? Some kind of a trick? Who are they?"

"No, it is no trick." It is Gendun who replies in awe, saying what they are all thinking, with the same conviction they are all feeling.

"It's the Lama. She has found the Child."

23

THE BATTLE

The canyon shakes with the clatter of the horses. In the shadows of a ravine, Karma rides with the mounted outlaws, winding through the narrow gully. The chill wind whistles shrilly over gaping holes in the rock, the walls as pockmarked as lesions of a dry bone. The ghostly sound makes him shiver, while the pounding of the hooves makes his heart race and his body quake at the thought. *Could it be? Could it be they have found the Lama Child?*

Could it be that it is fate that I should help them?

The passage narrows, room enough only for them to ride two abreast. They approach the mouth of the skull, shadows lifting, rock turning golden in the light.

The canyon opens. The echoes disappear.

Karma's face warms. His hair streams in the dust and the sun.

Karma squints out at the nun's lone figure in the basin ahead of them. She waits for them patiently. In the distance behind her, the caravan is visible, closer now than when they had spied it from the clifftop.

"Isn't it as we said?" the Reverend Mother says when she sees them. She has been crying, her face streaked with tears of joy. "Like I told you. It is fate."

The people in the approaching caravan appear to number in the dozens. As Karma peers into the dawning sun, he can make out animals as well. They seem to see them in return, warned ahead by the rising dust of the horses' charge.

"They're dallying," Surkhang says.

"They're afraid," Gendun replies. "They don't know who we are."

Nima leans forward in her saddle, shielding her eyes from the sun's growing strength. "Wait," she says suddenly. "What is that, on the other side of the basin?"

They squint to where she is pointing, far across the skull, past the approaching caravan, to some distant dunes. Tiny flecks stream down the slopes.

Other figures, like the caravan, only more of them.

Many more. Almost like . . .

An army.

"Those are patrollers . . ." Gendun utters in incredulity. "There must be a whole division of them, from the looks of it."

As if to confirm, tiny pennants appear, faint flags unfurling in the wind, the color still too distant to see, until they mass together.

Red.

The color of the tabernacle silks.

The color of Hanumanda.

Dorje's earlier elation vanishes. "They're coming for the Child!"

"Quick," Gendun gives the order. "Round up the caravan. Get them to the canyon."

But the caravan has stopped, apparently perceiving a threat from both sides. The phalanx of Gangdruk riders lurches forward. Instead of meeting them, the caravan begins to scuttle into a defensive huddle—afraid, as Gendun had predicted. As Karma and the other riders draw near, Karma makes out slender shafts jutting out from the makeshift redoubt.

They have rifles.

Gendun sees it too. "Guns!"

A rifle kicks, booming smoke across the way. Gendun signals and the Gangdruk fan out, veering to a stop.

"Don't shoot!" Gendun shouts, lifting his arms in a gesture of peace. "We are the Chushi Gangdruk—friends!"

No response from the caravan. Something from this moment seems familiar to Karma. Something about the appearance of the barricade and the animals. Perhaps it is the agitation, the reminder of the raid by the bandits on the monks.

There are voices from the huddle. Furtive peeks from behind the barricade.

The Reverend Mother has taken one of the horses and is riding forward, calling out to the caravan as well. "Do not be afraid! We are here to help!"

The long barrels of matchlock rifles bob through the barricade, training their sights at them. "Don't come any closer!" a voice shouts in reply.

Karma blinks.

That voice.

He knows it.

It can't be. But it is.

"Uncle Urgyen?" Karma says, calling out to the barricade. "Is that you?"

A moment of stunned silence. All eyes turn to Karma.

"It's me!" he waves, certain now. "It's Karma!"

Movement from the huddle. Then comes the most welcome sound he hears—his mother's voice.

"Karma?" Her head peers out from behind the barricade.

He sees her. "Mother!"

Another head pops up. Smaller. A child's. His cousin Lobsang.

"Is it Karma?"

"Heavens . . . could this miracle be?" his mother cries, clapping her hands to her mouth. "It's really you!"

Karma flings himself from his horse, bounding forward.

The redoubt spits another burst of rifle shot, though this time only fired into the sky.

Karma freezes midway there.

"Everybody, stay put!" Uncle Urgyen's voice shouts out. "Don't come any closer!" To those with him, he commands, "Keep those guns on them."

"What are you doing, Urgyen?" Karma's mother can be heard. "Can't you see it's Karma?"

"Yes, and I can also see an armed band with him, and on our other side, the patrollers he left behind to *guard* us. That's what I see," Urgyen snaps.

"Uncle," Karma begs, taking a step towards them. "These are the Chushi Gangdruk, protectors of the Four Rivers and Six Ranges. They are here to help."

The Gangdruk horses nudge forward.

Urgyen twitches his rifle in their direction. "I said—no closer!"

Again, they stop. All except the Reverend Mother Dorje . . . who dismounts and continues on foot, staring intently. But not at Urgyen. Not at the rifles.

At Lobsang. Karma's cousin.

She tucks her hands together, close to her robes. Then she bows gently. The realization of what is happening stuns Karma.

She thinks Lobsang . . . is the Child.

Gendun quickly addresses the caravan. "If you've heard of us, you know we've helped others cross the Borderlands." He points to patrollers in the distance. Now Karma can make out both horses and regiments on foot. "We're here to help you. But you don't have much time."

Before he can stop her, Karma's mother pushes past Urgyen. He tries to call her back, but then Auntie Pema follows, trailed by Lobsang, running to Karma.

One by one, the other Khampas come out from the barricade. Karma runs forward to meet them. This time, Uncle Urgyen does not threaten to shoot.

"Take only what you can carry," Gendun shouts. "Leave everything else!"

His mother reaches Karma, taking his face into her hands. "Thank the heavens," she says, weeping. "I thought we'd never see you. I didn't want to leave. But there was a mutiny when Lobsang woke up and told us the patrollers were the bandits who hurt him. We had to fight, Karma. The shaman was killed."

"It's true," Karma says. "It's all true. I am sorry."

His mother's face flashes in anger. "It's not your fault. I told Urgyen—it's not Karma's doing, he didn't know . . ."

Karma chokes back tears, his throat thick with emotion and relief.

"Karma!" Lobsang dashes forward. Karma drops to a knee, receiving the boy into his arms. He can feel him laughing and crying into his shoulder at the same time.

"It's all right," Karma whispers. "Everything will be well now."

From the corner of his eye, Karma sees the Reverend Mother looking at them with an expression of awe. She told Karma that their paths crossed for a reason, that her vision showed her the Child, that it was Karma who was meant to bring them here. And now, of all people . . . it is his villagers they have encountered.

His cousin is the Lama Child?

Lobsang? Could it really be?

"How miraculous, the workings of karma," Dorje marvels, not for the first time.

His cousin returns the Reverend Mother's gaze with a look of curiosity.

"They're coming!" Norbu calls out, interrupting the moment. Across the basin, a cloud of dust is growing, the dotted formations now a wave of riders.

"Get to the canyon!" Gendun begins to motion. "Everyone!"

"Take my horse," Dorje tells Pema. "And take your son and ride. Quickly!"

Auntie Pema and Lobsang comply, mounting the horse. Karma climbs back onto his own horse, helping his mother up behind him. Dorje rides double with Nima.

They gallop to the cliffs, the army still only a remote presence behind them, soundless and distant. At the entrance to the ravine, they slow, impeded by the narrowness of the opening.

"Swiftly, now! Hurry!" Gendun waves the riders in.

Inside the canyon, the sounds are dampened, the reverberations of their movements trapped against the rock. Against the blurring of the walls, the stillness feels suddenly stilted, unnatural. Like breaths held.

Or . . . something lying in wait.

Karma's skin crawls and something compels him to look up.

From a hollow in one wall, two eyes peer down at them. A single masked face.

Karma blinks and the apparition disappears, only to reappear in another hole. Karma stares, uncertain if he is seeing things, until he glimpses a bow, a shaft of sunlight hitting the tip of an arrow. Then a dozen more appear, in every nook and every crevice.

Karma's mouth jerks open, a warning shout forming on his lips—

Border bandits!

But it is too late.

Strings loose. Shafts streak.

A torrent of arrows suddenly fills the ravine. In front of him, Auntie Pema's horse lets out a shriek. It careens toward the wall as Pema cries out. Karma can hear the thud of their bodies. Karma wrenches on his reins. The horse rears, narrowly missing them.

Karma and his mother lose their balance. They hit the ground.

Auntie Pema is facedown. To their shock, an arrow protrudes from her back. Pinned underneath her—is Lobsang's small, unmoving body. Somewhere in the background, Karma hears his uncle's anguished scream.

"No . . ." Karma's mother begins to moan. "No, Pema . . . no . . ."

Karma reels.

How is this happening?

But there's no time. Shouts from the canyon walls, and another barrage of arrows hisses through the air. One lands beside his leg. The canyon echoes with shrieks and cries.

"Turn back!" shouts Gendun. Strained, distant. "Turn back to the basin!"

But Karma can only stare.

A movement beneath Pema. Lobsang's hand twitches.

Alive. He's alive.

"Dear God," Karma's mother gasps. "Lobsang . . . Lobsang, can you hear me?"

Together they lift Pema, pulling the boy free. Lobsang's face is inert, his eyes are closed.

"They're coming!"

Karma looks up. Ropes unfurl down the rock walls. In a chorus of wild ululation, a swarm of bandits rappels down the canyon rift.

"Get up, Karma!"

Nima and Dorje come galloping toward them, Karma's horse in tow. Dorje is frantic, but the look in Nima's eyes is a virulent rage.

"Take the boy! Ride!"

Karma and his mother climb on, hefting Lobsang into the saddle with them. Suddenly, a bandit is upon them, grabbing hold of the horse's bridle. Karma goes frozen with fear.

A sword pierces through the brigand's shoulder. The bandit drops away.

"Go!" Nima barks.

Karma doesn't stop. He flees, riding hard, following the line of horses as they wend their way back from where they had just come, back to the basin, out to the open, out before the charge of the army.

The bandits follow, streaming in droves. The Gangdruk circle around the Khampas in a protective ring.

Karma scans the field, his vision blurred by panic. With the Minister's army approaching on one side and the bandits blocking the ravine on the other, there is nowhere to go. They are trapped.

"*You!*"

A hand grips Karma's arm. Karma turns to see Uncle Urgyen's wild and enraged eyes.

"You did this! You brought this on us!"

Urgyen wrenches him from his saddle to the ground.

"No, Uncle—"

"You were the one! You . . . got Pema *killed!*"

Without warning, Uncle Urgyen strikes him in the face. Karma lets out a grunt, not so much from pain but shock.

"It's because of you! You and your cursed father, both!"

Urgyen hits him again. Again, it is the anger from his uncle that Karma feels, not the blows, his senses too stunned, as if it is happening to someone else even though it is his body that is reeling.

Karma sprawls on the ground, dazed. He sees the bandits fanning out to surround the caravan, the Gangdruk horses charging out to meet them in return. At the mouth of the ravine, fighters clash. As his uncle grabs him again, Karma's mother claws at Urgyen, still holding on to Lobsang.

"Stop," she screams. "Don't hurt him!"

A conflict within a conflict. His uncle pushes her away.

"They did this! They brought this on us. Your husband . . . and his son!"

Karma lurches out of his uncle's grip, but Urgyen chases him still.

A horse suddenly looms before them. Its rear swings around, knocking Urgyen to the ground. From atop the horse, Nima points her sword at Urgyen's face.

"Touch him again," she snarls, "and I'll kill you myself."

Karma's uncle stares at her, not daring to move.

A scream snatches away their attention. Three bandits surround Karma's mother as she clutches Lobsang in her arms.

"Lobsang!" Karma's uncle stumbles to his feet.

"Let me," Nima says. Wheeling her horse toward the attackers, she charges forward. She reaches the first bandit, the powerful horse crunching him instantaneously under its hooves. A stroke of Nima's sword, and the second bandit falls. But the third bandit manages to sidestep, sticking his weapon into the horse's side, the animal rearing, throwing Nima from her saddle. There is something familiar about the bandit—his red-painted face. The same one from the raid.

It is Drakpa, the bandit chieftain.

Nima lands on her feet, sword still in hand. The chieftain takes in the sight of the two other bandits she has dispatched. He grabs Karma's mother by the collar of her robe, raising his own saber to her throat.

"Mother!" Karma cries.

The bandit chieftain gestures to the caravan. "I have seen Hanumanda send a cavalry of fifty horsemen to ride down a defector. Even dispatch a whole company of patrollers to quell a rebellion. But a whole division?" He looks to Karma's mother. "You must have something they really want." He turns back to Nima. "What do you think, *Gangdruk*? Some large ransom for us to share? Enough to go around."

But Nima is not listening, not hearing, as if possessed by another thought. "Drakpa," she says. "It is you, isn't it?"

The chieftain cocks his head. "You know me, girl?"

"I know you," comes Nima's reply. "I know you as a murderer. I know you as a coward who raids refugee settlements and nomad caravans. I know you as the one who killed my parents."

The chieftain's painted face flickers with surprise, but quickly turns into a sneer. "I see," he says. "Then we are already acquainted." Without another word, he shoves Karma's mother forward, front and center like a human shield, swinging his weapon at Nima at the same time.

The air sizzles—a crackle of gunfire ripples from across the basin. The chieftain's body gives an unnatural jerk.

A hole suddenly gapes at the center of Drakpa's chest, blooming red and spreading.

A stray bullet.

Nima flinches, as if she herself has been shot. "No—"

The chieftain returns her stunned expression. His mouth opens in a gasp, but instead of air, there is blood draining from the hole, glugging down his front. Karma's mother scrambles back to her feet, eyes wide at the horror of the scene.

The chieftain's weapon slips from his hand to the ground. His body follows next. It seems to fold on itself.

"No!" Nima cries out again.

She thrusts her sword into his body, but it barely registers a response, his eyes already closed. All the same, she does it again, over and over.

The blade scrapes against bone and becomes stuck.

"No, no, no . . ."

The basin shakes. This time not with rifle fire and its barrage of stray bullets, striking the bandit chieftain, but the rolling bass of oncoming cavalry.

"Nima." Karma reaches for her. "We have to get out of here."

They hear shouts and commands. The border bandits are rallying, turning to meet the onslaught of Hanumanda's army. The wave of patroller cavalry comes, red banners waving. Bodies smash, weapons crash. The Minister's cavalry slams into the circle of bandits.

The voice of Gendun floats over the noise. "To the canyons!" he is shouting. "Retreat!"

The basin resounds with the indiscriminate clang of the soldiers' arsenal, the boom of their gunfire. Screams fill the air. Next comes the wave of foot soldiers. Facing the swell of bandits, they charge in a mass.

"Nima," Karma yells. "Nima, they're coming!" He touches her arm. "We *have* to go."

Dorje has joined them. The Reverend Mother's eyes go to the chieftain's body, then to Lobsang's slumped figure in Karma's mother's arms. Her face pales.

"He's dead." Nima sways over the brigand, as if the draining of his life had drained hers as well.

Rifles concuss, deafening in their echo. The wind blows gun smoke, stinging their eyes.

"We have to go," Dorje whispers.

Karma scans the cliffs for the mouth of the ravine. He spots it, a grey gash ahead.

"Come on, Nima," Karma says, his voice gentler.

Slowly, gradually, Nima peels herself away.

Together, they run.

Looking over his shoulder through the haze, Karma sees the full force of the border bandits' legions trying to reinforce their line, their center collapsing, though still slowing the cavalry's advance.

They reach the canyon, the mouth opening to them through the smoke and the dust. Together, they file through the passage. This time there are no arrows, no masked faces in the crevices. But there is blood on the ground, a red trail that has pooled like a stream.

Uncle Urgyen clutches Lobsang in his arms. "Hold on," Karma hears him pleading, his little cousin's limbs swinging limply. "Stay with me, son."

The sun is now high above the canyon and Karma can see the faces of the dead from the ambush. So many of the people he has known, now bodies lining the ravine.

Urgyen's footsteps slow.

There, lying in the twisting corridor of the canyon, is Pema. Still clutching his son, Urgyen drops to his knees beside her.

"She's gone, Urgyen," Karma's mother weeps quietly behind him, her lungs heaving. "We have to go too."

The clap of retreating hooves echoes around them. The Gang-druk are rounding up whatever horses they can find for those on foot, shouting for the people to ride. Urgyen looks up at Karma's mother, his eyes brimming with tears.

"For Lobsang," she says.

Urgyen clutches the boy close. With a last glance at his wife, he rises, trembling.

They mount the horses and ride through the canyon. Toward safety. Toward the west, and toward the Borderlands, leaving their dead behind on the skull-shaped floor of the jagged ravine.

24

THE CHILD

The harvest moon is a bright one. Wandering out from the camp,
Karma gazes up at the orb, full over the land, a circle ringed by
a halo. Tonight, everything seems heightened: the thin fragrance of
the air, the signal of a cold night ahead; the movements in the earth;
the wobble of the moon and stars, like the canopy of a tent on its last
legs; the wail of the ghost-winds, more mournful than Karma has ever
heard them.

Perhaps our dead have joined their voices already. Karma's heart
sinks at the weight of the tragedy. So many dead. His aunt—Lobsang's
mother—among them. His cousin injured again.

And still no sound of the horn.

At least we are together, Karma thinks. *At least we have gotten
away.* The village is safe for now. His mother. Lobsang. They are going
to the dzong. *But then what?*

He sits down on the cold earth, crossing his legs under him. The
camp under the night sky reminds Karma of another night many years

ago, before his father left. There was a moon such as this, perfect and round, at the time of the Mid-Autumn festival. He remembers children dashing around in the light of the moon, lifting the lids of the water pots as if to trap the shimmering discs of light, the grown-ups watching and laughing.

It is one of his fondest memories. The last happy one he can remember. Now the sounds are not of laughter and conversation, but of loss and mourning as his people tend to the wounded. The voice of his Uncle Urgyen drifts over now, cursing the gods and the Suns—and most of all, the day Sherpa Patrul's path crossed the valley. Against the backdrop of stars, their silhouettes resemble a pack of wolves, living out their existence in the night, free to roam but only in hiding. Nomads now, without so much as a hovel to call a home. Outlaws, on the run.

"How you were able to stand an uncle like that for so many years, I will never know," Nima's voice comes at Karma. She steps through the darkness. "With kin like that, who needs enemies?"

The words should sting, but they are a welcome salve. She is speaking to him again.

Karma rises from his seat. "I guess I hoped that one day I would earn his trust," he replies.

"Maybe that hope was misplaced," Nima snaps. But in the next moment her voice softens as she sits down at a small distance from him. "Maybe his fault was being too harsh a judge."

Karma lets out a silent sigh, allowing himself a smile. But he has more to say to her. "I should never have deceived you, Nima." He hangs his head. "It was inexcusable."

Nima snorts. "You could have left me in the cave, Sherpa," she says. "You could have gone for your mule and headed home to try to impress that bootheel uncle of yours. But you didn't, even before you knew who I was. You came back, though I had judged you a coward and self-ish—because you gave your word. Just like you gave your word to your mother and your people. You keep your promises. That's just . . . who you are."

Relief floods Karma, a weight taken from his chest.

"I should have seen it myself, anyway," Nima says with an ironic laugh. "Your hair was too long, even for a wandering monk. And your face, too soft. But I was fixed on Drakpa, on what I could learn from you about him. On what I was going to *do* when I found him." Her voice cuts off. "I'm as much to blame."

Karma thinks of the look on her face at the battle—the shock, the denial, followed by the pure rage—when, finally having a chance at revenge, the opportunity was taken from her. He could see it in her eyes, as if she had been robbed again—first of her family, and now of her vengeance, of being the one to take the life of her family's murderer. In an instant, the pain of the loss returned.

"I am sorry," Karma says.

Nima turns her face toward the darkness. "Fate is a funny thing. I should feel satisfaction, knowing that as I am sitting here, his corpse is growing cold, feeding the jackals." Her voice lowers now, like she is talking to herself. "Instead, it feels like unfinished business."

She starts when the ghost-winds wail ghoulishly, long and fading, then turns back to Karma, her eyes intent as she studies his face in the moonglow. "Maybe it's all just an illusion. Maybe in the end, none of what we do matters." She pauses then, working out her next words. "But . . . if there's a chance this cousin of yours is who the monks say he is, if you can prove to that bootheel that he was wrong about your father, and if it means we can be a thorn in the side of the Minister—then maybe that's worth fighting for."

Karma is uncertain what he should say. Many of the Gangdruk harbored doubts when they first left the fortress, including Nima. And then the Reverend Mother's vision came true. Yet, the idea that Lobsang is the long-awaited reincarnation of the Lama is a proposition difficult for Karma to accept. Not just because the boy is his cousin.

But to have a fate thrust upon someone who has not asked for it—a child, no less.

He says nothing. What is most important is that they are safe for now. If the Chushi Gangdruk believe that the Lama from the time before the Six Suns has been reborn, and if they believe that this Lama Child is, in fact, Lobsang, they will take them to the dzong and they will be safe yet longer.

From there, the journey could continue. Karma has not forgotten about his father.

"Come on," Nima says, rising, "the Reverend Mother is anxious to know how your cousin is doing."

She holds out a hand and pulls him to his feet. The two begin to head back to the Gangdruk's side of the camp. At the fire, the Gangdruk and Reverend Mother are waiting, speaking in hushed tones.

When she sees them, Dorje rushes out to Karma. "How is he—the Child?" she asks.

They have already taken to calling him by that name. *The Child. The Lama.*

"Still sleeping," Karma answers. As far as he is concerned, the longer Lobsang sleeps, the better. For rest. For delaying the inevitable knowledge of his mother's death.

But no sleep can last forever.

Dorje bows her head in silent prayer.

"I told you it was foolish," Surkhang calls out from the other side of the fire. "Did I not? Look at us now . . . half of our fighters dead. And for what?"

"This is the *Child*," the nun says. "The reincarnation of the Lama who will gather the people to be taught the lost dharma on the Mountain, where the Stone will reveal answers about the past and show the way to stop the Seventh Sun and change the future. Your comrades' sacrifice has preserved that. We are all in their debt, everyone in the entire Four Rivers and Six Ranges."

The reactions of the Gangdruk are mixed, some glancing at Gendun and Surkhang to observe their responses.

Gendun rises, giving a decisive nod. "The Reverend Mother saw a vision that the Lama Child would be there, and he was. As far as I'm concerned . . . she's proven herself. As did the Sherpa."

"Proven what?" Surkhang retorts. "The Lama has been gone for three generations. What makes you believe he's returned now in the form of a . . . child? And why *this* child? What's so special about him, over any of us?"

"Were you not at the battle, Surkhang?" Gendun counters his brother. "Did you not see the whole division of patrollers? Why would Hanumanda send that much of the Eastern Army if not to attempt to obtain the Lama Child? Is that not proof enough for you?"

"Are we speaking of different battles?" Surkhang shoots back. "Yes, I saw the Eastern Army. I also saw them firing their weapons indiscriminately into the fray, even at the border bandits, who everyone knows are the army's own pawns. *Attempt to obtain the Lama Child?* There was no attempt by Hanumanda to obtain anybody or anything, except to kill! How do you explain that?"

Gendun does not have a reply. But it is the Reverend Mother who does.

"Because the Minister didn't know," Dorje says. "It was Karma—his village—that Hanumanda was after, as leverage to obtain the Stone. That's why he sent his army. It was only destiny that the guide to the Mountain and the Child should find themselves from the same village, and their paths converge with ours."

"And ours too," Gendun says. He dusts his hands, a decision made. "Reverend Mother, whatever help and protection the Chushi Gangdruk can offer—you will have it. For better or worse, it seems that our fates are aligned as well."

The metal ringlets on Surkhang's hauberk smolder in the orange glow of the fire as he drops his head into his hands. "Help and protection?" he murmurs. "When we've lost half of our people, what help and protection do you intend? What will you do when the Minister's forces eventually overrun the Borderlands and come for us, only this time with the entire Eastern Army?"

Again, Gendun is quiet. The wind blows tautly through the dark hills, strained and fraying. Just then, a commotion stirs from the Khampas' side of the camp. Voices rise; the sound of excited activity grows.

They hear the words, "waking up."

The voices spread. They can see the villagers moving, crowding.

"He's waking!"

"Is it the Child?" Dorje asks.

Karma starts toward the other camp.

The Gangdruk and Reverend Mother follow him, rushing to the villagers. As Karma wades through the crowd, his mother sees him. "Karma, Lobsang's awake! Thank the heavens, your cousin is awake!"

Karma sags with relief. Perhaps it is true, then. Perhaps Lobsang is the Child. Beside him, Dorje immediately begins another prayer of gratitude.

Uncle Urgyen is crouching beside him, holding a water skin to his mouth. "Son," he coaxes, "can you hear me?"

Slowly, weakly, Lobsang's eyes blink up at their faces. His lips move, trying to form speech. His voice is a small whisper, yet clear.

"Mother . . ."

It is unbearable. Between the grimness of his uncle's expression and Karma's mother's hushed sobs, the silence that follows is longer than the lull of the wind on the loneliest stretch of the valley's plain.

"Where's . . . my mother?" Lobsang asks.

"My poor son," Urgyen's voice is choked as he says the next words. "Your mother is gone . . . to the mountain pass . . . beyond the veil of snows." The words are a euphemism, intended to be as comforting as they are beautiful in imagery, now seeming only to heighten the forlornness of death.

There is no reaction from Lobsang. Instead of tears, he squints into the night like someone trying to recall a distant sight. "Are we going to visit her now?"

Not a single person speaks, not even the ghost-winds, as if the entire world cannot bear to shatter the dream of the boy. Shakily, it is Karma's mother who tries.

"What your father is telling you, dear Lobsang . . . is that your mother is dead. She was killed by the bandits. I'm so sorry."

But Lobsang is shaking his head, as if they are the ones who do not comprehend. "I saw her there." His eyes glaze like he can still see it, like it had only just happened.

"Where, Lobsang?" Karma asks finally.

"On the Mountain," Lobsang says, "as bright as the sun. She is there. Waiting for us."

25

THE REBELS

The journey back to the dzong takes twice as long because of the number of wounded. When they reach the forest of lichen-stained pine, Karma knows the fortress is close. The evening sun weaves through spider silks, strands half golden, half gray, strung from limb to limb. A pair of greenfinches flits among the bald branches, beating the resinous light off their wings through the trees. Soon they will see the open field the Gangdruk have cleared for farming, and then the tall palings, and the long river.

For what feels like the hundredth time that day, Karma glances back at Lobsang, now riding with his father. There was a time when these forests, so different from the valley, would have fascinated the boy.

But since those moments when Lobsang first awoke whispering about his mother in the otherworld, he has slept, as if clinging to her in the in-between land of dreams.

Karma breathes a heavy sigh to himself.

From their place in the convoy between the line of Gangdruk and the Khampas, the Reverend Mother nods at him reassuringly.

"I hope you can see the hand of fate in all of this," Dorje says. "The destiny in this moment. The Child, none other than your cousin. It is karma."

In the silence of Karma's hesitation, it is the birds that reply: the caw of a monal pheasant, the distant whistle of a lone falcon.

Fate. Destiny. Karma.

Those words. Spoken like absolutes. Yet the meaning so unknowable.

"Your cousin sees his mother as if she were among the living. If I wasn't sure before, I know it now—this world may end, but there is an otherworld where our loved ones live on until a rebirth." She pauses then. "But a single thread doesn't make a cloth, and a single tree does not make a forest." She slows her horse.

"What I'm trying to say," she goes on, "is that you were meant to be here. We were meant to find the Lama, and you were meant to bring us to the Mountain. You can see that, can't you?"

Karma lets the question hang. He has interrupted his journey out of concern for his family. Now that they are together again, he plans to resume his search for his father, but she is telling him it is more than that. That all this is the gathering to the Mountain of the Lama.

Fate. Destiny. Karma.

Karma looks ahead at the convoy of horses stepping. Then he glances back at his people, watching their march, a trail of refugees treading along the path. His father was a refugee too, when the mountain range first began to crumble. He came to the valley, an outsider.

What else can they to do? Their home, gone. They cannot look back, only forward. They can only hope. And believe.

"I do," he says to Dorje. And then, more truthfully: "I'm trying to."

The old nun smiles at him. "How miraculous, the workings of karma."

The stillness of the forest is interrupted by the distant blare of a horn—a trumpet—ruffling through the leaves.

The convoy lumbers to a stop.

Karma cranes his ear. It is not the same sound he heard in the waters of the river—the deep, sonorous whirring like a yawn of the earth. Not even the sound of his father's Sherpa horn from his dream. For one thing, the entire convoy can hear it. Short and quick, coming from the approach of the clearing. A sound of warning.

"Was that the dzong?" Dorje whispers.

The Gangdruk are already whirling into action, dismounting from the horses and drawing their weapons. Nima comes running from the front, waving them back. "Find cover!" she signals sharply. "Right now!"

Panic erupts. The Khampas disperse, scurrying into the bush. Within moments, they have emptied the path. Nima reaches Karma and Dorje, hunkering down beside them.

"What was that sound?" Karma says.

"A signal from the guard tower."

"For what?"

But Nima holds up a hand for silence, keeping her eyes trained toward the clearing. Gendun and several Gangdruk are advancing to take a look, creeping in ready to attack to the edge of the forest. Slowly, they peer out through the foliage, and then . . .

Nothing.

No movement. No readying of an attack. No reaction. For what seems like a long time, they merely stare, as if in shock, until—one by one, Gendun and the others rise from their hiding places, stepping out into the clearing.

Karma and Nima exchange looks of confusion. "Come on," Nima says.

Watching her venture out, Karma tiptoes along behind her to the edge of the forest, the rest of the village's caravan slowly following. The open light of the clearing washes through the foliage, a contrast from the shadows of the trees. Then Karma sees what it is that has so arrested the others.

From end to end, the dzong's field—only a few days ago completely empty—is covered by tents. Yurts and lean-tos, shelters and wagons, pens of animals and crowds of people—the crop field is gone, replaced by a sprawl of camps. Everywhere they look, there are cook fires burning, tents being raised, people mingling, animals braying.

But this is no organized soldier cantonment or lumbering nomad caravan. There is no pattern to their congregation, but rather an agglomeration of many encampments, each of a different configuration, filling the field before the dzong with hundreds, if not thousands, of people.

Nima's eyes go to the fortress. The walls and gate are still intact; there's no sign that the fortress has been compromised. Two guards peer warily over the field.

"More refugees?" Karma says.

But Nima looks unconvinced.

A ripple of attention flutters through the field. Heads turn, fingers point. They have been spotted. Cheers erupt suddenly through the camps.

Surkhang gives a surprised laugh at the chorus of voices. "They're saying hail! To . . . the victors of the battle at the border, the liberators, the protectors—the Chushi Gangdruk . . . hail!"

The crowd swarms toward them, arms outstretched in praise, surging, circling, jostling one another. Karma blinks at the sight of the gaunt faces. Rawboned and tattered, they resemble beggars. Somehow they have heard. The news of the skirmish has traveled fast through the Borderlands. But from whom? And from where have they come?

One of them throws himself at Gendun's feet, mumbling garbled praises as he tries to touch Gendun's sword. The Gangdruk captain kicks the beggar's hand away instantly, reaching for his weapon.

"Don't be afraid, Gendun!" Surkhang chortles. "They're *worshipping* us!"

It is true. But a feeling of foreboding floods through Karma.

I've seen them before.

More come, trickling from the other camps. And then he sees a face in the rear of the crowd. A tall man in a fur-trimmed tunic, his face covered with tattoos of deer antlers. Karma turns cold.

The Khan.

Now he sees the guards too. Bataar and Chuluun—the same men who tried to have their way with Nima in the cave. The Mustang is nowhere among them; likely he did not survive the snakebite.

"Nima," Karma hisses, afraid to take his eyes off them.

She hears him and follows his gaze.

At the sight of the rebels, she stiffens. In the next instant, she is moving—without warning, one hand to her sword, the other pulling up the scarf around her neck to conceal her face. She reaches them just as Bataar's eyes register the loosing of her blade, though not before it has already begun its arc. He tries to duck but does not escape the blow entirely. Skin slices, blood spreads, and Bataar grips his ear with a howl of rage.

Pandemonium breaks out. The other guards whirl on her. Nima raises her sword, ready to meet them. Gendun and the other Gangdruk react, rushing to draw their weapons in turn.

"Stop!" The Khan's voice booms.

He holds up his hands. "Stay your weapons!" The rebel guards hesitate. "All of you!"

Reluctantly, the guards relent, lowering their weapons. All except Bataar, one hand gripping his ear as it gushes blood, the other still holding his sword.

"Not until she throws hers down too," Bataar demands.

"*Nima,*" Gendun says, "what in the Four Rivers are you doing?"

"It's him," Nima spits the words. "It's Altan. And his rebel *army.*"

Gendun's face registers surprise, then understanding, followed swiftly by anger.

The Khan steps forward, bowing deeply.

"Honorable protectors, the girl is correct. I am Altan, khagan of these people. But on my word, had she told us she was one of the esteemed Chushi Gangdruk, we would never have imprisoned her. We would have treated her as the friend and ally you are, not a spy. For *this* is why we have come," he says gesturing to the droves on the field: "To join in an alliance—with the Chushi Gangdruk."

26

THE COUNCIL

The next day brings more refugees, more who have heard the news of a rebel skirmish at the Borderlands, more who bring reports of the Eastern Army on the move. The camps spread farther to make room, the center of the field left open in a kind of arena, reminding Karma of the ring in the grotto, only larger. The Khan's men form troops from the clans, marching them around the perimeter, drilling them back and forth in a ragtag patrol. Others are already clearing trees and raising an earthwork, the beginnings of a second fortress.

A council meeting has been called for the afternoon. The light grows grayer, a storm at their doorstep, a cluster of clouds over the horizon like a curtain gathered, soon to drape the world in night. By the time the clan heads take their seats, the entire field looks to be on the brink of heavy darkness.

The sight evokes an uneasy recollection of the Minister's words in Karma's mind—at once foreboding and urgent:

Earthquakes and storms unceasing. More blood than water flowing.

Beasts become the hunters and man the prey. Stars losing their places and stranding the traveler.

We are running out of time.

Uncle Urgyen attends on behalf of the Khampas, sitting somber and silent amid the group of rebels. For the monks, Reverend Mother Dorje is present. The first drops of rain begin to fall, and there is no sign of Gendun.

Just when the crowd gets restless, the doors of the dzong open and Gendun marches out, a train of his Gangdruk outlaws behind him. Karma waves from the crowd at Nima and Norbu. Seeing him, they peel away from the group, joining Karma among the spectators.

"There must be hundreds here," Norbu says under his breath, looking around them.

Karma mirrors his amazement. "Maybe thousands."

Nima frowns, less impressed. "Thousand or ten thousand. What does the number of goats matter to a butcher? This is no army. If they think they can take on the Minister with this rabble, they are mistaken. No more than beggars or thugs, most of them. The Eastern Army is not a refugee caravan to be raided in the night." She shakes her head. "No, the Khan knows that to get the full support of the people, he needs Gendun. That's why he's here."

"Gendun won't do it, will he?" Karma says. After what the patrollers did, the thought of an army to challenge the Minister is tempting. But Karma's family is with them now, and the Reverend Mother is calling for the Gangdruk to join their pilgrimage. All he wants to do is resume his journey for the Stone.

Nima spits on the ground. "Gendun's no fool. He knows if you lie with a dog, you catch fleas."

Norbu looks unconvinced. "They may be rabble, but there are still a lot of them. Things could get ugly."

Norbu has a point. Altan wanted the Chushi Gangdruk to join his rebel alliance even back at the grotto. Now that he is here, will he take no for an answer? One thing is for sure: They will have to keep the Child—*Lobsang*, Karma corrects himself—secret from the Khan. If the Khan learns that the Gangdruk have the purported reincarnation of the Lama with them, he will never leave.

Karma suddenly has a dispiriting thought. "Do you think they followed us here, the night we escaped?" He recalls the presence that woke them up in the night by the river. It was dark, and back then his first thought was the migoi, but he wonders now if one of the Khan's men followed them.

Nima spits again as though she could care less, though Karma catches a flicker of doubt on her face.

A hush sweeps over the crowd. Gendun has entered the ring of chieftains. The last seat of the circle is directly across from Altan Khan. Gendun sits, crossing his legs stiffly. After a moment, Altan rises. Going to the center of the ring, he bows four times in the four directions. He scans the gathering.

"You have all answered the call to this council meeting for one reason. We face a universal threat together: the Minister Hanumanda. From the east, his army approaches. He wants nothing short of total control of the Four Rivers and Six Ranges, from the Territories into the frontier. Like the coming Seventh Sun, the danger draws nearer each day."

Altan sweeps a hand around at the multitude. "But today we see that he is not the only one with an army. Today we stand together, irrespective of people, tribe, or clan—united as one! Today we have an army of our own. The rebel army!"

Applause ripples through the crowd, then a cheer with a rising beat that again reminds Karma of the night at the grotto.

Khan. Khan. Khan.

Karma catches sight of Bataar watching from the side. One eye is obscured by bandaging. But with his other eye, he is staring, unblinking—at Nima. The look sends a chill through Karma's body.

"Yet," Altan goes on, "though we are many now, and many more join each day, we need every one of the people. We need their hearts and their minds."

He turns toward Gendun. "Gendun, the people know your reputation as captain of the Gangdruk. They know your abilities. Many of them are here because your band of outlaws helped them cross the border. And now your men have directly faced the Eastern Army and prevailed."

Gendun makes no response. Altan continues.

"You see the result before you now, the number of people who have flocked here because of what you have done, because of their trust in you. Therefore, on behalf of the rebellion . . . I ask you to join us in helping them. In return, we will make you and your fighters fellow-captains in our army, new lords of the lands once we take them back."

One by one, the chiefs turn to Gendun, waiting for his reply. His face is wooden, eyes neither meeting nor avoiding their gazes. The stares of the tribal chiefs flick from one to another in uncertainty.

"Will you join us, Gendun?" Altan urges. "Will you pledge yourself to our rebellion?"

A moment passes before Gendun rises. "A pledge has already been made by us," he says. "To help the pilgrims on their journey west. If we were to join your fight, we would not be able to fulfill that promise. They need us. For this reason . . . I must decline."

Murmurs ripple immediately through the gathering.

Altan's rejoinder is controlled, precise. "But Master Gendun, you are the Chushi Gangdruk, protectors of all the Four Rivers and Six Ranges, not just the monks alone. The *people* need you."

"We're not rebels," Gendun says.

The Khan makes a face of surprise. "With respect, you have been smuggling refugees across the Borderlands in *open* rebellion of the Minister's law. One might even say that it is your last act of rebellion that brings the army to the Borderlands now."

Gendun pauses at this. "When we faced the patrollers at the Borderlands, we did it because we had no choice. We did not intend to start a rebellion."

"Regardless, one has begun," Altan counters.

"If so, it's a fight doomed to fail."

Altan frowns, affecting the expression of one who has been wounded by an offense. "Do you really have so little faith in your countrymen?"

"Hanumanda is not the first of his kind," Gendun answers. "Nor will he be the last. Kill the Minister, there will be another."

If Altan suspects that Gendun is referring to him, he doesn't show it. "So, are you telling the people that they should simply surrender to his tyranny?"

"I don't presume to tell the people anything."

The Khan shakes his head as if he cannot believe what he is hearing. "And what about the rest of you," he turns to the Gangdruk in the crowd, "fighters that you are? Won't you honor your dead by avenging them?"

Gendun has been reserved, but now, his face flashes with anger. He rises slowly, every inch of his tall frame drawing the crowd's gaze. "We honor them," he says evenly, "by carrying through with the oath we made, so that their deaths might not be in vain." He gives a stiff nod to the clan chiefs. "You have our answer. There is no need for you to tarry here any longer. We wish you luck."

Altan crosses his arms, the fragments of bone on his necklace bunching into what looks like a twisted smile. His head lowers, the brim of his hat obscuring his face for a moment. But as Gendun turns to go, he speaks again.

"You'll need this alliance, Gendun . . . when Hanumanda comes for the Child—unless, of course, you think to keep the Lama for yourself."

Gendun stops. A babble of surprise runs through the crowd.

Gendun searches Dorje and Urgyen, but from the looks on their faces, the Khan's knowledge is just as unexpected to them.

"Don't be surprised," Altan says. "Word travels fast in troubled times. The people are looking for hope, no different from you. If the child is who you think he is, they will follow him as their rightful ruler. And every ruler needs an army." The Khan gestures to the expanse of the crowd. "One that will stop at nothing to keep him safe—*no matter what.*"

Gendun squares himself to face the Khan, a standoff between giants. "Is that a threat?"

"Of course not, Gendun," Altan replies lightly. "I only point out that if we can ensure his safety, there is no reason the Lama should run away when his place is here—with the people." He turns his attention to Dorje. "Surely, the Oracle would not deny the Child his very calling as their leader, nor the people the blessings of his gifts, Reverend Mother?"

Dorje's reply is swift. "His calling as a leader is in gathering the people to the Mountain. His gift is his ability to see the past and alter the future. That is his purpose. Not to fight your war."

Altan's voice is measured, relentless. "If you think the people will see their long-awaited Lama taken away into the wastelands on some pilgrimage from which he may never return, you underestimate their resolve. They have been waiting for three generations." His gaze roves now to Urgyen. "How about you? You're the father. Will you let them hide him away? Will you let them expose him to the dangers of the unknown frontier?"

The crowd begins to rumble in murmurs. Uncle Urgyen's face seems to ebb between grimness and surrender.

Gendun interjects. "Perhaps . . ." his voice rises, "it is a valid point about the Child's safety." The words surprise Karma—the slow delivery, his jaw moving as though forcing down an unpleasant bite of food. "Perhaps then an army *could* be of use, after all." He nods stiffly. "Let us think on it further."

A long silence follows. No one cheers, no one applauds. Uncertainty permeates.

He didn't really mean he might form an alliance with the Khan, did he?

Before anyone can say another word, Gendun withdraws from the council circle, striding unceremoniously away before the crowd. The rebel allies look at the Khan as if waiting for a reaction. But none comes from Altan, who merely watches Gendun leave.

The Reverend Mother follows. After a moment, Urgyen leaves as well. The crowd parts, giving way as they tread the path back to the dzong.

A hand reaches for Gendun's arm as he passes. It is Surkhang, close enough that Karma can hear his voice. "Brother," he says. "I am so glad that you are reconsidering. It is the right decision. We may not have trusted them in the past, but this is an opportunity for a new beginning. To be strong enough to take back what is ours."

Gendun levels him with the same look he gave the Khan a moment ago. "Get to the fortress," he says through gritted teeth. "*Right* now."

Surkhang blinks as if bitten. His hand drops away. Looking suddenly self-conscious, his eyes shift to the ring of rebel chiefs, to Altan's watchful stare. Gendun storms onward to the fortress gate, the trail of Gangdruk brushing by in his wake.

A confused mumble begins to reverberate through the crowd. It echoes the distant rumbling of thunder.

The light darkens. Thickening clouds roll in, covering the horizon. The wind rises, and Karma can feel the sudden chill, an electricity in the air.

Without a doubt, a storm is about to arrive.

27

THE STORM

Karma watches the chaos as the doors of the fortress close shut.
"Double the guards on the walls," Gendun shouts an order.
"Lock the gates—nobody in, nobody out."

A moment ago, Karma wondered if Gendun meant it when he said that the Chushi Gangdruk would reconsider joining the council's alliance. Now the answer is clear. There will be no alliance, at least not between the Gangdruk and the Khan's army. They are expecting a fight.

Worry grows in the pit of Karma's stomach. They just fled one conflict with tragic losses, outnumbered and surrounded. Will the same thing happen here? In the corner of the yard, he glimpses his mother and Lobsang watching, confusion on their own faces. He crosses quickly to them.

"What is happening?" his mother asks.

Gendun's orders continue to issue from the ward. "Norbu! Take a few of the monks and ready the rafts."

The rafts?

Lobsang looks at his older cousin. "Are we going to the Mountain now?"

"Come," Karma replies, taking Lobsang gently by the hand, leading his cousin and mother away from the activity to the shelter of one of the buildings. "Let's go where it's not so busy. Wait until things calm down."

"Why are the Gangdruk arming themselves?" Karma's mother asks.

Karma gives Lobsang a squeeze on the shoulders. "Everything is going to be okay. Just stay here with Auntie for now, all right?"

Turning back to his mother, Karma lowers his voice as he guides her out of earshot of the little boy. "Altan knows about Lobsang. About . . . the *Lama Child*," he says, the appellation still strange to use.

Now a fearful look comes over his mother's face too. She glances back at Lobsang, who is sitting obediently, watching them. "What are we going to do?"

"I don't know. All this talk about the Lama, I'm not sure what any of it means. But I do know that I don't trust the Khan. I think we need to listen to Gendun. He'll keep us safe," Karma replies.

As his mother nods her agreement, the inner door of the gate bangs open. Surkhang storms in, the only Gangdruk not yet behind the walls. "Gendun!" he shouts. "Talk to me! Tell me what's going on inside your head!"

Gendun shouts to the guards at the gate instead. "I said to lock it! Anyone else who tries to get in, shoot them."

Surkhang gapes at the additional guards on the wall. "Have you *lost* it? Are you deliberately trying to start a fight?"

"We're leaving the dzong, as soon as we can."

"What do you mean? We told the rebel council that we'd join their alliance. To fight the Eastern Army together!"

"We're not joining any rebel council. We're not joining any alliance. The only pledge we gave was our pledge to the Reverend Mother."

"You mean, the only pledge *you* gave," Surkhang shoots back. "I don't remember any of us choosing that!"

"No? And yet for that warlord Khan you stand ready to give that pledge now, is that it?"

Surkhang blinks. "If it means restoring what the Eastern Army has taken. If it means recompense and retribution for the people since the patrollers moved into the Four Rivers and Six Ranges—then yes, I *will* stand ready. I will gladly fight, now that we have a chance!"

"Oh, so it's the people you're concerned about," Gendun says ironically. "Glad to see it was that, and not that your loyalty had been compromised."

Surkhang's eyes widen to huge proportions. "If you want to accuse me of something, Gendun, come out and say it."

"How is it that they know about the boy? Who told them?"

Surkhang's face reddens. "If there's one good that can come out of the *Child*, it's that he can help the cause. We can unite the people to rally under him and strengthen the alliance."

Gendun blasts into him. "And who do you think this alliance would serve? Are you such a fool not to see it?"

"Is that what this is about?" Surkhang replies. "Are *you* so threatened, Gendun? So unwilling to share power? We have a chance now to change things. To fight and to win! That's what matters!"

"Open your eyes, Surkhang!" Gendun shouts. "The Seventh Sun is coming. Soon there'll be nothing left to fight over. Are you so blind that you can't see that, brother? Only the Lama can change our fate. We need to get him to the Mountain and the Seeing Stone. We have to look beyond this world!"

Surkhang's eyes harden. "No, Gendun. It is you who is blind. You who won't see. Look out there, look at how many have come. All these years, we've lamented how little we do will make any difference. Now, for the first time, we can have an army of our own. We can lead it, me and you, never mind about the Khan. They will follow *us*. Why would you put your faith in these monks, in a child who has never been proven, in a place we do not even know is real? You tell me—*brother*—which is more foolish?"

A sudden swirl of wind kicks up the dust between them.

Surkhang whirls to the others. "Don't you see? This is our world, even if it ends tomorrow. We're still here. So why should we run? But do what you want, I don't care anymore. As for me, I am going to stay and do what Gangdruk do best. Fight, *not flee*."

He storms to the gate, pushing past the Gangdruk guards who do not dare stop him as he throws open the bolt.

"If you leave, Surkhang—"

But the door is already swinging, ricocheting shut behind him.

"I'll go talk to him," Nima says after a moment. She starts after him.

"Don't," Gendun snaps. "Trying to talk sense into him now would be like trying to talk the snow out of falling. Pointless. But wait till it starts storming out there, you'll see how quickly he'll be back in here." He glances at the darkening sky. "At least he'd better—because we're leaving."

28

THE CROSSING

Karma knows that he is in the dreamworld again when his father appears in the darkened room, standing at the end of his cot. He knows it because under the wail of the ghost-winds, he can discern with his mind their whispers. And when he rises to follow his father to the door, instead of moving through space, it is as if he is standing still and time is the one passing him.

At the door of the barracks in this dream, Karma pauses. His father signals to him to go, and speaks.

Time to go.

While his father's image does not startle him, the voice does. Piercing, deep. One he has known but forgotten.

I am dreaming. This is only a dream. Just a dream, Karma tells himself, repeating the words.

As if to prove it, he steps out into the night. Even in the dreamworld, he can feel the gust of rain. It is an icy wind that blows. Something pulls at his feet, and he looks down.

The ground appears to move, a muddy wash lapping around his ankles.

Flooding?

Follow me, Karma, his father calls again.

Karma looks up, searching for him. On the other side of the yard, something else waits instead. Lightning strikes and Karma is startled by the appearance of a large beast, turquoise in the light, long and covered in scales like armor. Though it is no animal that he knows, he recognizes it from the Four Dignities of the prayer flags. This is the last of them, the final protector spirit.

The dragon.

It moves.

Its tail rattles against the pikes of the fortress walls as it unwinds to its full extent. In the burn of the lightning's afterglow, the creature slides toward Karma, its belly making a glissading sound like the clattering of hailstones.

At the same time, he hears a voice in his head.

I am the dragon, the last of the Four Dignities.

Large, yellow eyes expand before him. Whiskers probe the air through the rain. A snout flares, and Karma recoils at the mist of breath. The voice comes to him again.

Come, and see . . .

The dragon's head tilts down, presenting a pair of antlers like the branches of a tree. Karma hesitates, searching for his father again, wondering where he has gone.

Come . . .

Then he realizes that his father's voice is coming from the dragon. And now his initial fear cannot be ignored. Not fear of harm or fear of terror, but of the conclusion Karma is afraid to draw. That in this dreamworld, in this place where the living and departed meet—if they cannot commune except through this Dignity, then it must be that . . .

Father is dead?

The voice of the dragon that comes in reply is so firm, so reassuring, reading his mind, that no sooner does Karma hear it than the fear is replaced by a feeling of peace.

Do not be afraid, Karma.

Slowly, carefully, Karma stretches out his hand. The antlers have the roughness of tree bark, the rigidity of bone. When he sees that the dragon does not move, he closes his hand over the antler and pulls himself up, climbing into the cleft between its shoulders. The scales are hard as tortoise shells, yet when the dragon begins to move, they bend and flex as a whole, pliable as leather. Suddenly they are surging forward, the blood rushing to the back of Karma's head, followed by a lurch deep in the pit of his stomach as in the next moment they change directions, launching upward, lifting off, climbing into the sky.

The wind sears his ears. The driving rain cuts like shards of rock against his face. Karma grasps the antlers even more desperately, pressing himself against the dragon's neck, feeling the creature's shoulder blades locking back against his calves so tightly, almost as if they could break his legs, pinning him in place. The dragon banks to the side, continuing its lift. In a few moments they are clear above the clouds, Karma's head swimming from the dizzying height. Slowly, the boom of thunder and hiss of rain fades, falling away beneath them.

Karma steals a glance below. They have crossed the river, a long black snake beneath the flicker of a spiraling storm cloud. The terrain gleams, white and pale as the face of the moon. But then the dragon descends, and Karma sees that the whiteness is nothing more than the barrenness of a desert. For miles it stretches, empty except for the dragging of their shadow. He sees no mountains, no lost cities. Nothing but sand and dust.

Is this all that is beyond the Four Rivers and Six Ranges? Or is this . . . the otherworld? This wasteland?

His father's voice comes again.

Look and see . . .

In the distance, a small break appears on the otherwise flattened horizon. Slowly, incrementally, there is a slight change in the gradient of the land. A sloping rise, indistinct at first, then more pronounced.

Now he hears a noise, deep and low. An expansive sound, the contours of its timbre conjuring up a vision of a wide cavern of echoing walls in the earth.

This is the sound of a horn.

The pitch alters and so, too, does the vision, becoming a view of towering massifs and soaring clouds.

Look to the Mountain. Look to the Stone. A far-off glint ahead catches Karma's eye, a phantom glimmer. He searches the horizon, but the darkness seems impenetrable. Then he sees it again, a lone flicker, recalling the flame of the butter lamps in the windows of the Khampa village at night, beacons in the valley's stillness.

A light. I see it.

Could it be Mount Kailash?

Could it be that now I know where to find it?

Thunder rumbles behind them. Karma turns his head. The black mass of the storm cloud is directly at their backs. Somehow it has caught up.

The dragon dips its head, driving forward to escape it. The wind screeches in Karma's ears, tugging his hair at the roots. For a moment, it seems they are getting away. But then a bolt of lightning arcs across the sky, white and angry, followed by an immediate wallop of thunder, so close the boom rattles Karma's teeth. The dragon writhes, shrieking. It has been hit. The muscles of its shoulders slacken, releasing its grip on Karma's legs, the scales sliding apart. Its flight begins to slow.

Father!

All at once, they are enveloped, surrounded by the roiling blackness, a vortex of thunder and lightning obliterating the earlier glimmer of light and braying of a horn.

I can't see.

I can't hear the horn.

The dragon plunges in a spiral. Karma slips. His hands lose their hold. He plummets into free fall. Into an abyss of night.

This is a dream. This is only a dream. Just a dream

But he can feel himself speeding toward the ground, the torrent whirling around him. The earth rushes closer.

Help me, he pleads.

Wake up . . . wake up . . . wake up . . .

Father!

Wake—

———✦———

Karma jolts at the shock of cold washing over him.

A vision of a flickering beacon.

A memory of yellow eyes.

A flash of lightning.

A sound of a horn.

Water.

His mind reels as he splashes upright in the wet cold. He has fallen from his cot onto the floor, finding the floor covered in water. Voices of the Gangdruk men shout around him. Groping in the dark, he lurches to his knees.

Water in the barracks?

Again he feels the liquid drag against him. Icy.

Flooding.

He feels something else too. In the ground, a quivering. Not the usual swaying or shaking of the land during an earthquake, but sharper somehow, like the tremble of a lid before a pot boils over.

"Karma!"

He gapes into the swirling blackness of the room. Figures stagger through the chaos. Despite the darkness, he can make out Norbu stumbling toward him. A loud bang against the walls outside sends a shudder through the structure. He feels a sickening crunch through the entire building.

"We have to get out, Karma!" Norbu shouts at him. "The storm is going to blow the building down!"

Karma sways unsteadily, his legs still asleep as though numb from the grip of the dragon in his dream. Gendun grasps him, pulling him along.

A dream? But I saw it. The Mountain. I heard the sound of the horn.

He wades through the swirling water in a daze. Others splash alongside them. The room bobs with floating objects: clothing, bedding, pieces of the cots. The water is knee-deep and rising.

And I saw him.

Father.

A surge of water knocks them back against the wall. As they lean against it, they feel the surface bend, folding on itself.

"Quickly! To the door!" Norbu sloshes forward, Karma following. As they lurch into the yard, a flash of lightning ricochets from one end of the sky to the other, lighting the dzong. A crackling noise sends the barracks crumbling behind them.

Karma stares in shock and disbelief. Just as it had been in his dream . . . the dzong has become a pool, the ground awash in a swirl of mud and river water. In the sky, ghost-winds shriek from a column of air, smooth and moving. A knot forms in the pit of his stomach.

"Karma! Norbu!"

Nima splashes toward them. Behind her, Karma sees Dorje and his mother with Lobsang.

Karma barrels straight to them, lifting Lobsang into his arms.

"Are we going to the Mountain now, Karma?" the boy says.

Karma blinks back the rain, uncomprehending.

"The dzong is flooding," Nima exclaims. "The whole place is going into the river. We have to leave!"

Karma stares at her.

Now? In this storm?

A crackling noise directs their attention to the western wall. It is completely gone, except for a large section of palings that now begins to topple. It slams into the river in a spray of water and splintering wood, sending a tumble of debris downriver. With the wall gone, fortress and river become one. Flotsam rushes into the channel. Braying figures bob and scream in the whirling wash.

With sickening realization, Karma sees that they are the animals, their heads disappearing beneath the waters. In the afterglow of the lightning, he sees the Gangdruk by the riverbank, wrestling with the rafts.

Wrestling, and failing . . .

"The rafts! Hold onto the rafts!" Gendun is shouting.

But the barges tear away on the crests of the waves. The copious provisions they lashed onto the platforms disappear as if swallowed up by some hungry river god.

Just as it seems that the turmoil has reached its peak, a rumbling, not of the sky, but of the ground, begins. Some deep force, rising angrily from the earth, swaying the stupas like saplings in the wind. Erratic, fierce. Vibrating through his core.

Another earthquake.

Karma grasps Lobsang with one hand, his mother with the other. The tremors swell, stronger and stronger, bursting suddenly with a force that sends them to their knees.

Earthquakes and storms unceasing . . . From his mind, the words of the Minister come like a threat.

Karma glances out across the river. The quakes are not slowing. They are not stopping. It is an intensity of convulsions he has never felt, too many quakes to count. He flinches at a boom of thunder, so explosive he half expects the sky to burst into flames.

A string of prayers is loosed from his mind:

Please, not yet. We're not ready. We have not reached the Mountain. We have not yet had the chance to look into the Seeing Stone. To see what must be done to change our fate.

To see father—one last time.

Now it is the river's water that erupts, growing from disturbed to completely deranged. As Karma watches, something else happens. Another change. The river's flow suddenly stops, the current appearing to be in suspension. Then, all at once, it shifts course, reversing direction, suddenly turning south where before it was flowing north.

Karma remembers the day on the river, what Nima told him.

These quakes—the last was so severe, the river actually reversed course. Sent everything back upstream.

From around the bend where the water flowed out, the deluge returns, with waves like a stampede of horses. In its surge, Karma can see the items that washed away earlier, now tumbling back. The fragments churn, the river shooting jets of water into the air as it slams the debris into the bank of the riverbend, where it becomes suddenly lodged. The wreckage quickly begins to pile up, growing in size and height as more pieces of their belongings and parts of the fortress clump together. The channel stops up, clogged.

Almost immediately, the river's depth sinks. As the dam grows in height, the water drains away, before altogether disappearing under the continual gusting of the wind. The people stare, the water around their feet seeming to vanish as if by the work of some miraculous power.

"The water," Karma's mother says in amazement, "it's disappearing!"

"Everybody!" Gendun shouts. "To the banks, now!"

The Gangdruk are already mobilizing, their backs laden with whatever is left of the supplies they can gather. Several have reclaimed a few overturned carts and are dragging them toward the river.

The water's gone. Like a miracle, the riverbed stands dry, and we're crossing. Right now, we're leaving the dzong.

He feels the grip of Lobsang's small hand.

"We're going to see them, aren't we?" Lobsang says.

Karma glances back out at the river. The water is piling up at the blockage, nearly spilling over, looking ready at any moment to burst and turn the trough into raging rapids, but astoundingly, the ground on this side of the dam is now dry.

"My mother," Lobsang says. "And your father?"

The hand of fate. The destiny in this moment. Like the Reverend Mother said.

Fate. Destiny. Karma.

Karma squeezes his cousin's hand in return. "Yes," he says. "Yes, we are. We are going to see them now." One way or another.

Together, the people cross. Down the banks, the riverbed is a mire of mud and flotsam, little rivulets glassing over in the wind. At the riverbend, the wall of debris brims with the flow of the reversed current, piling higher by the second. Lightning renders the land in a deathly, eerie light, shadows moving like gathering ghosts. But there is a strange stillness as well, like the calm before a storm. The ghost-winds are muted, as if watching them with bated breath. The people's movements are slow as they pick their way through silt and sludge.

Halfway across, Karma stops to look back at the dzong. To his shock, he sees Gendun standing at the edge of the river, unmoving, his black hair as wild as the wind and lightning.

"What is he waiting for?" Karma's mother asks.

Karma scans the wreckage, the three other sides of the fortress walls now swaying precariously in the wind, buildings disintegrated into a morass of mud and wood.

There is no one else left in the fortress.

Then Karma remembers. Surkhang. "His brother is still out there."

They watch in worry, wondering what he will do. Gendun and Surkhang are kin. At times they have been foes. Still, Gendun never meant to leave without him.

But the storm is threatening to tear down all the dzong walls. If they are to avoid confrontation with the Khan's rebels, before the river's natural currents are restored, they must leave now.

"Why have you stopped?" Uncle Urgyen runs at them, wrenching Lobsang out of Karma's arms. "Can't you see that the dam is breaking?"

As if on cue, the dam crackles with the splitting of wood, a stream of water shooting through the air as a piece of the barrier gives way. Water gushes from the hole, the entire structure shuddering with the pressure. But it does not seem as if Gendun can see the water or hear their cries in the howling of the winds. The pilgrims break into a sprint, dragging carts and hauling baskets.

"Gendun is still in the dzong," Karma tells his uncle.

Urgyen follows his gaze to the figure of the Gangdruk captain across the river. "It's too late," he growls. "Nothing we can do."

Karma glances at the dam, then back at Gendun. "I'll go."

His mother shakes her head in protest. "No, Karma—"

But her son returns a look of resolve. "It's all right," he says. "I know, now."

His mother strains, confusion in her eyes as Urgyen holds her back.

"I saw it," Karma continues. "The Mountain. And I saw father too." His eyes well up. His mother's face changes, understanding what this means.

"He's dead, mother," he goes on. "It's true." But then an expression of faith and confidence comes over his face. "But now I know where to find him."

His mother goes limp in Urgyen's arms.

"Take her to the other side," Karma says. "I'll be right behind you."

Urgyen grunts in frustration and barrels away, Lobsang and Karma's mother looking back at Karma as he goes.

Racing now, backtracking. Karma scrambles up the bank, where he finds Gendun standing by a cart.

"Karma!" Gendun wheels around when he hears him. "What are you doing? Don't you see the dam is breaking? Go back!"

"I saw the Mountain," Karma says immediately. "You were right. The Reverend Mother's promise is true. It is real. I heard the horn, calling us there."

Gendun stares at him as if through his eyes he might see the vision for himself. A look of peace and relief comes over him. But then, loss.

"My brother," Gendun says. "I don't want to leave him."

There is a crunch of wood, followed by hissing of water. Panicked shouts trickle over as the last of the people scramble up the muddy riverbank. With a gushing roar, a wave of water cascades over the dam. Then the waves come crashing with the force of a herd of horses.

The bursting of the dam seems to snap Gendun out of it. He grabs Karma by his shoulder, pulling him down the slope.

"Run!"

Together they drop down the bank. The wind thunders in their ears, the mud flings from their feet. In the corner of their eye, the river closes in, pounding toward them. They sprint across the riverbed. A wall of wind strikes their backs, a blast of sound and spray. The Gangdruk's hands grasp them, pulling them in. Like fish netted from the water, they rise from the torrent. The river sweeps past in the wake of their escape as Karma and Gendun roll onto the shore.

They stare at each other. Karma's mother's and his cousin's arms are around him, their bodies heaving, their voices crying. Karma hugs them back.

Safe.

We made it.

The words are a mantra in his head, the closest thing to a prayer of thanks he has ever said—when a sound he heard once before on the river whirs suddenly through the air, humming in the skies. Low and trumpeting, expansive and deep.

Karma cranes his neck at the vibrations in his ears.

The horn.

The notes cut through the thunder and din.

I hear it. I hear it, and this time . . . it is certain.

Westward. Sounding from beyond the desolate bank. He can almost follow it in his mind, as clear as if it were a voice calling his name. And then softly, gently, it begins to fade. Still, he knows, he has heard it. It is real.

Karma begins to laugh, shaking with joy and relief.

"What is it?" Karma's mother says. He blinks at her, at the others.

She doesn't hear it. None of them do. Karma looks at the people, but now they are staring across the river, something else drawing their attention. Across the water, on the other side of the river, figures are gathering.

Where they stood only moments ago, the Khan's rebels now cluster, the tall gates of the dzong blown open by the storm. In the flicker of lightning and hurling winds, their silhouettes form a twitching outline along the ragged bank.

"Look!" Norbu points.

Gendun stands, wiping the wet strands from his face as he looks out. His eyes stop at the sight of his brother standing there. Too late, too far. A figure lit by lightning and storm. Karma sees Gendun raise a hand as if to reach out over the waters to him.

Surkhang's head moves, chin slowly rising at the gesture. Their eyes appear to make contact. But from across the river—the gulf too wide and too violent—he does not wave back.

PART IV

<hr>

And it will be like a pure bright mirror
in which forms and shapes are all reflected.
The bodhisattva in his pure body
will see all that is in the world;
he alone will see brightly
what is not visible to others.
Within the three thousand worlds
their forms and shapes in this way
will all be reflected in his body.

The Lotus Sutra (1st cen. CE)

29

THE FRONTIER

For the span of seven times seven days now, the land has climbed. Sloping, rising, growing westward. But still there is nothing resembling the Mountain. Only the rise. Unending, unbreaking, incessant. The lightning-shaped cracks across the ground. The desiccated mud. The fine, white sand. Only the wasteland.

Since the crossing, the earth has not fully ceased its convulsions. Tremors come and go, recalling the thundering from the night of the storm, like an echo trapped in the land. At night, the rumblings keep them awake. In the mornings after, they wake to a landscape reorganized. And there are the pools.

The displacement of earth has brought out fountains of groundwater in unexpected places. A gift, though it slows their travel. But even this abates as the pools drain to puddles, the puddles evaporate to sand.

Now, the land blazes with the heat of a desert, the sun's glare against the salt-white earth turning blind anyone who did not wrap their eyes. The pilgrims huddle now under their makeshift shelters, small squares of translucent shade. The air weighs down, stagnant and breezeless. Today not even the dust stirs, though still it clings to their hair and clothes like wood ash and soot.

Karma sits among the weary, his head bowed, eyes pinched shut behind his visor of yak-hair. There is no reason to look at the landscape. It has not changed in days. The horizon reveals nothing but a shrouded haze in the distance. The ground is so hot that he must squat to keep his legs from burning.

The movement causes a spectrum of colors to shoot from the crystal pommel of his knife. The sudden vibrancy seems unworldly to him, strangely unreal.

For weeks they have been climbing a constant slope, remnants of the once-towering Himalayas. Yet no summit, no end in sight. The higher they go, the more Karma has observed that their bodies deteriorate. They complain of headaches, nausea, stiff joints. He is tired too, but the thinning air seems to affect him less than the others. The heat does not help. Night would be a welcome relief, were it not for the sudden drop to freezing temperatures.

Karma rises abruptly, unable to stand the waiting any longer, his shadow melting into the blazing heat as he ducks out, away from the shade. For the hundredth time, he shields his eyes against the glare of the scorching sun as he squints into the western horizon.

Not so long ago, he was the son of a scoundrel, an outcast of his village. Now it is up to him to lead his people.

They follow him, heeding the fleeting sounds he thinks he can hear but no one else can. He felt a thrill of exhilaration at first, a feeling of purpose. He was doing what his father had set out to do so many years ago.

The son vindicating the father.

But then the horn stopped, as if in reaching the wasteland, they have come to the true end.

No Mountain.

No Seeing Stone.

No father.

Nima shuffles toward him, her face wrapped in a scarf, a wavy figure in the desert heat. He can't bear to tell her. He is afraid what the people will say—it has been days since he has heard the horn.

But Nima knows something is wrong. "Is it the horn?" she says in a low whisper.

"I . . . cannot hear it anymore," Karma finally replies. "I don't know the way." He presses his fingers to his eyes as if to squeeze out some memory, some image. "In my dream, there was a light. I could see it. I could hear the horn sounding. But it seems . . . there is nothing now. Nothing but desert, from here to the end."

"Maybe it just means we are close?" Nima replies. "Maybe it means that we are nearly there."

Karma shakes his head. "I don't even know if it's real anymore. All I hear are the sounds of ghosts at night." He scans the never-ending desert all around them. "Now it seems we may very well join them in the otherworld."

He turns to Nima, his eyes now searching hers, as if in them there might be an answer. "I thought if I could save them, I would redeem my father's name. But I have only sealed our fate, and soon it will be too late."

Nima twists the scarf off her head, letting the sun beat down on her exposed, browned face. "What is this? Beating up on yourself, like the villagers? Or just a moment of self-pity?" She lowers herself to a squat beside him. "So you can't hear the horn," she says. "Who says you need it to tell you the way?"

"You don't understand, Nima. Left, right—I don't even know which direction I should go."

"Left, right—maybe it's neither. Maybe it's straight. Maybe it doesn't matter. If the end is truly coming for us, maybe it makes no difference. Maybe," she pauses, "the only way to reach the Mountain is through the otherworld."

Karma looks at her. "You mean, by death?"

"So be it, if that is the way. We could have stayed back in the Borderlands, if we wanted to. But we followed you. The people followed you. And they will follow you still."

The bridge of her nose is cracked with dust, her skin bronzed with a patina of clay, her hair ashen as soot. Not an inch of her is not covered with the grime of toil and sweat. But—there is something beautiful about her. Just now, there is something as radiant as the rain on the day he watched her by the river.

"But we're not dead yet," Nima finishes. "So, choose. And if it be that we die, at least we die facing the sun."

She meets his gaze, eye to eye, and in that moment, Karma can see that she is every bit as certain as he is unsure. She is not someone who has spent years seeking the Lama Child and following the signs. She is no pilgrim monk. Karma is not even sure she has ever been convinced by any of it, having once said the end of the world could not come soon enough. But—in her eyes, he sees it. She believes in *him*. Prophecies and destinies aside, it is him she is following. Not an idea, or words. Not even a motivation, like revenge. She is following Karma.

And so is everyone else in this desert-banished pilgrim caravan. In the end, it is just as his father had said: *A Sherpa's destination becomes his destiny. Though he cannot always see the end. He leads so others can follow.*

Nima will not let him go back. She will not let him give up. She has a job to do. And he knows that he, too, will keep going, because she will keep following. Until the sooner of either a slow death or a miracle, they will keep on wandering. Like the pilgrim monks who roamed the lands looking for the reincarnated Lama, they will endure.

Staring at her, Karma is overcome with a deep feeling of gratitude. How glad he is for her strength, her companionship. Beside her, he has the feeling of leaning against the trunk of some great tree, resting in the shelter of its cool shade, the desert and sun suddenly inconsequential and bearable. Karma breathes, finally.

Their respite is shattered by voices, loudly cursing. Turning to the shouts, they see Urgyen standing by one of the carts, holding up two small sacks, eyes glazed with fury. The sacks are bags of meal. A startled Norbu is rising from his own patch of shade.

"I knew it," Urgyen shouts, shaking the bags. "You people have been feeding us like mice, lowering our rations, while all along there was always more food!"

"Put them back!" Norbu says. "Those are not to be touched."

"Why?" Urgyen challenges. "So you can let some of us starve?"

"Urgyen," Gendun gets up, ready to intervene. "We must conserve what we can. We don't know how much farther we have yet to go."

Urgyen's eyes bulge from behind the layers of his scarf. "How much farther we have to go?" he repeats. "Isn't the answer obvious to us all? As far before the food runs out, that's how far! Then we die! Because there is no Mountain, is there? The truth is, we've been wandering for weeks because the Sherpa boy is a fraud—just like his father. And you know it. That's why you're hiding this food. For the rest of us to die, and then you take what you want!" He shakes the bags again in the air.

"*Urgyen.*" Gendun's voice deepens. "The heat is getting to you. You're not thinking clearly. Put them down and go back to your place."

"Go back to my place?" Urgyen's voice rises at the injunction. "Oh, if only I *could*. If I could go back to the valley, back to the time before that Sherpa ever came and cursed us with his visions and stories. Back to the valley. Back when I was a headman, when my wife was still alive. We would even be better off going back to the Khan. Hell, not even death at the hands of the Eastern Army would be worse than this torture. The cursed leading the desperate, following that Sherpa. I tell you, if I could, I would go back. But we're doomed to die out here like the rest of his people."

His uncle's words sting, and the familiar sinking in Karma's chest returns, the one he has felt his entire life. That feeling of shame, even after all this time, even on the other side at the end of the world. The earth is doomed, but somehow it is him the curse follows. The karma of the father is the karma of the son.

Gendun lunges suddenly at Urgyen, grabbing hold of the bags. But Urgyen's grip is sturdy. The bag stretches. The burlap tears. Karma sees it happening, knows what will occur even before it does.

Meal spills onto the desiccated ground.

The two men freeze—Gendun's face twisting from shock to something darker. Urgyen lets go, only to spill the rest of the bag, the defiance on his face now joined by a look of nervousness.

He blinks.

The entire caravan goes still.

Then all at once, the Khampas rush forward, hands scooping up mouthfuls of the precious meal, dust and tsampa mixed together.

"*That . . . is . . . enough!*" Gendun roars, unleashing his sword in his fury.

The people cower, cringing before the weapon.

We're going to die, Karma thinks. *If not from starvation, or the harshness of this desert, then at each other's hands.*

In the moment of dissension, the heat of their strife, Lobsang suddenly speaks up, barely audible in the fracas.

"Look—!"

He says it again, speaking louder—pointing up now.

"There! In the sky."

Karma follows his cousin's finger to the starkness above.

At first, he sees nothing. But then . . . a dot. Moving. It could be an illusion, an aberration from the glare of the sun. They have seen nothing for days, after all. He blinks.

It is still there.

A speck in the hazy white.

The shape vanishes in the glare, then reappears again, suddenly closer, moving like . . .

A buzzard.

Suddenly there is another joining the first, soaring into view, followed by one more, then another. Four of them. Turning . . . circling . . .

Circling us.

There are gasps. Heads crane upward, the people trickling out from their shelters, shielding their eyes skyward.

"Vultures," Nima says, sounding stunned.

As if summoned by their name, the buzzards descend lower, their broad wingspans turning shadows over the ground to the terrified yelp of the pilgrims below. Someone begins to wail.

Urgyen's utterance comes like an accusation. "You see, what did I tell you? We're going to die. You can't hide it now. They'll be picking on our godforsaken bones, every one of us. Mark my words."

"Then we won't let them," Norbu declares, dashing forward to the cart. "We won't give them the chance." He rummages through it, pulling out his bow and an arrow. "We'll shoot them down."

"Wait!" Lobsang waves his hands.

The caravan isn't listening.

"It's a sign!"

The child shakes his head, trying to get their attention. "Don't shoot!"

An epiphany comes to Karma now, a sudden comprehension.

My cousin is right. It is a sign.

Quickly, Karma steps forward, catching Norbu by the arm even as he is notching the arrow. He can see the panic in the Gangdruk's eyes. Panic in all their eyes.

"Wait," Karma says. "Listen to him. Listen to the Child."

Now Norbu stops. All eyes turn to Karma.

"It's a sign," Karma declares, confident now in his realization. "Lobsang's right, don't you see? It's a sign of *life*. We're saved."

Murmurs of confusion, looks of bewilderment. How can it be so, when buzzards are the birds of death?

But then the Reverend Mother Dorje speaks up. "Of course! Where there is carrion, there must be other animals."

Silence follows, the sound of incomprehension. But then Karma's mother speaks up as well. "Why, yes. And if there are animals, there must be plants."

"Which means water"—Nima joins in with them—"which means . . ."

"That we can't be far from the Mountain," Gendun finishes.

It all takes a moment to sink in. But gradually, the cries turn into sobs of relief and murmurs of excitement.

Dorje turns now, lifting her hands to the skies. "We see you, vultures!" the Reverend Mother cries out. "But look! We're alive! Go back to your home, to your nests and your roosts, your burrows and your crags. Today is not the day you will pick these bones!" She jumps up and down, waving her arms in the air. "Come on!" she urges the pilgrims. "Let them hear you! Let them lead us to life!"

The caravan breaks into a cheer, the pilgrims clapping their hands and stomping their feet, doing whatever they can to raise a racket. The birds respond, widening their flight in light of the sudden burst of activity. Breaking their circuit, they turn, each banking off, heading westward for the sun, a trail like the waving of an arm encouraging them to follow.

The caravan breaks into applause. They are animated now, dashing about, scooping bundles, wheeling carts, rolling toward the direction of the birds. Karma doesn't know if it is from their movements or if something has changed in the air, but a breeze stirs, drawing his attention to the distance.

Directly beyond the flight of the buzzards, the shape of something begins to emerge through the haze.

A rise in the horizon. An earthen bulk.

Karma's heart skips a beat. He glances at the others to see if they have glimpsed what he sees. But the object is now faded, vanishing away to a chalky blur—the haze once again obscuring the horizon, yet not his recognition.

He has just glimpsed his first mountain.

30

THE SONG

The sun sinks like the slipping of a veil, falling away to reveal the vastness of night. Their walking does not cease. They want to continue, so motivated, so inspired by the sight of the buzzards, then of shrubs, then of small, gnarled trees growing that they do not want to stop. The higher altitudes are taking a toll on their bodies. But tonight, the pilgrims do not complain; the aches in their heads are nonexistent, their muscles and bones miraculously revived. They no longer grumble under their breaths about whether Karma can hear the horns. The people are pulled by their own hope. They follow the sound of their own footsteps, their own convictions, their own trail.

Karma and Nima walk side by side at the end of the line, where they can watch for stragglers. The moon casts silvery shadows from the east. In the black firmament above, the Northern Bushel emerges, seven dots of clear light, outer edge pointing toward the pole star, which sits like the center of a celestial prayer wheel, churning the milky stream of the Heavenly River below it.

In the beautiful night, among the long procession, he is reminded of a night from another time, from another world far gone from this one. The night of a wedding in the village. In a procession much like this, under a canopy of glittering stars, they delivered the bride to the home of the groom in the neighboring village, when there had still been other settlements nearby, before his father left Kham. Arriving at her new home, the bride dismounted from a mule onto a cushion filled with the strength of the land—salt, barley, and wheat. The groomsmen placed two large stones representing pillars, enacting the last ritual of the wedding: to the left of the newlyweds' door, a stone of black obsidian; to the right, a rock of white. Together the couple approached the door, the groom laying his khata scarf on the white stone, reciting the words: "Sacrifices to you, thirty-nine cities and ninety-nine slopes, for I am an incarnation of the Lama's sons from the ten places and three masters." He then turned to the dark stone, uttering the final words: "And it is I, who shall slay the monster." With the vow thus complete, the groom lifted the black stone, overturning it upon the earth. Oh, how the villagers cheered.

Karma slows his steps. In the clouds and twilight, the atmosphere is suffused with a rarefied quality, a thinness so refined it seems to alter even the sounds he can hear. He stops walking, cocking his ear.

"What is it?" Nima says.

"Everything . . . feels different."

"Different?" Nima asks. "The land?"

"The land," Karma replies, "the air, the altitude. It's like we're in another world, almost in between ours and the otherworld." He pauses, looking at her now. "But *I* feel different too. For the first time, I know where I came from, why I'm here, and where I'm going."

Nima considers this, following his gaze around. In one corner of the heavens, a soft, sudden glow washes the horizon, so faint, so barely detectable that at first, they are not sure they have actually seen it. Then, as ephemeral as a cloud, the light doubles, a tide of gold surging across the starry ocean. Soft flashes, the shimmer of distant storms. But no thunder, and the colors are like no storm light Karma knows.

Pink, green. Ribbons and tendrils. Soluble clouds. Ebbing, flowing.

The caravan emits gasps of wonder. The northern sky streams with light like waves on a heavenly shore.

As they lift their heads at the spectacle, Nima's and Karma's shoulders graze. Hands brush, their fingers touch. In the moment, in the immensity of the endless sky, under mysterious lights and distant worlds full of colors without name, their palms slip together into each other's. His into hers, hers into his . . . the universe in their hands.

Clasping the moment itself.

Time stills. The palette of colors grows. Beckoning, flashing.

"What are they?" Karma whispers, not wanting to disturb what may be a waking dream.

"Something beautiful," Nima answers.

The colors pulse as if to an instrument unseen and unheard.

Until suddenly—

It is possible.

He *can* hear it.

Louder and clearer than ever, as if not that far. Unmistakable. One note then another. Thrumming, echoing, filling the skies.

Karma can hear it as a heavenly song.

Not just of my father's Sherpa horn. But of the Mountain. Of the dharma horn.

After a moment, the lights begin to recede, the tide flowing back out into the depths of the distant night. The stars twinkle back into view. All is as it once was. The lights disappear, the moon once again the brightest object in the sky.

Still, the pilgrims stay transfixed and holding their breath. Karma's and Nima's hands remain clasped together under the cover of night. Karma is trembling. Not from fear. Not from cold. But from the reverberation of the horn, the resonance of the music.

"You're shaking."

From what she says and the excited chatter of the pilgrims, Karma knows—they did not hear it. He was the only one.

His eyes well up, filling with tears of joy.

At long last. At very long last.

He feels as if he could live in this moment. And then he knows what is different, what has changed about the land.

It is the ghost-winds. He cannot hear them anymore. Like the end of a long sigh, they are completely still, though not like that time by the river, that sudden gasp of air held tight when they had awoken in the middle of the night. But for the first time, as though with the pilgrims' coming arrival to the otherworld—they are at peace.

31

THE SNOWS

Snow comes, further evidence of the change. Not the light, drifting flakes that have come in the night or the usual ash-covered frost powdering the ground, but snowfall of a new velocity, growing in intensity with the rising of the land, sleeting down in a slurry of speed. Great, sizable clusters, borne by a new wind out of the west. Thicker and heavier, swirling and billowing.

By afternoon, the snow is burying the horizon, hiding the extent of the landscape. Every gust of wind is a squall of white and gray, every rumble in the sky like a tumbling of rocks unseen. The land treks upward, seeming to offer a way out of the snows. They follow it, moved by glimpses of life here and there. A scattering of lone trees. The peak of deep-green cotoneasters, red berries suspended in teardrop icicles, sealed in time, halted in space, promising life after the thaw.

But when they reach the top of the current slope, what they find is a portal to another, darker world. A world of twilight and ice with no end in sight. A storm.

Their movements slow to a crawl. Their voices are muffled, their vision reduced to no more than a few paces ahead.

Karma scans the figures around him, then stops abruptly.

"What is it?" Nima says, barely audible under the bundle of her scarf.

"I don't see Lobsang," Karma says.

They stop the caravan of figures. Karma finds his mother and Dorje. Norbu is with them, but there is no sign of either his cousin or his uncle.

"Where are Urgyen and Lobsang?"

They look around. "I thought they were with you."

The cold is deep and biting. Each extremity begins to feel as numb as wood.

"Could they be ahead of us?" the Reverend Mother asks. "With the Gangdruk?" The caravan had split into two, with the Gangdruk having gone ahead to scout the way forward and to look for possible shelter, leaving Nima and Norbu with the people.

"We would have seen them pass us," Karma says.

"Then they've wandered off course," Nima says grimly. "We'll have to spread out, look for tracks."

As some of the group peel away, Karma backtracks, trampling across their own snowy tracks now brushed by the drifting of the wind. He tells himself not to panic. Perhaps Urgyen and his cousin are only straggling. Perhaps they have stopped for a quick rest. Maybe they have even caught up with the others. He squints into the whiteness, calling out as loudly as he can.

"Lobsang! Uncle Urgyen! Where are you?"

Through the blur, he thinks he sees something—an indentation in the snow taking a different direction, seeming to veer aside. Perhaps just the shadow of a snowdrift, perhaps something more. He hastens to it. An irregular trench, a pattern of hollow bowls, is already starting to fill with fresh snow.

Footprints.

Two pairs.

One large, one small, icy and distinct. Sure enough, they wander away, blending into the whiteness.

Karma shouts to the others. They are winded when they reach him, heaving air in short, feeble bursts. The altitude, the cold, the strain from trudging back and forth through the snow is starting to show. How much more of these conditions can they take?

"It's them," Nima declares when she sees the tracks. "It must be." She turns back to the group. She scans the area, pointing to a copse of trees adjacent to the trail. "You two take everyone to those trees, see if you can set up some shelter until the storm blows over. I'll go after Urgyen and Lobsang."

"I'm coming with you," Karma says. "Lobsang may need me. And besides, it'll be better if there are two of us searching."

"He's right," Norbu agrees. "I'll manage all right with them."

Nima relents, nodding, though Karma can also detect a hint of appreciation in her expression. He can sense in her, like himself, a yearning for the prospect of being alone together, even if only for a few moments. She signals for him to follow, and their steps fall into a pair.

The tracks wander up an incline. On the other side of the slope is a snow-filled gorge, wind whirling through it. Large boulders line the face of the decline, some still partially bare, shielded from the wind.

"Urgyen!"

"Lobsang!"

The snow dampens their voices. They continue down the slope. Near the middle, the tracks take a turn at a cluster of boulders. Then, at a covered hollow, they disappear into the rocks.

Karma peers into the crevice. "Uncle Urgyen? Lobsang?"

A rustling escapes. Stilted silence follows. They glance at each other. Crouching, Nima sticks her head inside. In the dim hollow, the beleaguered face of father and son stare out.

The boy's small, bundled head moves at the sight of Karma. But Urgyen holds him back.

"What on earth . . ." Nima breathes in an astonished voice.

"We're resting," Urgyen bleats back at her, not budging an inch.

A stunned pause. "Like hell," Nima says. "We've been looking all over for you."

With the expression of a petulant child who's been caught in the act, Urgyen turns his face away. "We won't take another step. Not a single one."

"Now you've truly lost your mind," Nima says. "Can't you see the boy is freezing!"

She reaches for Lobsang.

Urgyen pulls him away, with a kick to her hand. "It's futile, can't you see? The world is ending. All of this—it's for nothing!"

Snapping, Nima seizes Urgyen's ankle, hauling him out with a force so hard his head bangs against the rock.

Urgyen hollers in protest, slinging curses at her. "Leave us! Just leave us be!"

Nima flings him to the ground, stabbing a finger at his face. "Your son is the *Lama*—"

"So what!" Urgyen shouts back. "We're doomed! Nothing can change our karma!"

Lobsang is crying now, crawling out after his father.

"You're scaring him," Nima says. "You have no idea what you're talking about."

Urgyen lets out a wild laugh. "Oh, but I do. I do. I know this journey was an illusion all along. *A lie.*"

"Come to me, Lobsang," Karma says, reaching for his cousin. "It's okay. The storm will pass, and then I'll take us to the Mountain."

Urgyen pushes his nephew away. "You still think you can save us? That you can change the outcome? That your father found something out here?" He shakes his head in an expression somehow both smug and bitter. "None of this is real. The Minister didn't just happen to find you—it was I who brought him. Your father didn't happen to go on the expedition—I sent him away."

The hollow goes quiet with Urgyen's voice, strained from shouting into the cold air. "But what I did, I did because I loved her. I swear I did it for us."

"Uncle," Karma says, "I don't understand—"

"It was because of me!" Urgyen cries. "Don't you see? Had your father never set foot in Kham, your mother would have loved *me* instead of him. So when his people were killed in the quakes, I told him their ghosts would not rest until he freed them from the otherworld and gave them peace. But he was worried about you and your mother. He didn't want to leave his family at first. But *I* convinced him. I told him he had a responsibility because of his gift. That he would be saving you too. And it worked: He left. And I thought finally, I am free of him. But still she wouldn't love me, not even after he was gone." His voice becomes weak, weeping now. "So I made a deal with the Minister. To send you away too."

Karma blinks, his mind not fully registering the words.

Urgyen begins to sob. The sound of each shudder reverberates in Karma's own chest like the blunt force of a stone. "It's because of me, we are cursed. Because of me, the patrollers came. Because of me, we had to leave the valley. Because of me, Pema is dead. Because of me . . . because of me . . ." He breaks down. "Now she haunts me. I can hear her in the winds. And your father too. I can hear them, all of them. I . . . I'm sorry, so sorry . . ."

It can't be.

But even as Karma struggles with the import of his uncle's words, everything suddenly makes sense. He has always suspected it, watching the attention his uncle directed to his mother. But he wanted to believe it was because his uncle was fulfilling a promise to his father to care for her, and so he told himself it was a sign that his uncle cared for him too, no matter how else his uncle treated him. But it was not that Urgyen loved them—just that he hated Karma's father.

And that is why he despises me too.

And my father's journey? Is it all, then, just a ruse? This search, a pointless quest?

Urgyen wheels on Karma, hands clasped, begging now. "Have mercy, Karma. Don't make me go to the Mountain like this. I can't face them." He grabs Karma's coat. "Just let me end it. Take Lobsang, go ahead. But let me die here like I deserve. I can't bear the guilt anymore."

Karma stares at Urgyen, at his uncle's grasping hands. He feels suddenly lightheaded, as if everything has taken on a tinge of unreality. His gaze centers on his uncle's face, but he doesn't recognize the face that pleads back at him—grotesque, pathetic—a face that has watched him, a face that has made him feel lesser, a face he has known his entire life.

The face of a liar. A coward.

It was not his father, but his uncle, who was the deceiver. He tried to send Karma away to hide the truth, history repeating itself. But here, between either death or discovering the otherworld, he cannot run away from his guilt. His karma has caught up to him.

An urge rises within Karma now—to lash out, to break something.

He wrenches his uncle's hands away. Pain and fear registers on his uncle's face.

Tears streaming down his face, Urgyen's eyes widen as now Karma takes Lobsang's hand—slowly, quivering—joining them together, a son's into his father's.

Urgyen stares at his hand, then at Karma. Karma can feel the sting of the ice on his own face. Not tears of sadness, not even of anger anymore. Only hurt. Heartbreak. But he also feels something lift from his shoulders. A weight.

"No," Karma says, expelling a breath of trembling air with his next words. "Take him yourself. A son needs . . . his father."

Urgyen buries his head into Lobsang's shoulder, slumping with the force of his sobs. Lobsang hugs his father in return. Together they weep. Karma watches them. In some ways, it is the scene he once imagined with his father if he ever saw him again.

If.

In that regard, Urgyen is right. If they do not make it to the Mountain, none of this would matter. All hope will have been an illusion. This will be their end.

Quietly, Nima kneels beside them. "Listen to me. Nearby is a forest. It's just over the hill and a short distance away. They're taking shelter as we speak. We can wait out the storm. Look, it's already stopping."

Sure enough, the snow has begun to slow. The pink glow of the setting sun diffuses through the clouds, touching the bottom of the gorge. As Karma's eyes follow the light, a sense of certainty rests upon him, like a mantle on his shoulders.

There is still the storm to endure. There is still the Mountain to climb. But more and more, he can feel the clarity of his mission.

Six Suns, six blasts in the sky. A seventh one, and the earth will die.

But gather to the Mount and the Seeing Stone, that the Lama may reveal yet a future unknown.

His part is to bring Lobsang up the Mountain. Not even his uncle will be able to stop him from doing that. What happens afterward may be unknown, but of that much he is now sure.

Almost as if in response to his thought, something on the ravine floor catches his gaze. In contrast to the smooth ripples formed by the wind, a wide swath of snow has been disturbed, trampled.

Karma squints. "Do you see that, Nima?"

The two of them troop toward it to look, stopping at what are clearly the tracks of a large caravan.

"It's Gendun and the others," Nima says in disbelief.

She breathes a sound of both relief and exasperation. They must have been blinded by the snowstorm, the group of Gangdruk ahead diverging from the Khampas behind. How fortunate that Urgyen had wandered off. Who knows how long it would have taken otherwise to discover each other's tracks?

"We can catch up to them," Karma says.

Nima glances at Urgyen and Lobsang huddled together and shakes her head. "Your uncle and cousin are in no shape to go any farther. We need to get them to a tent before anything else. Unless . . . do you think you can take them back on your own?"

It is the logical plan. Karma wants to answer yes, but inexplicably, an uneasy feeling comes over him.

Nima seems to read his hesitation. "Never mind," she says. "We can take them back to the others together, and then go after these tracks afterwards."

"No," Karma declares. "I can do it."

Nima stares at him.

"I'm not afraid of him anymore," Karma says.

Nima nods. Then she gives him a smile. "You've changed, Karma. You know who you are now." She nods once again, a short farewell, turning to go.

Wait . . . stop, Nima.

He only imagines himself saying this, as the plan after all makes perfect sense.

But still Nima stops, as if he has said the words aloud. To his surprise, she turns back to him as if on impulse, throwing her arms around him in a sudden, but fierce, embrace.

Instinctively, Karma hugs her back.

As they separate, Nima looks at him. "I've changed too. All these years, thinking I had nothing to live for but revenge. But I've found something else. Something better." She smiles, the corners of her eyes turning up. It is a miraculous look, half buried by the scarves around her face, but one that fills him with warmth and hope that all will be well. "Call it karma."

A swell of emotion rises in Karma, a sense of a future filled with possibilities he has never known before, and this time it is he who reaches to take her hand like that night under the northern skies. He can feel only the bundled layers of their gloves touching. Together, but not meeting. Close, but not enough. Yet the connection in that grasp fills him with the immensity of all the world.

Hope.

Slowly, she draws away. "Just follow our tracks." She glances at his uncle and then back at Karma, her voice still low. "You're in charge of your people now."

Karma nods.

My people.

"Wait for me at the trees," she says to him.

"I will," he replies. "Please be careful."

When they separate, Karma feels slightly embarrassed at the show of emotion, at the awkward parting of their embrace and the tears still warming his frost-rimmed eyes. But in the waning of the light as he watches her go—for the first time, he is not ashamed.

32

THE NIGHT

It is a clear night. With the storm having passed, the moon radiates its corona of white over a jagged horizon, the appearance of which is sudden after weeks of barren landscape and shrouded skies. A single peak, taller than the rest and almost perfectly pyramidal in shape, juts out from the center.

Karma sits outside his tent looking at the beauty, so otherworldly it could be a dream. No one else is out there with him to see it, to assure him that he is truly, finally looking at Mount Kailash. He should be inside his tent too, resting, keeping warm.

Instead, he is keeping watch.

He feels the same presence again. Like that night with Nima by the river. A sense of something waiting in the darkness, behind the trees, in between shadows and light. An ominous prickle. A tingle of trepidation. But why wouldn't he feel that? From this proximity, the rocky walls of the mountain seem unclimbable. How they will they find their way up, he has no idea. But most of all, he is worried about Nima. Why has she not come back after regrouping with the Gangdruk? What is taking her so long?

He goes to the fire, now burned down to a few sticks. He hears rustling behind him, and the door of his mother's tent opens. She crawls out, the breath from her mouth streaming frost on the air when she speaks.

"It's cold out there, Karma."

"I need to rebuild the fire," Karma replies. "So Nima can find us."

His mother looks out at the twilit wilderness of snow. "If she hasn't returned, I don't think she'll be coming back until light."

"Doesn't make sense," Karma says. "The others couldn't have been that far. Why is it taking so long?"

His mother joins him by the fire, gazing out at the landscape.

"When I met your father," she begins suddenly, "we were not much older than you." Her words form slowly, the movements of her mouth impeded by the cold. "He was to me this mysterious person—from far away, a Sherpa. He never talked much about his home or what happened. I had lost my parents not long before he came to the valley. He had lost everybody. Everyone is prepared for the eventuality of the Seventh Sun, but for us, it seemed like the end was already here. But then . . . somehow, when we were together, everything just seemed like it would be all right. Seventh Sun or not, suddenly the end didn't seem so near." She turns to her son, studying his face. "It was so good, finally, not to be alone."

"But then you were alone again," Karma says. "After he left."

His mother sighs, half a tremble, half a shiver from the cold. "Yes," she says. "And no. That kind of companionship, knowing he was at the Mountain, I never really felt that far from him." She looks into Karma's eyes. "I know we'll be together again. All of us."

Turning her head, she gasps at the sight of the Mountain.

"Karma," she says. "Is that . . ."

"It's Mount Kailash," Karma confirms.

His mother is speechless, her eyes welling with tears. "It's . . . incredible," she says.

So it is. And not a dream, after all. A calm fills Karma, the peace of knowing that they are so close, and he is glad for his mother's presence. Once it was the three of them: mother, father, and son. Then it became just the two. Will it be three again soon? It has been a long time.

"How quiet it is," his mother says. "I cannot remember a time when the ghost-winds were this peaceful." She looks back at Karma. "All will be well. *You've* done well. Father would be proud."

"We're not at the Mountain yet," Karma says.

"We're *together*," his mother replies.

Karma cocks his head at a sound. He scans the trees, then the area around.

Footsteps crunch the snow. Out of the shadows, a figure approaches. Karma's heart rises . . . *Nima?*

It is only Norbu, his silhouette familiar against the perimeter of gnarled birch and conifer, cradling a bundle of sticks in his arms. He has been collecting firewood.

Karma's heart sinks. He scans the surroundings again. Once more, he has the terrible feeling that something has gone wrong. Nima is lost. She is injured. She is trapped somewhere by something. Buried in an avalanche.

Norbu tracks toward them, setting the sticks down by the fire.

"I'm going to go look for her," Karma announces. Norbu blinks, glancing at Karma's mother.

"It's been hours," Karma continues. "She should've been here by now. Or someone from the Gangdruk. The storm's long over. They can follow our tracks. What if the reason they haven't come is because . . . something's happened? We can't just sit here and do nothing."

"It's freezing out there, Karma," his mother says.

"All the more reason I should go look for her," Karma responds. "The snow's stopped and the moon's out. I'll be able to follow the trail easily. If you keep the fire going, I can find my way back." He pauses. "She would do the same thing for any one of us."

Norbu glances out to the hills, to the black skies beyond. He shivers, as though imagining the cold out there. "Well, then," he says. "I should come with you."

Karma looks at him in appreciation. Norbu has become a good friend. Always selfless, always loyal and fair. Still, Karma shakes his head. "Someone needs to protect the people."

"You don't trust your uncle?" Norbu says.

Karma feels a pang of guilt. They *were* his people, his duty. Even more so now that his uncle, the village headman, has fallen apart. He is the reason they fled the valley and joined the pilgrims. He is responsible for all of this.

For them.

"Don't worry," Norbu says, as if he can hear Karma's struggle inside, "I would be happy to do it."

Karma nods, then quickly ducks into his tent to gather his bundle of skins.

His mother meets him outside the tent with a pair of the makeshift snowshoes they crafted earlier from branches and pine. The Reverend Mother Dorje has joined them. Karma expects that she will try to talk him out of it, but she says nothing. Now that he has made up his mind, he is anxious to go.

But the sense of foreboding returns.

Stop . . .

The impression comes almost like a voice in the air, though faded like an echo.

Go back . . .

A voice like the ghost-winds. Like someone speaking from a distance. Some seer beyond the hills. But at the same time, as if it were his own voice.

Don't leave him. Lobsang . . . go to Lobsang.

"I'll be with him," his mother says, as if hearing the words herself. "Set your mind at ease. Go find her."

Karma nods, grateful to his mother. He sets off, casting a final glance at the flicker of the campfire and the gazes of his mother, Norbu, and the Reverend Mother. Before him, the land extends to its full immensity, meeting sky and stars. Past the trees, the shape of the white range thrusts up like a saw's edge. Snow crunches as he walks. Finding his old tracks, he walks for minutes that stretch like miles because of the snow.

A loud bark shatters the stillness, coming from the Khampas' camp. The sound of an animal.

Karma freezes.

His head snaps back toward the camp, with its yellow glow of fire now tiny against the trees. Stillness follows, so absolute it is as if he only imagined the sound. All fates—safety, salvation, and peace—are still possible, still latent. But his hopes are torn down when from the woods, a chorus of growls and howls rises abruptly.

Wolves.

At the camp.

Stunned but already moving, he drops his pack, breaking into a run. He is sprinting, legs straining, snowshoes breaking apart as he lengthens each stride through the snow.

I should never have left them. Should have trusted my instincts.

A scream punctures his ears. Sharp, piercing.

Wolves are attacking.

How many of them are there? Where did they come from? He falls, scrambles back to his feet, snow flying in his wake. The screams turn to shrieks.

He enters a scene of confusion. Stumbling, flailing, the people scatter from the camp, trampling their tents, crushing each other in snow and mush. From the peripheries, yellow eyes blink into view, one pair after another, glowing through the trees. Shapes dart.

A man Karma has known since birth spins around, looking dazed. In the next instant, he goes down, dragged away by a triad of snarling wolves.

No. No, this isn't happening.

A woman has fallen. He bends to help her up and sees that it is the Reverend Mother. Streaks of red mark the snow.

Blood.

"To the fire!" he hears Norbu shouting. The people are huddling together in a defensive circle, waving sticks of flame, as wolves dart to and fro.

"Mother?" Karma bellows as he and Dorje limp toward the group. "Lobsang?"

"She went to check on the Child," Dorje mumbles.

No.

Karma turns, starting for the tents.

Please. No, no, no . . .

Through the chaos and the shadows, he runs. Toward the area of the darkened periphery, he sees them.

At least five—maybe six, maybe more—wolves are circling. Uncle Urgyen stands surrounded, holding Lobsang high in one arm, his other swinging a stick.

"Get away, you devils!" Urgyen is shouting.

Karma sees his mother then, clinging to his uncle, cowering behind his back, shielded from the wolves.

Until one springs from behind.

Karma lets out a shout, a cry of warning—but too late. The wolf lands on his mother, slamming her against Urgyen and toppling them both to the ground. Lobsang, too, falls to the snow. The screams of his uncle and mother pierce in unison. The sound seems to rend him to his core. It startles the wolves, and for a moment it looks as if they will abandon the attack. But they are only doubling back to gather more momentum, lunging forward again.

"No!" Karma screams. "Get back!"

His voice is drowned out in the cacophony of snarling. Karma reaches for his knife and draws the blade—when he sees the movement in the corner of his eye, a darting shape closing toward him.

Another wolf—this one coming for him.

It leaps, jaws open, fangs flashing. Teeth snap as they hit the ground, grazing his face. Karma plunges the knife into its throat. Its yowl of pain is an even more terrifying sound. The blood is hot on Karma's hands. He jerks the blade out and sends it stabbing right back in again. The wolf bucks, the yowl becoming a squeal and a whimper. Squirming loose, it hobbles away, claws dragging in snow and blood.

Karma scrambles to his feet, brandishing his dagger as he looks wildly back to where his family had been.

All he can see is a mass of fur, piling and snarling, mauling and tearing in a wild frenzy.

Lobsang. Mother.

No!

"Get away!" Karma screams, hurling himself at them.

At the sound of his voice, some of the wolves swivel to bare their teeth, ready to turn their attack on him. But then a glow of firelight flickers. Shouts yell out. The Khampas come charging, led by Norbu, waving torches, beating with sticks, and hurling objects through the air. The wolves stop their mauling, confused now by the rallying of the people.

Suddenly, the trees rustle with the movement of something large, rapidly approaching. A shifting of shadows, a rushing presence . . .

Something tall rears, black and formless, unfolding from the night. A stench saturates the air, bitter to every sense.

From the darkness, comes an ear-splitting roar. The sound knocks Karma back and sends the wolves scampering, but not quickly enough. One is seized, lifted into the air. In one motion, the massive shape hurls it. It hits a tree. The crunch of bones makes a sickening sound.

The wolfpack howls. A pair of green eyes pierces the night.

The migoi.

Karma goes cold with dread.

It must be.

Now the wolves scatter like cowardly children, retreating to the woods, some desperately trying to drag off their prey. A lone wolf seizes onto Lobsang's lifeless body. Before it can even begin to drag him away, the migoi catches the wolf by its muzzle, strong claws gripping both jaws, forcing the animal's mouth open. In a wrenching motion, it tears the wolf's mouth apart. The migoi tosses the wolf to the ground, the animal making a strangely graceful somersault into the snow, its head wrenched to the side at an unnatural angle.

The migoi gathers Lobsang's body now, lifting it overhead.

"No!" Karma gasps, not knowing what will happen next. "*Don't!*"

Swerving toward the source of the utterance, its eyes meet Karma's.

It screams a reply, the sound of the screech driving Karma to his knees again.

"Please . . ." Karma cowers. "Please, don't hurt him. He's . . . just a child."

But the migoi's claws nevertheless close around Lobsang, the small body contorting into a shape that makes Karma feel weak in his stomach, and he sees then that instead of claws, they are fingers. Fingers—and hands—of a man. Just as quickly as it had appeared, now the migoi begins to draw away, a figure melting back into the forest.

"No . . ." Karma's stunted sob is a plea before deaf ears. "Come back. Come back."

But it is no use. The migoi disappears into the night . . . along with any hope for the Child who was to be the Lama.

33

THE LAMENTATION

Daybreak brings no relief, no end to the nightmare. On the glistening snow, the dead number a dozen, gathered up in the middle of the camp, surrounded by burnt torches and huddled figures like some ragged vigil. At first, Karma held his mother, blood soaking the snows, waiting with her. But eventually her breath ran out, growing softer and softer, before finally ceasing completely, and then she was gone.

He turns to the woods now, chasing in rage and terror after the migoi's tracks and Lobsang's blood trail, determined for either vengeance or escape, until the red dregs too run out, and all that is left are his own prints in the snow.

He sinks to his knees, allowing the sobs to rip through him, the cold air to cut deep in his lungs, his shaking insides to moan like the cracking of timbers in the frost.

The Reverend Mother's voice accompanies him from behind.

"Oh, Karma," she says.

Then she says nothing more, kneeling to sob with him.

He shudders so hard it shakes them both, and she grasps him tighter, as if to muffle the sound lest it rend him in half.

"I couldn't stop them," Karma weeps. "Not even when the migoi took him, I couldn't."

"My dear Karma, my dear . . ." the Reverend Mother can only repeat.

"I'm sorry," Karma heaves. "So sorry . . ."

"No," Dorje whispers. "It is I who should be sorry. To have ever believed differently. To have ever given hope . . ."

Karma pulls back to look at her, his vision blurred by the tears. The Mountain has become shrouded again, clouds moving in, the peak now a floating mass, suspended and rootless in the sky.

"'Six Suns.'" Dorje's voice drifts on the air. "'Six blasts in the sky. A seventh one, and the earth will die.' All along, it was the only outcome. All along, it told us. This is our karma. A world at its end."

She says nothing then, a silence from the last patch of the world so absolute that they can hear the snow glisten. Karma blinks through his tears as she brings her gaze to him.

"It's over," Dorje says. "'Gather to the Mount and the Seeing Stone, that the Lama may reveal yet a future unknown.' But it is pointless. The Child is gone. Everyone we love is gone." Her face slackens into a numbed expression. "There is only the Stone now. All we can hope for is the chance to see their faces once more until we reap what has been sown. Perhaps in the Mountain, I can see the Oracle's face one last time."

Karma's heart sinks at the surrender in her words. It is truly over, then. Without the Lama, there is no escape from the Seventh Sun. No way to look into the future to see how the crisis can be averted. Only a last comfort, a tender solace if able to glimpse into the Stone to say farewell.

But then a thought enters his mind, stopping him. Like a clear signal, a distant call.

"Not everyone is gone," he says to her.

She looks at him. Dorje said that everyone they love is gone . . . but it is not true.

"Nima." Tired and broken, yet not yet beaten, he wipes his eyes. "Nima's still out there."

Dorje's eyes lift up. But still she shakes her head. "It makes no difference. Nothing we can do will stop the end."

He understands what she is saying. Without the Lama, they cannot escape the destruction of the Seventh Sun, no matter what they do; at least if they continue to the Mountain, they may yet have the chance to set their eyes on the Stone and glimpse their loved ones before the end.

But that is not what he means. Despite knowing that Dorje is right about the futility of it all, he cannot leave Nima. He will not.

"I have to look for her," Karma says.

"The people won't wait, you know," Dorje replies. "Not with the wolves and migoi about."

Karma swallows. "I've failed them. They will do what they will."

Dorje says nothing. There is nothing more to say; they both know their paths are chosen: the Reverend Mother to continue with the pilgrims to the Mountain, Karma to find Nima.

Rising from his place of mourning, Karma takes his leave. His footsteps tread heavily, despite being with purpose. This time, he avoids his tracks, the bloodied snow, and the waiting Khampas. He avoids the bundled dead.

He has already said goodbye.

34

THE TOMB

The group's tracks have all but disappeared under the winds of last evening, but in the gorge, shielded by the cliffs, there are still traces of footsteps, grooves like the waves of a white river. Through these ripples, Karma can detect the hint of a single, more recent set of furrows.

Nima's footprints.

He follows them through the ravine. The gulch widens, becomes deep. The passage alternates between drifts of sunlit snow and mist-covered ridges, hinting of higher passes yet to be ascended. Distant booms of icefall echo across the cliffs. Abruptly, the tracks disappear as a turn in the gorge exposes the ravine to open winds, the surface now smooth and swept. Karma sees a shoulder of rock that ascends to a ridge. From its vantage at the top there will be a view for miles around. Perhaps he will spot something from this higher ground—more tracks, possible signs of their camp. He decides to make the climb, scaling the boulders at the base to work his way up, when he comes across a pronounced indentation in the snow.

A footprint.

Distinct and unmistakable, nestled between a pair of rocks—unblemished by wind or snowfall.

He swoops on it, studying the track.

It's her.

He is sure of it. She came this way, seeking higher vantage, just as he is now. He hurries on, hastening up the ridge at the sign of more tracks. He follows them, carefully scaling each boulder. Nearing the top, the height is taller, the slope steeper than he had expected. All around is an expanse of blue and gray, deep walls of glaciers brimming blurrily in the clouds. The snow is returning. Karma glances down, and the view takes his already-winded breath away. The edge is a sheer drop, a vertigo-inducing plummet to rock and snow. To slow down—to grip the wall—would be to fall. Swallowing, he looks back up, keeps going. He can only climb upward.

He reaches the top of the ridge. The view to the west reveals a mountainous shadow behind a shroud of mist. It is Kailash, only the tip of the massif showing, faintly glinting beneath turbulent clouds.

The light from my dream.

But the prints have disappeared. Continuing, he inches along the ridgetop, scanning the ledge for other tracks. A strong gust of wind pushes him into a low crouch. Flakes swirl, with snow slowly accumulating. The steepness of the cliff looms dangerously beside him. Despite the precariousness of the drop, something compels him to glance over the edge again.

A lower ledge juts out, its surface shielded from most of the snowfall by the higher promontory. A pattern of flurried tracks is scattered across the rock, appearing like footsteps. Karma kneels to study the marks. They are blurred by the wind, and he is uncertain if they are in fact footprints. But then his gaze stops short at a patch of red, out of place on the white snow and gray granite. His heart quavers.

Blood.

But whose?

His eyes flick back and forth across the ledge, but he does not see anything else. To see beyond the lower edge, he would have to go down. His head feels light, his palms grow sweaty. The air is strangely calm, the snows suspended in silence. The drop to the ledge below is not far, but the drop beyond the precipice certainly is. Breath shaking, he dangles one leg over, then another. Slowly, he lowers himself. His feet touch down. Safely on the ledge, he inches toward the red stain. The sight recalls the gore of the wolf attack, and his legs suddenly feel wobbly. Slowly, fearfully, he tiptoes forward. Reaching the precipice, he peeks over the edge. Glitter of snow, flutter of white.

He sees something.

A shape at the very bottom. A form foreign to the terrain and contours of the boulders at the base.

"Nima?" he says, but it comes out barely a whisper, as if deep down he did not truly want to be heard, did not want to confirm what he is afraid of.

Karma swallows, a gulp of cold air. He makes himself say it again. "Nima?"

Between the sky and snowy hollow, his voice does not seem to carry. Quickly, he backs away from the edge, going back to the wall. Within moments, he is scrambling up, climbing back over the overhang and onto the ridgetop. Then he is on his way down, back down the shoulder of the escarpment, down the slope of the gully. His movements are those of someone in a dream. Not seeing his own feet, he speeds along the surface. By some miracle he does not fall, though a few times he slips on the uneven rock, sending a cascade of snow tumbling behind him. He clears the boulders, clamoring to the bottom.

It's snowing heavily. Blinking back the rushing flakes, he sprints alongside the cliff. In the muffled silence, the thumping of Karma's heart is thunderous, the rush of blood in his ears a roar. His steps shorten, his pace slows.

An incongruent form sprawls before him, distorted by snow and shadow. The shape of a body.

His world falls away.

Her face is turned up, her eyes half closed in repose as if to catch the falling snowflakes. But a thin, dark trickle of fluid belies her condition. Beneath her body, a web of red bleeds through an icy crust.

The walls of the canyon seem to lean in. The ground seems to fall away.

"Nima—"

He rushes forward. The leaden feel of her body shocks him. Her skin is the color of granite, her face covered in frost. He shouts, shaking her shoulder and brushing away the snow as if that were all it would take. He tries to raise her. The frozen layer of ice on her back stuns him and he lets out an anguished cry, trying frantically to rub some warmth into it.

"Nima . . ."

If only he had a fire. An image from the night after they escaped the Khan's grotto flashes through his mind. By the river, they collected sticks. She showed him how to light kindling with his knife and flint from a stone she had found. It burns bright in his mind now. He sees their fire, its warm light, the smoke rising, safe from the rain.

If I can get her back to the woods.

I could relight the fire.

I could warm the life back into her.

His thoughts are illogical but he strains to pick her up. She is heavy, as though she is resisting him. Her hat, somehow having remained in place until now, tumbles away, her hair untouched by snow, as dark as when he had first seen it in the sunrise.

He grasps her in his arms, stumbling forward. The ground is icy from the blood. Karma curses the snow and everything it touches. He feels sick, weak limbed. The gorge darkens under a cloud. Karma cowers against a sudden, furious gust of wind, yet spurs himself on.

"Talk to me, Nima," he says into her ear. "Please."

But the only reply is the storm, a wall of white. Still, Karma plows forward, back up the gorge the way he came. Pushing, slogging, until his arms and legs become numb of any feeling, like phantom limbs.

He follows his own tracks up the slope to the same place where they parted just yesterday, where they found his uncle and cousin hiding in the hollow of the rocks. *If only*, Karma thinks. If only they stayed together. If only he went with her. If only one of any hundreds of things happened instead. The regrets swirl with each step. Unanswered, they heap in the wind.

His movements become slower, the heaviness of her body in his arms weighing him down. Progress ceases, the pull of the slope now an immovable weight against the wild and impenetrable barrier of snow and ice. Karma stumbles to his knees. He hunches over to keep her from landing in the snow. But the snow does not bother her. Nothing will, ever again. Her eyes are open. Thin slivers, unseeing.

"Not you, Nima," he begs. "Please. Don't leave me too."

Tearing off his gloves, he touches her forehead and then her cheek, gently feeling. Her skin is so cold, so stiff. She is not going to wake up. Not ever. No fire, no heat is going to bring her back.

She is already gone.

And now he leans into her, touching his forehead against hers, the way he saw his father and mother say farewell when he watched from the darkness of the wreckage. He holds her hands so softly that it convinces him that they cup his in return.

"Nima," he utters her name one last time.

For the second time that day, the tears come.

The wind blows. The snow swirls.

Shadows creep. Daylight wanes. He does not know how long he stays there.

When he finally lifts his head, darkness has set in.

Karma buries his head beside hers, unable to stop shaking.

"We're not dead yet, you said," he says to her ear. "Not yet."

Despite her newfound hope, nothing changed. Whether by the Seventh Sun or some other way, apocalypses great and small come for them all. In the end, it is the same.

A scream rips from his lungs, so forcefully it throws him back, wild and insensate, and he cranes his neck to the skies, dark now, damned if the world and the heavens would not hear him. The sound is beyond pain, beyond anger. Beyond flesh or blood, hope or reason. He is a ghost-wind. He collapses, an empty shell. Nothing left.

When the moonlight settles on the snow and the cold saps the tears from his eyes, Karma sees the stone crevice of the night before. He carries her to the rock, legs and back trembling. The gusting of the wind makes a low moaning through the hollow. In the end, a tomb after all.

Gently he lays her inside the receptacle. Gently again, he wipes the snow from her face.

A slab of rock seals the entombment. He rolls it shut—delicately, sliding the stone into place. Then, fearing the wolves, he fills the pockets and holes with other stones.

By now he is shivering, from the cold or fatigue or something else, he cannot tell, but when the task is completed, he crumples beside the makeshift tomb, his exhaustion complete. The sky is a streak of night now, the snow invisible as it drifts through the silvery gulch. The wind sighs in and out.

All along, it was the only outcome. All along, it told us. This is our karma. A world at its end.

He leans against the stone. His eyelids droop.

It's over.

Something is moving out in the snow. A four-legged animal lumbers through the dark. It is joined by another, creeping, hunched in the shadows. A group of them now, closing in.

Have the wolves returned?

Yet Karma does not reach for the silver dagger on his belt. Does not even think to try. His eyes close. Giving in. To the darkness, to the inevitable.

And now he feels the truth of what the Reverend Mother said.

Nothing we can do will stop the end.

Around him the animals converge, silently, invisibly.

But he is already gone.

35

THE HERD

H e can tell it is a dream.

It is summer, back in the valley.

The hills crouch low and serene in the distance. The meadow ripples, green in the wind, with grasses longer than he has ever seen. There is the herd. He has never known a stock of yak as full and fatted, as numerous as they are. Yet they are his.

They lounge beneath an endless sky, the air bluer, the color more vibrant than he has ever beheld.

Karma stands as a herder in the middle of the flock, amid the rustling and the lowing. He can breathe the smells, feel the warmth of the sun, the brush of the breeze.

His heart fills with the peace of it.

A boy's laugh floats over. Karma turns. He stops.

There is Lobsang, coming toward him. He is skipping over the grass, Auntie Pema there too.

And Karma's own mother.

The colors of her apron are bright again, her hair ungrayed—the way he remembers it as a child. All together, all coming to meet him from the village.

But it's not possible, is it?

They're dead.

And we're not in the valley anymore.

Karma does not say anything, does not want to disrupt the moment. The herd parts lazily as Lobsang flicks his sling, making way. The warm air blows, rippling the thick coats of the yaks as they stir.

Karma startles.

White fur dashes into view, bounding toward them.

A snow lion.

A shout forms in Karma's throat. His hand goes instinctively to where he once carried a sling. *Run!* he wants to shout. *Run!* But his family shows no sign of concern. Neither do the yaks. They do not scatter, do not panic at the sight of the lion's presence. Instead, they make room, allowing it to dart through the grass, to stretch its back and kneel beside them.

Karma stares in confusion. The snow lion yawns and stares back. Then it turns to regard the yaks. But rather than stalking its prey, it eyes the flock with a gentle gaze, like a guardian keeping watch.

Another animal appears, this one from another corner of the herd, parting the drove from the east. It is a tiger, tail swishing, whiskers twitching, the ripple of its stripes blending with the shifting of the grasses. It comes to a perch beside the snow lion. From the west, a winged shadow swoops overhead. A brightly colored bird, feathers rippling. From a fourth direction still, follows the long tail of a flying dragon, disappearing in the sun only to reemerge against the sky, turning black, circling the flock.

The Four Dignities.

Just a dream.

Or have I, too, reached the otherworld?

A noise trumpets in answer, a low burring from far beyond the valley, beyond the hills, rattling the air . . .

Ommmm . . . Ommmmm . . .

A pause. Then a rumble follows, in the hills, in the earth. A bottomless reverberation, like the stirring of a giant, waking from the deep.

It is the music of the dharma horn, calling the people to gather.

A hopeless call, if the world must end.

Still, it persists. Trembling through the valley, echoing in the hills, spreading through the rocks and the cloudless sky. Deep into his bones, far into his sinews.

Shaking him. Rousing him.

Wake up, it seems to say. *Awaken, Karma.*

———

Karma blinks in the weak light, blue and shadowed between his eyelids.

His head thrums, his body pounds.

But he is warm. Steaming mists breathe down in a cloud of animal musk and sounds.

He is surrounded. Hulking, hairy figures—huddled about him.

He recoils, drawing back against the rock of Nima's tomb.

Wolves?

No, not wolves.

It is wool, not fur. Instead of claws and fangs, there are massive bodies, snorting noses. As a shepherd, he knows the smell.

They are yaks.

Karma stares incredulously. Their large heads hang low, they band together, smaller calves in the center. He has seen his own herd do the same thing, grouping together by a mound of earth to share one another's body heat, to form a barrier against the cold. But these are wild yak. Larger, with taller shoulders. More numerous.

The low croon of a trumpet reverberates suddenly over the sound of the wind and the herd. It summons immediately in Karma's mind the images of the green Khampa valley of his dream.

Is the sound imagined, or is it real?

To Karma's surprise, the wild yak lift their heads, ears waggling, seemingly able to hear the noise as well. When the horn blares again, still muted but distinct, they turn toward the sound. Then they begin to move. The larger yak on the outside are the first to lumber forward, their bodies like plows.

Nodding behind, the calves follow. Their displacement leaves a void filled by twilight and the falling snow.

The horn blows once more, clearer than before. In the contours of the sound comes another impression. A picture—this time of whistling winds and rushing waterfalls, tinkling springs and echoing chasms. All echoing through great winding tunnels in a palatial mountain under the sky.

He knows what it is, a voice suddenly coming as the ghost-winds through the dusk.

Look to the Mountain. Look to the Stone.

Hidden in the shape of the echo, in the contours of its thrumming and the timbre of its notes, he can feel it out there. Waiting.

Then he hears the ghost-winds whistling through the cracks in the rocks, and it is another voice that whispers from the grave. Nima's voice, he imagines.

We're not dead yet.

And if it be that we die, at least we die facing the sun.

Karma squints through the flurries. Seeing one of the larger calves cross before him, he reaches for the animal, grabbing onto its hair. The young yak bleats, its steps speeding up. Though fighting exhaustion, Karma holds on, pulling himself onto its back. With his sash, he makes a harness around its neck. Tied together, they barrel forward, crunching through the snow, merging with the rest of the herd.

The wind picks up, blinding the way with ice and snow. Karma slumps over the yak's hump, closing his eyes, letting himself go—back to the vision of the valley, back to the green field and blue sky—as now he floats aloft the herd of snow, visions of the Mountain calling.

To the place beyond.

36

THE FRIEND

The whispers of the ghost-winds fade as the swaying of the yak comes to an abrupt stop. In the sudden stillness, the world comes in and the world goes out, darkness to light, night to day.

Karma's eyes blink open to a dazzling whiteness of sunlight and snow. Beneath him, he can feel the pleasant heat of the yak's body. Warm, comforting. He can hear the heavy sounds of its breathing, the drag of air into its icy nostrils and out in wet puffs. But otherwise, it is a crisp silence that surrounds him, a stillness unperturbed by cloud or storm.

A sharp *thwack*, and the yak's entire body twitches, struck. Braying, it lurches into a trot. The sudden movement sends Karma tumbling from the yak's back, landing in the snow. He thinks he imagines the sound of voices, of people drawing near, coming toward him.

On the ground, Karma squints in confusion. A white peak blurs in the haze of his vision, penetrating a blue sky.

Is this the Mountain?

But the sun, in its brightness, blinds him. Figures suddenly converge, not imagined after all, clamoring all around.

Karma turns his head. He sees the calf collapsed on the ground, arrows sprouting like sprigs from its body. It makes a bleating wail at him.

Karma opens his mouth in protest while at the same time a figure's shadow looms, darkening his view. Karma looks up.

Who?

It can't be.

The face he sees is one he has been surprised by before.

But not now, not here . . .

He feels himself reeling. Vision dims. Consciousness falters.

Not him.

He begins to slip. Other figures swarm around, but it is this face that stays with him.

The face of Altan,

Khan of the rebel army.

He's found us.

And then the thought, as the world slides back out: *He's found the Mountain.*

What rouses him is the aroma of cooked meat, at once sweet and nauseating. Karma opens his eyes to find himself in the dim interior of a tent. Across a blanketed floor of skins and furs, he sees Altan—sucking the marrow from a shard of bone.

"The Sherpa awakes."

They are in a yurt. The smoke from a pan of coals trails through the vent to a white sky. Altan tosses the bone aside, reaches to a platter of meat for another. In another corner of the yurt, Karma sees Surkhang crouching, watching him.

Karma's stomach murmurs loudly at the sight of the roasted flesh. Altan laughs. "Eat. Drink. There is plenty, thanks to you. A whole herd of wild yak. The men have been slaughtering all day." He picks up a large hunk of meat and walks over to Karma, holding it out to him.

Karma draws back in revulsion, thinking of the calf. It must show on his face, as Altan gestures with the piece of meat, coaxing him.

"The beast has done its part. It brought you here to the Mountain, now let it sustain you so you may climb it."

Karma's stomach twists again in hunger.

Altan takes Karma's hand and thrusts the meat into it. Karma tells himself to throw the food aside, but before he knows it, he is gnawing at it, his stomach aching violently from both the regret and the need.

Altan smiles. "You've made it," he says, nodding toward the yurt's door. "Just outside is the pass leading to the Mountain's caves."

The Khan watches Karma, studying his reaction. "You're wondering, how did this happen? From the time you set foot in the grotto, I knew who you were. Those patroller deserters—the brothers—they did not need much convincing to talk."

The food sticks in Karma's throat. "You followed us."

"You might say, you *led* us," Altan replies.

Karma drops the food like it is poison.

The Khan goes on. "Gendun may have succeeded in spiriting you away the night of the storm. But he is not the only one capable of intrigue."

"That uncle of yours," Surkhang interjects from across the tent.

"He came to us," Altan says. "Because he wanted you gone. So we made a deal with him if he would leave a trail for us to follow. Between that and the writings of a certain Oracle that were obtained by the border bandits who joined our rebel alliance after their rout at Skull Lake, we were able to find you easily."

Karma is stunned. "You brought the border bandits here? What if the Minister followed them?"

Altan appears unperturbed. "The battle is inevitable, Sherpa. The Eastern Army is nearing. That is why you need us. That is why there is no time to lose. We must find the Seeing Stone before they do, no matter the cost."

Karma feels sick. The meat in his belly. The smoke.

"But the only guide who can lead us is you," Altan continues. "You've made it this far. Now you must find the Stone."

Karma sets his mouth in defiance. "The Stone is worthless without the Lama."

"Where's the boy, then?" Surkhang demands, growing impatient.

"He's dead," Karma declares simply. At least he knows that his cousin is forever safe from their grasp. "He was killed by wolves."

Surkhang frowns. "What do you mean, killed? What wolves? What about all the people who were with him? What about my brother?" He pauses, and Karma knows the question that is coming. "What about Nima?"

Karma's reply comes slowly and heavily, like stones too heavy to move.

"She's dead too."

Surkhang's face loses all expression. As Karma meets his eyes again, he realizes something about Surkhang that he suspected, the way someone recognizes a piece of themselves in someone else: He loved her. They both did.

Still do.

The tent falls silent. From his seat, the Khan's face becomes stony. But then . . . a glint in his eye, like a spark from a fire. "And yet, here you are."

Karma stares as the Khan steeples his hands.

"Could it *be*, then," Altan says, an inflection in his voice as if a discovery is dawning on him, "that when one door shuts, another opens?"

Something burns inside Karma. He feels his heart racing. "I don't know what you mean."

"Hanumanda came to you," Altan continues. "The Mountain calls to you. The people follow you. Because *you* are the guide."

Karma is fearful. Somehow he knows what is coming.

"*You* are the Lama."

"No," Karma refutes. "It's not true—"

"What if I told you your loss need not be permanent?"

"What are you talking about, Altan?" Surkhang trembles beside him.

"Nima, your father, anyone you may love." Altan holds up a hand. "Look inside yourself, Karma. Tell me you don't already know it. Tell me you don't want to at least believe. The Seeing Stone has the power not only to see the future and the past—but also, to change it. With such an object, no loss need be final. Imagine, looking into the Stone, to see a way to pull someone back from the void. Back from the other-world. Back, as it were, from the cliff's drop."

"That's impossible." Karma shakes his head.

"Not for the Lama," Altan states. "The rest of us can only look, but if *you* are the Lama, you can literally pull Nima back from her fall. Back from death."

The sheer hope of the pronouncement is at once alluring. Until something inside Karma stops him, clicking in his head. He blinks hard. "What was that you said?"

"I said the power is yours to wield. If you bring me the Stone, I can show you how."

Haltingly, Karma rises, his strength slowly returning from having eaten. "Not that. What you said . . . about Nima falling. How do you know that?"

For a moment, the Khan has no reaction. His face then lets slip a mild look of surprise.

Karma continues, "I never said anything about how Nima died. Yet you just said I could pull her back from the cliff. How did you know that?"

From the other side of the yurt, Surkhang's gaze swings from Karma to the Khan. "Altan," he says. "What is he talking about?"

But Karma understands. Suddenly and intuitively, he feels it.

"He knows," he says, his teeth and hands clenching with the growing revelation, "because it was not an accident. It was him. His men. Those tracks in the snow, and on the cliff. They were the ones who killed her."

Surkhang stares at the Khan. "Altan?" he repeats. "What is he talking about?"

The Khan makes a sucking sound between his lips, caught. "The truth is—she surprised the advance party. When they tried to take her alive, she attacked. She killed two of our men, maiming several others, including my own bodyguard Chuluun. He survived. But she did not."

The floor seems to fall away. Surkhang's voice fills the tent as he steps forward. "You told me no harm would come to her or my brother. You said this was about the war with Hanumanda!"

"This *is* about the war," Altan replies. "You can't start a fire without burning a few sticks."

Surkhang's hands clench as he faces Altan. "She was not the enemy!"

"Anyone who isn't with us is against us," Altan answers. "You understood the stakes. The Minister is coming, and this time he will stop at nothing to get the Stone. And neither will I. Ten years ago, we were this close to obtaining it. Even if it costs every life in the rebel army, I will not fail again!"

Surkhang looks stunned. "Ten years ago . . . you were searching for the Stone?"

Altan merely nods. "When the father of the Sherpa here disappeared, Hanumanda hired us to track him down. That's when I learned about it."

Surkhang's face contorts as it works out the meaning of this admission, finally seizing into an expression of absolute rage. "You . . . were . . . working . . . for the Eastern Army?"

"Still am," Altan replies. "Call it an alliance of convenience, just like the rebel council. Until I can get my hands on the Stone. Then the Eastern Army will work for me."

Surkhang's voice brims with rage. "Now I see," he says. "Now the snow reveals the muck. You talk of the threat of the Minister, tell of the horrors the Eastern Army has done. But all this time . . . you were one of them. You talk of traitors. But it was you who betrayed your own people."

Altan's face changes, any guise of congeniality now erased. "Careful, now." His voice is cold and sharp. "I should think you are on thin ice."

But Surkhang is beyond heeding the warning. "How do you think the rebel council will feel, knowing they have been lied to—by a *traitor*? That you would use them to take on one tyrant and replace him with another? That's your plan, isn't it? Use the boy to find the Stone, then use it to take Hanumanda's place. My brother was right: Kill the Minister, another takes his place."

"Bataar! Chuluun!" Altan calls to the door of the tent.

The two bodyguards enter, hands on their swords. On Chuluun's left eye is a bloodied bandage. Nima's handiwork, according to Altan. Bataar's own ear is deformed. Another gift from Nima's sword.

"These two," Surkhang taunts. "Between the two of them, half a brain and one bollock."

"Remove this churl from my sight," Altan snarls.

Bataar and Chuluun hesitate, eyes going to Surkhang in a moment of confusion before piecing the situation together.

But the pause is all the time that Surkhang needs. As they reach for their swords, he moves. He reaches Chuluun first. By the time Bataar charges at him, Surkhang has already gained control of Chuluun's arm and thus his body. As Bataar lunges with his weapon, Surkhang yanks Chuluun into its path.

The sword thrusts. The blade stabs . . .

Into Chuluun's gut.

Both emit a grunt of surprise, more out of shock from Bataar, who recoils, pulling his sword away as if to undo the error. But it is the wrong move, as the ground he gives is the ground Surkhang takes, returning the attack instantaneously with Chuluun's own weapon. With almost practiced precision, he runs the sword through Bataar's neck, his mouth opening in soundless shock. As though with choreographed timing, Bataar and Chuluun's bodies fall together, hitting the ground at the same time.

Surkhang turns now to face Altan.

"The swordsman Surkhang!" Altan claps. "As impressive as they say!" He draws his own saber, sidestepping to maintain distance. "But tell me this isn't over the girl! Tell me she isn't the reason you turned, when it was you who came to me! Unless . . . Was it *because* of her you left the Gangdruk in the first place? It wasn't because she had fallen for the boy over you, was it?"

Surkhang charges in a rage. But Altan is ready, timing his remark to slip behind Karma, and shove him into Surkhang. The two collide, sending the pan of coals scuttling across the tent. The scattered embers glow as Altan seizes on the opportunity, lunging out to slash at Surkhang's leg with his saber, sending him to a knee.

"You should have let it go, outlaw," Altan chides. "I could have made something out of you."

I have to do something.

I have to help him.

The dagger. The Khan's back is to him. Karma reaches into his robe. It is there in his pocket; they have not removed it. He grips the crystal handle, drawing the knife.

The Khan spins around, hearing the blade zing as it unsheathes, only to realize that the bigger threat is not from Karma, but from the ground as Surkhang lunges at him. Altan whirls back to face him. Their swords clang.

Altan grunts and staggers back. Slowly, he looks down at his side. His hand comes back red with blood.

"You fools," he growls. "What do you think you have accomplished?" He takes a step toward Surkhang, but instead drops his saber on the carpet.

Surkhang rises. "What I should have let Nima do when she had the chance. Maybe you'll cross the mountain pass after all, but you'll never see the Stone."

The Khan slides to the ground, his face spiteful as his eyes take in a dark trickle down Surkhang's torso. "Neither will you," he hisses in reply, before slumping slowly under his own weight.

Surkhang teeters a moment. He touches a hand to the area below the rib cage.

It comes back bright red as well.

Karma gapes at the color, the amount of blood revealing the grievousness of the wound.

"You're hurt, Surkhang," Karma says. He scans the tent, looking for something to use as bandaging.

"Don't bother."

"I can go get—"

"I said, don't waste your time. You think I don't know a fatal wound when I see one?" Surkhang takes a step, staggers. The blood is coming fast. Haggardly, he lowers himself to the floor. He touches the wound again, gingerly, then rants a string of curses. His hair dangles over the increasingly pallid sheen of his face.

"What should I do?" Karma asks.

"What can you do? Just *go*."

Karma shakes his head. "I won't just leave you here. Not after what you just did."

"I didn't do it for you," Surkhang snaps. His breathing turns heavy, grows labored. "It's no use, anyway. The end has come. My brother was right. I was blind all along."

"No," Karma replies after a moment. "In the end, you acted well. In the end, you saw the truth." He nods as reassuringly as he can. "I will tell Gendun."

Surkhang grimaces, shutting his eyes. His breathing becomes short. "You still here, boy?"

Karma kneels beside him. He wishes he could say something. Some words to guide the dying to the otherworld. But he *is* a boy, neither shaman nor monk, and he does not know them.

"I'm right here," Karma says.

Surkhang's stare dissolves, as if drifting to some unseen place beyond the walls of the yurt, beyond physical sight.

"Is it real?" Surkhang stammers. "Is there really another world beyond the Mountain? Something more after the end?"

Karma is silent. In the face of doom, how comforting to believe there could be such a place. An opportunity for redemption and rebirth. For recompense and reunion.

A refuge.

He does not know the answer. Not even for himself.

"I hope so," Karma finally replies.

The answer holds a promise and Surkhang begins to murmur. "I . . . see it."

His eyes have a far-off gaze.

"There's . . . a light . . ."

Karma swallows. What he had seen in his dream with the dragon. "Yes."

Surkhang's voice is a whisper now. "As bright as the sun."

There is a look of peace on Surkhang's face.

But then, something happens. Another look replaces it, creeping slowly, sliding across his brow like a shadow at dusk.

Fear. It seems to eclipse Surkhang, the tranquil expression of a moment ago crumbling away. He lets out a whimper, a sound that sends a chill through Karma.

"It's not a light," Surkhang gasps. "It's a fire."

Karma goes cold.

"It's the whole of the earth," Surkhang says now. "The heavens, everything, burning—"

Surkhang's words become garbled, small, cutting off suddenly.

The whole of the earth. The heavens.

The Seventh Sun.

Surkhang's breath catches. "In the end . . . nothing."

Slowly, his eyes close, this utterance his last.

Karma can sense him slipping away, can feel him drifting from the room in this world to the beyond in the unseen one. From this tent, across the final pass.

Leaving Karma now, alone.

37

THE LABYRINTH

Karma's shrouded face and bundled figure goes unnoticed as he rushes through the camp, putting as much distance as possible between himself and the Khan's tent, the rebel fighters too busy devouring the boon of yak meat to pay any attention to him.

Karma flinches at a sonorous boom—whether the sound of thunder or falling snow, he cannot tell. Another storm is moving in, thickening the pass with shadows and snow. The Mountain looms over the void, yet its peak is still hidden in the clouds.

To the Mountain then. Before the rebels discover what has transpired. Karma walks faster, trying to outrun them—but also the voice that has been following him from the Khan's tent.

Enticing, subtle, a pervading dirge that he fears he cannot exorcise except by facing it.

With such an object, no loss need be final. Imagine, looking into the Stone, to see a way to pull someone back from the void. Back from the otherworld.

Then comes Karma's own voice, soft and whispering, fearful to once again believe . . .

Is it true?

Can the past be undone?

A way to save Mother. And Lobsang. To pull Nima back. Even . . . to stop Father from leaving?

If the past can be changed, then what about the future? Can the people be saved after all?

And the most vital question to him now:

Am I the one to do it?

He glances back over his shoulder toward the rebel camp. No one is following.

One last hope. It is not the end. Not yet.

He turns to face the pass.

Flurries fill the gap. Still careful to stay undetected, he keeps close to the walls rather than traversing openly through the heart of the vale. The land slowly ascends through the mists. The Mountain begins. A steep face, impossible if one were to climb it. But just below is a deep drop, leading to an icy blue world: caves. The way within the Mountain. He hastens on.

The winds gust, threatening to blow him from the face of the slope. He hugs the wall, shivering in the bitter chill as he edges his way slowly down. The going is precarious. A few steps farther and he can no longer see his feet, much less what is ahead. He breathes to steady his nerves, but, unable to see where he is going, he is terrified that he will soon be stuck, stranded on the side of the Mountain with the full brunt of a storm bearing down on him.

This is too slow. I must move faster.

In the growing blindness of the snow, he cranes his neck forward. Where is the horn to lead the way? He shuts his eyes to listen. But there is no horn sounding, no blowing other than that of the wind and the ice.

His foot misses a step. Where there was ground, now there is only air. Heart lurching, he makes a leap, trying to regain his footing—but it eludes him. He feels himself dropping, tumbling down the slope. If he cries out, the sound of his voice is long behind him.

His body collides against a snowbank.

Unhurt. He can still move.

But where is he now? The cliff above has vanished, with only the cool canyons of ice around him to be seen.

A low braying sound startles him—through the frigid air, a deep, haunting burr, rolling toward him through the gorge like a river's swell.

Ommmmm . . .

He can hardly contain his relief. It is the horn, its music begun again, the sound deep and full, coming from the narrows ahead.

Karma climbs to his feet, pausing unsteadily. Blue walls rise in alternating slots of light and shade. Through these walls run other fissures, deep passages of ice and rock, wide enough for a person to enter—a network of glacial corridors. A vision comes to him of an imaginary summer of long ago—long before the snows, when the ice once flowed in streams, emptying through these channels into a glassy lake bearing a reflection of the peak.

But now everything is frozen, the ground a fogged mirror holding only a shadow of the Mountain as it once was.

Ommmmm . . .

The throaty bass of the horn flows deeper, the sound recalling the guttural chanting of the pilgrim monks.

Cautiously, Karma ventures forward, coming to a branch in the canyon. He goes one way. The sound of the horn sours, turning more dissonant with each step. He stops.

It's the wrong way.

He reverses course. The dissonance wanes. As he switches paths to the other artery, the horn's pleasing resonance returns.

Ommmmmmm . . .

Louder now.

This way.

He continues, following the sound through the maze of corridors. When at the next juncture the pitch again sours, he veers course as he did before until he finds the resonance restored once more. Reaching the end of a corridor, he turns a corner.

A mountainous pile of boulders, debris from a rockslide, appears to block the way. Two oblong stones lean precariously against each other—one a solid shaft of granite, the other cracked—both looking at any moment ready to fall. But there is something about their size and appearance, their uniformity, that hints of more. Not random but ordered by the wisdom and beauty of a structural plan. A pair of totem columns hiding a shaded opening. It is a door. The entrance to a cave.

Karma approaches. The columns are twice his height. He peers into the hooded gap. Stray light from the gully falls across his back, thrusting a deep shadow into the opening.

A deep bellow booms forth from the depths of the cave.

Ommmmmmm . . .

The reverberations raise the hairs on Karma's neck and tingle down his back. Enter, it seems to say.

Beyond the dusky entrance is a spacious cavern. Karma's eyes adjust. The tall ceiling commands his gaze. Gray icicles droop like overgrown beards. Echoes cascade as he displaces gravel with each step. The ground glimmers with flecks of gold, the walls with glints of silver. Farther in, the cave floor becomes a mirror image of the ceiling as the mineral deposits pile up in heaping towers, matching the stalactites above, ceiling touching floor to create a colonnade of tapered pillars and solid walls. They form passages, branching and dividing, spawning and reconnecting—a labyrinth of tunnels.

Karma stops before the first passage. From within comes the whistling of wind, ghostly, mingling with the humming of the horn. The combination of the notes is off-key, discordant.

He moves on, ear cocked to listen at each of the subsequent openings. The tunnels that follow produce a similar trill, each of a different pitch, yet none is a match with the horn. At the final tunnel, Karma pauses. The whistling from within makes a perfect complement to the sound.

It's this way, then.

He steps inside. The volume is immediately amplified, enveloping his body in a tide of reverberation. He continues. The passages change shape—dividing and merging, splitting and rejoining, widening and narrowing. At every junction, Karma listens, feeling the changes in his body, the resonance telling him where to go. By now he is in complete darkness, feeling the walls with his hands. The blackness that engulfs him is the blackness of a tomb, darker than a starless night. All sense of time is suspended, and soon he has no idea of how long he has been wandering. He is seized momentarily by the panicked thought that he is lost, doomed forever to roam this labyrinthine cavern, an underground world with no end, nothing on the other side.

The hum of the horn fades abruptly under another, competing sound. A low buzzing, tinny and metallic, emanating from the passageway ahead. A faint glow of green pulses within his view.

Karma goes still, but his heart is racing.

What is that?

The smell comes first, like an answer. An overpowering stench. The stink of rot just before decay. Neither alive nor dead. But something in between, festering. Like the smell that day they found the calf, but worse. It fills Karma's nostrils. He gags, bile rising in his throat. He wants to scream but cannot. His mind tells him to run, to flee the way he has come. But his body is immobile, paralyzed, every sense deadened.

Except the sense of fear.

A shadow emerges from the green light, advancing toward him, each step dragging on the ground. Claws on a stone.

From the blackness, two deep sockets glister out at him.

Karma bumps back against the wall, nowhere to turn.

The hollows enlarge as the creature approaches. Karma has the impression that they are the eyes of a man.

Just as its fingers were the fingers of a man.

"Who are you?" Karma blurts out. "What do you want?"

But he knows.

This is a migoi. And what he wants is death.

The hollows seem to stretch toward him, taking him in. But it is when he hears its voice that Karma's blood turns cold. Coarse and unused, but still the voice of a man.

"The liberation that was promised me after I paid my penance," he answers. "The liberation of which I was robbed—*by you.*"

"What do you mean?" Karma trembles. "I don't know what you speak of."

"Only the Lama has the power to free me from this curse. To release me from this prison between the world of the living and the otherworld. And you killed him."

"No." Karma shakes his head. "It was you."

The migoi screams, and Karma shrinks as if the sound has withered his insides. "I stopped the wolves. He was the Child. But you let him die!"

"I . . ." But no other words come. Wasn't it true? Lobsang was his responsibility. He left him despite sensing the danger. Karma's legs buckle, weakened only further by this revelation. But the migoi is not finished.

The words come out, feral, volatile: "For ten years I have waited. For ten years, suffering the price of my actions. Banished from the world, while deprived of the reprieve of death. Forbidden from interacting with the living, except if they should come into range of the Mountain."

Something in the migoi's words stands out.

Ten years. Ten—the time when Father left on his journey.

Karma is suddenly fearful. All this time believing that his father was a hero. But what if he discovers something different? Doubt floods him.

"I was only going to use the Stone for good," the migoi rages. "I left my village, my family. I abandoned everything for this!"

No. It can't be. Not Father . . .

"My only crime was spilling blood in the sacred Mountain. But karma is a heartless judge. You don't know the pain of paying for your own deeds. But soon you will. We *all* will."

The migoi seizes Karma by his shoulder, nails piercing his flesh, and Karma cries out at the violence of this action.

Not the liar, the scoundrel, the thief.

The migoi begins to stalk down the dark corridor, dragging Karma who moans with pain. A pain not of flesh, but of something deeper. Something dying inside him, never to live again.

Why . . . why, Father . . . ?

He can only ask the question in his mind, too broken to articulate. "If the only hope of deliverance is the deliverance of destruction, and the only liberation is the liberation of annihilation, then let it be. If I will have no release, then let the whole world burn with me."

There, in the dark of the caves, lit by a pulsing green light, Karma beholds a gaping cavern: half-collapsed, a silo of metal and broken rock. In the middle of the chamber, a long, tower-like cylinder stretches toward the cavern ceiling. The faint glint of its surface reminds him of the wreckage of the iron bird by the village.

Metal. It is perforated in the middle, toppled against the far wall. The very top tapers into a conical tip like the point of an arrow's shaft, obscured in darkness and shadow. Stencils of unfamiliar lettering mark the side.

A low hum emanates from the object, tinny and metallic, the noise mixing with the green glow and squeals of a colony of bats writhing from the ceiling. The air is warm, festering with a strange heat, dead and stagnant.

The migoi lets go of Karma.

"This is the *Surya*. This is the Seventh Sun."

The horror compounds as finally Karma realizes what he is looking at. This is the weapon the Reverend Mother mentioned. The thing that will destroy the world. Is this what his father found? Here at the Mountain? Their refuge turned to their ruin. Is this truly the fate of mankind, everything subject to corruption to the point of destruction? Truly then, his curse is real.

Karma groans with heartbreak. After all they have gone through. And his father?

"Why?" Karma whimpers. "Why you?"

This can't be how it ends. Not yet. Not after all this.

Look to the Mountain . . . look to the Stone, you told me.

"What did you think you would find here"—the migoi's voice rumbles against the hum of the Seventh Sun—"without the Lama?"

Karma feels like he can barely get to his knees beneath the oppressive atmosphere. It chokes him. The sense of betrayal weighs on him. It's what will kill him—it's too much to take. He longs for air, for the sky, for the valley again. For a green tree. To be away from this darkness of hell.

"My father," his words trickle out. If it is forgiveness his father was seeking, then it is forgiveness he will give, even if he is not the Lama. "I came to find my father."

The migoi's eyes flicker. "Your father?"

Yes, don't you recognize me?

"Sherpa Patrul."

The migoi's head rears, eyes expanding to drain the room of the pool of green.

"Sherpa Patrul?"

Something is wrong, Karma realizes. It is not as he thought.

Not as he had feared.

"Not . . . the Sherpa who put me here?" the migoi's voice rises. "The one who I followed because of his promises of the Stone, only for him to be too afraid to use it? The one whose blood I had to spill when he tried to stop me? The one . . . who cursed me?"

Karma reels at the words.

The migoi is not my father.

Karma almost crumples with relief. But then he realizes what the migoi just said.

He is my father's murderer.

Now another feeling rises in him. No longer fear, but something potent, growing to a degree Karma has not dared to allow—until now.

Fury.

The migoi's eyes narrow on Karma, and he begins to move toward him. "How cruel, the workings of karma. How fate must laugh. For it was the father who cursed me, and now it is the son who has sealed my curse by depriving me of the Child. But fate is not without irony, and I shall have my revenge again. For it was the father I killed, and it will be the son I kill too!"

The migoi's shape shifts in the dark, losing any semblance of man as it suddenly screeches and rushes Karma. But Karma is already moving, the rage that is in him turned to motion. He grips the dagger, pulling it from his robe, lightless in the dark, the black of the sky-iron betraying no warning. The migoi reaches him just as Karma thrusts it forward. The blade goes in easily—surprisingly so. The migoi's scream is not so much a cry of pain but of shock. The migoi gapes down at the knife, buried to the hilt in its chest. The eyes of the creature begin to change, shrinking from the hollow reflections of green to the small, round pupils of a man's.

"What . . . have you done to me?"

Karma staggers back, equally astonished. Now the glow of the green is replaced by another light—as the shaft of the crystal handle begins to glow, flashing brilliantly. The migoi's face reshapes itself, shadows morphing into the features of a man, one Karma vaguely recalls from his village's past.

It's Tenzing—Urgyen's brother, who went on the expedition with Karma's father. And who now, Karma can see, is dying.

But a migoi cannot be killed.

Yet it is happening. And the migoi can feel it too.

"How can this be?" the man gasps. "When the Lama is dead?"

Perhaps not, after all.

Was Altan right?

The migoi crumples with a tormented screech. The sound of its scream echoes, shattering through the cave. The bats break forth from the ceiling, swirling in droves through the cavern, shrieking.

Karma runs—away from there, away from the nightmare of the migoi and the Seventh Sun—back into the labyrinth of corridors.

The thrum of the horn echoes as all at once the tunnel opens up before him, the notes louder now, sounding closer than ever before, the entire labyrinth vibrating in accord. A light appears, growing distinct. Karma's footsteps quicken, his strides lengthen. Sunlight penetrates, waters hiss and burble.

Through a veil of rising vapors, spires of sunshine slash the darkness, catacombs meeting windows of sky. They illuminate springs of liquid running down rock, pooling in bowls aquamarine and milk-white. Sulfuric elements fill the air, the smell of the deep mixing with the breath of the heavens.

The end of the labyrinth.

The beginning of a bridge.

A stairway to light.

The otherworld.

38

THE MOUNTAIN

Mists envelop the bridge, thick and billowing.

Through the swirl, Karma has the impression of walking on clouds. Occasionally, the mists part long enough for him to glance over the edges, glimpsing a crevasse so deep it seems to go to the very center of the earth itself. He glances behind him.

No migoi.

No creature following. No evil lurking. It was Tenzing who murdered Karma's father. And now he is dead.

But how? Karma thought it was not possible to kill the migoi, but he has done it. And in slaying it, he released the creature from its atonement of misery, its curse. Something only a Lama can do.

The doorway of light ahead grows larger, brighter.

With something to guide him, his steps become more confident. The horn is a constant hum, driving into him. But he begins to hear other sounds too. Distant twittering, birds chirping. Sounds of summer.

Am I hearing things?

The veil of mist becomes thin, gauzy, reaching his head, along with the unexpected smell of cinquefoil and moss, sunlight and grass. The doorway softens, vapors growing translucent, fading out of darkness into a burst of gold.

He is in a garden, wild and untended, teeming with varieties of plants he has never before seen, gigantic growths with fronds as wide as arms. The air is as heavy as the valley after summer rains, tittering with life—the chatter of birds, the chirping of insects, the gush of water.

Karma cranes his head up toward the radiant daylight, staring in awe. He is inside a vast space, wide open yet enclosed. Expanding, rising. Walls of rock vaulting the skies. He is inside a hollow mountain.

Along the crater, a long stone staircase wraps in a massive spiral, past innumerable doorways, one height to the next. A river gushes from the walls, miraculously suspended in a perpetual cascade. And at the very top, as bright as the sun itself, a ray of light shines through the spray, projecting rainbows like multicolored bridges, over which a flock of birds passes back and forth. There are other animals too—*tahir* and *bharal*, rarely ever seen, scampering up the precipitously steep rocks.

The sibilation of the waterfall. The caw of the birds. The cooing of the wind through the caverns. The scent of the flora and the grass. The warmth of the sunlight on Karma's skin. All are conjoined at this moment. A unity of light and sound, of time and space.

And from this union hums the horn's call, welcoming him into the hallowed mountain. Greeting him at the cavern of the sun.

Look to the Mountain. Look to the Stone. Listen for the sound of the dharma horn to take us home.

He reels with the revelation.

I have found the Mountain. Now I will find the Stone.

39

THE STONE

Karma's ascent up the stone staircase winds with the internal contours of the Mountain. As the sun begins its descent outside, the crater's rocks turn pink and golden, holding the light of the sunset like a bowl. Still, he continues climbing. Onward, never losing his stride, over steep steps and broken stones. Past dark doorways flickering with ghostly illuminations inside, torches lit in perpetuity by flames of gas. Their shadows hint of an endless web of passages snaking through the recesses of the Mountain, and secrets they might hold.

But they do not call to Karma. Only the echoes of the horn beckon to him.

His mother's words come to him as he climbs: *My husband was a dreamer. He heard sounds. Sherpa horns blowing from afar. He thought it was the dead calling to him from the otherworld for help.*

His father believed the horns sounded from beyond the Mountain, from the dead. Where, then, are the ghosts?

Where are the dead?

Karma cranes his neck to see the summit of the cavern, the top of the vast staircase.

Where are you, Father? Mother? Lobsang? Nima?

To look into the Stone is to see beyond.

Will it show me where you are? How to bring you back? How to save us from the Seventh Sun in the Mountain?

In the absence of an answer, it is the apex of the Mountain that he climbs toward, the oculus of fire on the roof that he resolves to pursue.

The top of the staircase looms; then it stops abruptly. It is the end of the climb. The capstone peak comes into full view, a lid atop a massive jar. But it has the look of glass, like the handle of his dagger. Crystalline. Still out of reach.

The ground is paved, but not with ordinary rock. The cobbles are colorful, precious stones like coral, pearl, ruby, and turquoise. Others he cannot even recognize. They are polished and inlaid in an elaborate pattern of geometric forms, staggering to behold. The path leads to a wide doorway, flanked by two large columns beneath an outcropping of rock, the entrance to a building multiple stories high carved into the hollow, lined with windows.

Karma teeters before the edifice, awed by the sight.

I am here. At last.

He approaches the entrance. The threshold is a raised ledge, a precaution against the creeping evil spirits who slink on their bellies, should any make it this far. On the lintel above is a carved face of fierce expression, with small, glinting gemstones for eyes. He pauses as he recognizes the face of an animal, and then sees that there are four of them—a snow lion, tiger, phoenix, and dragon—making up the Four Dignities altogether. A feeling of reassurance comes over him, like seeing a friend on a long road. He steps inside.

From the light streaming through the windows, he can see that the interior walls are gilded, though the gold is tarnished with age. There is furniture. Benches and tables made of stone, shelves carved from the walls so seamlessly it is as if they had grown out of the rock. The stairs and the passageways are the same way, everything in the Mountain appearing as if it were part of one massive natural formation, a place birthed out of the earth as a conscious whole.

The floor slopes under his feet, a great ramp rising with the curvature of the peak, leading him through room after room. But Karma finds nothing more than some bat droppings and moss growth on the empty surfaces. No treasures. No pillowed jewels, no locked chests. No polished pearls or gleaming gems—nothing resembling what could be the Seeing Stone.

But at the next room, he stops. In this great, darkened hall, the shelves are not empty. Instead—cluttered, crammed, lined from floor to ceiling, end to end, seemingly infinite with the curve of the Mountain—they are filled.

With books. The hall is full of them.

Stunned, Karma steps inside. Rope scaffolding strings across the uppermost levels of the bookcases like the web of a giant spider. Scrolls, parchments, tablets. Metal plates, cloth bundles, animal-skin folios. There are all kinds, volumes of every shape and size, more than can be numbered. He traces the spines with a finger, wandering through the stacks. Strips of leather hang beneath them like black tongues, darkened with dust and age, inscriptions barely legible. Some of the marks and letterings appear familiar. Others, containing strange characters, he does not recognize. Dorje spoke of a sanctuary of learning where one day the pilgrims would be taught by the Lama. Are these the great books of the dharma? From the looks of these volumes, at the sheer variety and age, he can only guess that this repository dated not only from the time before the Suns, but much, much earlier. And the quantity. Up until now, he could count the number of books he has seen and handled in his life. To read all these . . . how long would it take?

A lifetime.

No—many, many lifetimes. An eternity.

A low and hollow cooing, like wind as it blows over a well, hums through the hall of books. The sound is sharper, but he recognizes the tone that called him here. He steps away from the books, following the haunting notes.

The bookcases wrap the mountain walls in an ever-tightening curve. The warm colors of sunset flood through the stacks. As Karma rounds the curve, he comes upon an open porch—a veranda overlooking the belly of the mountain hollow.

The intensity of the brightness tells him he is near the summit. He steps outside, passing into the wash of light, squinting up like one cringing before a forge. Overhead, so close it seems as if he had only to stand on his tiptoes to reach it, the vault of the Mountain's pinnacle blazes above him, now iron-red from the color of the setting sun. At this distance, Karma can see it for what it is.

A crystal glass.

Solid, yet transparent as ice, the capstone is a massive pyramid. It holds the light like a prism of molten liquid, the rays trapped and refracting before diffusing, leaving behind an afterimage of their glow.

He steps out onto the veranda. Over the low parapet plunges the yawning cavern. The view makes his body tingle. From this height, the roar of the waterfall below him and the whistle of the wind come as a rushing hiss.

A breeze sweeps over him. The air trembles, alive with a hum from the horn. At the end of the balcony is a long, cylindrical object. Shaped like a giant smoking pipe, it extends from a stone pedestal to the end of the veranda.

A horn!

He approaches it. Made of brass, its metal is dulled and blackened. Studded jewels run down the length of the shaft, their luster obscured under a layer of dust. Carvings adorn the surface, intricate designs of interweaving patterns running from a small aperture on one end to the flared bell on the other. The wind rustles again, and as the air glides over the mouthpiece of the horn, the sound emanates once more, a tremulous vibrato into the air, expanding through the Mountain, even to the belly of the cavern.

Ommmmm . . . Ommmmm . . .

Karma touches the instrument in fascination, his fingertips tingling with the vibration of the brass. The music ripples from the sunlit veranda to the shadowed walls, mingling with the echoes of water and whistling of winds.

The sound of the dharma horn.

Glancing back across the veranda, he notices a series of grooves, concealed in the striations of rock in the wall. On closer look, the pattern becomes distinct.

Steps.

He surveys their progression.

Leading up to the pyramid, to the glass capstone.

Where he makes out an opening in the ceiling.

A door.

One more room. One more place to search for the Stone.

He ventures to look. The grooves are narrow and steep, like the rungs of a ladder. Reaching to grab one of the notches, he steps up. Stretching a hand, he ascends to the next footing. One rung after another, he continues to climb. Gradually the stairs curve, inching past the veranda. Karma steals a quick glance down. It is a sheer drop through the mists to the mountain floor. He forces his gaze back to the ladder, stomach wobbly.

At the final handhold, he reaches the summit. The surface of the wall changes from rough to smooth rock. The steps level out.

He enters.

Expecting brightness, he finds instead the light subdued, as if most of it has been refracted outward, leaving only a soft illumination within.

He startles at a movement beside him, what appears to be a column of persons animating at his presence. He halts, surprised. The figures likewise freeze. He blinks. The figures blink back. They are not the movements of other people, but his own.

My reflections.

He turns to regard himself. The images turn to regard him back. The walls shine like still water, mirror smooth, echoing his likeness and movement. In the reflection, his face is frost-burnt, hardly recognizable. There is age in his eyes. His cheekbones are sunken. His long, black hair is now natty and ashen, unwashed for months. His clothes hang in tatters, the shoes worn nearly to mere wrappings on his feet. The sorry sight reminds him of the Reverend Mother's story of the faithful who once conducted pilgrimages to the sacred Mountain in the time before the Suns: traversing a step, then bowing a step, prostrating facedown in prayer. Circling it once would erase a lifetime of sin. A journey of years that would transform the pilgrim. The Mountain was sacred then, Dorje had said. A pillar to another world.

This is Karma's own pilgrimage, then. Looking in the mirror, he too has been transformed.

Karma peers deeper into the images. Behind the pale reflections, he perceives that the rock is multifaceted, a crystal lattice of smaller pyramids making up the cluster of the whole, each reflecting another. As he moves, the images multiply. Not just reflections, but reflections *of* reflections, duplicating across manifold surfaces and planes in a never-ending ripple of his movements. All simultaneously clear, all simultaneously real. Karma reels from the whirl of images, pausing to steady himself.

But then he detects an anomaly. While the reflections closest to him appear to be perfectly synchronized mirror images of himself, in the ones farther away, his actions seem delayed. Staring down the row of facsimiles, he spots a reflection in which he is no farther than the doorway, only now just about to enter the room. The effect is as if he is looking at another person entirely, the past a wholly separate, yet parallel, world to the present.

He turns his head in the other direction. Again, he finds the first few images in the series mirroring him almost exactly. But as before, the farther he looks, the less synchronized they are—only now the images appear to *foretell* his movements. As he picks up a foot to take a step, the reflections already show the same foot falling to the ground and lifting for the next, cycling ahead in an ever-increasing blur. Somehow, in its bending of the light, the crystal not only holds reflections of the present, but also a memory of the past . . . and the haze of the future.

The Seeing Stone is the key. To look into it is to see beyond—what has happened in the past, what will happen in the future.

Karma goes still.

The Stone. The crystal walls.

Is this the Stone? The capstone of the Mountain itself?

Disoriented, he drops his gaze to the floor, away from the inundation of images. The ground is like ice, at the same time translucent and clear, with the spaciousness of the mountain beneath him visible at parts as if warped through a lens. But as he looks at the floor, the view through the rock begins to change, the light bending, the image of the upper walls of the crater now warping into something else.

A picture of the mountain floor rushes toward him, like a dive from a bird's-eye view. In the next instant, the garden in which he had entered the mountain hollow appears suddenly, foliage of green choking the crystal's floor. Karma reels in surprise.

The crystal is magnifying his sight, like a massive spyglass.

He turns his gaze from left to right. His vision sweeps from one tree to another. As his eyes linger, the crystal floor now fills with the close-up of a single frond, the veins of the leaf suddenly as large as the limbs of a whole tree.

Karma's breath catches. He stills himself, afraid to move now for what else might happen. Slowly, tentatively—he trains his gaze past the garden floor, toward the entrance of the cave. The crystal viewer responds, the picture of the leaf whisking away now to the blackness of the tunnel. It seems to linger, as if awaiting further command. At no more than the mere nudge of a thought, his vision eases onward, picking up speed, plunging swiftly—into the mists, through darkness visible, passing at a blink the heap of the migoi's body, twisting down turns and winding hollows, finally to emerge . . . in the gray whiteness of the canyons.

The icy walls come next. Then, over the cliffs, to the fork of the snowbound pass, stark wedge of sky juxtaposed against rocky ravine. The Stone can see it all. On to the mouth of the pass itself, blocking the entrance toward the Mountain—the rebel camp on one side, and on the other . . .

He sees the pilgrim caravan!

Karma leans forward at the sight of them, and the Stone immediately focuses on the image. He sees the monks, the Gangdruk outlaws, the people of his village. Reverend Mother Dorje, Norbu, Gendun, too. It is as if they are right below him. He wants to call to them. Their faces are worried. Perceiving a presence beyond the pass, Karma follows their gaze eastward.

Beyond the shadows of the pass, the light of the sinking sun bleeding into the snowy valley, a sea of red moves. An army amasses on the slope, descending from the crest like a cup overflowing, trickling down the sides.

As he stares, the crystal pulls his view up close in a whoosh. But he already knows who they are.

The Eastern Army.

Banners stream, red tails blowing like flames. Soundlessly, boots march alongside the stomping of hooves. But most frightening of all, a crush of strange, hulking machines Karma has never seen before— metal, like the scraps of the rusting heaps near his village home—trundles forward, spewing smoke and snow, their violence felt despite the soundlessness of the quivering image in the viewer.

And in the midst of the march, borne by poles on the shoulders of men, red drapes swishing against flaking snow—is the covered palanquin, the Minister's carriage.

Hanumanda is here. He has followed the tracks of the Khan's rebel army and found the Mountain.

He is coming for the Stone.

Before Karma can stop himself, the Stone's gaze focuses on the covered litter, penetrating past the red veil. Inside, he sees none other than the Minister Hanumanda aloft the moving throne, eyes almost serene, staring ahead—as if looking straight at him.

Karma flinches. The vision whips aside like a blindfold snatched from one's eyes, retreating in a flash, the viewer whizzing out to a single dot of light in the floor, and he is once again back in the crystal prism among his myriad reflections—some mirroring his reeling movements, others still on their hands and knees staring through the viewer, while still others have already begun getting up and turning for the door.

Karma thinks of the pilgrims, of the thousands of troops and machines now headed directly their way.

I've got to warn them. I have to gather them into the Mountain to safety.

He clambers to his feet. He whirls toward the door but stops.

But how? I'll never make it. The pass is blocked, and there's not enough time.

The thought comes to him in the voice of the Minister, from that first meeting in his tabernacle.

They say that the Seeing Stone is the key, that anyone who can look into it can see what has happened in the past, but only a Lama can also see how to change the future.

The Stone.

Karma turns back around, scanning the room. A flurry of images flutters by, facsimiles of himself, watching himself.

The Stone will show me how. The Stone will show me what to do.

He casts his eyes back to the viewer in the floor. The same images zoom up to meet him. The rebel fighters on one side, the Minister's Eastern Army on the other. In between, the pilgrim caravan. He is running out of time. But there is no hint as to how to alter the scene that is unfolding.

Because it is not yet either the past or the future, only the present?

Or maybe . . . it is because I am not the Lama, after all.

Karma closes his eyes as his heart drops. He doesn't want to, but he hears the Reverend Mother's conclusion in his head.

Six Suns, six blasts in the sky. A seventh one, and the earth will die. All along, it was the only outcome. All along, it told us. This is our fate. A world at its end.

I cannot watch this, Karma thinks. *I cannot bear it.* He turns, starting again to flee for the door. His reflections follow him, some trailing, some darting ahead. He ignores them, racing past the infinity of images that reach further out, going further back.

He stops suddenly, his gaze stalling on a far reflection of himself. To his surprise, instead of being inside the crystal pyramid, his image is somewhere else—another place, another time. It is evening, darker than it is now. There is a snowstorm, the background a wash of white. Karma's skin shivers involuntarily at the memory of the swirling blizzard, the icy winds, the biting cold. As he looks closer, he sees that there is someone with him in the image. He flinches in recognition. His heart stops in his chest.

It is Nima.

Alive again.

They are talking. Though Karma cannot hear the words, the scene is familiar. Nima pointing to a slope where he sees Lobsang and Uncle Urgyen—all just as alive as she is. He sees himself, in the reflection's image, lowering his head in a reluctant nod, and then . . . their embrace.

"Wait—" Karma shouts, rushing at the image, realizing now what he is seeing. "Stop! Nima . . . !"

But Nima keeps walking, while his reflection only watches. The image changes suddenly, to a place Karma recognizes. The cliff he climbed, following Nima's tracks. But now a squad of the Khan's advance party is making their way up the rocks.

What is this . . . what's happening now?

Suddenly, Nima leaps out as they near the top. A slash at one and thrust into another. Her sword becomes stuck. As the other rebel scouts barrel up the path, she throws herself at one of them. It is Chuluun, Karma sees. The two of them wrestle to the ground, rolling closer to the brink of the cliff.

"Nima!" Karma pounds his hands against the crystal, feeling the smack of solid rock against his fists. "Watch out!"

They drop suddenly, disappearing over the edge.

He presses on the glass, helplessly screaming and pushing as if it were not a slab of crystal stone but a door.

Suddenly, the stone feels as cold as the snow itself. Karma backs away in confusion.

The words of the second verse of the prophecy echo in his own voice.

But gather to the Mount and the Seeing Stone, that the Lama may reveal yet a future unknown.

Is this what the Khan meant when he said that Karma could reach out and literally pull Nima back from her fall?

"The Stone is a portal," Karma whispers aloud. His gaze swerves from the snowy image to the multitude of other reflections around him. "These are *all* portals."

He turns back to the image, now clouding and swirling with snows.

I can choose to open this door.

I can go back and save her.

He shivers, blinking in surprise to see his breath clouding with frost. The coolness of the crystal is now a chill in the room. The glassy surface of the stone becomes hazy, dissolving. Flecks of snow drift onto his feet. He inhales sharply.

It's already happening.

He moves forward, eager. But something stops him. What will happen to the people if he leaves the Mountain now?

The monks, the villagers, the Gangdruk . . . who will help them?

What about Father?

He hovers now. Instinctively he knows—if he goes through the portal, he will not return. His body strains, weighed down by the burden of his choice. He shuts his eyes, afraid of the power of the images to lure him further. Reluctantly, he draws back. When he reopens his eyes, the surface of the crystal is hardening, slowly becoming whole again.

I'll be back, Nima. Like that night in the grotto. I won't leave you.

Karma turns, tearing himself away, trembling. A dark glimmer from another wall catches his eye, another image.

Black, twinkling. Karma blinks at it.

An image of night.

In the darkened landscape, a figure moves across a desolation of white—it is himself, trampling through snow. He is alone, with nothing but the bag on his back, walking away from the smoldering glow of a campfire in the background.

What now?

And then Karma's heart twists in realization of what he is seeing.

The night of the wolves.

The night we lost Lobsang.

He starts toward the crystal's image, where his reflection continues to stride, unsuspecting, through the night's terrain.

"Stop!" Karma shouts at himself. "Go back. Don't leave him. Lobsang . . . go to Lobsang."

His reflection pays no heed but treks into the moonlit wilderness without slowing. Karma knows what will soon come. He thrusts his hands to his head. He has seen this before. The mere memory turns his insides sick, as if he can already hear the growling.

I cannot watch this. Not again. Please.

What if I told you your loss need not be permanent?

The Khan's question comes like a taunt.

Karma grasps the glass. He begins to pound his fists against it. The reflection of himself perks up, ear cocked as if toward some noise. Only moments left before the wolves come.

Mother! Uncle Urgyen! Lobsang! Get away! Run!

But nothing changes. The past goes on. He sees himself continue to trudge away in the snow.

I'm sorry . . . I'm sorry . . . It's not working. Eyes clenched shut, he tears himself away. Away from the image, away from the sight. Away from the inevitable, he staggers.

Fleeing, into another wall of the prism.

He opens his eyes to an image of a vibrant sky, clear and blue. Once again, fearfully, he sees his reflection, but in another form, different from the first two. It has gone further back in time—much further. He is a child now, hiding inside the rusted ruins of the iron bird, watching the people of his village. The fact that he is hiding—while everyone else is gathered as a crowd—reveals to him the date and the occasion. The place is Kham. The day, his father's departure. The time, the hour of farewells. But not by him.

His father is just as Karma had retained deep in his memory, only now he can see him, all the blanks filled in. Sherpa Patrul wears his hair like Karma's, or rather Karma like his—free flowing but for a single braid. No jewelry, no adornment. His brow is already lined, though he is young. But his face is smooth and clear. Except at his eyes, crinkled now as he squints at the dunes. They are worried eyes. Desperate. Searching, Karma knows, for him.

His mother's voice is calling to him now: "Karma-la. Karma-la. Your father is going to the Mountain. Come and embrace him."

Go, Karma thinks. *Go—you fool! This is your last chance. You will regret it.*

But he does not go.

Slowly, his father turns his back, and the sun obscures the boy's vision, already blurred from tears as he watches from inside the jagged mouth of iron.

I wish, Karma thinks. *I wish I could stop him. I wish I could race toward him once more.*

Something is moving, a ripple in the vision. The image skips. From the rusted ruins, young Karma is suddenly outside, suddenly teetering toward his father.

Karma stares, stunned at the image. It's not real . . . yet it is. It *could* be.

Patrul drops to his knees, arms outstretched. He smiles to his son, their eyes level to each other's as they embrace.

The child's lips are moving.

"Don't go," Karma mouths now, only in a whisper.

He does not know his father's reply because he never heard it. For the last ten years, he imagined this scene, but now that he is beholding it as reality, he does not know what his father would have said. Until suddenly he hears the sound, even if only in his head—of his father's voice.

Look to the Mountain. Look to the Stone. Listen for the sound of the dharma horn to take us home. Look before it crumbles, returning to the sea. The sea of fire, the sea of glass. The sea that sees all, and what will come to pass.

You will know when I am there. The whole land will know. By my sounding the dharma horn, calling you to the Stone.

Karma's body heaves with a wave of longing. The glow of the image flickers within the crystal. He bows his head.

"I heard the horn, Father," Karma whispers. "I am here."

His father smiles as he leans toward the little boy in the reflection, touching his brow against his. Karma does the same, his own forehead pressing up to the image, amazed to feel the warmth of the illuminated slab on his skin. Dust rises in the image as the horses whirl, about to bear away his father, along with Tenzing, the man who Karma now knows will one day kill him.

Is it this, then, the truest desire of his heart, his reward after his search, the thing that he will leave this world for? His journey to the Mountain, a journey back to the time before it all began—a journey home. How easy it would be to cross the threshold toward the warm, dusty light.

But still, he cannot do it. Casting his eyes once again to the viewer in the floor, the approach of the mountain's pass appears. Hanumanda's army looms through the gap, a red river through a channel of white, and he knows what he must do instead.

The horn . . .

Just as it called to Karma, now he will use it to call to the people.

The images flicker, the portals seeming to wane. Karma's eyes sweep back to the image of his father.

Wait, Father. I will be back. Just as you called to me, and the Mountain called to you, now will I call to them.

And then I can return with you.

At last he turns away. His reflections seem to linger as well, giving chase only at the last moment, converging on the exit of the crystal room, losing him as he descends through the door.

Down the ladder steps to the stone pavilion. He reaches the old brass dharma horn.

With a glance back up at the distorted glow of the crystal pyramid, he presses his lips to the mouthpiece. Drawing a deep breath, he blows into it. The pipe stirs. Karma takes another breath, then blows again, cheeks expanding with the force of air. The horn finally fills, tingling in his hands and coming alive with a deep, rumbling note from the bell.

Ommmmmmm . . .

A long, otherworldly sound. A sound seemingly too large and too deep to come from himself—but it does. It ripples through his being like the swell of a river. Karma pauses, then blows once more, even harder this time, giving everything he has to it. The blast fills the air, stretching through the mountain. He blows again. The notes overlap, merge, join into a single strain, unified and prolonged as if building off each other, multiplying in force and power as it reverberates from one end of the cavern to the other like an infinite echo. He can feel it in his bones, emanating from his lips to the walls of the mountain, to the passages and the tunnels, into the very depths of the earth itself, to fill the entire land.

Hear it. Heed the call. Find your way into the Mountain!

He starts back to the pyramid. Rushing, he climbs the rungs again into the upper room, to the images of the Stone. But something is happening.

A trembling rumble. The room shakes, then the ground bucks. Karma drops to his knees. Something booms in the distance. The whole mountain sways, and he hears rocks cracking.

The reverberations. They've started a quake.

Another lurch. Karma goes sprawling. The floor is like a raft on a river, pitching and heaving. A loud snap draws his eyes down to the viewer. A crack has formed across the crystal. He can see the glow of images flickering.

No . . .

He considers going back to the veranda and stopping the horn, stifling the reverberations somehow. But he knows it is impossible now. There is no calling back the emanations. The lights of the pyramid blink like the flickering of a lamp in the wind. Then one by one, the glows of the crystal images darken.

Not the portals!

The room lurches. There is a splintering noise, a sound like smashing pottery. A crack zigzags across the ceiling, the crystal lattice glassy and uniform one moment—a web of fissures the next. It comes shattering down.

Karma dives. The fragments of glass rain in a shower of glittering shards. He collides, head against rock, a vision of stars bursting, before his field of vision is restored to the sight of a pillar toppling—a shadow of glass and rock suddenly rushing upon him.

He never feels the impact.

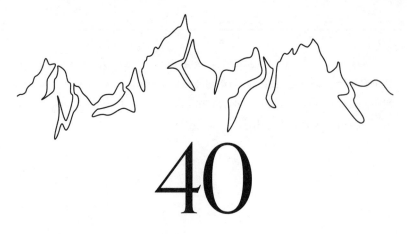

40

THE BEYOND

K arma twitches awake to darkness.

The night sky stretches overhead. It teems with stars. Infinite numbers, infinite worlds. Infinite distances, looking down.

The wind lashes. The cold turbulence makes him shiver.

The pyramid roof is gone. The floor is strewn with crystal. The shards tinkle as they stir. Glittering pieces, fragments of shattered worlds.

As above, so below.

The Stone.

He looks at the area where the glass was. Portals to his father, to Lobsang, to Nima.

Gone.

His heart sinks.

All of it . . . forever.

He rises, crunching broken rock, hair whipping in the wind. The brim of the crater's edge smolders with a molten hue, the vestige of a departed sun. He sweeps an area clear, peering through the darkened floor. Nothing stirs, as if the space beneath were a bottomless pit. The moan of the wind is a desolate sound, the sound of empty space, any sign that the pilgrims made it into the Mountain nonexistent.

As he stares into the void, the void stares back.

A splash of light appears suddenly, glowing around him on the floor. Karma shrinks at its presence.

Is this it? Is this the end? Has the quake triggered the Seventh Sun, with fire and destruction to follow? Is this oblivion?

It spreads. A growing whiteness. A brightening beam of daylight.

He cringes in anticipation of the impending blast.

What appears instead is something like the morning star, harbinger in the east—not in the sky, but in the midst of space before him. Very clear, very bright. Yet growing in size, getting nearer. Its light touches him, and his body tingles, as if it were passing through him. Then it floods all about.

The walls change, flickering with a translucence, turning crystalline in appearance, shimmering beneath the surface. The radiance spills down into the crater now, lighting caverns, filling cracks. Bending and bouncing, refracting and reflecting, it turns the Mountain into a pyramid of white.

And then Karma feels a presence, a feeling of warmth like summer days in the Khampa valley, and he hears a voice he remembers.

"My son."

He turns to see a figure walking toward him out of the luminescence of the walls, as if the rock is not solid but a corridor of light. Standing there, they face each other.

He is just as he remembers him.

The same single braid of hair down the side of his head. The same smiling corners of his eyes. Only there is a newness to his robes, or perhaps it is just the brightness of the room. And whereas once Karma had to look up to him, now they are the same height.

Karma's heart leaps within his chest.

"Father," he says, "is it really you?"

Then he asks the next question.

"Am I dead?"

Though he thinks this could be true, he says this without fear, without irony.

Sherpa Patrul's eyes gleam.

"Karma," his father replies, "I assure you, you are very much alive."

"Then am I dreaming?"

"You are awake."

"But how is it . . . that you're here?"

His father smiles. "Because you sounded the horn, calling to those above the earth and below, in the otherworld and in the physical world. And we heard you." He gestures to where the shattered ceiling was. "The seal between our worlds is now reopened, the link restored."

Karma looks around but can see no one else. Beyond the immediate light, the contours of the mountainous crater are visible. A broken world in the dark.

"But it doesn't matter, does it?" Karma says. "Everyone is dead. The Seeing Stone is destroyed. In the end . . . I failed."

His father returns a patient gaze. "This is not the end, Karma. Look again and see. Listen and hear."

A noise like a gradual whooshing of the wind begins to grow. As it becomes louder, it fills with the whisper of voices. Many of them, rustling together. He recognizes them. The ghost-winds, only this time they do not sound pained. In the facets of the now crystalline walls of the mountain crater, their figures materialize. First a handful, then several more, growing to dozens, hundreds, and before he knows it—far, far more than he can ever count, filling the entire view. Whole nations, it seems to him, seen through the light of the walls.

Karma reels at the sight.

Then his heart soars.

There, amid the multitude, is his mother. There is his aunt and his cousin Lobsang. There is Nima. All of them, coming forward. All of them, together. All of them . . . *alive.*

Relief and sorrow come pounding through him as he sees their faces as they were before.

"Death is but the passage to the next life," Karma's father continues. "And so long as there is life, there is always hope."

Karma's mother comes forward now, at her husband's side at last. Like him, her robes are clean, the colors bright again.

"My dear son," she says to him. "You must finish what you started."

The words overwhelm him.

"Mother," Karma says. "What more can I do?"

"You've sounded the call. Now gather the people."

Karma is lost. "Other pilgrims?"

"All who dwell in the valley. Every ear who will hear. They need a guide to gather to the Mountain."

Karma is dumbstruck. "You . . . want me to go back? But Hanumanda's army—"

"Look and see again," Karma's father responds.

The crystalline walls of the Mountain begin to brighten, the luminescence intensifying across the entire face of the crater.

"There are more of us than there are of them."

The Mountain trembles, the earth stirs. But unlike the earlier tumult, the vibration is gentle, a purring like the *Om* of the throat song of the monks. As Karma watches, the rocks transform, suddenly appearing to lose their opacity, colors coruscating and rippling until becoming transparent, as if washed of all impurities by the light, the whole mountain appearing now as one massive crystal.

Glowing, the crust of the mountain dematerializes to reveal a vista of night lit bright by the aura. What the floor of the Stone had been, now the Mountain has become—calling images from every direction—an all-seeing, all-penetrating tower. Through these lenses, Karma looks.

Down, way down at the mountain's approach, the aftermath of an earthquake clogs the pass. Avalanche of ice and rock, flecked with the littering of bodies. The sight chills him. But he does not have long to dwell on the scene. Just beyond the clot of ice and debris comes the army of red—scaling their way over the range, men and machines trundling through snow. The vision whisks into their midst, and again Karma sees the covered palanquin of the Lord Minister, the curtain slid open to reveal Hanumanda's face.

The brightness of the Mountain intensifies, growing. A searing light streaks out in all directions, striking the ranks of the Eastern Army like the blast of a furnace. The soldiers recoil.

Something else is happening. Back on the slopes of the Mountain's crater, a multitude of figures emerges. Ghostly lights in the thousands, descending. As Karma watches, the crystal hones into a view of their luminous bodies, each bearing a stone of light themselves, brilliant weapons of flame.

He can hear them now, their voices no longer a wailing in the night but loud cries of war in the day.

They are the ghost-winds embodied. Come to fight the army.

Karma looks toward the Minister's troops. The approaching army has halted its advance, the covered palanquin hesitating as Lord Hanumanda peers through the parted curtains. His mouth moves at the palanquin bearers. Cumbersomely, frantically, the litter circles, laboring to turn itself around. The army begins to break rank. A retreat forms, the troops scattering helter-skelter before the multitude of beings.

The ghosts lash with their stones of fire. Snowfields vaporize, jets of steam scalding the men as they attempt to flee. Hanumanda shrinks into his palanquin, pulling shut the drapes, only to have the cloth ignite in his hands. The servants writhe, dropping the carriage. Men and armor melt in the brilliance. The Minister tries to escape, leaping, but the movement fans the flames and sets him ablaze. The heat must be searing. He spins madly, his screams silent. He crashes, whirling into a heap of cinders, the rest of the convoy combusting in terrible bursts of burning.

The inferno rolls. The Mountain's walls begin to shake as if now they, too, are in danger of being incinerated. The land turns white-hot. Too bright, suddenly impossible to look at, impossible to withstand. It will surely burn his eyes.

Karma cries out, turning his face away, shielding himself.

Then all eyesight goes blind.

The brightness has subsided. But still Karma's eyes cannot see, burning with the afterimages of fire, dark whirls, and white flashes. He thinks he hears a voice.

Karma . . .

Reaching blindly, he stumbles in the shadows. He can see just enough to make out the outline of a figure.

He stops. Despite his blindness, he knows her presence.

His throat tightens and his eyes well up. "Nima?"

The darkness fades like a veil removed. Slowly, the light of his surroundings creeps back. His vision refocuses.

He sees her, just as he saw his parents. Suddenly alive, suddenly standing before him. Only now with a radiance like a phoenix reborn.

A whirl of emotion flows through him, unlocked at her sight.

Nima's voice is clearer now, audible as speech.

"It's time for you to wake, Karma."

Karma realizes what she is saying.

His shoulders droop. "But what if I want to stay here with you?"

"You rejoined our worlds," she replies, "when you blew the horn and caused the Mountain to shake, breaking the Stone that sealed them off. But your time to cross to the otherworld has not come."

Karma feels his heart sink. "How much longer, then?"

"Until the gathering is done."

"And . . . what if it's never done?"

"The Seventh Sun will always be waiting."

Then she adds, her voice softening, "But because the worlds of the living and the dead are connected again—you can know that our separation will never be for long."

The light flickers between them. A whorl of shadows hastens, and she stretches out her hand. Eager to feel her, Karma reaches out in return. In the radiance, their fingers meet, not a touch of flesh and blood, but of light and life.

"This is not the end," Karma says at last. "Not yet."

"No, it is not," Nima replies. "Now, wake. Rise, and return to the Mountain."

41

THE OTHERWORLD

His eyes fill with the haze of daylight. Something heavy is pressing down on him. It moves, lifting from his body, a slab of rock propped up by another, sliding off him.

"Karma . . ."

Stained faces stare down at him, coming into focus: the Reverend Mother Dorje. Norbu. Gendun.

Karma blinks, not certain at first if he is still seeing a vision of the otherworld, or if it is really them. But the pull of the physical world—the weight of the fallen debris, the throbbing ache of his head—tells him that it is very real.

That he is awake.

And alive.

He scans the faces. The Khampas and monks are there too, along with the Gangdruk.

They all made it into the Mountain. But how?

The surprise and confusion must be apparent on his face.

"We heard the sound of your horn, Karma," Dorje says. "We followed it here, to you."

Karma's gaze flicks across the room. To the open ceiling, exposed now to a sunlit sky, touching clouds like a window to the heavens. The air is warm, calm.

"The Mountain started to shake. Rocks were falling. But then we heard a sound from above," Dorje says, her voice deep with emotion and gratitude. "It led us to the caves. As soon as we were inside, everything outside collapsed. It was an avalanche. The armies didn't stand a chance. But we made it, Karma. Because of you, we did it."

Karma strains to lift his head. They help him, moving rock fragments that crunch on the littered floor, then give him space as he sits up. He looks down the hollow of the Mountain.

Where once there was dull stone now shines the brilliance of glass. The walls of the crater are translucent. In the sun, the land spreads in all directions, an endless vista.

The transformation has remained.

All is as one massive crystal.

The Mountain is the Stone.

Wonder floods through Karma.

"I saw Nima," he says. "I saw Lobsang, my mother, I even saw my father, while they were still alive. I could have reached out and touched them."

"All is one glass, all one Stone," Dorje says. "Our worlds are joined together again. Yet you stayed here. You could have left this world. You could have saved any of them, but you didn't. Why not?"

"I wanted to," Karma says. "But there were a million pasts, a million times where things had gone wrong. And then I realized, if I change the past in order to alter the future, I would lose the present. I would give up on this world, and then it would be as good as gone, Seventh Sun or not." He looks at the Reverend Mother. "They're still with us, never far away."

Dorje's face is contemplative. Karma knows she is thinking about the Oracle. "How about the Seventh Sun?" she says. "Have we stopped it? Or is the world still doomed?"

Karma ponders this. The Seventh Sun is buried under the rubble. But it is still there, a reminder of the world's potential fate.

"I don't know," he replies finally. "But as Nima said, we're not dead yet. As long as there is life, there is always hope. For our people, and even for our dead."

Dorje is silent for a moment. Finally, a look of peace comes over her. She smiles at him then, displaying a book in her hands. "From the Mountain's library," she says. "One of the Oracle's favorites. I thought I would never see it again." She turns to the first page. "'Smoke a sign of fire is,'" she begins to read, "'the Southern cloud a sign of rain. The little child will be a man, the foal a stallion one day.'"

She shuts it gently, mist and marvel in her eyes. "I was wrong, so blind to despair, when all this time, it was you. You were the Lama Child. Yet I never saw it."

"No," Karma says, remembering suddenly the words spoken at that wedding so long ago and so far away. "We are all the children of the Lama." He looks at the Gangdruk. "We assumed it was a reincarnation in the form of a child, but in truth we are all the sons and daughters of this land, all its protectors." Then he turns to the monks. "And all of us are pilgrims seeking our way, all calling to one another—just as the Mountain called to my father, and he called to me."

Karma gazes out to the veranda below. Despite the fallen rubble and fragments of ruptured crystal strewn about—the brass dharma horn is still intact, its long barrel extending its length to the edge, projecting its aperture over the drop of the pavilion.

He looks out. The walls shine as the sun climbs, prisms scattering rays, brightening the space of the Mountain out to the heavenly blue above and the vastness of the land beyond.

The earth is all aglow, as far as the eye can see.

42

THE BEGINNING

In the spring, the snows of Kailash have melted, yet the Mountain still beams white, a beacon in the sun. From the outside, the peak is a perfect pyramid, rough surfaces scoured away by the quake, now smooth and translucent as glass.

A towering massif of crystal. The rivers once again flow unfrozen, four great tributaries gushing waters and ice melt in the directions of the Four Dignities.

In the months that followed the events on the Mountain, the wild yak have returned, flourishing in number. Karma stands among a team of them, provisions loaded on their backs. Norbu checks the harnesses. Around them, the people gather.

"Are you sure you must go?" the Reverend Mother says. "The Minister is dead. So is the Khan."

Karma nods. "But there will always be another minister and other warlords. Just like there are other people, other villages, who are seeking refuge. They will find it here in the Mountain, where we can begin again." He gives Dorje a reassuring smile. "This is not goodbye," he assures her. "No more than it is the end."

Dorje inclines her head in a bow. "I wish you blessings and good luck, dearest Karma. May many hear your call."

Next comes Gendun, pressing his hands together.

"You are certain you will not take more of us with you?" Gendun asks. "You know well that the road is full of danger."

Karma shakes his head. "The monks have work to do in the libraries, and the Mountain will need protectors. Besides," Karma adds with a smile, "I won't be alone."

"That's right," Norbu joins in. "He'll have me to keep an eye on him."

It is time to go. As the people wave their farewell, the herd moves, Karma leading at the front, Norbu behind.

In the pass, the melted snow reveals a constellation of cinquefoil and lichen, white stars of edelweiss. A mirror image of the Mountain is reflected on the lake, the two images forming a diamond-shaped gem. Overhead, in an otherwise cloudless sky, a single tuft of white hangs above them like a shelter from the sun. Its shade appears to lead them, a guide toward the east.

Karma smiles to himself as they continue on their path.

It is a good omen.

ACKNOWLEDGMENTS

There are many people to thank, but the first would be my mother, who instilled in me a love of books and a desire to be a writer of them.

To my friends and colleagues who patiently endured the creation of this book, I cannot thank you enough. Of note are members of the Carpe Noctem writing group, especially Sheldon Gilbert (first reader of my earliest draft), Eric J. Goodemote, M.M. Gallatin, and Paul Glyn Williams (a true writing buddy when it was needed most). To Brandon Ro, a gifted scholar of sacred architecture, who provided invaluable inspiration during the conception of a journey to a primordial Mountain, I say thank you, my friend. To the Lanes, for our weekly "Mahjong/Bridge Nights" that kept us sane during turbulent times—you're on this ride now! To the Peaks and countless others; writing is often a solitary journey, I am so blessed to have your company on this road.

To my agent Tamara Kawar at ICM, who impressed me with her understanding of this novel from the first read, thank you for helping me realize this book in its fullness and your unswerving search for the perfect home for it. Thank you also to Hillary Jacobson for introducing me to said amazing agent. To the team at CamCat Books, especially Sue Arroyo, Laura Wooffitt, Bill Lehto, Maryann Appel, Abigail Miles, Gabe Schier, Jessica Homami, and my wonderful editor Helga Schier and her assistant Elana Gibson who helped me cut and polish the manuscript until I could see the past, present, and future of this story as clearly as if I was looking into the Seeing Stone itself—thank you for taking on this esoteric tale set at the ends of the world. To the many other publishing professionals for the support, mentoring, and positive reinforcement, I count Kathy Kidd, Betsy Mitchell, Ammi-Joan Paquette, and my SFWA mentor Elizabeth Bear.

There are many others to thank, but most of all, thank you to my family for being hitched on this wagon and never doubting, celebrating every milestone on the way. Without my children, there would be no inspiration. And without my wife, there would be no story. This book is for you.

ABOUT THE AUTHOR

Born in California, Brandon Ying Kit Boey spent his childhood in China, Singapore, and various parts of the US. He graduated from New York University and Brigham Young University Law School, subsequently working in Asia, the UK, and across the US before settling in coastal Maine, where he currently lives with his family. When not at work on his next novel, he can be found wandering the woods with his children, practicing law, or writing poetry. He decided to write this book because he had never seen a novel about the end of the world from an Asian perspective despite a richness of eastern cosmological and eschatological traditions.

If you enjoyed
Brandon Ying Kit Boey's
Karma of the Sun,
you will enjoy
The Secret Garden of Yanagi Inn
by Amber A. Logan

Chapter One

December 24th
Chicago, Illinois

I'd always been told hospitals were a place to heal and rest, but my mother's hospital room was an assault on the senses. The stench of decaying flowers and cloying cherry disinfectant clung to my skin, invaded my nose. A wave of nausea swept over me. I couldn't breathe, couldn't think.

"I need to get some air."

I rose to my feet before Risa could object, although I knew she wouldn't. My sister had been trying to convince me all day to leave Mom's hospital room, to go get some real food or take a walk.

"Sure, Mari, go ahead. I'll stay with Mom." Risa nodded without looking up, her short blond curls bobbing. She leaned back in her bedside chair, still absorbed in her book. I glanced at Mom, now a papery, skeletal version of the woman she once was. But at least she was peaceful, sleeping.

As soon as I stepped through the hospital's sliding glass doors, the blast of cold air sent an involuntary shiver through my body. I pulled my hair back into a ponytail, knowing the chill wouldn't last, that five minutes in I'd be sweating, my muscles warmed. Maybe the fact I already wore running shoes was fate, or maybe I'd just gotten lazy—too exhausted after so many long days split between the gallery and the hospital to care about my appearance. Either way, I'd dressed in sweats that morning and I was going for a run, damn it.

I turned north and ran down the nearly deserted sidewalk. Streetlights were wrapped with faux greenery and twinkling lights, and last week's snowstorm had left lingering mountains of gray snow on the edge of parking lots. The morning air stung my throat, but the cold was a welcome change from the stifling hospital room.

I ran for most of an hour, my pace too fast to fall into a comfortable groove. But the burn in my muscles and the emptiness of my mind renewed me. No worrying about the doctor's cryptic prognoses, about visits from the counselor who peeked in occasionally to "see how we were doing." I could just run—it was me and the cold air and the thud-thud-thud of my feet on the pavement, and all was right in the world.

But it wasn't. This was a dream, and reality waited for me back in that suffocating room. Risa would be wanting her midmorning coffee, and I, being the good big sister that I was, ordered two drinks from the Starbucks around the corner so she didn't have to settle for the unbranded kiosk in the hospital's lobby.

I expected to return a hero, sweaty but triumphant, brandishing two grande peppermint lattes as I opened Mom's door. But as I carried the drinks down the hospital corridor, I saw Mom's door was already open. My hands trembled.

I sped up.

Sounds of movement and talking inside the room. And crying—Risa was crying. I broke into a run, burning my hands as peppermint latte sloshed over them onto the pristine polished floor.

Risa was still in her chair, sobbing behind both hands, her book dropped at her feet. Two hospice nurses stood at the foot of Mom's bed, speaking in quiet, respectful tones.

Mom didn't look any different, looked for all the world like she was still sleeping.

But the whirring, dripping sounds had stopped. They'd turned off all the machines. Only Frank Sinatra's crooning "Silent Night" drifted down the hall from a distant room.

Mom had died.

And I'd missed it.

Chapter Two

Two months later
En route to Japan

The dimmed cabin lights brightened to a rosy glow, mimicking a sunrise though it was late evening in Kyoto. I wiped the drool off my lip with the back of my hand, glanced at the passengers on either side of me. The elderly woman to my right was awake, watching *Roman Holiday* on her seatback screen—Mom's favorite movie, one I'd watched with her three times in the hospital alone.

The smartly dressed blond woman on my left had her laptop out on her tray table. Her stockinged feet rested on carry-on luggage with the same floral print as the weekender bag Mom had picked up in England years ago.

An optimistically small bag for her hospital stay.

The woman was probably working. Her nails on the keys tick-tick-ticked away, knocking on the door to my brain, reminding me I should check my work email. I reached for the bag between my feet. And Risa would need to be reminded of where I'd left Ginkgo's pills. She needed to know he wouldn't take them without sticking the pills inside butter. She needed to know—

STOP IT, Mari. I pictured my little sister smirking at me, arms crossed, standing next to my white puffball of a dog. *Relax—I've got this.*

I leaned back in my seat, rhythmically twisting the too-loose ring on my middle finger.

The flight attendant pushed a drink cart down the aisle. She wore a fitted top and pencil skirt, a jaunty kerchief with the Japan Airlines red crane logo tied around her neck. "Green tea, coffee?" Her voice was quiet, soothing.

I raised my hand. "Coffee would be amazing, thank you."

She smiled a practiced smile, set a small cup on her metal tray, and poured the coffee from a carafe. The two women on either side of me asked for green tea.

Even over the aroma of my coffee, I could smell their tea. I'd missed it, the slightly bitter scent, the warmth of it. A scent from my childhood. Japan. *I'm really going back. This is real. This is NOW.*

I took a sip of the coffee, hissing as it stung my tongue. A sharp, cheap flavor like the instant crap Thad used to buy when he'd finished off my good stuff.

I should've asked for tea.

"Ladies and gentlemen, we will be landing at Kansai International Airport in approximately half an hour. We anticipate a slightly early arrival. Local time is 7:14 p.m."

My cardigan was damp with sleep sweat. I'd take it off, but I was afraid of elbowing the ladies next to me, so I made do with pulling my hair back into a ponytail and hitting the button for my personal fan. It whirred to life, but the clicking annoyed me, and I turned it back off. In the row behind me, someone sneezed.

What the hell was I doing running away like this—abandoning my sister, my now ex-boyfriend, maybe even my job? Tears welled in my eyes and I fought them back, staring at the screen in front of me, at the image of the tiny airplane and the dashed-line trek it'd made across the Pacific Ocean. Even if Risa had made all the arrangements and basically shoved me out the door, it felt wrong to just leave. Even if it was for only four weeks.

Deep breaths, Mari, deep breaths.

At first the timing of the grant had seemed fortuitous, if a bit rushed. But the closer I got to Japan, the more reality set in and the vague details of the NASJ grant paperwork felt more and more inadequate. Photograph an old, isolated Japanese inn "for posterity's sake"? It wasn't much to go on.

Had I brought the right camera lenses? Would four weeks be enough time? It seemed an eternity to me right now, but I'd never been asked to document an entire estate, never even received a grant before. I was an artist, not a documentarian.

At least, I used to be an artist.

Maybe I should've splurged for the upgraded camera bag with better padding. I pictured the *Roman Holiday* woman next to me opening the overhead compartment and my camera bag tumbling out onto the floor. Contents may have shifted during flight.

Could she even reach the overhead compartment? She was a tiny Japanese woman—probably in her seventies. I snuck a glance at her.

But Mom was sitting next to me.

I froze, my entire body turning numb.

Mom, leaning back in her seat, was watching the movie with a slight smile on her lips. Her platinum blond hair was tied back in a loose ponytail, but tufts had fallen out and were dusting her shoulders, her blouse, like dead leaves. She sipped her green tea.

I struggled for air. The sweat dotting my skin turned cold, clammy.

No, no, no. I'm just tired, didn't get enough sleep. I closed my eyes, inhaled deep, gasping breaths. Mandarins, I smelled freshly peeled mandarins.

"Are you all right, honey?"

My eyes flew open. CEO woman on my left, with her slim laptop and flowered bag, stared at me. Her eyes were wide with concern.

I shot a glance to my right. The little grandmother had returned and was happily watching her movie, oblivious to my distress.

Am I all right? The dreaded question.

Did she mean "do I need medical attention?" Or was it more of the existential "all right" we all seem to strive for but never quite manage?

I smiled at the woman, responded with the only reasonable lie one can give to that question: "I'm fine."

Deep breaths, Mari. Deep breaths.

The flight attendant in her perfect pillbox hat and red bandana came by again, this time with white gloves and a plastic trash bag. I handed her my half-empty cup of coffee with an apologetic smile.

I should've asked for tea.

Like an orderly river, we flowed off the plane and down the jet bridge, then spilled out into the brightly lit airport. I squinted, one hand carrying my camera bag, the other pulling my square carry-on luggage.

The stop at the bathroom with its private floor-to-ceiling stall doors, the polite customs workers, the wait for baggage—it was all a blur. A foggy-headed, clips-and-phrases of Japanese and English blurring together kind of chaos. But I was an ignorant American, the tall, brown-haired white lady looking like a confused tourist, so of course I was funneled through with utter politeness and a tolerance I was grateful for, yet also resented. I didn't need their help.

I say that, but when I finally stepped out into the arrivals area and scanned the crowd for a sign or a screen or a hand-scrawled note featuring "Marissa Lennox," I found none. My heart leapt into my throat for a moment, but I swallowed it back down. No worries, the plane had landed a few minutes early.

Maybe my ride was running late. Maybe there was a miscommunication about the terminal. Maybe . . .

I scanned the line of men in suits and white gloves again, watching for a glimmer of recognition in their alert faces, but each one's eyes slid past me to the next arriving passenger. I didn't match their profiles. Of course I didn't.

I found a bench nearby where I could keep one eye on the sliding glass doors and the other on my oversized suitcase and assorted bags. But no drivers came rushing in, embarrassingly late to pick up the unfortunate foreign woman. I considered buying a coffee at the kiosk or indulging in my love of Japanese vending machines, but decided against it. I didn't relish shoving all my luggage into a tiny bathroom stall if I had to pee before I left.

And so, I waited.

A handful of older businessmen passed by, glanced surreptitiously my way, chattering amongst themselves with the self-assuredness of men who assume I can't understand them. One laughed and nodded. I caught a few of their words in passing: foreigner, tall, Chelsea Clinton. I chuckled and raised an eyebrow. Maybe Chelsea Clinton on her worst day—my frizzy brown hair with graying roots was already sneaking out of its scrunchie to spill across my oily face.

I tucked a strand of hair behind my ear and turned on my phone, careful to keep it in airplane mode. Damn it, I hadn't thought I'd need an international plan. I pulled up the email from Ogura Junko at the Yanagi Inn—no phone number, not even in the email signature. I leaned my head back against the hard wall, practiced the breathing technique Risa had taught me in the hospital months ago. *Breathe in, one-two-three, breathe out, one-two-three.*

I double-checked the email, noted the inn's street address. If no one came to pick me up, I could just step outside, find a cab, and give them Yanagi Inn's address (though the long ride from the airport to the remote inn would probably cost a fortune).

I wasn't helpless, after all.

But still, having no one to meet me . . . not a good omen.

Half an hour passed before I thought to check the printout of the grant paperwork Risa had sent me. I dug through my bags until I found it tucked in the pocket beside my laptop. I balanced the computer on my lap and smoothed the sheet of printer paper across its flat top.

I hadn't bothered printing the front page, only a few paragraphs from the middle, with highlighted parts I'd thought relevant. No contact info.

. . . for the purpose of documenting, via artistic photography and for the sake of posterity, the property known hereafter as YANAGI INN . . .

"Lennox-san?"

I glanced up sharply, nearly toppling the laptop. A sixty-something woman with graying, short-cropped hair stood over me. She wore a simple indigo kimono with a wide cream-colored obi belt, and a grandmotherly air of silent disapproval.

"Ogura-san?"

For a moment, she just towered over me, scrutinizing my face as if searching for something. Then she gave a barely discernable nod and turned toward the glass doors. I scrambled, shoving the printout and my laptop back into their bag. I didn't even have time to pull out my jacket.

"Wait!" I called after her, frustration creeping into my voice as I grabbed the handles of my various bags and rolling luggage.

It seemed like every one of the airport's many patrons turned and stared at me. I flushed and scrambled after Ogura, the only person in the building who hadn't bothered acknowledging my cry.

I tripped out of the automatic doors, following the old woman into the brisk night air. She was surprisingly quick in her traditional wooden sandals, weaving between travelers toward a slick black sedan waiting at the curb, its lights flashing. A driver in a black suit and white gloves hopped out of the car and started loading my bags into the spacious trunk. I thanked him, my cramped arms lightening with every bag removed from my care.

Ogura climbed into the passenger seat before the final bag was stored in the trunk, so the driver opened the door to the back and I slipped inside, grateful to sink into the soft leather interior.

It's dark, I thought vaguely, for both the car's tinted windows and the sky outside were inky, seductive, and as soon as I set down my camera bag, clicked my seatbelt, and rested my head against the cold window beside me, I was out.

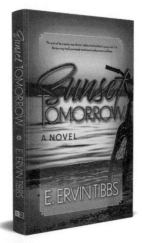
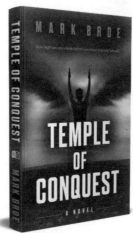

CamCat Books